THE OTHER
MARCH SISTERS

THE OTHER MARCH SISTERS

LINDA EPSTEIN
ALLY MALINENKO
LIZ PARKER

KENSINGTON
PUBLISHING CORP.

www.kensingtonbooks.com

KENSINGTON BOOKS are published by

Kensington Publishing Corp.
900 Third Avenue
New York, NY 10022

All Kensington titles, imprints and distributed lines are available at special quantity discounts for bulk purchases for sales promotion, premiums, fund-raising, educational or institutional use.

Special book excerpts or customized printings can also be created to fit specific needs. For details, write or phone the office of the Kensington Special Sales Manager: Kensington Publishing Corp., 900 Third Avenue, New York, NY, 10022. Attn. Special Sales Department. Phone: 1-800-221-2647.

The K with book logo Reg. US Pat & TM Off.

ISBN: 978-1-4967-5025-9
First Kensington Hardcover Edition: March 2025

ISBN: 978-1-4967-5027-3 (e-book)

10 9 8 7 6 5 4 3 2 1

Printed in the United States of America

This advance edition represents the manuscript being distributed for prepublication review. Typographical and layout errors will not be present in the final book available to consumers.

For Anna, Lizzie, and May, and all those who haven't had a chance to tell their own stories.

"I have a foolish wish to be something great and I shall probably spend my life in a kitchen and die in the poor-house. I want to be Jenny Lind or Mrs. Seguin and I can't and so I cry."

—Anna Alcott Pratt

"Miss Hinkley was horridly shocked at my devouring meat . . . and stared her big eyes at me. [She] will probably come to deliver another lecture soon. I don't care for the old cactus a bit. . . . Write often to your little skeleton."

—Elizabeth Alcott

"I often wonder if I could step back into my old life and feel at home there, for I seem quite a different person from the woman who bade you good-bye so long ago, and you would find me greatly changed."

—May Alcott Nieriker

Contents

Contents

DEAR READER

I'm sure you believe you know their story from reading that other book, which told you an inspiring tale about four sisters. It told you a story, but did it tell you the whole story? That book was written by the second sister, who was known to occasionally take some liberties with facts. In her beloved book, the author recounted some incidents which, had they been written by another sister, might have shown that author in a most unfavorable light.

Of course authors may take that liberty, to craft their fictions out of fact. But let's step back for a moment, if you will, and consider the untold stories of the other sisters—interactions both small and large—of which that author wasn't privy. Private moments, confidential conversations, intimate and undisclosed connections and correspondence. These pages contain some of those moments.

PART ONE

~ Amy Curtis March ~
The Art of Courting

London

PROMENADE ON THE MALL

There was nothing back home in Concord—or even in Boston or New York—that compared to the Mall at St. James's Park. The Mall was a place to see and be seen, and St. James's Park was a thing of beauty, a lovely bit of green amidst the grand buildings of London's City of Westminster. Amy and her cousin Florence had been invited to promenade the Mall with the Vaughn twins, Fred and Frank, on this rare sunny afternoon in London. It was slightly breezy, and a small flurry of wind pulled at Amy's parasol, which she wouldn't dare walk without, lest an intrepid beam of sunlight have the temerity to freckle her fair face. They were to stroll toward Buckingham House, past St. James's Palace and, Amy hoped, perhaps enter St. James's Park itself. As exciting as promenading was—and she was excited—what she desperately wanted to do was sketch in St. James's Park. She yearned to stand on the Blue Bridge and view the famous pelicans. But her aunt and uncle had deemed it improper for a young lady to spend a day sketching unaccompanied, and it was certainly not something Cousin Florence would ever want to do. She was grateful that Aunt Mary and

Uncle Edward had invited her to accompany them on their grand tour of Europe. She was sometimes concerned though that she was interested in different things than they or her cousin were. So, she tried to take her pleasure where she could, and today's enjoyment was promenading.

Although it was a rare occurrence, Amy's first thought this day hadn't been about drawing. Instead she had spent hours worrying about what to wear. It was very important that she dress exactly right. Too much, and she'd look as if she was trying to elbow her way into high society, too little and she'd suffer the scorn and judgment of upper-class promenaders who rejoiced at looking down their collective noses. She didn't know if Fred Vaughn might be the sort of gentleman who would notice a fashion misstep, and she definitely wanted to avoid that kind of attention. As she and Florence had readied themselves earlier in the day, it had been all that Amy could think about, worrying that she'd miss the mark. Finally, she had settled on a cornflower-blue silk walking skirt with a small bustle, a modestly trimmed overskirt in a slightly darker blue, and a paletot over top, cinched at the waist with a simple sash. She'd tied and retied the sash until she'd gotten it perfect. Now, as she and Florence waited for Fred and his brother Frank to arrive, Amy nervously smoothed at the sash. Florence was holding Amy by the arm, and her fingers were beginning to dig into the flesh.

"You're hurting me, Florence, dear," Amy said softly, managing to maintain a smile as they spotted the Vaughns.

"I can't remember which is which," Florence replied. "Am I really to walk with the handsome one?"

Fred and Frank greatly resembled each other although they weren't identical twins. Frank was slightly taller, leaner and, truth be told, *was* more handsome. His lips were fuller, his eyes held more of a sparkle, and he had the most enviable Roman nose. He was always impeccably dressed in the latest fashion.

There was something a bit coarse to his brother's features, who leant so far toward proper and conventional that one might accuse him of being a bit stodgy. As the young men walked toward them, Amy noted that Frank's hair was the color of golden-hued maple wood, with a healthy complexion to match, whereas Fred was a faded strawberry-blond with a complexion like rising bread. Which was not *exactly* unpleasant, yet was also not quite as charming. Amy and Florence stood taller and straighter as the young men drew near.

The nervous little sparrow that seemed to have taken up residence in Amy's chest fluttered against the confines of her rib cage.

"Frank is the one on the left," Amy replied, giving her elbow a little shake to hopefully loosen Florence's viselike grip. "And I think they're both quite handsome." She wanted to convince herself of this anyway. Amy was too polite to point out that the only reason Florence and Frank had been asked along at all was due to Aunt Mary's notion that Amy and Fred promenading unaccompanied would be inappropriate. Besides, it really didn't matter which brother was more good-looking, as the always proper Fred, not the livelier Frank, was the brother who had been paying Amy attention. *Comme il faut,* thought Amy, practicing her French in her head, *correct in behavior or etiquette.* That was a good thing, was it not?

As they approached, Amy couldn't help noticing Frank's effortless stride. This was a surprise as she remembered he had suffered an injury when he was a boy and had used a cane. In contrast, Fred's gait seemed a bit stiff. With a slight bow and a tight smile, Fred said, "Lovely to see you, Miss March." She could tell by his eyes that he *was* genuinely pleased to see her, which fact was very agreeable to her. He gave a quick nod to Florence.

"Mr. Vaughn," Amy said, addressing Fred; then, turning her pretty face to Frank, continued, "and Mr. Vaughn!" Amy blushed as Florence let loose a giggle. "You remember my cousin Florence Carrol?"

"Why of course," Frank said. "Miss Carrol, it's so lovely to make your acquaintance again." He bowed with an exaggerated flourish, took her hand, and kissed it. Florence laughed again. Amy hoped and prayed Florence wouldn't start prattling on, as she sometimes did when nervous. There was a slight breeze, and Amy caught the scent of Fred's eau de cologne, which had the dry woody scent of vetiver.

Fred cleared his throat and said, "Shall we walk?" and immediately they were paired. Frank and Florence trailed behind as the four of them began their promenade down the Mall.

If Amy could watch herself walking beside Fred Vaughn, her nerves might have been calmed and the frantic bird would have tucked its head under its wing and taken a little nap on its perch. The four young people made a pretty picture—two handsome young men, clearly brothers, accompanying two proper, pretty young ladies. The plainer girl in the finer dress was endlessly chattering to the laughing, dandily dressed young man. The more serious brother held the arm of a very attractive blond girl in a blue walking dress, that perhaps would have been a touch more fashionable the previous season. This fact would have been lost on any observer though, as the young lady was the picture of beauty, poise, and breeding. She walked with the grace of a dancer, her dignified demeanor hiding the actual state of her nerves.

"Have you been enjoying London?" Fred asked.

"Quite," Amy replied. "I love hearing the chime of the Big Ben and we've been to Westminster Abbey, to Poets' Corner, and the beautiful memorial to William Shakespeare." A barouche-landau pulled by a pair of high-stepping Hackneys sedately made its way past them, and Fred's attention wandered to the horse and carriage. In her nervousness Amy had begun to chatter almost as much as her cousin. "Oh, and I've been to visit the

British Collection so many times now that the guard has begun to recognize me," she continued. "I've gotten permission to sketch there," she said. "It's quite glorious! Have you seen the Elgin Marbles?" she asked. Fred nodded at the two young women in the barouche, which had slowed, allowing its inhabitants to make a full appraisal of the young ladies accompanying the Misters Vaughn.

"Well, we are donors to the British Collection," he answered. Amy's brow furrowed as she tried to make sense of his response. Did that mean he *had* or *hadn't* seen the Elgin Marbles? She heard Frank and Florence laughing behind them. It sounded as if they were getting on well. The spring breeze picked up again and suddenly a spot of soot found its way directly into Amy's left eye. "Oh!" she exclaimed, and her hand automatically shot to her face, where she promptly poked herself with a gloved finger. The assaulted eye began watering, and she couldn't help winking and blinking in discomfort. She gazed straight down the Mall, at the looming Buckingham House, and tried to pretend her eye wasn't doing what it was clearly doing.

"Miss March," Fred said, "may I offer you my handkerchief?"

Amy cleared her throat, mortified. "Thank you, Mr. Vaughn," she replied, taking the bit of embroidered cambric, and daubing at the tears. But it was of no use. Her irritated eye wouldn't stop watering. She heard Frank's deep resonant laugh and Florence's twitter again. Fred said, "Perhaps if I wet the handkerchief in the fountain?" He took the scrap of linen from her hand and proceeded toward a drinking fountain topped by a statue of a boy resting comfortably on a plinth. Florence and Frank came up to her. Seeing her tears, Florence said with concern, "Oh dear, Cousin, you're crying! What's happened?"

"What's the blundering chap done this time?" Frank asked.

"I'm not crying," Amy said, gently swiping at her tearing eye with the back of her gloved hand. "He didn't do anything,"

"Allow me, Miss March," Fred said, now holding a dripping wet handkerchief. Standing straight as can be and holding her breath, Amy wished she could sink into the ground as Fred clumsily blotted at her eye. Droplets of water splattered the bodice of her dress, leaving dots of cerulean on the cornflower satin.

Amy swallowed. "Thank you, Mr. Vaughn," she said. She was fairly certain the tears streaming from both eyes now were from mortification only.

"Leave her be, Freddie," Frank said. "You're making quite a mess of things." Frank took out his own handkerchief and began to blot at the water droplets on her dress. "Not to worry, Miss March," Frank said. "I don't believe the spots will stain."

"What an unfortunate turn," Fred said. He looked flustered.

"It's nothing," Amy said. She tried to keep the quiver out of her voice but failed. She had worried so about what to wear, about minding her manners, and successfully promenading the Mall. And here she was, being fussed over in such an undignified way by the Vaughn twins, in public. At long last, she convinced Fred and Frank to put aside their handkerchiefs and they resumed their stroll. When her dress dried, which it did quickly enough, you could only see where the water droplets had stained the silk if the light was just right and you squinted your eyes. Or so Florence assured her.

Frank and Florence returned to their laughing and chatter. Fred offered Amy his arm at even the slightest crater or acclivity on their walking path, which at first Amy had found endearing but soon began to wear on her nerves. By day's end everyone had forgotten the unfortunate soot-in-the-eye incident. Except Amy, of course.

Another Assignation

Amy enjoyed being courted. It made her feel grown-up and worldly; as if she was no longer the unsophisticated youngest sister from a small town in Massachusetts who had embarked on a grand tour due to the charity of her aunt and uncle. The enterprise of being courted made her feel she was actively doing something to secure her own future, which endeavor her parents had gently suggested to her more than once before leaving home. She was getting accustomed to meeting with Fred, and as the weeks went by Amy's anxiety regarding him judging her harshly had lessened. He was clearly enamored of her, which felt quite gratifying. It was only recently though that she'd thought to examine whether her feelings for him were reciprocal.

They weren't the first people to get spun around in the Hampton Court hedge maze, and surely wouldn't be the last. But Amy and Fred were, indeed, quite lost. Fred had insisted he knew exactly how to lead them out, but it had been almost twenty minutes now, with him frantically searching for the exit after they'd left the center. Now he confidently strode before her saying, "It's just a right up here! I'm certain that on our way in we passed this very branch that's a bit broken." Amy was getting tired. She daren't say anything though. Fred seemed a bit upset that he wasn't in control of this situation, and she certainly didn't want to add to his dismay. As she'd spent more time with him, she had learned Fred very much liked to know exactly where he was and where he was going.

He continued walking confidently, Amy following behind, skimming one pretty gloved hand on the leaves of the tall wall of yew beside her. She loved the way the light hit the dense, dark evergreen. She trusted that eventually Fred *would* figure it out and lead them out of the conundrum of the maze. She smiled to herself. There was nothing complicated about Fred Vaughn, and of that she was appreciative.

When they had arrived at Hampton Court, they had first visited the gallery to view Raphael's Cartoons. Standing before the great paintings Amy had remarked that the original cartoons were actually at the Victoria and Albert, and the ones they presently were gazing at were copies that had been painted in the 1690s by a man named Henry Cooke.

Fred had nodded and said, "Well, I suppose it makes not much difference who paints something then, does it?" Amy tried to explain to him how although a copy of a painting could *attempt* to capture what the original artist intended, at the end of the day it was still a copy. For Amy, that meant something, especially given that she was learning to be a copyist herself. Having gotten permission to paint at the V&A she had stood in awe in front of a Turner, feeling entirely amateur from her top to her toes. How could anybody adequately copy a Turner sky? The despondency she had felt had been immense, even as she tried and retried.

How much easier it would be to live in the world like Fred Vaughn. Everything was so straightforward for him. Raphael's Cartoons painted by Henry Cooke were on equal footing with Raphael's Cartoons painted by Raphael.

She was lost in her thoughts when Fred abruptly came to a halt, as they arrived at yet another turn in the maze where a choice needed to be made. Left or right. Amy stopped just short of running into him. He scratched his head, looked to his left then right. Finally, he turned about to face her directly. "I believe we might be lost, Miss March," Fred said. His face was red with embarrassment. He cleared his throat. She smiled sweetly up at him.

"Oh, I'm sure you've been guiding us quite perfectly," she genially said. "I think we must be very near the exit." She pointed left and said, "Isn't it just around there?" Fred turned and Amy followed him. "Here we are!" he said, as they bid farewell to the maze. "I knew I'd figure it out!"

Amy didn't tell him that she'd never been lost at all. When Amy and her sisters were children, they had built a small maze of hay bales, and Laurie, their neighbor, had told them about the beautiful Hampton Court hedge maze. Before moving to Concord, Laurie had been to boarding school in England, until he came to live next door to them. Amy had somehow tucked a bit of hedge maze information away for years. Laurie had told them that the hedges had been grown in a fashion whereby placing and keeping one's right hand along the wall would lead one to the center. And reversed, out again.

She had tried to let Fred figure it out and feel manly, even as she had known where they were the whole time. She was pleased to be able to gently nudge him in the right direction and let him think he was a hero. But it was Laurie who was the true champion, as he had often been for her as she was growing up.

"I knew you would find our way," Amy said, looking up at Fred, as he took her arm. He fondly smiled down at her, and then they went to find the rest of their party. He stood a bit taller, and had a satisfied look on his face, when they recounted the adventure to their friends and Amy called him her hero.

Telegram

Amy couldn't imagine how much money Laurie had spent to send her a message via telegraph. And it only read: *Coming to London. Letter forthcoming. Laurie.* She knew that more than ten words per message was even more costly, so she didn't fault him for being brief. But she wished she knew when he was coming. Or, for that matter, *why* he was all of a sudden coming.

Of course she would be very glad to see him. She had rarely seen Laurie in recent years as he had been at college when she'd left for Europe. He had been part of her family in ways that her cousin, aunt, and uncle weren't. The Marches only saw the Carrols at holidays, funerals, and weddings. But she had grown up side by side with Laurie. When she was twelve years old, he was the handsome, lonely young man who came to live with Mr. Laurence, his grandfather, their next-door neighbor. Amy's sister Jo, being friendly and bold—although sometimes over-bearing—had quickly befriended him, as they were nearly the same age. Jo and Laurie became fast friends, but all the March sisters had welcomed him into the warm embrace of their family.

Laurie was there when Beth, her sister, fell ill. And when

Amy was sent away, so as not to contract the scarlet fever too, Laurie had made the banishment to her Aunt March's house bearable. He'd come to visit her every day. That was when she and he had truly become friends, apart from the rest of the family. He had been there for all of the Marches when Mother went to Washington to nurse Father back to health during the war. And Laurie was the dear who sent flowers to her and her sisters on their birthdays, who made certain there was always a beautiful Christmas dinner on the table each year, even when they couldn't afford it. He was generous and kind and she loved him dearly. They all did.

But what had happened to provoke an unplanned European trip? Why did he send her a telegraph? She hoped he wasn't in any kind of trouble. She knew Mr. Laurence had extricated Laurie from numerous scrapes whilst in college—one of the privileges of the rich—but she certainly hoped Laurie hadn't continued with his devilish shenanigans after graduation. She would need to be patient and await his letter. But it was all very curious.

At the Ball

Being in England had been a dream come true for Amy. They had visited museums and galleries, palaces and cathedrals, places that she'd only read about, but had never imagined she'd have the great good fortune to visit in person. She reveled in these travels, eagerly soaking up the art and architecture. There was nowhere she was more comfortable than gazing at a painting or sculpture, immersed in understanding or experiencing it. Viewing art was like being with an old friend. She was also enrolled in a painting class for ladies. Standing at an easel painting she felt quite at home. Amy had always been comfortable meeting new people and visiting acquaintances. She was usually very self-possessed. So the anxiety she had been experiencing since being abroad, was a very new feeling.

None of the March sisters would particularly be characterized as insecure, even though her sister Beth was shy with anyone outside of the family. It was easy to have self-confidence being a member of the March family, even if they were no longer a family of means. Father's connections in the Concord community were with philosophers, poets, and prominent transcendentalists. Mother had been active in the abolitionist movement, as well as working for women's suffrage. Her oldest sister, Meg, had seemingly transitioned effortlessly from being an intelligent, patient governess, to being a loving young wife and mother. Amy and her sister Jo had always been strangely competitive and were frequently at odds. Jo was not gentle with Amy. She mocked her and judged her and often made Amy feel small. And dear Beth, although quite content in her own company, was an accomplished pianist. Back in Concord, with the strength of her family's connections and accomplishments, Amy had been at ease and confident in most social situations. She was one of those people whose charm and beauty drew others to her. She was well-liked and comfortable in that role. That wasn't the present case though.

Amy unconsciously touched the lace at the neckline of her dress, as if it might give her some strength or ease her social anxiety. Back in Concord, when they had packed Amy up for this European adventure, Mother had lovingly trimmed Amy's sky-blue tarlatan herself, adding delicate ivory lace scavenged from one of her own old gowns. It was a remnant from Mother's youth when she still held a genteel position in society. That was before father's poor business decisions had changed everything.

As Amy fretted about the ball, she felt the return of the panicky sparrow in her chest. She wasn't worried about the dancing, at which she was, of course, adept. What she feared was an inadvertent blunder, accidentally saying or doing something inappropriate, or wearing the wrong thing. She was ever vigilant to the many ways she might misstep and cared greatly about the good opinion of others. And, for pity's sake, she wanted to avoid another fiasco like the soot in her eye at St. James's Park.

"Oh, I hope they've put a varsoviana on the dance schedule!" Florence chittered, grabbing Amy's elbow. Florence, Amy, and

Aunt Mary strode two paces closer to the ballroom entry, where a servant would take their names to be announced. Past the servant, who was dressed in livery, they could see the widow Lady Willoughby, their hostess, hovering near the entrance, greeting her guests.

Aunt Mary whispered, "Well! I'm certain that won't be the *first* dance." They took another step forward. She continued, "And I'm sure Lady Willoughby has arranged whatever is *de rigueur* here in London." She pursed her lips and whispered, "I know Lady Willoughby conducts herself strictly according to the code of good breeding." As they took two more steps toward the entrance Amy heard the tinkle of a piano and croon of a cornet, shortly followed by a violin and violoncello in conversation with each other, as the musicians readied themselves to play. Aunt Mary snapped open her fan and whispered behind it, "Of course even the slightest departure from the code of etiquette would be a grave offense." Amy's gloved fingers left the lace at her throat and moved to the nape of her neck, checking for errant curls escaping the combs on either side of her braided bun. Thankfully, it was a mild summer day lacking in humidity and her hair was behaving.

"Oh, Mother, stop making Cousin nervous," Florence said. "I'm sure etiquette here in London isn't all that different than at home." Cousin Flo had no idea the effort Amy had put in at home to learn and follow all the formalities of proper conduct. Amy had only recently begun to move about in society. Of course, her sister Jo had given her such a ribbing about her efforts, mocking her and saying she was putting on airs. But Amy wouldn't allow herself even the slightest slipup.

Jo didn't care about manners or improving her social standing, as Amy did. Jo went through life like a bull in a china shop, ready to smash everything around her with her careless impulsivity and boyishness. But Amy had ever been a careful doe, stopping to admire the beautiful china, perhaps moving a pretty teacup to a spot where one might better see its delicate artistry, and wishing and hoping to take said teacup home. Amy had done her fair share of damage, as an ungainly doe might, but had always returned to her pursuit of excellence in the social graces.

Amy often imagined her Aunt March's voice, sometimes as a guiding angel, sometimes as a warning devil, but always paying attention to Amy's actions. Amy eagerly sought the approval of her fictitious version of Aunt March in her head. In the confines of her home life with her sisters and mother, they had rarely spoken of etiquette. Rather they spoke of things like goodness and kindness. "You have not lived today until you have done something for someone who can never repay you." The words of John Bunyan were etched on her soul in a way that choosing the appropriate first dance at a ball, never would be.

It wasn't that Amy hadn't read Bunyan's *Pilgrim's Progress* with as much enthusiasm as her sisters or didn't want to be a good little pilgrim. It was that somehow along the way she had *also* learned that upward social mobility was not only an attainable goal, but one that she, of all her sisters, might be capable of realizing. She endeavored to be good *and* improve her social standing. And, although nobody said it aloud, she knew that her parents were counting on her to deliver their family out of poverty through an advantageous marriage.

Aunt Mary fluttered her fan and continued to whisper behind it. "Florence, whether at home or abroad it is essential for a young lady to master the etiquette of the ballroom."

"Mother," Florence said, "Amy needn't worry about mastering etiquette. She has her beauty." Florence tilted her head, looking at Amy, and said, "I believe her comely visage inspires forgiveness whenever she misses the mark." Amy knew Florence wasn't mean-spirited, she just had the tendency to be a tad unsophisticated, which made this conversation about etiquette ironic.

Amy blushed and faintly smiled at Florence, wondering when

she'd missed the mark, and who she had needed forgiveness from. She stifled a sigh. Mention of her pleasant appearance felt like such a burden. It was tiresome that her family—even dear cousin Flo—felt need to always drag out her physical appearance and discuss it in front of her, as if she weren't there, as if it were all she was made of.

"She does indeed have her beauty!" Aunt Mary crooned, looking at Amy fondly, and reached out to touch Amy's cheek with her pearl-white lace-gloved hand. Amy stiffened, but didn't draw away, letting her aunt pet her face, as if she were a beloved kitten. They took three last steps and finally reached the ballroom entrance. Aunt Mary handed the servant their cards, and he announced in a booming British voice, "Mrs. Edward Carrol, Miss Florence Carrol, and Miss Amy Curtis March."

As they stepped into the ballroom a few heads turned, and Lady Willoughby greeted them with a polite smile. Aunt Mary began speaking immediately. "We appreciate the invitation to your lovely home," she said, extending her hand. Lady Willoughby genteelly took it to shake, even though Amy was pretty sure shaking hands was no longer the fashion.

"It is my pleasure to welcome the family of my dear friend Josephine Curtis March," Lady Willoughby said, looking at Amy rather than Aunt Mary. She delicately dropped Aunt Mary's hand to give Amy her full attention.

"And how is your Aunt March?" Lady Willoughby asked welcomingly. Amy wasn't sure if she was supposed to answer, or if Aunt Mary would take offense. She glanced her aunt's way, to see her looking expectantly at Amy, as if she, too, wanted to know how Aunt March was.

Amy hadn't spoken a word since they'd entered the manor house, she had been so intent on controlling her nerves. It had been easier to let Aunt Mary and Cousin Florence prattle on about manners and etiquette and just politely listen. She timidly said, "Aunt March is well, thank you." She cleared her throat and said in a more confident voice, "She particularly asked me to send you her regards, Lady Willoughby."

Lady Willoughby's smile warmed even more as she leaned in toward Amy and said, "Josie and I share a love of the arts and patronage. One might say we've gotten a bit competitive about it at times."

Amy grinned. "Aunt March might have made mention of that," she said.

Lady Willoughby chuckled. "And you are the niece who paints or the niece who writes?" she asked.

Amy blushed. "My sister is the one who writes," she said.

Cousin Florence clutched Amy's arm and said, "Our cousin Amy is a talented painter. She's a wonderful artist, really."

Lady Willoughby's eyes dimmed a bit as she gazed towards Florence, as if she were just noticing her. "Ah!" she replied. Then she turned her attention back to Amy. "Well, you are welcome to come back to Clarke Manor anytime to paint or sketch." She smiled conspiratorially, and the corners of her eyes crinkled with laugh lines. "It would also be very agreeable to me to have a nice gossipy tea with you!"

Amy smiled back. "Thank you, Lady Willoughby," she said, "it would be agreeable to me, as well."

"Enjoy the ball, Miss March!" she said warmly. "Miss Carrol, Mrs. Carrol, thank you for coming," she said, dismissing them.

As Lady Willoughby turned to greet more guests, Aunt Mary snapped her fan open, gleefully whispering to Amy and Florence, "We've been invited to tea!"

Amy relaxed a little, now that she'd met Lady Willoughby, who was clearly cut from the same cloth as Aunt March. She could imagine Aunt March saying, "I've trained you well, Amy March. You're more a lady than most of the others in this room, and my friend Willoughby has seen it. Now go enjoy the ball!" Then Amy sighed, remembering her parents' directive to

"Make this trip worthwhile," by which she understood them to mean, *come home with a lucrative promise of marriage.*

Aunt Mary broke Amy's reverie when she said, "I am to meet Katherine Vaughn in the rose parlor before the first dance." As Aunt Mary swept away, Amy stood for a moment longer, wondering if she was the only person who noticed that poor Aunt Mary's anemic champagne moiré gown was the exact same hue as the wallpaper.

Florence was already on the move. She looked back over her shoulder at Amy. "Why are you lingering?" she said excitedly. "Let's go stand where the Vaughn twins may see us, so they might come say hello!" Amy gazed across the large ballroom and saw Fred and Frank Vaughn. Fred was looking in their direction.

"We have spaces to fill on our dance cards," Florence said with glee, as she began weaving her way through the crowd. Amy could see Florence meant to position herself at a large Grecian urn packed with pink chrysanthemums and pale yellow roses. Gaining the attention of young men was just a game for Florence, a merry entertainment. Given her family money, there was no imperative to her finding a wealthy husband, although she would of course not want to marry beneath her. The violin began playing a lively tune, and over the heads of the other guests, at the far side of the room, Amy saw Fred smile directly at her, as he lifted his chin in greeting. She smiled back, hoping she came across as encouraging without seeming crass or overeager. It felt like such a fine line sometimes.

Squaring her shoulders, she began to weave her way through the crowd to take her place next to Florence at the urn.

The room began to feel a bit stifling, amidst all the milling people. She knew exactly what the rest of the evening would look like. Of course Fred would claim the first dance on her dance card, as well as the one before supper. Etiquette dictated that a gentleman who dances with a lady in the last dance before supper has the opportunity to escort her to the supper room, attend her while there, and accompany her back to the ballroom after. As she smoothly navigated her way through the throng of people toward Florence, across the room she could see that Fred was on the move too. Frank was busy laughing and chatting with a handsome young man, but Fred resolutely made his way through the crowd, like a shark parting the waters, headed directly for the Grecian urn.

Sometimes the rules of etiquette were comforting, as so little was left to conjecture. Some things were correct, and others were not, so Amy felt she mostly knew how she was faring. But sometimes, like this evening, the rules of etiquette, when put up against the judgment and expectations of her family, felt stifling—not comforting at all. *I like Fred Vaughn*, she thought to herself, *so why do I feel so trapped?*

Afternoon Refreshment and Whist

Aunt Mary put on her spectacles and leaned over to look at Mrs. Vaughn's needlework. "Such delicate stitching, Katherine," she said. The older women chattered on, heads together, occasionally glancing at the younger set, who were busy with a card game. It had been a couple of weeks since the Willoughby ball, and Amy had found herself frequently in Fred Vaughn's company. That afternoon she and Florence sat at the card table playing whist with Fred and Grace Vaughn. Apparently, Frank was under the weather and had stayed home to convalesce. The older sister, Kate, was not going out in society at the moment, as she was confined yet again, expecting another child.

Amy picked up the trick. "It's difficult to believe you are engaged to be married, Grace," she said. "It seems like just yesterday we were little girls at a picnic, meeting for the first time."

Grace discarded a card. "That will be six years ago this summer!" she replied.

Fred said, "I find it intriguing how in six years the age difference between us has narrowed so much." He laughed and discarded a card.

"Why, what do you mean?" Florence asked, discarding her own card.

"When Kate, Frank, Grace, and I picnicked with Laurence and his odd group of little women friends, Laurence and I were near seventeen years old, and certainly felt ourselves almost men."

Grace muttered, "You might have *thought* yourselves men, but I can assure you, you still acted like children." Amy remembered Fred's older sister Kate being quite condescending to Meg, and Fred himself had tried to cheat Jo at croquet. Which of course had been a great mistake.

Fred continued, unperturbed. "You and Amy were actual children at fourteen years old," he said haughtily to his younger sister. "And it was then that you and she first became friends."

Amy smiled weakly, trying to be polite. He was recalling the story as if she and Grace hadn't been there. It was slightly irritating that he went on as if it weren't her life he was discussing. She lifted her chin and urged her face to smile more authentically. She didn't want to be rude. She discarded her card and picked up another trick.

Fred continued. "Who could have foretold back then that one day we would meet again here in London? That we would look fondly back at our youth, Grace an engaged woman, and you, Miss March, perhaps on your way to the same."

Amy cleared her throat and kept her eyes intently on her cards, as she felt her face begin to blush. Fred smugly took the trick, looking very satisfied with himself. Grace shook her head and let out a loud sigh. Florence said, "And how is your brother Frank faring?"

"Oh, Frank," Fred said, shaking his head. "He'd be much better if he'd just . . ."

Mrs. Vaughn interrupted, loudly saying, "Put the cards away now! Shall we have a light refreshment, Mary?" Then continued in a softer voice, "Frank is on the mend, dear Florence.

Thank you for inquiring." If Amy had had any doubts as to whether Aunt Mary and Katherine Vaughn had been eavesdropping on their conversation, that was cleared up now.

"Some refreshment sounds delightful, Aunt Mary," Amy said, rising to join the older women. "And what a lovely assortment of canapés!" Florence, Grace, and Fred followed Amy's lead, the half-finished game of cards quickly forgotten as they happily indulged in dainty dishes, oysters, and chilled Pimm's cocktails.

Later, as the girls readied themselves for bed, Florence was brushing out her hair and said, "Well, if the meaning behind Fred Vaughn's recent attentions hadn't been clear until now, I do believe he made them obvious today at tea."

Amy was brushing her own long blond curls. She smiled and started to make a braid. "He certainly tipped his hand during whist, didn't he?"

"Indeed!" Florence said. As Amy turned away from her cousin, though, her smile began to fade. If all kept going as it was, she and Fred might be engaged within the year. She knew that *should* make her happy, but something about it was not sitting right with her.

She'd always understood Father and Mother's unspoken expectation of her, but it wasn't until now, when she was faced with its impending actuality, that she'd begun to realize she'd never given thought to what she might have wanted for herself. As a young girl she'd always said she intended to fall in love with a rich suitor, because she loved fine things. She hadn't realized that falling in love wasn't so simple though, or what one might have to give up of oneself.

Fred was a perfectly fine man, of course. She didn't like to admit that she found him a bit dull sometimes. But she did. It was as if the steadfastness that she admired in him was also one of the things that irritated her about him. If only he had more of the playful nature of his brother Frank, who reminded her of

Laurie. Laurie could make her laugh and sometimes even cry, but certainly never made her yawn. She hadn't heard anything more from him since the cryptic telegram. But best to think of pleasant things, not drive herself mad wondering what Laurie had gotten himself into, or considering the possibility of other prospects for her future—especially when it looked as if she and Fred were fated.

Sighing, Amy said, "Good night, Florence," and Flo responded, "Sweet dreams, Cousin."

Painting in the Park

A warm, soft breeze rippled through the park, sending strolling ladies' hats flying. Amy held the top of the canvas with one hand, so it wouldn't blow right off her easel. With the hand holding the paintbrush she pushed a stray lock of her golden hair behind her ear, carefully avoiding smudging paint on her face. The pallid London sky was washed out compared to the robin's-egg blue on her canvas. Florence fidgeted on the blanket, which was spread beneath a tree.

"Cousin, shall I turn my head just so?" Florence asked, "or would it be best this way?" She tipped her chin down. It didn't matter at all to Amy what Florence did with her head. She was more interested in figuring out how to capture in paint both the warmth of the sun and the movement of the breeze. Cousin Florence's likeness was merely a blob of olive green on a daffodil-colored blanket, a slash of ginger at the top indicating her hair. Amy didn't reply, thinking about all the mail she had received that morning: a letter from Meg, about the twins and how tired she was; a letter from Beth about a new piano piece she was learning; a long letter from Mother and

Father, which began quite lovingly but ended instructively; and a thick envelope from Laurie that she'd put aside to read when she had some privacy. Florence chattered on and on, as always, oblivious to the fact that Amy wasn't paying attention. Amy mixed another bit of blue paint into the white and dabbed at the canvas.

As it took weeks to receive a letter in London from the States, Amy had waited impatiently after receiving Laurie's telegraph. Ever since she had been sent to stay with Aunt March when Beth had first fallen ill, Amy had counted on Laurie's friendship. He'd promised her he'd visit her at Aunt March's Plumfield, and for all the weeks she'd been forced to stay away from home he had devotedly shown up every afternoon. When she thought about it now it seemed extraordinary that a young man of not even seventeen years had been so kind as to play savior to a sad, homesick fourteen-year-old girl. Before then she had never been away from her home, and it had only been through Laurie's tender concern and attention that it had been the least bit bearable.

Aunt March had been quite bristly at first. Jo had spent much time at Plumfield, as Aunt March's companion, and that had been fairly disastrous. Aunt March wasn't used to young people, and Jo was impulsive and impatient. Not knowing what to expect from Amy, whom she'd been led to believe was a bit of a ninny by Jo, Aunt March had taken a while to warm up. Amy felt that Laurie's daily visits had saved her, and it had been the true start of their friendship, born outside the dynamics of the March family. Because of that their relationship had always been private and special to her.

They had spent many companionable afternoons back then, walking in the gardens of Plumfield, riding in Laurie's carriage throughout the countryside, and always talking and laughing. But he hadn't laughed when she'd shared her aspirations to become an artist of renown; to one day perhaps have her work hung at an exposition. He had regaled her with stories from his boarding school days in England and Switzerland and Italy, telling her of some of the shenanigans he'd gotten himself into in each place. And he'd shared his own romantic fantasies of someday composing a symphony or opera.

When Beth was somewhat recovered and Amy finally returned home to Orchard House, Amy sensed Jo's jealousy upon seeing the shift in her friendship with Laurie. Amy sighed, remembering it. Jo had never understood that Amy and Laurie's mutual attachment had nothing to do with her, that it was something unique and separate from his friendship and relationship with the rest of the March family and with Jo. That seemed so long ago now. The breeze in the park picked up, and Amy steadied her canvas with the hand not holding the paintbrush.

She daubed a touch of white into the sky, tilted her head as she looked at the canvas, and daubed again. As they'd both grown older Laurie had continued to be a dear friend to her. Now, he was newly graduated from Harvard and a ripe old man of almost twenty-one. Feeling mature herself at eighteen years, Amy was concerned about him. She could feel that something had been brewing. She was almost sure it had to do with Jo. And that never boded well for anyone.

That morning the post had come just as Amy and Florence were leaving on their expedition to the park. In her painting class they'd been working en plein air and she wanted to do so on her own. She'd quickly read the letters from her family, but from the heft of it she knew she'd want to read Laurie's letter privately, so she'd safely tucked it away in the pocket of the linen pinafore she'd buttoned over her light summer day dress. Now, it felt as if the letter was burning a hole in that pocket. Florence was saying something, but Amy had ceased listening quite a while before.

"I think we're done for today, Florence," Amy said, beginning to wipe her brushes and pack them back in their case.

THE OTHER MARCH SISTERS   31

"Cousin, have you not heard a word that I've said?" Florence asked, trying to rise to her feet in the most ladylike way possible.

Amy said, "Of course I have, dear," and smiled, whilst folding up the easel.

"So then, shall we?" Florence replied happily.

"Shall we . . ." Amy's attention was finally fully on Florence. She exhaled with a big sigh, hoping she'd be able to figure out what she was agreeing to, without letting on to Florence that she hadn't, indeed, been paying attention at all.

"Shall we return to the hotel and have a cool beverage?" Florence asked, as if *today's* afternoon refreshment would be any different than any other day's. As if having a lemonade at the hotel were somehow a novel suggestion.

"Oh, yes," Amy said, smiling and trying to look pleasant. "We shall." She put her hand into the pocket of her pinafore and ran her fingers over the envelope, wondering what news it held inside.

A Letter from Laurie

Concord, Massachusetts
My lady,
  I trust you received my telegram. As
promised, I will explain myself more fully.
I am leaving with Grandfather tomorrow,
disembarking at Southampton ten days
hence. After a certain recent
conversation—about which I will apprise
you later in this letter—I have decided to
accompany Grandfather, as he attends to
some family business in London. I hope the
itinerary your uncle has set for your travels will coincide with my arrival in London
as I am in dire need of a good family sit-
down, and who else could I possibly confide
in besides you, dear Amy?

Amy stopped reading for a moment, her brow furrowed. Who,
indeed? Although Laurie was always there to listen to Amy,

usually when he confided in *her* it was because Jo was being a scold or a nag. What on earth had Jo done to warrant a hasty departure out of the country by Laurie? She continued reading, skimming the letter past the parts where he detailed the different choices of accommodation on the ship, his arrangement for fresh flowers to be sent weekly to Beth at Orchard House whilst he was away (dear boy!), and his suspicion that life at the Dovecote wasn't as cheery as Meg was leading others to believe. On the third page, near the bottom, she finally got to it.

After graduation, this past spring, Jo had been acting queerly. As you know, this is not unusual for your sister. I believe I'd mentioned it to you in my last letter. Well, she and I had a bit of a falling-out, I'm afraid. I don't like to put you in an uncomfortable position with your sister, as that relationship is often already fraught, but I think you of anyone will understand my feelings regarding what happened.

When we were all children, Jo did the honor of welcoming Grandfather and me into the March family, and our lives would surely not be the same had she not. You know I love Jo like a sister, and with all my heart, although she always calls herself a brother. I share this next part of my story in utter confidence. As Jo's sister I think you might understand it in a way no one else can. I'm certain were she to relay it to you herself, she'd likely tell a different story.

Amy couldn't imagine where this was going. She rifled through the pages of the letter and saw that it went on for some time.

> *During one of our romps through the woods, Jo and I stopped to rest and chat. We casually spoke of future plans now that I'm graduated. It had been a pleasant afternoon, but then, as she does, Jo began telling me what I should do, when I should do it, and exactly how it should be done.*
>
> *Deciding to turn this back upon her, as I had no intention of ruining a pleasant afternoon by making any sort of grand life decision, I steered the conversation back to Jo's own plans for herself. I know she has been worried about family finances. She told me her stories weren't selling as she had hoped.*
>
> *Now we know how prickly Jo can be, so I thought to soften what I wanted to say to her about writing. So I began by telling her that I've loved her ever since I'd met her, that I couldn't help it, and that she's been so good to me. When I said that, though, she got the most queer expression on her face, interrupted me, and began speaking all in a rush. She told me I was too good for her, she was proud and fond of me, but that she was sorry she couldn't love me as I wanted her to. I didn't understand what she was saying, and then she told me that she couldn't change her feelings. She said, "It would be a lie to say I do when I don't."*

I was totally confused, because I'd wanted to talk to her about other ways she might use her writing skills to bring in money for your family. Then it dawned on me that she thought I was professing my love for her because I wanted to marry her. I tried to cut in, but she just powered forward, not letting me say a word. But then, much to my surprise, Jo suggested she and I should get married, live under the same roof, but without the intimacy usually enjoyed by a husband and wife. She said we could be married in name only. She told me she had no inclination for intimacy with a man and she didn't care a fig for romance, with me or anyone.

Amy read and reread the last few sentences. It did not surprise her that Jo could be so brash. But that Jo would bring up the topic of intimacy with a man? Even Laurie? Well, Amy felt embarrassed for her, especially seeing Jo's misinterpretation of the conversation Laurie had intended to be having with her. Amy read on.

She had confirmed the suspicion you and I had that she has no interest in romance or intimacy with men. As you and I have always said, we love Jo for the person she is. I almost laughed aloud at her misunderstanding, until I realized that my dear friend had begun to think of me as a means to an end. I became speechless and as she continued on I could feel my heart break. She said by marrying me, she would be able to provide for your family and also be with her closest friend. You know how much I would love to be a member of the March family, but to marry without that sort of love? To forsake intimacy for the purpose of the economic security of your family? I couldn't begin to understand how Jo thought that would ever be acceptable.

Here, Amy paused in her reading. She set the letter upon her lap, her eyes wide, as she realized she and Jo weren't that different after all. For so much of her life she'd accepted Jo's characterizations. Meg was the pleasant, motherly sister; Jo claimed intellect as well as creativity for herself; Beth was relegated to merely sweet and simple; and she, Amy, had always been drawn as a silly, spoiled, frivolous little girl. But here she was, halfway across the world, spending her days in hopes of securing a proposal from a man of means, while her sister had tried to take matters into her own hands at home to accomplish the same goal. Amy didn't blame Laurie for not wanting to enter into a marriage based only on convenience, but he couldn't begin to comprehend the difficulties a woman faced when born to a family of only sisters.

Amy took a deep breath and read further.

I'm sorry to say I lost control of my emotions then, and rather than express my disappointment or hurt I became belligerent and indignant. Trying to control my temper is the bane of my existence! It is only with you that I never seem to get angry. Upon seeing my reaction, Jo tried to explain that it wouldn't be only for the money but that such a marriage would ben-

efit us both. She insisted my character is the same as hers—that where she is boyish and manly for a young woman, I am more gentle and tender than most young men. She isn't wrong. We all know that. Then she inferred certain things about this fact, which I will not commit to paper, nor will I deny.

I told her that I love her dearly as a sister--she corrected me and said brother, as she always does--but I could never consider a marriage of this sort and I was insulted she would even propose such a thing. Now she will barely speak to me. She makes excuses if I try to call on her. She leaves my notes unread in our post box! I fear I've lost my dear friend.

I didn't mean to shame her, and I'm very sorry I wasn't delicate in correcting the misunderstanding. I think she is stewing in humiliation. So I am running away, as it were, to give her time to sort herself out, in hopes that when I return, our friendship might be restored. You know how I wish our dear sister a life of happiness. I think Jo might be able to have the sort of companionship that she seeks in a Boston marriage, although I'm not sure she will ever admit that to herself.

Amy didn't know what a Boston marriage was, and she also only wished happiness for her sister. That Jo, who had always said she would never marry, had been willing to push aside her feelings on the matter for the benefit of the family, truly spoke of Jo's love for them all. Amy wished she could take Jo's hand

and tell her that she completely understood why she had been willing to do that.

Laurie's letter ended shortly after that, with him saying he looked forward to seeing her soon. He signed off as "Your lord," in the private joke they shared between them. Laurie's letter had stirred her in unexpected ways. It was perhaps impolite to discuss, and yet Laurie had confided in her how unacceptable it would be for him to marry someone without romantic love, for convenience only. Amy could see that Jo's misinterpretation of the conversation had probably been fueled by her motivation, but there was something else too.

There was a facet of Laurie that Jo just didn't understand, as she seemed devoid of it herself. He was a sensual person. It was so much a part of him. Amy could see how Laurie would be hurt that Jo—his dearest friend—could ask him to put that part of himself aside.

Amy sighed, neatly folding the letter, and slid it into the desk drawer for safekeeping. She stood and smoothed down the fabric of her skirt. Before she went down to tea with Florence she stopped at the small mirror on the wall next to the door. She shook her head at her reflection, unfurrowed her brows, and smiled. It wasn't very convincing, even to herself. She tucked an errant curl back into her plaited hair and lifted her chin.

The letter also mirrored some truths about herself Amy would rather not look at. She was trying to do what was expected to help her family, in much the same way Jo had tried. Amy didn't like to think about whether Fred would also be hurt were he to know why she entertained his affections. But Laurie and Fred were both men, and had financial security. They had the luxury of choosing to marry for a particular *kind* of love, for romance or passion. Women without financial security didn't have that privilege. They had to do what was necessary.

She tried smiling at herself in the mirror again. She wished she had the freedom to decide who she would be in the world, who she would be to her family or Laurie, and even perhaps to Fred. But mostly, when she thought about it, she wished she had the freedom to decide who she would be for herself. Her smile seemed slightly more convincing now, and that would have to do. She nodded at her reflection and went to meet Florence.

Paris
A Letter to Laurie

Paris

Dear Laurie,

I trust you are finding London to be all that you had hoped by way of escape. I'm very sorry that we missed each other. It seems we have much to discuss about Jo. When I first read your letter I was surprised by her behavior, but upon contemplation I can understand her thinking, even if that thinking failed to take your desires into account. The gist of your letter, though, feels as if it might be better discussed in person. I look forward to seeing you when you arrive on the Continent and having the family sit-down that you desire. As you had told me I would, I adore this City of Lights! Paris is absolutely divine!

Will your grandfather accompany you to Paris, Laurie, or is he set on returning home to Concord? I would love to see him. Please give him my fondest regards. And do tell me your plans so I know when to expect you.

We are soon off to visit the Cathédrale Notre-Dame de Paris with the Vaughns. Aunt Mary and Mrs. Vaughn have become fast friends. Fred and Grace have proved attentive travel companions to Florence and me. I will catch you up on all the latest gossip in case you hadn't heard. Frank stayed back in London; I'm led to believe he's convalescing from something. Have you been to see him? The Vaughns often speak of him being unwell, but I don't know the nature of his illness. I don't want to be rude and ask Fred, but I am feeling nosy about it. Was his health poorly when you knew him as a boy at school?

Grace is to be married next year to a young man named Spencer Green Myers, who's accepted a position as vicar in a country parish outside of Bath. I met him when we were in London, and he is very pleasant. He was unable to travel with us because of his responsibilities. I believe he was a few years behind you, Fred, and Frank at school? Grace tells me that she misses him horridly. Truth be told I can't imagine Grace a vicar's wife!

In other news, Fred and I have become quite friendly. I'm not sure why, but I feel shy about telling you it. I am trying to figure myself out. I feel unexpectedly topsy turvy about it all. I don't have anything further to report yet. We shall see.

As for Paris, our rooms are quite close to many of the touristic sights. Florence and I try to visit something of cultural import frequently. Unfortunately, the École des Beaux-Arts won't accept women students and most artists won't accept women in their studios as well. So I'm in a painting class exclusively of women, where we are charged twice as much and get half the instruction. We do paint from live models but only draped, as it's considered unseemly for a woman to paint from a nude model. I've requested dispensation to train as a copyist at the Louvre. I was fortunate to draw at the British Collection and copy at the Victoria & Albert when we were in London. Since I have these credentials, I'm hoping to be approved by the Louvre.

In the meanwhile, I try to behave like a good little woman as Mother raised me to be, being gentle and kind to all, and minding my manners. I think Aunt March would be proud of me. Sometimes, though I can't pinpoint exactly why it is, I feel like I can't breathe. I look forward to seeing you, My Lord, and being in the company of someone with whom I can always exhale. Ever your lady,
ACM

Cameo

Aunt Mary and Mrs. Vaughn lingered in front of a shop window. Flo was up ahead with Grace, whilst Amy and Fred ambled along behind. They were strolling in the gallery of the Palais-Royal, which Amy thought was heavenly. There were so many lovely things, it was distracting!

"Allow me to buy you a little gift," Fred said. "Would you accept a trinket to remind you of me?"

Fred can be such an agreeable young man, Amy thought. Of course, the fact that he was clearly enamored of her was flattering. She hadn't a lot of experience with courting. At home in Concord she'd always done what was expected, visiting with neighbors, while Aunt March had provided entry to a social circle Amy and her sisters might not have had access to on their own. But mostly Amy had been quite sheltered. She had kept her focus on studying painting in Boston. So Fred's attentions were complimentary and gratifying in a way in which she was unaccustomed. The only young man who had ever looked at her the way Fred did was Laurie. And of course Laurie had looked at her through the gaze of an older brother. She couldn't help it, but when she looked up at Fred with his milky pale skin and ashy blond hair, she thought *I wish he were dark like Laurie; I'm not sure I fancy light men.*

"Perhaps you would care for one of the cameo brooches we saw in the window?" Fred continued. Of *course* she would like a brooch, who wouldn't? But accepting a gift from a young man was no small thing.

"Let's catch up to the others," Amy said, trying to avoid the question. But Fred was persistent. He took a step closer to her and lowered his voice. "Amy," he said, "it's just un petite bibelot! Let me! Won't you?" He took her arm and led her back to the shop they'd passed. In the window was an array of shell cameos, brooches, and pendants, artfully displayed. They *were* lovely. But they were also far beyond her means. She felt certain Aunt Mary would think it inappropriate for her to accept.

"Perhaps that one?" he said, pointing. She looked at him and thought *Fred Vaughn is very rich and does come from an excellent family, so I shan't find fault with his pale hair.* She swallowed a sigh because as much as she wished it otherwise, a part of her recognized that her heart was not doing its job of aligning with her head.

"Either that one with the three Graces or perhaps the one with the face of Aphrodite?" He smiled at her. "Either would suit you," he said, in an intimate voice. He looked so earnest. He looked, indeed, as if he was falling in love with her.

Of course, it was flattering that he wished to buy her something, and that he was flirting. But then out of her mouth popped the words, "Oh, but that's Athena, not Aphrodite." She immediately regretted it. She put her hand before her mouth and bit her lips. How could she be so rude to correct him when he was trying to be kind? He looked back at the cameos in the window and then to her. "But she's quite beautiful," he said. "What makes you think she's not Aphrodite?"

Amy and her sisters had all studied both Greek and Roman mythology. An appreciation of art demanded it. How else could one understand Caravaggio, Rubens, Botticelli? And Raphael! She had viewed paintings by Raphael with Fred.

She cleared her throat. "Well . . . there's an olive branch in her hand," she quietly said. He leaned toward the glass a bit, trying to get a better look. It was like a spigot had been turned and she couldn't stop more words from pouring out. "If she were Aphrodite the artist would have used myrtle, a pomegranate, or a dove." He stepped back from the window and looked quizzically at her. She shrugged, blushing. "Mother and Father insisted we know our mythology."

"Quite so," he replied. "Well, then Athena she is! And shall you have her?"

"Thank you very much, Mr. Vaughn," Amy said, trying to sound appreciative. "I regret that I can't accept though." He frowned. "I'm certain my aunt would not allow it."

He nodded, took her arm, and they turned to catch up to the others. As they walked, he leaned into her a bit, and gently said, "Soon, Miss March, I hope to be able to offer you something finer than a shell cameo."

Her heart sped up and she felt herself blush. If you'd asked her what she was feeling in that moment, she wouldn't have been able to name it. It might have been happy anticipation, or it might have been worried apprehension. But she was not trying to name her feeling, she was trying to avoid it altogether. So she changed the subject.

"Florence and I shall go to Fontainebleau," Amy said. "We are to visit with a great artist. Aunt March's friend Lady Willoughby arranged the invitation."

"How wonderful! Your enthusiasm for painting is so charming," Fred said. "I'm sure you will enjoy yourself. Is he someone of whom I would have heard?"

"She's a she," Amy said. "The painter's name is Rosa Bon-

heur. Her paintings *Ploughing in the Nivernais* and *The Horse
Fair* are quite famous. She received the French Legion of Honor!"
This was better. Talking about art was soothing. It was much
easier than navigating conflicting emotions about Fred's attentions. Back on comfortable footing she gayly said, "Florence
and I leave in the morning!"

At Fontainebleau

"She seems so . . ." Florence whispered, "I don't know . . ." She looked around the beautiful sitting room where they were having tea, as if the word she sought might be resting amongst the settee cushions, atop the pianoforte, or hidden somewhere in one of Miss Bonheur's paintings hung on the wall. "She's just a queer sort," she settled on.

"She's a renowned artist," Amy whispered back. "She's the only woman to have had her work shown at the Paris Salon, Florence!" But Flo didn't seem very impressed.

"Well, just because she's a famous artist," Florence replied, sitting up a bit straighter and sniffing, "does not excuse her poor manners."

"Poor manners?" Amy said. "What poor manners are you speaking of?"

Florence took a demure sip of her tea. "Why on earth would Miss Bon-hore think we were interested in watching her horse give birth?"

Amy smiled. "Florence, she's the most acclaimed *animalière* in France! You really must work on your French, dear," she said. "She invited us to *visit* the colt that was just born, not witness its birth." Amy laughed, shaking her head and sipping her own tea. Florence sniffed again.

"Well, I also find it very rude that the French refuse to accommodate their visitors when we can't understand what they're saying."

"The whole world isn't obliged to speak English, Florence, just because Americans aren't well educated."

"I had a French tutor for years," Florence said. "And even so," she continued, "I have no interest in going to Miss Bonhore's stables to look at a colt."

"Her intention was for us to see two specific horses of hers, not just the colt," Amy replied. "She was explaining a particular aspect of painting them."

"Oh, painting! She reminds me of your sister," Florence said, delicately spearing a piece of cake from her plate, "when Jo goes on and on about her scribbles—as if anybody *truly* cares—and how to show a character through dialogue, et cetera et cetera et cetera." Florence daintily placed the piece of cake in her mouth, pursed her lips, and chewed in a most ladylike way.

"Yes," replied Amy. "She does put me in mind of Jo."

Florence swallowed her cake, took a sip of her tea, and continued. "And why would any lady want to wear a man's outfit? It's positively scandalous. And to do so in public?"

They heard someone coming.

"Florence, please," Amy whispered. "Gossiping doesn't become you."

"She's a queer sort," Florence muttered.

Rosa strode back into the room, holding a stack of papers.

"Mademoiselle March," she said, "these are the sketches of which I spoke." Her English was heavily accented, *these* sounding like *zeese*. She spread the sheets of paper out on the floor in front of them. "You see the progression here?" She pointed from one sketch to the next. "When I was younger, I found it particularly difficult to truly recreate the musculature, not knowing the mechanism of what was underneath."

To Amy even these rough sketches looked like works of art, beautiful in simplicity and anatomic specificity. It was apparent Miss Bonheur's knowledge of structural anatomy was the foundation of her work, literally creating artistic form from knowledge of function.

"My papa encouraged the artistic education of all of his children, beginning with me," she said. "I was not exempt because of my sex. We all worked for years helping Papa with his commissions."

Florence was looking out the window, uninterested in the conversation about art. But both Amy and Miss Bonheur's attention were on the sketches.

"I was fortunate to study for a bit at Boston's Museum of Fine Arts," Amy replied. "My Aunt March sent me. She's always been supportive of my artistic education."

Miss Bonheur smiled. "Yes, it is important to have someone in our lives who understands the artistic drive, the soul of an artist, *non*?" She gathered up the sketches at their feet.

"I don't know that Aunt March understands the soul of an artist." Amy laughed. Florence's attention was caught. "But my whole family has long been supportive of the rights of women in attaining equality in education," she said. Florence's eyes opened wide in surprise.

"You're not suggesting Aunt March helped you with painting lessons because of a political leaning," Florence said. "I thought she just wanted to encourage you to be more of a gentlewoman than your family could help you be."

Amy blushed at the mention of her family's diminished circumstances and was about to reply when Miss Bonheur said, "Mademoiselle Carrol, my father raised me with the ideals of the Saint-Simonians." Florence stared blankly at her. Rosa continued. "We ardently believe in the equality of women and men and the abolishment of all class distinctions in society." It was Florence's turn to blush. "If it weren't for that, I don't think I would have had the opportunity to achieve anything that I've achieved."

"*Pardonnez-moi*, Miss Bon-hore," Florence said. "I most certainly didn't mean to offend in any way."

"*S'il vous plaît, n'y pensez plus*," Rosa replied. "We French are quite different than the Americans, and *la famille* Bonheur is most certainly extraordinary even for the French."

"Mademoiselle Bonheur . . ." Amy said, trying to steer the conversation back to art.

Miss Bonheur interrupted her. "*S'il vous plaît, appellez-moi RB*," she said.

"Oh! *Merci beaucoup!* RB, I thank you for inviting us to tea today. It's been such an honor to have the opportunity to discuss art with someone of your stature."

"Ah! *De rien!*" She warmly smiled again. "The pleasure is all mine. It is not often I have the opportunity to speak to a young artiste anymore. It is all work, work, work!"

Amy gathered up her nerve. "I wonder," she said, "do you know, perhaps, of a painter in Paris that might welcome female students to draw from a live model?" She swallowed and continued. "I've found one studio that allows women to draw from a draped model, but I want to learn more." Amy heard Florence sigh.

"Ah! The challenge is real," Miss Bonheur replied. She rose from her seat in agitation. "We are told we cannot be great artists, that it is not in the nature of women." Striding back and forth, she ran her fingers through her short hair. "They point to the great artists and say, 'there are no women' as if that is the proof!"

Florence's eyes glazed over, and she poured herself more tea. Amy wasn't paying attention to Florence in that moment though. She felt as if Rosa Bonheur was speaking to her very soul.

"How can we be great, when we are excluded from learning and mentorship?" Amy said.

"Indeed!" Miss Bonheur replied. "If it were not for my papa's views on socialism and *le féminisme* I would not have been able to learn all that I did, studying and working for him in his studio." She sat back down in her chair, reached over to the side table, opened a small silver box, and withdrew a cigarette, which she proceeded to light. Florence's eyes widened in disbelief as she and Amy watched a woman smoke in front of them for the first time in their lives.

"*Bien sûr!*" Rosa said, exhaling a plume of smoke. "I reject the notion that a woman cannot achieve greatness, given the opportunity. And I wholeheartedly reject the roles that society insists we play."

Rosa's companion, Miss Micas, entered the room then. "*Tu devrais fumer dehors, ma chère.*" she said.

Rosa turned to Florence and laughed conspiratorially. "*Ma petite femme* does not approve of my smoking inside!"

Copying at the Louvre

After her visit with Rosa Bonheur, Amy strengthened her commitment to her painting. She was granted permission to be a copyist and spent most of her days at the Louvre. When she wasn't in a class or painting at the museum, she kept company with Fred. Although they were rarely alone, one would think that Amy might begin to let her guard down with him a bit. Fred was an amiable sort. Not unkind, if a little blundering. Amy was diligently polite and impeccably well mannered. She was deferential to him and rarely stated her mind. Her actions were never anything but exemplary of graceful femininity.

As such, Fred really didn't know her very well. He didn't know Amy as the little girl who used to pinch her nose because she didn't like its shape. He certainly didn't know the youngster who once undertook to cast her own pretty foot and ended up hopping wildly about the shed with said foot held fast in a pan of plaster, which had hardened with an unexpected rapidity. He definitely didn't know the Amy who, after being mocked one too many times by her sister, had fed the manuscript Jo had been working on for over a year, straight into the kitchen fire.

It was the worst thing Amy had ever done and she had regretted it immediately. It was an awful thing to do. And even though she had only been twelve years old at the time, Jo had never let anyone forget about it. It was the one horrible thing Amy had ever done.

What Fred *did* know was that everybody liked Amy, for among her good gifts was tact. She had an instinctive sense of what was pleasing and proper. She always said the right thing to the right person and did just what suited the time and place. Which is why it was surprising, both to her and to him, that one day she spoke quite sharply to him at the Louvre.

Amy had spent the morning copying in a portrait gallery. She knew her technique was improving but she still didn't feel her work was where it should be. Fred had insisted on meeting her in the gallery. The copyists were allowed entry from 9:30 until 1:30. He'd said he wanted to see where she was spending her days, time he'd rather she spent with him.

Her easel was set up in front of a portrait of a Black woman. Amy had done a rough sketch on her canvas and was laying down paint, layer after layer. The original work had been painted in 1800. She wondered if the model had a choice of whether or not to sit for the painter. She thought of her own country's horrific treatment of Black people, and how even now they weren't truly equal. She was curious who this woman had been and whether the artist had been an abolitionist, like Amy and her family.

"Ah, there you are, Miss March!" Fred said, striding into the gallery.

Amy didn't take her eyes off the painting, her eyebrows drawing together as she frowned. "Oh, you're a bit early," she cried. "I believe I'm allowed one more hour. I just want to finish . . ." Her hand moved as she focused on the portrait, forgetting she was in the middle of a sentence, and daubed another bit of paint on her canvas.

"I thought we might have a nice luncheon, so I arranged a table for us at one o'clock," Fred said. He looked from her canvas to the portrait on the wall and then back to her canvas. "Perhaps a bit of blue just over there?" he said, stepping too close to her and pointing. She huffed and put her paintbrush down on the edge of the easel, finally looking up at him.

"I wasn't aware you'd taken up painting, Mr. Vaughn," she said. Her voice was clipped, yet still polite. Fred looked at her, to see if she was joking. For a brief second, she looked irritated, but she quickly composed herself and shone a smile at him. "I meant, how lovely of you, to arrange a luncheon for us," she said.

Closing one eye he looked from her easel to the hung portrait again.

"I'm still in the beginning stages," she said. He didn't reply.

"I know it's not very good," she said. He took a step toward the hung portrait and looked at the name of the artist.

"I feel very privileged to have the opportunity to practice in this way," she said.

"Ah! A woman copying a painting of a woman painted by a woman," Fred said. "How funny!"

"Funny?" Amy said quizzically. She began gathering her things and cleaning her brushes.

"It's funny that an obscure painting of a Negro woman, painted by another woman, has made its way to the walls of this museum."

What did Fred know about it? Why would he think the painting was obscure? This was the Louvre, after all. How obscure could it be?

"It's quite famous, actually," Amy said in a small voice. "The artist is Marie-Guillemine Benoist." She cleared her throat. "She became an advocate for women's causes when she stopped painting," she said, and finished putting her things away.

"Well, I think you've done a fine job copying it," Fred said.

He clearly was trying to make her feel better. It wasn't even complete.

"It needs quite a bit more work," Amy said. "But I do think I've improved since I began copying."

"I'm sure you have," Fred said, as his eyes flitted back and forth between her canvas and the original, and finally returned to her face. He smiled at her.

"Well, your Miss Benoist sounds as if she was quite a spitfire," he said.

"Madame Benoist," Amy said. "She was married." She took off her linen smock and neatly folded it.

"How odd," Fred said. "May I carry your case?" he asked, reaching for the satchel that held her brushes and paints.

She tucked the smock into the top of the satchel. "Thank you," she said, handing it to him.

"Odd how?" she asked, as they walked together.

"For a married woman to be a painter whose work might end up at the Louvre," Fred replied. "I wonder what her husband thought of that. Did they have children?"

Amy didn't know much about Benoist's personal life, other than she'd stopped painting. "I don't know if they had children," she said. "And I certainly hope her husband was proud of her accomplishments."

"I would imagine so," Fred said. "I think the portrait quite good, even if the subject is a strange choice." For the second time Amy wondered what Fred knew about portraiture, if anything. And they had never discussed abolition. He did know she and her family had been abolitionists, didn't he?

"Of course," he continued, "a woman's greatest achievement would be creating a family." He looked fondly at her. "Perhaps your interest in painting will wane when someday you have a nursery full of babies of your own."

Amy felt her face flush red. She could feel her pulse thumping in her neck. His assumption that having children would impact her interest in art was infuriating. Her nostrils flared and just as she was about to speak her mind, she pushed the impulse down. She took a deep breath, regained her composure and, as she was wont to do when feeling irritated, changed the subject.

"My visit to Fontainebleau with Florence was quite interesting," she said pleasantly.

"Ah yes!" Fred said, oblivious to the energy it had taken for her not to explode. "How was your visit with that woman artist?" He laughed. "Are women artists and those that work for the rights of women a particular enthusiasm of yours then?" he asked. "Your aunt told Mother that your family holds an interest in women's suffrage, is that right?"

Amy wanted to tell him about her visit with Rosa Bonheur, who had been so inspiring to her. She wished she could talk to him about Miss Micas, and RB wearing men's clothing, and how Cousin Flo just couldn't seem to rise to the occasion. But without waiting for her answer he moved on from women's suffrage, nattering on about his impending trip to Switzerland with Frank, how he was looking forward to playing games of chance, and how the railroad had made travel into the Swiss Alps so much more convenient. She smiled and nodded and felt like screaming.

A Letter to Laurie

Paris, France
My lord,

  I hope you are well, and the weather has been fine. London can sometimes be so damp and dreary one must be grateful for every nice day. Oh, Laurie, I must tell you about an excursion that Florence and I made! We are recently returned from Fontainebleau, where we were privileged to visit with a great artist named Rosa Bonheur. She requested I call her RB, which apparently is what her friends call her. I'm sure they say it with a much better French accent than I can produce. I fear my American French doesn't sound as romantic. Madame Bonheur is quite famous, and Florence and I had tea with her. Aunt March's friend, Lady Willoughby, arranged it through one of her associates in the world of art patronage. What would I ever do without Aunt March? At Fontainebleau we talked of art and women's education and all sorts of fascinating topics. Poor Flo was quite bored. Sweet Cousin Florence doesn't exactly excel at intellectual discourse.

But RB! I can hardly believe my good fortune! She is the only woman of whom I've heard who is not only artistically successful but also financially secure from the sales of her work. When she was merely nineteen years, she'd already started taking commissions. I'm eighteen years, and I fear I will never achieve that.

As you know, I've always tried my hardest, and yet I can't count the times Mother and Father have told me I'm a silly girl to think I might support myself as an artist. You know that's why they sent me on this European quest, to barter my "pretty face" and manners for a husband. When I compare myself with someone as talented as Madame Bonheur, I think perhaps they are not wrong. Jo always says talent isn't genius, and no amount of energy can make it so. Be great or be nothing. I know I have talent, Laurie, and I yearn to have the opportunity to let it grow and blossom. And yet every day it feels I'm one step closer to attaining the goal my parents have set for me while stagnating in my artistic pursuit.

I know I don't have the genius of Madame Bonheur, but I believe our intentions are different. My paintings don't capture the realism hers do. They rather come from somewhere else, from expressing a physical manifestation of emotion on canvas. I don't know if I am making sense of it to you. And yet, I'm also hard pressed to copy a Turner sky, which is all emotion. Alas, my lord, I fear the work of Amy Curtis March may not contain the seeds of genius.

Besides leading to this artistic introspection, our tea with Madame Bonheur was educational in so many other ways. I've never met a woman like her, either at home or abroad. She lives her life so blatantly in opposition to societal expectations. Florence thinks her scandalous because she wears clothing like a man both at home and out in society, and styles her hair short in a masculine fashion. She even smokes a cigarette, Laurie! I believe her more comfortable and confident than any woman I've met.

RB made me think about what you wrote in your letter to me before you left Concord. I think our Jo might be such a one as Madame Bonheur. Jo has always been greatly influenced by Father and Mother's way of looking at the world. Even though they are forward thinking, they would never bless a life for our Jo such as Madame Bonheur lives. RB companionably resides with her Miss Micas, who has been her helpmeet for over twenty years. Imagine that, Laurie! Can you? Is this what you inferred when you spoke of "a Boston marriage?" Are there indeed women at home who do that? I think our Jo might be able to find happiness in that way.

I hope my letter finds you well. I miss you, kind sir, and very much look forward to seeing you. Please leave word at my hotel as soon as you arrive in Paris.
Your lady,
ACM

Surprise in the Louvre

Amy began to enjoy a sense of freedom in Paris that she hadn't felt in London. And she most certainly hadn't felt it at home with her family in Concord. Partially it was that Cousin Florence had become infatuated with wax flower-making and spent much of her time with a group of genteel young ladies who were similarly obsessed. At first Amy didn't mind joining in the occupation, but in the end, it was the inane conversation that she couldn't bear. Her aunt and uncle had loosened the reins a bit regarding where and when she was allowed to comport herself unattended. That had certainly helped. As had Fred's departure to Interlaken, which had freed up her spare time. It was as if Paris itself was blowing a warm breeze toward Amy, spun of *liberté*, *fraternité*, and *égalité*. She inhaled it greedily. It kissed her fair cheeks. It ruffled her neatly plaited and pinned hair and playfully fluttered the skirt of her dress. She was filled up with it.

One afternoon she was gathering up her painting supplies, ready to depart the Louvre with the other copyists. It was one thirty and time to go, when a shift in the air carried a scent reminiscent of home. It tickled her nose. It had been a frustrating day for her. She knew what she wanted the paintbrush to do, and sometimes it just wouldn't oblige. She was weary. Her brow furrowed. What was that scent? She rolled her brushes up in their canvas and neatly placed them in her satchel. Although her copying had definitely progressed since her early attempts in London, she was not pleased with today's work. She wished her skills would have improved more than they had.

There it was again. Was it sandalwood? She folded up the museum's loaned stool and placed it with the others beneath the window. Hoisting the strap of the satchel onto her shoulder, Amy gave one last dissatisfied glance at her painting. She knew that scent, yet she couldn't quite put her finger on what it was. Was that a hint of patchouli?

Amy smiled. Of course! As she felt a firm hand on her shoulder, she spun to face the tall, handsome young man with dark, wavy hair, olive skin, and an impeccably tied cravat.

"Miss Amy Curtis March," he said softly, still touching her shoulder. "Your cousin told me I might find you here."

Sandalwood and patchouli!

"Laurie!" Amy smiled. "When did you arrive?"

Letting decorum and manners slip for a split second, she dropped her satchel, leaned into him, and gave him an enthusiastic hug, which he heartily returned. He held her at arm's length for a moment, a funny smile on his face, and kept her gaze.

"Paris agrees with you, *ma chère*!" he said.

Laughing, she replied, "*Merci beaucoup*, my lord!"

In an instant they picked up their childhood game of "playing posh." She repeated, "But when did you arrive? Why didn't you tell me when to expect you?"

He picked up the satchel containing her painting things and hooked his other arm through hers. "Let me escort you back to your hotel, mademoiselle," he said, as they began to walk.

She couldn't stop smiling. "So, this is how it will be then, my lord?" she said. "You keep me guessing as to when you might arrive and then sneak up on me in a museum?!"

"It is!" he replied. "And I'm afraid I only have a few weeks, soon I'm off to Greece," he said, "but I couldn't bear to only correspond via post anymore, especially knowing we would be on the same continent."

She smiled happily up at him, holding his arm, as they companionably walked through the galleries to leave the museum. "It's so good to finally see you," she said, a feeling of contentment replacing any lingering bad feelings she'd been having over her frustrating day of painting. As they chatted and joked and laughed and caught up, they passed masterpiece after masterpiece, and yet only had eyes for each other.

Speaking of Pleasant Things

With Laurie in Paris, Amy still spent her mornings devoted to painting, but most afternoons were with him. Before this it had been over a year since they had seen each other back in Concord. In the intervening time their correspondence had been robust, particularly when he was in London and she in France, as the post took much less time. Now, with the opportunity to spend more time in each other's company, Amy appreciated the easiness of their relationship. She felt as if she'd been holding her breath since she'd stepped foot on the ship that had first brought her across the Atlantic. Being with Laurie allowed her to finally exhale.

One afternoon he hired a horse and carriage, and they took the hour-long ride to Bois de Vincennes. They skirted tourists at the café-restaurants surrounding Lake Daumesnil. The Temple of Love, perched on a promontory over an artificially created grotto on Isle de Reuilly, held no interest to them this day. They'd been to the marionette theater and many pavilions in the Bois de Boulogne; gone with Aunt Mary and Uncle Edward to see the animals at the Jardin Zoologique d'Acclimatation; strolled amongst exotic plants in the gardens of the Tu-ilieries; and braved the heat visiting the Palais de l'Industrie with Cousin Florence at the Jardin des Champs-Élysées.

Today they had planned a picnic, so they meandered their way through the winding paths of Bois de Vincennes until they found a peaceful place to stop. He'd brought a camp stool for Amy to sit upon, so she might draw, and he was sprawled languidly on a blanket. Amy felt content. The air had a crisp, invigorating quality, like a sip of champagne, sweet and bubbly and intoxicating. Laurie held up a sprig of lavender, looked at it, then lazily brought it to his nose to smell. He closed his eyes and tilted his head back, looking like a cat basking in a ray of sunshine.

He'd come round to collect her early that morning. Amy asked him to arrive before Aunt Mary or Uncle Edward awoke, so as to avoid their questions or the possibility that she wouldn't be allowed to go with him unaccompanied. It wasn't anything she would have had to contend with back in Concord, where he was just Laurie from next door, like a brother to her and her sisters. It never would have occurred to Mother or Father that there was anything improper about it. Aunt Mary took her role as chaperone a bit seriously sometimes though, and when she did Amy felt her lack of freedom keenly. Uncle Edward occasionally protested Aunt Mary's dictums on Amy's behalf, but she could tell he'd rather not have to challenge Aunt Mary.

"Don't move," Amy said to Laurie. Her charcoal scratched at the paper as she tried to capture the tilt of his head, his hand delicately holding the lavender to his nose, his long, lithe body stretched out on the blanket, propped on one arm, his leg bent nonchalantly.

"I love knowing you're looking at me," he said. He didn't move a muscle, expertly holding the pose, but the corners of his mouth tilted up in a satisfied smile.

"Shush, I'm looking at your form," she replied as she continued to sketch. "Not at you."

"And do you like what you see, mademoiselle l'artiste?" He turned his head and looked at her.

"Laurie!" Amy cried. "You ruined it! I'd almost captured your languor."

"As long as you want to keep drawing me," he said, "I'm certain there will be ample opportunities for you to reproduce my laziness on paper." From his spot on the blanket he looked at her, sitting in the shade of a tree. He squinted his eyes in the sun as he gazed up at her and a slight breeze ruffled his dark hair. She wore a hat with a wide brim to protect her fair skin from the sun, with a daisy chain woven like a band around the crown. Her pale blue day dress brought out the brightness of her eyes. She was a picture of innocent beauty.

As the day had warmed, and since nobody was about, they'd both relaxed their proper manners as if they were home in Concord. He'd taken off his stiff collar and her feet were bare. Had there been anyone there to observe, they'd have seen what appeared a rustic tableau, a young couple having a country picnic. Had the observer been her aunt or uncle they might have been scandalized by their absence of propriety. Had the observer been Amy's parents, they would have seen two young people who needn't take airs with each other, whose familiarity bred ease. Had the observer been Fred Vaughn though, he might have noticed the contented look on Amy's face and noted that it was one he'd never observed in his presence. As she put aside her paper and charcoals and went to sit next to Laurie on the blanket, Mr. Vaughn would have wondered why she never looked at *him* in the same manner, with as much tranquility as she gazed at the young Mr. Laurence.

"Don't do that," Amy said, leaning over to see what was in the picnic basket.

"Do what?" Laurie replied. "I brought *le fromage que tu aimes*," he said, nodding toward the basket.

She reached in and pulled out a baguette.

"Don't pretend that you're lazy," she said. "And *merci pour le fromage*."

"I *am* lazy," he replied. "You just said you were trying to capture my languor!" He took the bread from her, ripped a piece off the end, and took a bite. She took a hunk of cheese wrapped in paper from the basket, followed by a pear and a bottle of cider.

"There's a difference between having a relaxing picnic in the country, free of responsibility for a day, and portraying yourself as a man of indolence," she said. She handed him the bottle of cider.

He pulled the cork from the bottle and took a long draw.

"And you and I agreed we wouldn't use the characterizations that *certain people* burdened us with in our youth," she said. "So, if I'm not allowed to call myself silly and spoiled, you're not allowed to call yourself lazy or . . . spoiled."

He smiled. "Our youth," he said, "because now you are an old woman at nineteen and I'm a very old man of twenty-one!" He had another sip of the cider then tipped the bottle toward her. She took a deep drink too. Laurie laughed.

"Why are you laughing?" Amy said. She wiped her mouth with the back of her hand.

"If your Aunt Mary could see you now, with bare feet, drinking cider straight from the bottle . . ."

"Oh bosh, Laurie! I can't care!" she said. "I'm so tired of worrying what other people think of me. I know I'm very good at being proper and polite. And I *do* value good manners. But honestly, it's exhausting. And it's not funny." If at first she'd just looked like a pretty young girl pouting with a complaint, by the end it was obvious she was quite serious.

He looked chagrined.

"Aren't you weary of always considering what everyone else thinks?" she said.

"I rarely consider what everyone else thinks," he said. "But I see that it wearies you, Amy. And I'm sorry," he said. "I shouldn't tease you."

"No, you shouldn't tease me," Amy said. "You've always been the one to *protect* me from teasing. Please don't become like everyone else."

"Would that I could be like everyone else," he said. "Let's eat our lovely picnic and speak only of pleasant things." He unwrapped the cheese, which was soft and pungent, and sliced the pear in quarters. He ripped another hunk off the bread and put two portions of all atop the pretty serviettes he'd tucked into the picnic basket.

"Yes! I want to speak of pleasant things, and appreciate the beauty of our little paradise," she said, throwing her arms up. "I want to sketch pictures of the flowers and you and this sweet, happy horse, and pretend the world doesn't exist outside of our lovely private picnic!" There was a gentle breeze, and the sun was shining. The landscape around them was indeed a tiny slice of heaven, abundant with lavender and wildflowers. The horse was loosely tied to their carriage and grazing on tasty clover. He let out a soft, contented snort.

"I want to pretend that nothing came before this moment and there is nothing that will come after. We are just here. It is just now. It is just us." She closed her eyes and took a deep breath and the expression on her face was a portrait of serenity.

He didn't say anything in response. Her eyes fluttered open, and she looked at him. He had picked up a slice of pear to eat, but as she had passionately spoken of beauty and their private Eden, it had ended up delicately held between his two fingers, stopped midway to his mouth. He sat staring at her, open-mouthed.

"What is it," Amy said. "What's wrong?"

"I just . . ." he tried to say. "I can't . . ." He shook his head.

"Please, Laurie," Amy said. "Tell me."

"There is nothing to tell. You are just so yourself, Amy March," he said. "Even if you aren't quite traveling the path yet," he said, "you know which way you're going. It is stunning to observe, my lady."

She shook her head. "I don't," she said. "I maybe can visualize which way I *should* go, but I fear I'll never have the fortitude to walk a path of my own choosing rather than the path expected of me."

"Oh, but you will," Laurie said. "I can see it so clearly for you. You will paint and draw, and your work will be hung in the Paris Salon!"

She wished she could see herself the way he saw her: strong, capable, confident. It was only here, on a stolen summer day, where they played at Paradise, away from the scrutiny and expectations of her family and society, that she felt she could breathe and dream.

She swiped at her eyes. She didn't know why his saying she was so herself elicited tears. Laurie handed her a handkerchief from his pocket, and she dabbed at her eyes. She looked down at the beautifully embroidered stitching.

"Your sister's work," he said.

"Dear Beth," Amy said. She looked up at him. "I believe only she, of all the people in the world, sees me as you do."

Laurie looked away. "You'd do well to seek that quality in a suitor, *ma chère*," he said. Amy dabbed at her eyes again. She looked at Laurie, looking away.

"What are you saying?" Amy asked.

He turned back toward her and leveled his gaze, staring directly into her eyes. He was quiet for a heartbeat, then said, "You are an artist, Amy Curtis March. If you truly are to marry—and I'm not saying you must—you should select someone who can see you as such, who can dream with you and help you walk that path of your choosing."

She didn't say anything in reply. She chewed her bottom lip

for a moment, not breaking the connection of their eyes. Laurie was the first to look away. He took a bite of cheese and bread, chewed, swallowed, and changed the subject completely. "Now tell me of your new friend, Mary. She's also a copyist?"

Amy was glad to ignore Laurie's pronouncement about what kind of man she should marry and switch to a less fraught topic of discussion. "Yes! Mary Cassatt," she said. "She's also an American. From Philadelphia."

Laurie smiled. When Amy was enthusiastic about a topic she was a delight to watch.

"We met copying at the Louvre, and I quite enjoy her company. We paint together in the studio her mother procured for her. Well, recently I've been sketching, and she's been working in pastels but . . ." Amy talked, and Laurie listened. She told him all about her friend Mary, Mary's work, and Mary's studio, Mary's friend Berthe, who also was a painter. She prattled on and on, glad to be speaking about something she felt passionately.

In the afternoon Amy and Laurie headed back. They didn't speak much on the way home, riding in companiable silence as the horse clopped along. Although it had been a lovely day, they had changed the subject twice to try speaking of only pleasant things. Lying awake that night, with the sounds of Florence softly snoring in the next bed, Amy couldn't stop thinking about the avoided topics, weighed down by the pressure of trying to meet other people's expectations and the economic imperative to marry and marry well.

Decent Work

The following week Amy visited Mary at her studio. Coming from a well-to-do family, Mary Cassatt didn't have the same financial concerns Amy did. When Mary told her father that she wanted to study art abroad, after learning as much as she felt she could in Philadelphia, he tried to dissuade her. Mary had told Amy her father had said he'd rather see her dead than become an artist. Not to be deterred when her father refused to pay for art supplies, she spoke with her mother, who herself came from a prominent banking family in Pittsburgh. Katherine Kelso Johnston Cassatt was quite in favor of Mary's pursuit of art and had accompanied her daughter on this extended stay in Europe.

Now Mary stood behind Amy, gazing over Amy's shoulder at the paper on the easel. "I think your work decent," Mary said, "as I think mine."

Amy looked over at the other young woman's paper, the pastels blending together in a symphony of color, vibrant and alive, then back to her own still life.

"Although I haven't seen your sculpture," Mary said, "I've

seen your work on the portrait at the museum. I believe your strength lies in paint, rather than drawing."

Amy smiled. "On that we agree," she said. She thought her own work decent, too, especially compared with Mary's, which Amy considered more than decent, perhaps on its way to genius.

Mary returned to her own easel, and the women worked quietly, side by side.

According to her sister Jo's beliefs, and their father's teachings, genius was what one either had or did not. In her family they danced around Jo and her writing, as if there could be only one March sister who was truly creative. Some believed—although not the Marches—that genius wasn't something which women were even capable of embodying. What Amy had been told, what she'd been taught, was that genius was something innate, something that couldn't be learned. Jo had always scribbled, as she called it, and as a family the Marches encouraged and nurtured her talent, as if it were intrinsic to who Jo was.

Amy's love of beautiful things—having them, making them, being among them—was looked upon as a weakness, an indulgence they allowed her because she was the spoiled, youngest child. What her family didn't understand was that Amy walked through the world looking for beauty, searching it out wherever she was, and so finding it.

Even as a young girl she noticed things others didn't. Her delight in the pale pink blush at the tips of the white hydrangeas—which she'd then tried to reproduce in watercolor. Seeing the intensity with which her usually placid sister Beth sometimes played piano, she had tried to capture the beauty of that transformation in a sketch. Amy sat quietly on the couch as Beth played and had drawn and drawn and re-drawn her sister's face, until she'd finally caught that quality on paper. Amy's family saw Amy as a hard worker, not a genius. And until now, she had always second-guessed herself, trying to determine whether genius was in her or not.

What of Rosa Bonheur? She surely embodied genius. But Rosa attributed her expertise to instruction, practice, and being given the same opportunities as her brothers. RB had been raised with the support of her father, and the safety net of family money, to either fail or succeed as an artist.

And even though her friend Mary was defying her father's wishes by going abroad and seeking the life of an artist, she still had her daily living supported by him. Refusing her art supplies just wasn't the same pressure which Amy faced.

Her avoided conversation with Laurie at their picnic in the Bois de Vincennes kept nagging at her. "Mary, let me ask you something," Amy said, putting down her charcoal and wiping her smudged fingers on a rag. "If you had to choose between painting—or creating art—and the love of a husband, of having children and a family, what would your choice be?"

Mary didn't lift her eyes from her paper. Her hand swept across the sheet and her concentration was palpable. She answered, still engrossed in her drawing. "Well, as I've already decided I shan't marry at all," she said, "I suppose you have your answer."

"Shan't marry at all," Amy softly repeated to herself, testing the sound of the words uttered from her own mouth. She took up another piece of paper and began again. "I don't feel that's an option for me," she said.

"Of course it's an option," Mary replied, still working on her pastel. "When we are willing to give up everything for art—love, financial security, even social standing—we court our muse in a different way. You aren't quite there yet, friend." She gave a nod toward Amy's paper. "I think when you are, though, perhaps you'll put aside your *sketching* of the thing, and finally go at it with the oils." She closed one eye and took a step away from her paper.

"You do have the capacity to be more than decent," Mary said. "I know I do, as well." She took a long breath then put down the pastel. "Many women choose not to marry," she said, looking at her friend, "and for reasons less compelling than the pursuit of art. But tell me, Amy, how are we to create when we are expected to bear and raise children, and take on the burdens of running a household?"

"I don't know," Amy replied. "I see my oldest sister, Meg, being consumed by the chores of motherhood and being a wife." They unbuttoned their linen smocks and folded them neatly. They cleaned their hands at the wash basin together, pouring the pitcher for each other.

"I have the greatest respect for women for whom being a wife might be enough," Mary said. "And there is, perhaps, nothing greater than the love between a mother and her child. Yet I find I have no desire for that, no impulse to *be* that."

Amy sighed. "I don't know if I desire to be a mother, or not," she said. "I do know I desire to be a better artist though."

"Then make art, Miss March!" Mary said. "Perhaps you have your answer, yes?"

"It's not that simple," Amy said. "Because what of love, Miss Cassatt?"

"Love!" Mary scoffed. "I say choose art, for it will not diminish you, in the way love may. Even if we women artists must dance at the edges of acceptance of our work."

Mary's painting, *The Mandolin Player*, had been shown at the Paris Salon the year prior, yet even she was still barred from the École des Beaux-Arts because of her sex, as all women were.

"Art will feed your spirit, and if you're lucky, might put money in your pocket, too. With art you are the master, in control of the outcome. It is your hard work and perseverance that influences what makes it to the canvas, what you put on paper, mold with clay, or carve into stone."

Amy knew what Mary said was true. Copying had already made such a difference in her skill with a paintbrush. The hours she devoted to art, painting with Mary and the other copyists at the museum, engaging in long discussions of brushwork or technique, or just sketching at the park, these were the happiest hours for her. Gone was her anxiety about doing or saying the wrong thing, looking the right way, not slipping up, when it was just her and a paintbrush and canvas, or a bit of charcoal and paper, surrounded by like-minded folk. Those times were when she felt her truest self.

"Would that it could be possible to have both," Amy said.

Mary replied, "It's rare for a man to look at a woman and see an artist, and even more so to want that artist as one's wife."

"Indeed," Amy replied. "A family friend said much the same to me just the other day."

"And that is why I shan't marry at all!" Mary said, with a smile. "Now, shall we have one more lunch at the café? I'm famished."

"Yes, let's!" Amy said.

Mary looked Amy up and down. "Pretty and presentable as ever, Miss March!" Mary smoothed her own skirt and tucked a lock of hair behind her ear.

"As are you, Miss Cassatt!" Amy replied. "We look to be quite a pair of proper young ladies." Every time she left Mary's studio or detached herself from painting or drawing to return to the world, as it were, she girded herself for the return to polite society. For that was also the return of her social anxiety, and the knowledge that she was expected to return home to Concord with a marriage proposal from a gentleman of means.

"Let's not disabuse anyone of the notion that we are indeed

the most proper of young ladies by speaking of the merits of
the artistic life over men and mundane choices," Mary said. The
girls closed the door to the studio and descended the stairs, single file.

It was to be a farewell luncheon, as Mary and her mother
were leaving for Rome. Amy would miss her new friend, not
only for her companionship, directness, and inspiration, but
also for her understanding.

A Letter from Fred

Amy opened her letter from Fred. She'd barely missed him since Laurie had arrived, but she tried to ignore that truth. Reading Fred's letter was very much like being with him. It was slightly pleasant but only mildly interesting.

> *Interlaken, Switzerland*
> *My dear Miss March,*
> *It seems as if all of Continental society is on the move. The new rail system made our trip to Interlaken so much more agreeable.*

He waxed prolific about the railroad, clearly forgetting that he'd already spoken to her of it, multiple times, in depth. She sighed.

> *Frank has been enjoying the spa waters and seems quite rejuvenated every time he returns from the bath house. I have been amusing myself at the gaming tables, and I'm sure my luck will turn around soon.*

He blathered on, and although she was glad for a newsy letter, she found it very easy to put it down at the end.

> *I look forward to our time in Germany together. I hope you think of me, as I do you.*
> *Humbly yours,*
> *Fred W. Vaughn*

Quite Unexpected at the Louvre

Mary and her mother had departed to Rome and as much as Amy enjoyed Florence's company, spending many an evening sitting and talking on the balcony of their rooms on the Rue de Rivoli in Paris, gazing up and down the long, brilliant street, Amy's days had been filled with Laurie. Aunt Mary had begun to frown upon it. Then Amy and the Carrols were busy with preparations for their departure from Paris to tour Germany in the autumn—Frankfurt to Nassau, Koblenz and Heidelberg in between—and eventually the trip south to winter in Rome. She hadn't seen Laurie in over a week and when she packed her last trunk she asked Aunt Mary and Uncle Edward if she might visit the Louvre one last time before they departed. She didn't mention it was to see Laurie.

Uncle Edward had an affinity for antiquities, so he said he would accompany her, and she was hard-pressed to say no. Once at the museum she placed her satchel of paper, graphite, and rubber down next to the museum's sketching stool and she waited impatiently for Uncle Edward to leave.

Taking his watch from his vest pocket, Uncle Edward said,

"I will meet you in one hour, my dear," and he gave the watch a little wind.

"Yes, Uncle," Amy said, trying her hardest to look as innocent as possible. It wasn't very difficult. In her whole life Amy had only ever done that one thing that was truly bad. She was an honest, sincere, kind young lady. Yes, she was adept at bending the rules of social convention to suit her needs occasionally, but not any more than other young ladies her age. She always managed to do so in the most well-bred way, with so much grace it usually went unnoticed.

Demurely lowering herself onto the sketching stool and arranging her skirts around her, she smiled up at her uncle. "Go on now!" she'd said kindly. "I know you want one last look at the *Great Sphinx of Tanis*!"

Returning his watch to his pocket, he turned on his heel and virtually scampered to the rooms of antiquities.

She experienced a tiny eruption of freedom as Uncle Edward walked away. Life at home in small-town Concord hadn't been as restrictive for young ladies, and she and her sisters always gadded about the countryside and into town unchaperoned. In all the time she'd been abroad, the hardest thing had been getting used to her lack of freedom.

She looked up at the *Venus de Milo*. Amy had sketched this beauty many times now. Tilting her head, she tried to look at the Venus anew. She rose, picked up the sketching stool and her satchel, and poised herself behind the statue, with a view of her back. She reached into her bag, retrieved paper, graphite, and rubber, and began to draw. At first the lines she put to the page were light and indistinct, as she was barely giving any effort to the sketch. It wasn't what she was there for. But as the minutes ticked by, she couldn't help herself, and she was swept up in the act of drawing. Beauty and Form. Shadow and Light. The museum around her dropped away and it was just Amy and Venus and the page. The scratch of graphite on paper was the only sound in the room, as it was morning and not a time most people chose to visit the museum. Amy was totally lost in the act of drawing, deep in her own thoughts.

The young man stopped at the entrance to the gallery. He reached his hand out to the wall, as if to steady himself. He looked across the room, and illuminated by the sunlight streaming through the large windows, was a beautiful vision. Amy's blond curls were swept up and gathered on the sides with combs, a small spray of pale pink roses tucked into the braid that wound around her bun. She was wearing a simple walking dress, in her favorite azure blue, a bit of lace at the neck, but otherwise lacking decoration. Her black low-heeled shoes just peeked out from beneath her skirt. She was behind the statue, so he could see her face, which looked serious as she concentrated on her task. She didn't notice him, and he stood watching, enraptured.

Softly he had made his way across the gallery, but she was so intent on her drawing she didn't hear him approach. Finally, when he could stand it no longer, he said, "The Goddess Aphrodite's beauty pales in comparison to yours, my lady!"

"Laurie!" Amy exclaimed, putting aside her drawing and rising. She quickly looked around, to make sure the room was empty, and then fell happily into his embrace. She took a deep breath in, inhaling his familiar scent. Then she stepped back, putting some distance between them. Their picnic in the country felt like a lifetime ago. Day to day living with her aunt, uncle, and cousin had been full of obligations and expectations, and preparations for leaving France had been consuming. The feeling of contentment, of being caught in the present, that she'd experienced the day of the picnic, had been fleeting.

They spent the next hour together amiably, walking around

the gallery, commenting on and wondering about the statuary. No other patrons disturbed their time together.

"Uncle Edward will return for me soon," she finally said. He nodded somberly then swallowed, looking very much like the young boy he had been when they first met.

"But we must arrange to see each other when you return from Greece," she said, taking his hand, trying to reassure him. "And I promise to write to you from Germany." He nodded again, but now he looked distraught. "Germany," he whispered.

"Might you arrange to come to Rome in the winter?" she asked.

"Germany, Rome," he muttered. "And what of Fred Vaughn?" he asked, his dark eyebrows drawing together.

"Fred?" Amy said, in confusion.

"Frank tells me Fred is prepared to ask for your hand in marriage," Laurie said, his voice breaking on the word *marriage.*

Amy withdrew her hand from his. "You've seen Frank?" she said. "I hope he's well." She began to walk across the gallery and back toward the sketching stool and her forgotten satchel and supplies.

"Is it true then," he said. He followed behind her, like a forlorn puppy.

"You know this isn't a new conversation," she answered.

"You don't have to do this, Amy," he said.

Then she turned to him, her eyes flashing with anger. "Of course I do," she said. "It's the reason Father and Mother allowed me to come. You know it is."

"But do you love him?" Laurie said. His voice pleading, his eyes near tears.

"Oh, Laurie," Amy said sadly, shaking her head. "You know as well as I that I don't have the luxury of marrying for love. I am expected to drag the March family back to respectability with this marriage, which was very likely the same thing on Jo's mind when she misunderstood you back in Concord."

"But Amy," Laurie said, with the funniest expression on his face. Then he took her by both hands and pulled her into another embrace. He wasn't someone who was usually at a loss for words, but he didn't seem able to say anything besides her name.

"Laurie?" she questioned, tipping her head back to look up at him.

"My lady," he whispered, looking down at her, with tears in his eyes.

And then, much to her surprise but certainly not unwelcome, he leaned in and kissed her gently on the lips. She pressed up against him, her eyes closed, and he kissed her again, more deeply. As he did she reached up and touched his cheek, her hand lingering for a moment before smoothing its way into his hair. He pulled her closer, and she felt as if time had stopped. The museum dropped away, and it was just the two of them. It felt so right, as if she was exactly where she was supposed to be, in his arms.

Then they heard the tap of a walking stick, heralding the return of Uncle Edward and they pulled away from each other. Laurie straightened his collar and combed his hands through his hair. He looked at her, as if he was going to say something, then he turned on his heel and purposefully strode out of the gallery, not looking back.

Amy's heart was beating in her chest, and she could feel herself flushing. As Uncle Edward approached, she tried to look as busy as possible, putting away her art supplies. Her hands were shaking. What had just happened? She kept her face turned away from Uncle Edward, for she knew she must look different. She couldn't possibly look unchanged.

"Thank you, dear, for encouraging one last foray into the Egyptian exhibit!" Uncle Edward beamed. Amy cleared her throat, hoping her blush had subsided, and handed him the satchel holding her art supplies. She took his other arm and together they left *Venus de Milo* to herself. The following morning Amy received a short note that Laurie had decided to leave for Greece early. He assured her he would write.

PART TWO

~ Margaret March Brooke ~
Finding Meg March

A Good Man

Meg March—no, Brooke. She was Meg Brooke now and had been for quite some time—knew she had married too young. But in her day, in her financial state, and with her upbringing, there was little to be done about it. While one of her sisters was off painting and promenading in Europe and the other working in New York, no doubt writing her next great novel, Meg was stuck here in this small house with these small children, little more than a child herself, her ambitions long buried, more bones than seeds.

"You are barely twenty-three. You can still have a life, you know," Sallie Moffat said as she leaned across the table and filled Meg's teacup.

Sallie had been Meg's closest friend for years, one of the few people who truly saw her—not the way her younger sisters did, as a sort of stand-in for their mother, someone meant to keep them on the right path, bearing life's burdens with a smile—but as a person in her own right. Back before they had become Mrs. Brooke and Mrs. Moffat and were simply Meg and Sallie. Before Meg had ignored Ned Moffat's flirtations and he had moved on to marry Sallie, before Meg had agreed to a marriage of her own to a man with far less wealth and social standing.

"I am simply saying that life need not be only you and the twins all the time," Sallie said.

"That is easy for you to say," Meg murmured.

Sallie arched an eyebrow. "Ned was prepared to be smitten with you," she said. "But you turned him down. For love."

For *love*.

Meg laughed at the word, then found herself wanting to cry. She had hoped it had been love that had led her down this path, but if she was honest, she found herself here partly out of stubbornness and partly out of a desperation to be *good*. That, too, was another word Meg no longer felt she knew the meaning of.

"Do you not love him?" Sallie asked.

Meg waved a hand. "John is a good man."

"That is not what I asked," Sallie said.

Meg planted her elbows on the table, dropped her head into her hands, and sighed. "What difference does it make if I love him or not? I am here." She gestured to the ceiling where the twins napped in the room upstairs, blessedly quiet for the first time in hours. "They are here. And John, as usual, is nowhere to be found. You know my mother told me it was *my* fault he spends his afternoons and evenings with our neighbors, that I ought to make myself up for him as though I am a doll here for dress-up and nothing more."

Sallie pressed her lips closed as she considered this. "While I do not agree with your mother, I do think you could do with dressing up once in a while."

"The last time I tried buying nice silk . . ." Meg trailed off. She had never seen John so angry. Yes, Meg had spent fifty dollars on it, but in the end, Sallie had purchased the silk from her so that John could use the money to buy a new coat—something he needed far more than Meg had needed a new dress.

But Sallie grinned. "You ended up pregnant."

Meg didn't need that reminder. She took a long, sobering sip of her tea.

"They do say making up after a fight often makes the fight worth it," Sallie said.

Meg only shrugged. John had been tender beneath the sheets that night, but it had been the last time they'd been together in almost a year and a half now. And it had only come once Meg admitted she had been wrong, whether she'd meant the confession or not.

"Then don't dress up for him," Sallie said, her blue eyes gleaming. "Do it for you."

Sallie stood from her spot on the couch and went to the gown she'd hung in the corner upon her arrival. They had gone into a shop together a few weeks ago, Meg's children left under the care of Sallie's nursemaid. Meg had fallen in love with a particular pale green silk and even went through the motions of having her measurements taken, though she knew she would never have the dress made. Sallie, it seemed, had an eye for the same silk.

Sallie held the dress out toward Meg.

"It's lovely," Meg said, trying to keep the disappointment out of her voice.

"It's for you," Sallie said.

Meg's eyes widened. "You . . . what . . . I couldn't possibly afford it."

"It's a gift," Sallie said.

"I've nowhere to wear it," Meg said. "Especially not now."

"You act as though you have been put on a shelf since marrying John," Sallie said. "I won't have it, which is why I'm planning an afternoon tea in a few weeks. You can wear it there."

"But the twins . . ." Meg started.

"Will be in good hands with my staff," Sallie said. "Like they always are."

Tears pricked Meg's eyes as Sallie pushed the dress into her arms.

"And because I know you don't only like pretty things, contrary to what some of your sisters seem to think, I also got you this," Sallie said as she handed Meg a small gift wrapped in brown paper.

Meg gently took the package and started to open it until she held in her hands a volume titled *The Complete Herbal* by Nicholas Culpeper. Meg's eyes widened as she ran the tip of her finger over the title. It was an older book detailing plants and their properties.

"How did you know?" Meg asked.

"I saw you eyeing it when we were out last week," Sallie said with a smile. "You picked it up and put it back down enough times for me to know you'd have bought it if you could. Now you can finally get to work on your garden."

Meg's garden had been one of the few things she had looked forward to about starting a life of her own with John, but in all of her efforts to learn to properly care for a house during their first few months of marriage, followed by her sickness during pregnancy and the arrival of the twins, all she had grown were weeds. These days she spent more time tending her roses back at her mother's house than she did the patch of yard behind the Dovecote, if only to have someone watch over the babies so she could have a moment alone.

Meg bit her lip. "Why do all this for me?"

"You would do the same had I married John and you'd married Ned," Sallie said. "It's time you make your own happiness, and if I can help with that, even in a small way, you know I will."

Meg knew she wouldn't find the secret to happiness in a single dress or a book of herbs, but it was a start. She grabbed Sallie in a hug.

"Thank you," she murmured into her friend's blond hair.

"You have brought so much joy to my life," Sallie said. "It was the least I could do."

An Argument

The moment Meg closed the front door behind Sallie the now all-too-familiar sound of the twins' cries filled the house, almost as if they had sensed Meg had a precious moment alone to use her time as she saw fit and decided it would be better spent taking care of them.

She grabbed the dress and the book and started upstairs. After dropping the gown off in the bedroom, she went into the nursery and found the twins sitting up in their cradles. They had only just started walking, and that meant keeping an even closer eye on them. After Meg fed them, she set them on the floor of their bedroom along with a handful of toys Aunt March had given them. Then, she settled into her chair in the corner of the room and started to read.

She paused first on the illustrations that came before the title page—mallow and St. John's wort, chickweed and violet. She traced the tip of her finger over the flowers and leaves and thought of her sister across the sea, wondered what art she might be making in that moment, what life she might be yet building for herself. Then, Meg commenced to reading the actual words.

The book was arranged alphabetically, with all included plants listed in the contents. After the herbs came a host of instructions from harvesting and preparation to making everything from decoctions to poultices.

She flipped first to the entry for roses, her favorite flower.

> *I hold it altogether needless to trouble the reader with a description of any of these, since both the garden roses and the roses of the briars are well enough known. . . . To write at large of every one of these would make my book swell too big, it being sufficient for a volume itself to speak fully of them.*

Meg imagined an entire book on roses, and a smile broke across her face. Culpeper might not have dedicated the full volume to them, but he had included six full pages detailing their benefits and medicines. With each word Meg read, it was like coming to see an old friend in a new light. For Meg knew roses, had tended them for years at Orchard House, brushing her fingers over their soft petals, clipping errant branches, even getting stuck by a thorn when she didn't take the time to be careful in her work. But only now was she learning that they could be used to cure headaches, to ease inflammation in the heart, to help digestion, and more! All this time Meg had admired them for their beauty and washed her hair with water steeped in their petals, but there had been so much more to her beloved flowers than even her years of experience with them had suggested.

By the time the twins had worn themselves out enough for an early evening nap, Meg had already made it through thirty pages of herbs, flipping backward from the roses. She hurried back to her room, set the book down, and pulled her new dress from its hook. She stood before the mirror and pressed the silk against her frame, a soft sigh falling from her lips.

She tucked a strand of brown hair behind her ear as she

swayed, eyes closed, humming contentedly for the first time in she didn't know how long. So lost was she in the moment, that she didn't hear the door open, didn't notice the footsteps on the stairs, and when she glanced up in the mirror to find John's face reflected back at her, brow furrowed, lips turned down, she almost dropped the dress all together.

Her eyes widened, and she turned, quickly.

"You bought a dress," he said, slowly. "It looks expensive."

"It's not—"

But he didn't let Meg finish the sentence.

"We have two children in the other room and an entire house that I'm working to maintain every day, and yet, you've spent my hard-earned money on something you can't even wear."

"What do you mean *can't*?" Meg asked.

"Can't. Won't. You have nowhere to go dressed like that." He waved vaguely at the silk in her arms.

"And so what if I don't? Am I not allowed to have nice things?"

John took a step toward her, and as much as Meg wanted to hold her ground, she stepped back, bumping into the mirror. Despite her mother's suffragist leanings, she had warned Meg more than once not to stoke John's anger, and though he had never raised a hand to her, the fear still clawed at her belly in moments like these.

"How much was it this time?" John asked. "Another fifty? One hundred?"

"You're never going to let me forget that, are you?" Meg asked, voice small.

"If you had learned from it, I wouldn't have to," John said.

"I'm not some student of yours, here for you to teach the proper way to be a wife," Meg murmured. When they'd first met, John had been Laurie's tutor. That seemed like a lifetime ago.

"I should think not," John said. "Were you, you'd certainly have learned by now."

Meg stared at him, her own anger starting to rear its head. "And are you a proper husband? Coming home for a few minutes every night before you're off again, leaving me to take care of the children?" As if on cue, crying started up down the hall. Meg shot a glare toward the door as she carefully hung the dress back up, keeping it as far from John as she could.

"I never asked for you to care for the children all on your own," John said. "I'm their father just as much as you're their mother."

"Is that so?" Meg asked. "Then are you going to go in there and soothe them?"

John, too, looked at the door, but he didn't so much as take a step toward it. "We're not arguing about who is the better parent. We're arguing about you spending money we don't have when we have a family to raise."

"Do you really think so little of me?" Meg asked. She almost backed down, almost told him Sallie bought her the silk and there was nothing for him to worry about. But this was about so much more than the dress. She shook her head and pushed past him into the hall, but instead of making her way to the children's room, she started for the stairs.

"Where are you going?" John called.

"Out," Meg said. "It'll give you a chance to try a hand at raising this family you claim to care so much about."

And with that, Meg hurried down the stairs and out the door.

Every Ingredient You Need for Happiness

Though tears stung Meg's eyes, she refused to let them fall, refused to look back at the Dovecote as she made her way toward her childhood home. The walk wasn't as quick as the ones she used to make to make when visiting John during his days working as a tutor at Mr. Laurence's house, but Meg needed the time to think, and that's what this gave her.

She repeated the words her mother had told her so long ago, as if they were some sort of spell that could bring her the happiness a home and a husband and two healthy children were promised to offer.

"When you feel discontented, think over your blessings, and be grateful," she whispered to herself. "Be grateful," she repeated again, this time a little louder with a bitter laugh that drew the look of a passerby making his way in the opposite direction.

Meg flushed and ducked her head and tried her hand, once again, at gratitude. "My blessings," she murmured. "Daisy, Demi, even John." She counted their names on her fingers, tried to summon their faces in her mind's eye, but even the mention of John incensed her all over again. Though she'd never admit it out loud, those supposed blessings were the very things that had robbed her of her joy, of the girl she'd been before she dove headlong into the expected path of womanhood.

Orchard House came into view, and with it a sense of relief. She wondered if Beth was feeling well enough to join her in the garden, almost went to the door to knock, but that would mean alerting her mother that she was there. And as much as Marmee had become Meg's confidant, with Amy and Jo gone on their own adventures, guiding Meg whenever there was trouble at home—despite her assurances to John that she never, ever let those troubles leave the threshold—today, she wasn't much in the mood for confiding. Today was a day for brooding, and the sky had started to darken overhead with the threat of rain, as if it knew as much.

Meg slipped the shears from her pocket as she made her way around the side of the house. Concord had long since shaken off winter. Weeds poked through the ground, pulling nutrients from her roses, encroaching on the flowers her sisters had long since abandoned. Only the vegetable patch Hannah—the March family's housekeeper—tended looked cared for regularly except, of course, after Meg came to take out her frustration with John on the weeds that threatened her roses. Because, even though Meg had left this life behind—running through the fields with her sisters, trying her best to bear the burden life had given her by acting the good little pilgrim for her mother, and ultimately being one of her father's little women—these roses *were* hers, and always had been. Without her to tend them, to pour her own heartache into their soil in so many whispered words, to cut them back at the end of each season, they'd have long since given way to the wild.

Meg pulled her pinafore apron over her walking dress and tied it tight around her waist before she grabbed her bench from by the door and took a seat. While she had many varieties—

even one of the newer hybrid tea roses Mr. Laurence had gifted her after receiving a specimen from France—she found her favorite was the Rosa rubra, which she'd been delighted to find in her quick pass of the herbal that afternoon.

Though her mother had always been more enchanted by the rare blooms, Meg had felt a special connection to this particular rose and early on had used its petals in water when washing her hair. John had mentioned on more than one occasion how he'd loved the scent. She'd been so proud to tell him it was from a plant she'd grown herself. When they'd first moved into the Dovecote, he'd suggested she root some of the roses there, but she'd never gotten around to it. She held her clippers up to a spent blossom as the memory crossed her mind, and she bit her lip, wondering if she had loved him then, if she had ever really loved him at all. Tears stung her eyes, as she brought the blades to the stem.

"Sorry," she murmured to the plant before she snipped. She gathered the wilting petals in the pocket of her apron.

"Meg?" Her mother's voice cut through her thoughts as the back door opened with a creak.

So much for her private brooding.

Maybe it was for the best. Her mother always had a way of helping Meg see her place in the world and in her marriage. While Meg had yet to find her mother's promised contentment, talking with Marmee at least gave Meg what she needed to shift her mind away from all those things she wanted so she could focus on what was supposed to matter in life. Ambitions were, after all, for men.

"Where are my favorite grandchildren?" her mother asked.

Meg bristled.

"I'm doing fine, thank you for asking." She snipped a branch that was beginning to outgrow the shrub. She set it gently on the ground in front of her as she pointedly avoided making eye contact with her mother.

"I needn't ask," Marmee said. "It's written all over your face."

"My discontent?" Meg asked.

Her mother sighed the same way she might were she speaking to a petulant child before she reached out and plucked a rose from the bush and tucked it into Meg's hair. "Your life has every ingredient you need for happiness—a good husband and two beautiful children. What greater kingdom could you need than one ruled as bride and mother?"

Meg shrugged as she moved onto another branch. What more indeed.

"What was it this time?" Marmee asked. "Were the twins too much for you again today?"

"The twins are the twins," Meg said, finding that for once, she didn't want to pour her heart out to her mother. She wanted to be left alone to tend one of the few pieces of her old life she had left.

"You know I'm here to help. You could always drop them off for a few hours while you're taking care of the house. You're lucky, you know, having us so close. And of course, sweet Beth loves cuddling with them. She's such a dear. Perhaps if you tried to echo her disposition, you wouldn't find yourself in need of counsel quite so often."

Meg gripped a branch, and a thorn pierced her skin. She only just managed to keep from crying out and giving Marmee yet another thing to criticize. Her mother may have done important work for their community, but inside the grounds of Orchard House, Meg knew Marmee lived by the realities of the world rather than her hopes for it, and that extended to her daughters. A sweet disposition meant a better match. It meant less of a chance of a man's anger falling on you, no matter how good a man he might be.

"Not that I mind, of course," her mother said. "Nor would I ever tell your sisters about your troubles at home."

"No," Meg murmured. "Of course not."

"But you can trust me with the twins," Marmee said. "That's what mothers are for. You'll understand some day, when Daisy is grown." She rested a hand on Meg's shoulder and gave it a soft, somewhat possessive, squeeze. "But she'll never be fully gone. She'll follow in our footsteps, I'm sure of it." Marmee laughed softly. "Find a good man, like your father or John. Start a family of her own. It's years away, I know. But it'll happen faster than you think."

What then? Would Meg find herself where her mother was now? Helping Daisy sort through her decision to marry a *good* man, a man her mother and father approved of, a man who didn't have the means to give Daisy what she really wanted so she'd always find herself running back into Meg's arms . . .

Meg's eyes widened, and her clippers slipped from her hands, landing softly on the soil below as the realization hit her.

She wasn't happy.

Her mother *knew* marrying John wouldn't make her happy, and yet she'd pushed her toward him—rebuffed every man of means who showed interest in Meg, like Sally's Ned and even the Vaughn twins, those friends of Laurie's—knowing full well it would bring Meg back, crying into her mother's arms every time.

"Meg?" Marmee asked. "Are you even listening?"

But Meg had heard enough. She lifted her shears from the ground, grabbed the few branches she'd clipped from the rose bush she'd loved for so long and tucked them into her apron. Then, she turned on her heel and started around the side of the house.

Her mother called after her, but Meg didn't respond, didn't even look back to meet her gaze. Meg had tended her mother's garden long enough. It was time to grow something for herself.

An Abundance of Nettles

Meg ran more than walked back to the Dovecote, not even bothering to remove her apron. The darkening clouds overhead threatened to break open at any moment, and part of Meg wished they would. Let her get caught up in a storm, arrive home soaking wet and washed clean from every word her mother had ever used to direct Meg's path.

By the time she arrived home, her hair had fallen loose from her braids. She lifted her skirt as she pushed through the gate and made her way around the side of the house, with only one glance spared for the twins' upstairs bedroom.

She surveyed the small patch of land. It hadn't even been two years since she drove stakes into the ground and marked out her plan—vegetables, a handful of herbs, the respectable sort of plants a young bride of her social standing was expected to grow for her family. And while she knew weeds had settled into her meticulously planned beds, she hadn't realized it had gotten quite this bad.

The lines she'd so carefully marked were no more. Plants grew up all around her. Leaves reached skyward. Stems tangled themselves together. Wild flowers sprouted from all that green where they spilled seeds into the soil.

In the back corner, a once-scraggly linden tree she'd intended to remove to free up space in the already cramped yard had spread its branches wider. She'd likely need John's help if she wanted it gone. For now, she'd let it keep building the buds that would turn to flowers in a week or two and focus on what she could handle on her own.

Meg pulled her shears from her apron and glanced from the blades to the plants as she considered her options. She'd need a lot more than these were she to clear this ground and make something of her own. First thing was first. She took the two shoots she'd snipped from her roses and, using her bare hands, dug a small hole on either side of the back gate. She gently rested the cuttings into the ground.

Now, it was time to get to work.

With a sigh and a small smile, she wrapped her hand around the closest weed that had overtaken the space, ready to pull it free and clear the land for whatever she wanted to grow— maybe the vegetables as she'd originally planned, or more space for roses that would be all her own—but when her palm met leaf, pain shot through her skin, sharp and fast. She let out a small cry and clutched her hand to her chest. When she looked down at it, she found small, hair-like needles sticking out of her skin.

She dropped to her knees beside the plant and bit her lip, tears welling in her eyes.

"Of course the moment I try to do something for myself I get hurt," she murmured, looking at the clouds overhead. A drop of water landed on her forehead, and she let her tears fall to join it. "Maybe Marmee was right. Maybe the only happiness this life has for me is in being a wife and a mother, in accepting what's available to me rather than trying to make myself something more."

As she spoke the words, the wind whipped up around her, sending the plant she'd try to pluck free from the earth into her dress, where it stuck against the fabric. She dug into her apron for her gloves, only to discover they'd fallen out somewhere between Orchard House and home, leaving only her bare hands to remove the plant. She reached for it gently, and as she pulled the leaf free from the muslin—getting stung once again in the process—she murmured, "It would seem you don't want to be uprooted."

She didn't blame it. Had Meg found her way to fertile soil instead of the sandy stuff her marriage seemed made of, she too might want to dig her roots deep and make it her own.

"Seems appropriate, that instead of the garden I'd set out to grow, I find myself in possession of an abundance of nettles," she said to the little plant as she shook out her now stinging hand. She looked up, assessing the other weeds that had taken root—dandelion, bee balm, marjoram, mugwort. Once, Meg had sought to grow such wild herbs as these. All those years ago when her mother had given each of her sisters a quarter of the family garden to make their own, Meg had thought to nurture what had already been growing there, but Marmee urged her to be sensible. To choose respectable flowers like roses and heliotrope, not the sort of undesirable specimens that could take root anywhere without a watchful hand to guide them.

Now, as she recognized the plants that had overrun her carefully planned, if not quite as carefully planted, rows, she realized that she had read about many of them just that afternoon in the herbal Sally had given her. There was far more to these wild plants than her mother had ever realized, and because of that, Meg felt a certain kinship with them. Even the nettle who'd left several memories of itself still buried in Meg's hand had simply been asserting its boundaries.

These herbs weren't weeds. They were healers, maybe even friends.

Yes, Meg would try to grow her roses here. But this wouldn't be a garden like the one she'd tended under her mother's watchful eye.

"Thank you, little plant," Meg said with a whisper to the nettle, and as the words left her lips, the sky opened up over head. All around her, the plants seemed to tilt back and drink the water in, their leaves and stems and flowers tall and wild and free. Just as Meg herself longed to be.

An Apology

Meg went back into the Dovecote, soaked through and shivering but, for the first time in a long time, happy. As she pushed open the door, dripping water on the floor, and shrugged out of her apron, she thought she just might have a chance to carve something out of this life she'd been pushed into. Something her mother couldn't direct from her place at Orchard House.

She slipped out of her dress, hung it up to dry near the fire that John must have lit while she was out, then sat down beside it, letting it cast its shadows over her and this brief moment of joy. A garden wasn't a life—it wasn't the sort of ambition she'd had as a girl—but it could be something that might just give her the money she needed to build the life she *did* want. Especially with all the remedies she'd skimmed in the herbal.

But more than the money, Meg could make a difference.

She'd seen how women were treated when sick or in need. Many were ignored, others told to bear the burden they'd been handed in this life so that one day they might find paradise. Even in her own family, her parents had purchased every medicine for her sister they could afford, and while such things might have temporarily relieved Beth's symptoms during her worst spells, little thought was given to ongoing nourishment. No one considered that they might be able to strengthen Beth's heart rather than wait to treat the pain when it became too much to bear.

Did Meg think her little garden, should she foster it, could heal her sister? There was a glimmer of hope, certainly, but more she wanted to provide something to help Beth—and others like her—live their fullest lives with whatever time they had left.

But in order to even start to make a difference, Meg needed to understand what it was all those weeds could do. And that meant research.

Meg glanced up, listening for John or the twins. Then she pressed her hands to her full breasts and felt the familiar ache. The children would be hungry soon. At the realization, Meg's own stomach grumbled. She stopped by the kitchen on her way up and found that John had made a cold slaw, a few flapjacks, and had heated some of the string beans Meg had canned with Hannah at the end of last summer.

It wasn't a feast by any means, but it was something. Even more, he'd prepared a plate for her. She felt a pang in her heart and wondered if there might still be hope for love in this life they were building together.

Beside her plate, he'd left a note.

M—
I checked your ledger and don't know where the money for the dress came from. I know you keep your expenses meticulously, so I expected to find the cost here. As I'm writing this, I realize I could just ask you, but after you left, I was too angry to come after you and went looking for the answer myself.
Obviously, I didn't find it. It hadn't

> *occurred to me it could have been a gift.*
> *Now that I have calmed down (and the*
> *twins have calmed down), I'm thinking*
> *more clearly. It must have been a gift. You*
> *certainly would never steal it.*

Meg bristled, not because he didn't think her capable of stealing, but because he didn't think her capable of earning. The only reason she was in this house instead of out working for some family, teaching children she didn't have to tuck in at night, was because she'd taken up with him and now had her own to raise—without anyone to pay her for doing it.

She took an angry bite of slaw and continued reading.

> *Sometimes I wish we'd waited longer to*
> *marry—so I could get more established, give*
> *you the life you deserve. But your parents*
> *were so excited... It doesn't do any good to*
> *dwell on the past. This is where we are now.*
> *I made a commitment to you, vows to take*
> *care of you, and you walking out of the*
> *house after I'd been a complete ass—forgive*
> *me for saying it, but it's true—doesn't*
> *change that. But I'm trying to allow you*
> *more independence, something your mother*
> *mentioned you needed.*

Her mother? Meg hadn't realized Marmee and John were close enough that Marmee would relay Meg's worries to him. Seeing it here on paper only served to strengthen her resolve to not return to her mother's garden.

> *I sat with the twins until they fell asleep*
> *again and found I'm tired myself. It's a*

*wonder you can do this all day. While I
didn't have the time to prepare the sort of
meals you put together for us, I was a bachelor once and do know how to feed myself.*

*All of this to say, I am sorry. I should
have trusted you, because if we don't have
trust, then what do we have?*
—J

It wasn't some deep profession of love, but it was an apology. Part of Meg was angry that he'd apologized first, and she
could almost hear her mother's voice in her head, telling Meg
she had to be the sunshine of the family, that it was her responsibility not to anger her husband. And yet here he was, being
that good man her mother told her to marry. On the other
hand, she felt she fully deserved an apology and a plate of dinner and a night to herself instead of caring for the twins after
the things he'd said.

Marriage, it seemed, was as confusing as ever.

Meg finished her plate, cleaned it, then made her way up the
stairs, lamp in hand. No need to light the gas with the house as
quiet as it was. She paused at the bedroom she shared with
John, peeking in to find him asleep in the dark. She set the lamp
down outside the door and slipped in to grab her book. Then,
she went to her children.

At the light, Daisy blinked her eyes open sleepily while
Demi covered his own face with his hands and rolled over onto
his side with a little grunt. Meg laughed quietly as she reached
for her daughter and ran her fingers through Daisy's soft hair.

"Hello, my sweet little Daisy," Meg murmured. Her daughter cooed softly.

"Mama," Daisy whispered as she opened and closed her tiny
fists.

"Are you hungry?" Meg asked.

Daisy popped a thumb in her mouth and nodded. "Hungry," she repeated.

Meg smiled as she brought her daughter to her breast to feed. While Meg might want more than a life of *only* this, she did find a sweet satisfaction in her time with the twins, and with Daisy especially. Even the girl's name was a reminder of Meg's youth—before the twins and the Dovecote and even John. For Daisy was Meg's own nickname, one given her by her dear friend Annie Moffat, when Meg spent the week with her and Sallie. Though that time was now no more than a memory, it was a cherished one. Little compares to the wonder of friendship shared among young women—the fears and the secrets, the heartaches and the joys. Meg rarely saw Annie these days, busy as they both were with their firstborns (and Meg's second born), but that didn't keep Meg from thinking of her fondly.

With a contented sigh, Meg rested Culpeper's herbal on top of Daisy and flipped straight away to the entry on nettles.

> *Nettles are so well known, that they need no description. They may be found by feeling in the darkest night.*

Meg laughed abruptly, startling Daisy, who looked up at her. "Funny?" Daisy asked.

Meg nodded. "Quite," she said, the nettle stings still much more than a memory in the palm of her hand. But she didn't let it bother her because, as she expected, nettle was far more than a weed. It was a healer with the power to aid the lungs, to expel kidney stones, to counteract a venomous bite, to ease pain in the joints, and much more.

And so it was, with a smile on her face, that Meg continued to read.

The Linden Tree

Meg spent the next two weeks on her hands and knees digging in the dirt whenever she could. The summer solstice had passed a few days prior, and with spring turning to summer and John still off with friends in the evenings, she had plenty of time with the plants. When she had to break to entertain the twins or stir a pot at the stove, she turned to the back of the book where Culpeper had outlined various diseases and directions for making remedies. Though Meg's copy had been published in 1860, the herbal itself dated back almost two hundred years prior and paired plants with their astrological planetary influences, making some of his methods seem dated. While Meg would have much preferred to find a teacher, the book was all she had. For now, it would have to do.

In the garden, she made sure to respect the nettles, though she did end up having to remove a few—with gloves—that were choking out a patch of vervain. The vervain hadn't yet begun to flower, but it was a plant she'd recognize anywhere even though its purple, almost lavender-like flowers were still a month from blooming. Vervain had lined the meadow behind

Orchard House leading all the way to the water. Meg had been delighted to find it at the end of Culpeper's herbal. The description showed more uses for one little plant than she thought possible—from healing jaundice and easing gout to strengthening the stomach and cleansing the skin. To think, it had been yet another weed her mother had suggested she clear out to make way for something more beautiful.

"Thank you for choosing to take root here, little plant," Meg said to it while also apologizing to the nettle for removing it.

She continued on that way, recognizing weeds and wildflowers from her childhood and finding them in the book. It made the work slow-going, but in that slowness her discontent eased as though it were only her and the plants—and the twins, who seemed to enjoy picking wildflowers and digging up fistfuls of dirt as much as Meg did.

Every time Meg found herself turning to the book, she discovered yet another reason to let the plants stay where they'd taken up root. Yes, she pruned a few, like the nettles, making a path for her to walk among them without crushing their leaves and stems underfoot, but for the most part, Meg tended the weeds rather than clearing them. Those she did cut, she hung to dry in the kitchen.

It took a full week before she'd made her way to the tree in back that was no longer the easy-to-remove sapling she'd hoped for. She stood with Daisy propped up on one hip and Demi on the other as she looked it over.

"Flowers!" Daisy said as she reached for the plant, grabbing a handful of blossoms that had just started to bloom. She held them out to Meg. "Mama! Flowers!"

Demi, too, grasped at the tree, a small laugh slipping from his lips as he took a fistful.

"Careful," Meg said. "You don't want to hurt it." As the words left her lips, Meg realized that *she* didn't want to hurt the tree either. So, like the others, it would stay. She set the twins down, and as they shared their discoveries with each other with wide eyes and open hands, Meg pulled out her book once more. Once she found the linden tree—or the lime tree as Culpeper had categorized it—she ran her finger over the description, stopping on the section that read, quite clearly, that linden was both healing and strengthening to the heart.

Her eyes widened as she thought of her sister Beth.

She examined the tree, considered what she might be able to take, how much she needed. She pulled her shears from her pocket and filled her basket with yellow flowers and heart-shaped leaves, gathering enough for several tinctures (as outlined in the book) and a month's supply of dried plant for tea. Once she'd filled her basket—still leaving plenty of flowers for the bees who happily buzzed from branch to branch—she turned back to the twins, who sat playing with the flowers they, too, had harvested, and decided from that moment on to approach every encounter in her garden with the wonder of a child, lest she fail to see the power in working with a particular plant.

The twins clung to their linden flowers while Meg worked in the kitchen that afternoon. First, she set to drying several bundles, hanging them from any available space she could find. Then, she filled a glass bottle with the leaves before topping it off with distilled alcohol she'd purchased in town earlier that week with her allowance from John. She'd recorded it in her ledger as cooking supplies, not yet ready for John to see proof of her work beyond tending the garden itself. She poured boiled water over a teaspoon of the flowers and held the jar up to the light, watching as the liquid began to turn a soft peachy hue.

As she waited for it to cool, she sipped her own cup of linden tea and was delighted by the taste—at once sweet and earthy. It went down gently, and with each sip she felt her discontent ease and a new calm sort of joy slip into its place.

Once the jar she'd steeped for Beth had cooled, she packed the remaining fresh flowers into a basket along with the tea. The tincture would need several weeks before it was ready, but the tea her sister could start drinking straight away.

Meg wrapped Demi in a sling she wore on her back and began to prepare Daisy for one on the front. Though Aunt March had gifted her with an expensive pram that could hold two children, it was unwieldy and more a symbol of wealth than a practical way to take her children long distances. The family had been in awe over it, expecting Meg to be overjoyed, but while Meg liked nice things, she also liked practical things. The carriage was good only for pushing around town and pretending to have wealth that her ledger didn't reflect.

She packed her basket with the tea and flowers, then started for the door. She opened it to find Sallie on the other side, her hand raised for the bellpull.

"Sallie!" Meg said.

Her friend stepped forward for a hug, trying unsuccessfully to fit Meg and the babies in her embrace before falling back with an infectious laugh that had both women in tears.

"Where are you headed?" Sallie asked. "I'll walk with you. I can help with one of them if you'd like."

"No need," Meg said. It had been work enough to get them strapped in.

"I wish Ned would let me get away with the sling outside the house," she said, shaking her head. "The carriage is pretty enough, but ..."

"Not good for getting anything done," Meg finished.

They shared a grin.

"At least give me that," Sallie said as she reached for the basket, glancing at the contents. "Flowers? Tea?"

"It's for Beth." Meg closed the door behind her. "Look," Meg said with a smile as she grabbed Sallie's free hand and took her around the side of the house to the garden.

Her work had transformed it. Yes, the plants still grew where they'd rooted, but rather than a tangle of weeds, it looked cared for, if wild. Bees and butterflies buzzed from flower to flower. Birds had taken up in the linden tree, filling the world with song.

"Meg, it's breathtaking," Sallie said. "Your old rose garden was beautiful but this . . . this feels like you."

"I've been reading the book you gave me," Meg said. "There was so much growing here that I can use, not just for me, but for other people. Plants to treat illnesses and blemishes and pain, and to nourish the body and mind. They were here all along. They just needed a little love to help them flourish."

Sallie held up the basket. "This is from the garden?"

Meg nodded, her smile lighting up her face "The linden should help strengthen Beth's heart. I'm making a tincture, too."

"You're becoming a regular herbalist!" Sallie let the basket slide down to her forearm and clapped her hands with delight.

Meg flushed, then untucked and retucked a lock of hair behind her ear. "I'm dabbling."

"No," Sallie said. "Don't discredit yourself. This is important work." She tapped a finger against her lip. "This is work people would pay for."

This was why Meg and Sallie had stayed friends for so long. They thought the same way, and always with the other's best interest in mind.

"How quickly could you have a few things ready?" Sallie asked. "Especially what you mentioned about blemishes or really anything for beauty. And pain, too, particularly for monthly courses."

"Tinctures and vinegars take weeks but teas, like that one"—

she nodded to the basket in Sallie's hand—"are an overnight infusion."

"So you could have the herbs with instructions on how to use them in, say, a week?" Sallie asked.

Meg nodded. "If I started drying them today and tomorrow, sure. What is this about?"

"The tea!" Sallie said. "Next week we'll have Annie and my friends all in one place. Women who can afford to pay you for remedies like these and who would feel much more comfortable asking for them from a woman than the family physician."

Meg's eyes widened. It was what she'd wanted, the same thought she had only a week ago after she'd first found the nettles growing behind the Dovecote. But she hadn't considered how to make it possible. Women in need were abundant, but women who could afford to pay her—who *would* pay her? Without Meg seeming desperate?

"You are brilliant, Sallie," Meg said. "You really don't mind me selling herbs at your gathering?"

"Not at all," Sallie said. "I'll start the conversation. All you have to do is come ready with the teas." She held up the basket. "Now let's get this one to your sister."

When Meg and Sallie arrived at Orchard House, Beth wasn't in. She'd gone into town with Marmee for a walk in the early summer air. As much as Meg had hoped to see her sister, she didn't mind missing her mother. They hadn't spoken since Meg had absconded mid-lecture over a week ago, and Meg still didn't know how she'd handle facing Marmee again. Likely her mother would pretend nothing had happened. She'd carry on as she'd always done, waiting for her next opportunity to direct Meg's path. And while Meg was finished with that sort of relationship, she wasn't quite certain what sort of seeds she wanted to plant in its place.

"Did you buy this in town?" Hannah asked as she peered into the basket Sallie handed her.

"She grew it herself," Sallie said, brimming with pride on Meg's behalf.

"At the Dovecote?" Hannah asked. "Well done! Linden by the looks of it?"

Meg nodded. "It's supposed to help strengthen the heart. I thought . . ." She trailed off, biting her lip.

Hannah gripped Meg's forearm. "For Beth, of course. She'll be delighted you thought of her."

"The tea will be ready in the morning, but to make more you'll need to steep a teaspoon of the flowers in a quart jar like this one overnight." She pulled a slip of paper from her pocket and handed it to Hannah. "All the instructions are here."

"Seems easy enough," Hannah said.

"I'm also drying flowers to carry Beth through to next season, and I have several tinctures steeping for when we run out of the flowers or if she's not feeling well enough to drink a full quart of tea in a day. It will be a few weeks before those are ready."

Hannah nodded as she took the bundles of flowers and leaves Meg had brought her and hung them up to dry.

"And, Hannah?" Meg asked.

"Yes, dear?"

"Perhaps we just keep this between us and Beth."

Hannah arched an eyebrow.

"It's just . . . Marmee has her own way of dealing with Beth's illness."

"Right you are," Hannah murmured, shaking her head.

Meg and Sallie shared a surprised look.

"Your mother is a good woman to be sure," Hannah said. "She's simply protective of Beth."

"A bit too protective if you ask me," Sallie said.

"Aye," Hannah said. "She'd probably be afraid that anything not directly prescribed by the family doctor will send Beth into a fit rather than strengthen her. Plants like these are good medicine."

As the words left Hannah's mouth, Meg's heart swelled. For the first time in a long time, she heard the word *good* and it felt right. It felt true.

"Good medicine," Meg said. "I like that."

Truth Between Sisters

Meg spent the next day cutting herbs with her heart full of gratitude, offering thanks to each plant before her shears ever touched stem. She harvested cowslips for wrinkles, lovage and Solomon's seal for skin spots, and mallows for strengthening hair. Then, as Sallie had suggested, she turned to plants that could call down a woman's courses—mugwort, which made the blood flow freely while easing pain; comfrey, which could slow the bleeding in a woman whose course was too heavy; and chickweed to ease the sores that many women developed between their thighs as the cloths that held their blood rubbed at their skin.

John found her in the kitchen, hanging plants to dry and combining herbs with oil or vinegar or alcohol, depending on the intended use.

"Where did you get all this?" he asked, as she stood pouring oil over fresh lovage leaves. Once ready, it could be applied to blemishes on the face to reduce their appearance.

"It's from the garden!" she said with a grin before capping the jar, setting it in the sunlight streaming in from the window, and starting another.

"I love what you've done with it." John pulled aside the curtain and glanced out into the yard. "It's very whimsical."

"You think so?" Meg turned around to find John standing just behind her, looking over her shoulder at the jar of oil. He leaned forward and brushed the tips of his fingers over her cheek, pausing with his thumb on her skin. Their eyes locked, and they stood like that for a few seconds, a flutter in Meg's chest.

John cleared his throat. "There was a bit of dirt on your face." He stepped back. "What's all this for?"

"This and that," Meg said, afraid to tell him too much of her plans. John wanted to provide for them, but if he learned Meg wanted to make money of her own? She hoped he wouldn't try to stop her, but she didn't want to give him the chance. "Just trying to make the most of what we have."

She nodded to a pot that sat simmering on the stove. "I made some soup with the nettles," she said. "And of course a few vegetables Hannah gave me from her garden when I stopped by Orchard House earlier today."

"You stopped by Orchard House?" John asked, voice tinged with concern. Unless they went to visit her family together, Meg's solo visits typically were a result of discontent at home. John knew as much. "Is . . . is everything alright?"

"Everything is perfect," Meg said, and she meant it. "I was dropping off something for Beth from the garden. She was in town with Marmee, so I spent the afternoon chatting with Hannah."

The tension drained from John's shoulders as he started to serve himself a bowl of soup. "I was planning to go over to the Scotts' this evening, but I can stay here if you need a hand? Or perhaps you want to join me?"

Meg waved at him from where she'd started a third jar of lovage oil. "I've got this under control. Besides, I wanted to write to Amy. Go out. Enjoy yourself."

"You're certain?" John asked.

Meg nodded and was pleased to find she meant it.

"I could take the children," he suggested. "Give you more time to focus on all this."

Meg's eyes widened. A night completely to herself? "That would be lovely. You really wouldn't mind?"

"Not at all," John said. "Mrs. Scott keeps asking after you and the twins. You're busy here, but I can at least bring Daisy and Demi."

Meg placed the cap on her jar, then she turned and wrapped her arms around John. "Yes, thank you. I accept."

He laughed as he pulled back from her. "Anything you need before I go?"

"Just to nurse them," Meg said.

Once the twins were fed and gone, Meg sat down at the kitchen table, pen in hand.

> *Concord, Massachusetts*
> *My dearest Amy,*
>
> *I'm sorry I haven't written much since you've left. I'm certain mother has told you all about the twins, but I wonder if she's written much about me? And if she did, what would she tell you?*
>
> *Certainly not that she and I haven't spoken in over a week. That I realized she set me down a path that there's no turning back from—not now that I have two children depending on me.*
>
> *When we were still girls, Jo asked me what I'd do if John asked me to marry him. You know, I told her I'd say no. That I was*

much too young to become a bride. There were so many things left to do before I gave it all up for a family. I had ambitions of my own—not to become an author like her or even a renowned artist like you, but more than a wife and a mother, belonging to anyone but myself.

Aunt March showed up that day when John made his intentions clear. Not only had I planned to turn him down, I did turn him down! But then she told me how wrong I'd be to marry a poor man. At her words, everything Marmee had taught me about being a good little pilgrim bubbled up to the surface and before I knew it, I found myself defending him and accepting his proposal.

Now, I wonder if mother hadn't planned out the whole day, down to Aunt March's appearance at the most opportune moment. I've begun to realize just how heavy a hand she's had in the life I'm living, and it's like seeing the past through new eyes.

For so long I thought she wanted us to make the right matches—especially with you in Europe and the unspoken expectations we all know she sent you with—because as women we're so limited by what we can do in life based upon who is supporting us. Her work for suffrage is for the future, but she's also keenly aware of the present. At least, that's what I had told myself for so long. Yet it seems if she had wanted me to have the means to push the cause forward, she wouldn't have turned me away from Ned and set my sights on John. It's troubling, but I suppose one can work diligently for a cause without putting it into practice in their own life.

I'm sorry to burden you with my thoughts. I'd intended this to be a happy letter, and here I am prattling on about Marmee and my troubles. I am writing to tell you that I've finally found work of my own, something that not only brings value but that I enjoy!

I'm sure you remember our garden from when we were girls? Your honeysuckles and morning glory, the tall white lilies and delicate ferns. All perfect specimens for you to draw and paint! You might remember how manicured my little corner was.

Well, no longer!

I have finally started a garden here at the Dovecote, but rather than red roses and purple heliotrope, I am nurturing the plants that have decided to make a home here, just like me. It's funny—these so-called weeds are beautiful in their own right. Many are beginning to flower, and they bring in the most magnificent butterflies in colors that I think would make your artist's heart sing.

I'm not only tending to the garden, Amy; I'm learning to use it. All these plants, there's so much they can do. I've been reading Culpeper's Complete Herbal, and it

seems everything growing here has a use.
Even the linden tree I thought to cut down
has come into its own.

The twins noticed the flowers first, and I
am so happy they did. Linden, it seems, is
strengthening to the heart. I took some tea
over for Beth—she wasn't at home, which I
hope is a good sign. Marmee keeps such a
close eye on her, I fear for Beth's happiness.
We all know she's unwell, but that shouldn't
keep her from being alive here and now. I
can only hope the flowers give her at least a
touch more life, for however long she has it.
Not that you need to worry after her. She is
well enough for now.

I've included a sprig of linden for you as
well. To think the very flowers our Beth is
drinking will travel across the ocean to
you! Maybe it will inspire you. Every day I
spend with my plants I think of how beautifully you could draw or paint them.
Culpeper's herbal is useful, but it would be
far better if it had more pictures. The few
illustrations at the beginning are nice, but
every plant should include a drawing or a
painting. Perhaps when you return home
we could work on one of our own. Me to research, Jo to write, you to illustrate. Beth
can compose a song for us while we work!

It is nice, dreaming again.

But enough about me! What of you? What
of Paris? Have you been able to paint at
all? Marmee tells me you and Florence are

spending time with the Vaughn brothers, something she seemed awfully pleased about, but I'd much rather hear of your art than mother's machinations for the right match.

I hope you are well, dear sister. Sending you all my love.

—Meg

A Reunion Over Tea

It had been a full month since Meg started working in her garden, and the day of Sallie's tea had come. Meg packed up several jars of now-dried herbs. It would take a few more weeks before the oils would be ready, but if today went well, she'd have buyers for them before she ever strained out the leaves and blooms. Meg found herself as excited to show off her plants as she was to wear her new silk. She mentioned the tea to John that morning, and he had said he only hoped he got home in time to see the dress for himself before she changed out of it— without a single mention of the argument that had driven Meg to the garden in the first place.

It wasn't the sort of love she'd dreamed of as a girl, but it was a start.

She readied the twins in the carriage Aunt March had purchased. As much as Meg would have preferred to make the walk to Sallie's with her babies in slings, this was one time where appearances mattered. Yes, some of these women were her friends, but mostly they were friends of Sallie's. While Sallie said she would lay the way for Meg's new business venture,

Meg had to do the rest, and making a good impression was a part of that.

As she packed her basket with as many jars of dried herbs as she could and nestled a few in the pram with the twins, the house filled with the ringing of the bellpull. She opened the door to find two members of Sallie's household staff on the other side.

"Christopher?" She asked. "Sophie?"

"Mrs. Brooke," the older man, the Moffats' carriage driver, said. He'd taken Sallie and Meg on many a shopping trip over the past year. "Mrs. Moffat sent me to bring you over for the tea."

"Sallie sent you? For me?" Meg asked.

"Yes, ma'am," the woman said. Sophie couldn't be much older than Beth. She watched over Sallie's daughter, Eleanor. "She asked that I take care of the twins to protect your silk. We both know how babes can be." She reached for the pram and lifted first Daisy onto one hip, then Demi onto the other. "No need to bring this," Sophie said. "I'll take your little ones straight to the nursery when we arrive."

"Mrs. Moffat thought there might be a few additional items you'd need to bring as well," Christopher said, holding out a hand for the basket of jars.

Meg let him take it. "I'll be just a moment," she said, running back to the kitchen for another basket, which she quickly filled, leaving space for the jars she'd hidden in the carriage. Christopher took those from her, too, and then they were off.

Meg was the first to arrive for the tea, and it quickly became clear that was by design. Sallie welcomed her with open arms and took one of the two baskets Meg brought with her for the gathering.

"I knew that silk would look divine on you," Sallie said, wearing a dress of a similar fabric but in a cornflower blue, the color of her eyes. Both day dresses had been cut in the latest style—as anything Sallie had made always did—with narrow shoulders, tight sleeves and tall, fitted collars. Similarly, both women had pulled their hair up and back in chignons, though Sallie had likely had help that Meg didn't. "What did John think of it?"

"Other than that it was expensive?" She hadn't told Sallie how upset John had been when he'd discovered the dress. She didn't want to make her friend feel in any way guilty for such a generous gift.

"Don't tell me he made a fuss about it," Sallie said.

Meg waved a gloved hand. "Nothing more than to be expected," Meg said. "Though he did mention he hoped I'd still have it on when he got home this evening."

Sallie waggled her eyebrows. "Now that's a good sign."

Meg lowered her voice. "If I wanted to add to my already full household, it might be."

"Surely you've found something in all your reading that could help avoid that?" Sallie asked.

Contraception was on the rise, but Meg wasn't sure how to have that conversation with John. Luckily for her, her courses hadn't yet returned since the twins had come into the world. Still, she had found more than a few herbs Culpeper had listed to cure the disease of motherhood, as he put it—mugwort, tansy, pennyroyal, and rue, to name a few—and Meg had made sure to give them plenty of space when she found them already firmly rooted in the garden.

"After your recommendations last week, you know I have," Meg said. Women their age knew what herbs to avoid during pregnancy, but identifying them without assistance was a different matter entirely.

Sallie gave her a small smile. "I knew you'd read between the lines." She took a quick look around, then lowered her voice. "I for one would happily purchase any teas that can help keep another child at bay anytime soon."

"You would have them free of charge," Meg said.

"Nonsense!" Sallie said. "You're just getting started in your trade."

"And you are making that possible." Meg held her arms out at the room before them, where cakes and jellies and treats covered the table. "Consider it my way of thanking you."

"Don't thank me just yet," Sallie said. "I've brought you the customers, now we have to convince them they need what you're offering."

As if on cue, the bellpull rang and the guests began to arrive. Meg joined the ladies as they crowded around the treats and filled their teacups. They asked after John, after the Dovecote, if marriage and motherhood were all Meg hoped they would be. They complimented her dress and expressed how happy they were to see her out again, assuring her they understood how difficult adjusting to children could be on a woman, and Meg with twins!

Though Meg would rather have talked of her garden and her ambitions and the little book Sallie had given her, she indulged them with the expected answers, saving her teas and tinctures for the right moment.

As Meg popped a cake into her mouth, Annie Moffat—no, Williams, Meg reminded herself—walked through the door. Meg studied her as she took in the room. She held herself tightly, her mouth in a flat line and her hands pressed against her stomach. There was a weariness about her that Meg recognized instantly because she'd seen it in the mirror. But when Annie's eyes met hers, they lit up, and for a moment that heaviness lifted. She raised a hand, and then she was running toward Meg.

"Meg!" she said as she neared the table before she threw her arms around Meg and held her close for a few seconds longer than most would.

"It's been so long," Annie said when she finally pulled back, keeping Meg's hand clasped tightly in her own. It had been almost a year since they'd last seen each other. Annie had given birth a couple months after the twins were born, and while Meg's labor had been long, it had been easy compared to Annie's. From what Sallie had said, Annie had lost a lot of blood and had spent the next month in bed. She still hadn't gained all of her color back.

"I've missed you," Annie said. "How *are* you?"

Not: *How are the twins?*

Not: *How is married life?*

Not: *How is John?*

"I am better than I've been in a long time," Meg said, lowering her voice. "I think I might actually be happy."

Annie appraised her, looking her over from head to toe. "Please tell me your secret, because it can't be motherhood or marriage."

Meg laughed out loud, drawing the eyes of a few of the other women. She flushed and popped another cake into her mouth. Then, she said, "No, it's not the twins. It's me. I'm finding Meg March again."

"And where did you find her?" Annie asked.

"In my garden," Meg said with a soft smile. "It isn't much, but it's mine to tend."

Annie nodded slowly, then whispered with a look in her sister-in-law's direction. "To think, you could have had all this had you returned my brother's attention."

Meg shook her head. Even without her mother's objections to Ned, he would have never been a fit for Meg. "We weren't meant to be sisters, I don't think," Meg said, slowly. "Becoming a Moffat would not have been right for me."

"Would that I could have stayed one." Annie took Meg's hand and gave it a gentle squeeze, planting a warm, soft peace in Meg's chest. At this point, the life of a spinster was out of the question for either of them, but it couldn't hurt to imagine.

"Is Mr. Brooke better than what you imagined you would have found with my brother?" Annie asked.

Meg considered this. Her marriage to John was part of what had led her to her state of discontent, and while she wanted more than what John could give, getting into the Dovecote *had* gotten her out of Orchard House. It wasn't the life she'd dreamed of, but she was finally starting to craft it into something she might be happy to live.

"He is tender," Meg said.

"That, at least, I am glad to hear," Annie said.

"More importantly, he's been taking the twins out in the evenings to visit a neighbor so I can have time to myself," Meg said.

"Perhaps I should stop by some evening for tea," Annie suggested. "It could be like old times, only, made new."

"Perhaps," Meg said. "And what about you? Is life as Mrs. Williams everything your mother promised it would be?"

Annie let out a sharp laugh. "Hardly," she said. "After little Andy was born, the doctor put me on a regimented resting schedule—all alone in my room for weeks. It helped my body recover, some, but I cried at nothing and cried most of the time."

Meg gripped Annie's hand tighter. "Oh Annie, I'm so sorry."

Annie's answering shrug said more than words ever could.

"Perhaps I'll take a page out of your book and see if I can't find Annie Moffat again." She picked up one of the cakes, examined it, and looked down at her stomach. "I'm going to start by not worrying about every little thing I eat, much to my mother's terror." She popped it into her mouth with a satisfied smirk. Then she wrapped an arm around Meg's waist and led her to the couches.

Once everyone had their fill of gossip and tea, Sallie clapped her hands and said, "I am pleased you could all make it out today."

"This has been absolutely lovely," one of the women said.

Another nodded. "You always help us make time for ourselves."

Like Meg and Sallie and Annie, all of the women in the room had at least one child, if not more, and Sallie made sure she had plenty of staff today to care for them.

"Just because we're married and mothers now doesn't mean we should be set aside to languish! Many of us aren't even twenty-five yet," Sallie said. "Take Meg. I for one envy her perfect skin despite having had twins less than a year ago!"

Several of the women nodded.

"I asked her if she would share her secrets with us," Sallie said. "Anyone interested?"

Meg flushed, then shrugged as if to dismiss Sallie, feigning embarrassment, then did her best not to laugh when Sallie grinned at her. When Annie caught her eye and arched a brow, Meg gave the slightest nod.

"Oh yes, please," Annie said, pinching her own cheeks. "Anything to give me a little color back."

"I don't know," another woman, Tracey Miller, said. "I hate the blemishes myself, but I'm not quite ready to look so flawless and have Mr. Miller . . . well . . . you know." She bit her lip, looked around at the others. "One child is a lot already, and I know there's been talk of voluntary motherhood among suffragists, but when I even tried to broach the subject, he . . ."

"Said it was unnatural?" one of the other women, Sara Hutton, suggested. "As if yearly pregnancies are God's will and not our husbands'."

She was met with nods all around.

"Most plants have something to offer us, but even with those benefits, there are certain herbs that those seeking to have a child should avoid," Meg said, as she took her baskets out from behind the refreshment table. "Much the same as there are herbs for clear skin and healthy, shining hair."

Though she had only been working in the garden for a few short weeks, she had already known many of the plants she had discovered growing there, from years of playing in the fields. Yes, she was coming to understand them in a new way now, but it felt like talking about old friends.

She held up a jar of dried herb material, still green. "It turns out I'm growing an abundance of mugwort at the Dovecote. It's deeply relaxing and can help you get a good night's sleep." Meg had been drinking it herself for the past week to see how it interacted with her own body before recommending it to anyone else.

"I have never slept quite as well as I have when I take a cup before bed. Not only that, it can help ease the pain of your monthly course. And, if that course happens to be delayed, it can help bring it around faster," she said with meaning. She paused, let the words sink in. "Not an herb for mothers, to be sure."

Eyes widened all around her.

"Truly?" Tracey asked.

"And which one do you use for your skin?" Sara asked.

Meg held up a jar of dried lovage and mallows. "This tea blend will help both skin *and* hair," Meg said. "And I have oil that will be ready in a few weeks which you can apply directly to spots on the face to ease their appearance."

"Oh, put me down for one of those!" Sara said.

"I'll take two," Tracey said. "And the other tea—the mugwort—if you don't mind."

"Yes, I'm a nervous sleeper," Sara said. "Should I drink it daily or . . ."

"Two or three times a day leading up to and throughout your monthly course," Meg said. "You can also add sugar and milk to the tea if you prefer."

The women gathered round Meg and started picking up her jars, asking after the contents of each, and Meg found herself smiling more broadly than she had in years.

Meg Gets a Request

By the time Sallie's tea had ended, both of Meg's baskets were empty, but her purse was full. Every jar of oil she had bottled was spoken for, and she already had requests for more, which meant she had a busy week ahead of her.

With each purchase, she wrote down the woman's initials, the herbs, and the total. For the mugwort — of which everyone left with at least one jar — she provided the same instruction for each person, with the caveat that, if it felt too strong, they should come see her at the Dovecote so she could tailor the dosage for their needs.

One by one the guests left until only Sallie, Meg, and Annie remained.

Sallie glanced between the two women and said, "Shall I prepare more tea?"

Annie grabbed her sister-in-law in a hug, then nodded. "Yes, please. Thank you for arranging this."

"Arranging . . . ?" Meg trailed off, her eyes meeting Sallie's.

"It's not my request to make," Sallie said. "Let me have a pot of tea brought to the parlor."

Annie gripped Meg's hand and pulled her back from the entrance and toward the room from which they'd just departed.

"What's this about?" Meg asked.

But Annie held a finger to her lips until they were seated at the couch and the door was closed tightly behind them. Then, she turned to Meg.

"When Sallie heard about your garden, she came to me right away," Annie said, taking Meg's hand and pressing it to her stomach. "I need your help."

Meg's eyes widened.

"My husband doesn't want to admit it, but my first pregnancy almost took my life and the child's," Annie said, eyes gleaming as tears spilled down her cheeks. "I don't know that I can survive another."

"Your monthly course is delayed?" Meg asked with meaning.

"I've waited for it every day, but . . ."

Meg nodded slowly. She knew what Annie was asking—she'd known getting into this work would likely lead to this very kind of request. But prevention and termination were two different acts entirely. It hadn't even been forty years since Massachusetts outlawed intentionally bringing about miscarriage, labeling it a misdemeanor punishable by no less than a year in jail and a fine not exceeding two thousand dollars—a felony if the mother died in the process.

"Has the child quickened?" Meg asked, referring to the first feeling of movement in the womb. When she'd felt it with the twins, it had been at once a joy and a terror, the hope that this path would bring her the contentment her mother had promised but the reality that Meg's ambitions had been left at the Dovecote's threshold in exchange.

Annie shook her head. "It's only been a few weeks."

"Then we've no time to waste," Meg said.

"You'll help me?" Annie asked. "I know it's a risk . . ."

Meg took Annie's hand. "It sounds like having that child

might be an even greater one. But I have to tell you, I've never done anything like this before. Yes, I have the plants, and Culpeper's book details the process, but . . ."

"I trust you, Meg," Annie said.

Meg pressed her lips together. Before she could say more, Sallie returned with a servant and more tea. After the servant left, she glanced down the hallway and closed the door. She glanced between the two women.

"Well?" she asked.

Meg nodded, and Sallie gripped both her hand and Annie's.

"We must move quickly," Meg said. "We'll need a tub and plenty of boiling water. Do you trust your servants?"

Annie considered this, but after a few moments, she shook her head. "I don't know."

"Ned has business in Boston this week," Sallie said. "He leaves the day after tomorrow. We can do it here."

"We'll have privacy?" Meg asked.

"And help," Sallie said. "A year ago, Sophie needed the same."

"Then let's go to whoever helped her," Meg said, still uncertain of her yet unpracticed hands. "She can make sure Annie is safe."

But Sallie shook her head. "She doesn't do the work anymore."

Meg bit her lip. "Does she teach?"

Meg Finds a Teacher

With one babe strapped around her back and the other slung over her front, Meg made the walk from the Dovecote to the edge of Concord, just a stone's throw from Walden Pond, to the home of one Rebekah Mayer. Meg stared up at a house not much bigger than her own. Sallie and Annie had both offered to go with her, but if discretion had driven Rebekah to stop her work, then the fewer people who visited her, the better.

Meg pushed open the gate and followed the walk to the front door. Plants lined both sides of the path—many of which she recognized and many of which she did not, evidence of how much she still had to learn. But here, if she were lucky, she might just find a teacher.

After she rang the bellpull, she took a step back and waited. A few moments later, the door creaked open, and a child stood on the other side—nine or ten years old if Meg had to guess.

Meg's eyes widened. "Hello? Is Mrs. Mayer in?"

"Who are you?"

"Meg Mar—Meg Brooke," she corrected herself. "I was hoping she might help me with . . . a personal matter."

Meg worried at her lip. Sallie had said the woman was a widow, but she hadn't mentioned grandchildren.

As the young girl assessed Meg, a woman appeared behind her and rested a hand on her shoulder. Meg had been expecting some sort of old wise woman to guide her with her garden and tell her how best to help Annie; instead she found a woman who could have been her older sister.

"Mrs. Mayer?" Meg asked.

But the stranger's eyes narrowed as they skipped over the twins. "Run inside and get your mother," she said to the girl.

"Her mother?" Meg asked. "You're not . . . ?" Before she could finish the question, another woman appeared. She couldn't have had more than ten years on Meg.

"You're Mrs. Mayer, then?" Meg asked.

"You may call me Rebekah," she replied, resting a hand on her daughter's head as she, too, assessed Meg's children, before her eyes fell on Meg's stomach. She leaned out the door and glanced down the path. "You walked here?"

"My friend Sallie Moffat told me how important discretion is to you. You helped her servant, Sophie."

Rebekah's face softened and she nodded slowly. "I'm sorry, but I don't offer those sorts of services anymore."

"I know, I—"

Rebekah held up a hand. "Please don't try to convince me otherwise. I understand why you have come. Twins, and now another . . ." She offered Daisy a sad smile, hiding her face behind her hands then exposing it again. Daisy erupted in laughter, which had Demi squirming at Meg's back to see what fun he was missing out on.

Meg reached a hand over her shoulder and ruffled his soft hair to keep him from trying to climb out of the sling. "It's not for me," she said.

Still, Rebekah shook her head. "It doesn't matter who it's for. The answer is no."

"Becks," the other woman said.

"I can't," Rebekah said. "*We* can't."

Meg blinked as Rebekah gripped the other woman's hand, understanding dawning on her.

"Please," Meg said. "I only want to talk."

"At least hear what she has to say," the other woman said, extending a hand toward Meg. "Marianne Smith."

"You both live here?" Meg asked. "Together?"

"Widows," Marianne said. "I lost my husband in the war, and Rebekah . . ."

Rebekah rubbed at the space between her eyes. "My husband passed a little over a year ago."

"At least you don't have to bear the weight of it alone," Meg said, her gaze dropping to the women's clasped hands. When she looked back up, Marianne arched an eyebrow, and her lips curved upward.

"Some things are easier as a widow, but others are not," Rebekah said. "He supported my work, and without his protection, I can't risk the work any longer. Especially not now."

Marianne leaned in, whispered something in Rebekah's ear. With a heavy sigh, Rebekah nodded and waited for the other woman to go back into the house with Rebekah's daughter. She gently closed the door behind her and started down the steps and into her garden. "Walk with me."

Meg followed after her. She'd only gone a few feet before she paused to stare at the plants all around them. "You have everything here. And so much of it," she whispered as she dropped into a crouch to cradle a pale blossom between her hands. Daisy struggled against the sling as if she, too, wanted to hold it. "My nettles were choking out my marshmallow, so I had to cut them back. I thought that would solve the problem, but that plant is still struggling."

"How damp is your soil?" Rebekah asked.

"It's been drying out now that we're well into summer," Meg said.

Rebekah nodded. "Mallows prefer a moist environment, but still plenty of sun. Try covering the base with mulch."

"Thank you," Meg said. "I've been learning from Culpeper's herbal but . . ."

"There's only so much a book can teach you," Rebekah said, her earlier wariness falling away as her lips turned up. "That's why you're here."

"And to help my friend," Meg said.

Rebekah considered her. "Would you be open to helping others?"

"Yes," Meg said. "I've already provided a few women with preventative teas—something I felt much more comfortable offering because I've been using one myself."

"And tell me about your home life." She nodded toward Daisy. "Your husband, is he . . . amenable to the suffragist cause?"

Meg's own mother had long been a suffragist, though Meg wondered what Marmee might say if she knew what Meg was doing here, now. John knew her family helped those in need—it had been one of the things that had drawn him to her in the first place after he'd gotten to know her parents when her father was ill. But neither of them had gotten much involved with her parents' work.

"He's never expressed anything against the cause," Meg said. "And he allows me my independence. But he doesn't know how I'm using what's growing in our garden beyond clearing a blemish or making someone's hair shine."

Rebekah tapped a finger against her lip. "If he were to discover what you want to do for your friend?"

Meg considered this. She'd married John, borne his children, chosen this life her mother had pushed her into. She didn't love him, though she was warming to him. The words from his letter came back to her: *I should have trusted you because if we don't have trust, then what do we have?*

John might have decided he trusted her, but did she trust him? She shook her head. "I don't know."

"Can you keep it a secret from him?" Rebekah asked. "This work doesn't put only you at risk, it can threaten any of the women you see regularly, anyone who could be blamed should someone unsympathetic to the cause discover it—and worse, should any of the women you wish to help, die in the process."

"And you," Meg said. "And your family."

Rebekah glanced back at the house, where Marianne stood watching them through the window. "If I'm going to teach you, yes."

Meg had kept the truth of her feelings—of her unhappiness—from John well enough. "It won't be a problem." She hoped.

Rebekah watched her in silence for a few moments before she gave a short nod. "Then we better get started."

A Stirring of the Heart

Meg spent the afternoon with Rebekah Mayer, learning all that she could—how much plant matter to prepare, how to deliver it, how to hide the evidence of what they planned to do, and what to give Annie to help her recover once the work was complete. Now, she sat in her kitchen making sure she had everything she needed for tomorrow measured out and prepared.

Rebekah told her it would have been safest for Meg to prepare a tea, give it to her friend with instructions for use, then wash her hands of the whole thing. Yes, there was danger in it for Annie, but if no one else knew where she received the tea, then Meg would be blameless should anyone discover what they'd done. But Meg wanted the safest option for Annie's health, and that meant more than a simple tea. She'd start with a steam, then leave Annie with herbs to drink over the next two weeks.

As Meg counted everything for the third time, popping a violet blossom into her mouth, Daisy let out a squeal from where she sat beside her brother in the highchairs Aunt

March had given them. She held out her hands toward Meg and said, "Flower!"

Meg glanced down at the handful of soft purple blooms she'd plucked from the yard that morning alongside the herbs Rebekah had recommended—chamomile and agrimony, yarrow and feverfew, mugwort and cohosh root, the latter of which she'd had to borrow from Rebekah's garden along with a jarful of seeds to sow among Meg's own plants. She picked up one of the small purple flowers and offered it to her daughter. Daisy took it gently between both hands, bringing it to her nose to smell it. Demi, too, reached out.

"Me!" he said.

Meg laughed and handed him a flower of his own. While they played with them, she took a handful of violets and dropped them into her mortar. "Thank you," she murmured to the plants before she began to crush them. As she finished, the front door opened. Meg set the pestle down, eyes sweeping over the table, worried what John might see. She almost tucked the jars into a basket and hid them in the corner, but there wasn't enough time. Besides, she'd spent the last week drying herbs and preparing oils for Sallie's gathering. She could only hope John would think this was more of the same.

With a steadying breath, she started scooping up a spoonful of the violets. John stepped into the kitchen, a certain heaviness in his shoulders and tightness at the corners of his eyes. As the children erupted in a new set of squeals, waving their arms above their heads, flowers in fists, a smile broke across his face, and his weariness melted away. But rather than going straight for the children, he came up behind Meg, wrapped his arms around her, and looked into the mortar.

"You've been busy," he said, resting his chin on the top of her head. "I like it."

"You like it, do you?" she asked, letting herself relax into his hold, imagining that he knew exactly what she was doing, and he supported every herb she'd picked and every jar she'd packed.

"You seem lighter since you started working in the garden," he said.

"I feel lighter," she said.

"And what's all this?" he asked. "More oils for your friends?"

Meg opened her mouth, almost told him everything, but it wasn't a risk she could take. "Something like that." She finished scooping up the crushed violets and turned out of his embrace. She grabbed another soft purple flower, looked up at him, and said, "I have something for you."

He raised an eyebrow.

"Open up," she said.

He did. Then, she placed the flower on his tongue. He closed his mouth slowly and started to chew, his eyes brightening. "Delicious." He peered around her at the few flowers left on the table. "Violets?"

She nodded as he looked over the rest of her plants.

"Feverfew and chamomile. And this is ... agrimony?" he asked, with a nod to the bright yellow blooms.

"It is." Meg tried to keep fear from creeping into her voice. She needn't be afraid that John recognized the herbs. It didn't mean he knew what they would do, or why she'd have them together.

"And mugwort!" He rubbed a fresh leaf between his thumb and forefinger and breathed in the sharp scent. "Is all of this from our garden?"

"Most of it," Meg said.

"You've truly transformed it," he said. "Here I thought you were going to stick with vegetables, but you're building us our own apothecary."

Meg's eyes widened. "It's nothing like that," she said, only just managing to hold her voice steady.

"It's wonderful is what it is." John laughed softly, and the fear drained out of her. "What's this for?" He nodded to the mortar and the spoonful of violets.

"The twins," Meg said with a grin. "They're enamored by the violets, so I thought I'd give them a taste."

"And did they like it?" John asked.

"Let's find out." Meg handed him the spoon before getting out a second. John went straight for Daisy, Meg for Demi. They brought the mashed violet to the babies' lips. Demi opened wide, while Daisy reached for the spoon in John's hands.

He laughed and said, "By all means."

Demi, seeing what his sister had done, took the spoon from Meg. Then, they both licked up the contents. In tandem, their eyes widened.

"Mmmm," Daisy said.

"More!" Demi replied.

John laughed softly, then planted a kiss on each of their foreheads.

"That's enough for now." Meg collected the spoons and set them back down on the table.

"May I?" John asked, pointing toward her stack of violets.

She laughed. "Certainly."

He took two flowers, popping another in his mouth; then, he offered one to her. Meg placed it lightly on her tongue.

"This reminds me of our old walks through Mr. Laurence's hot house," John said. Those were their earliest days together, when Meg left her glove behind, and John had tucked it away. Before her mother got involved with whatever had only just begun to sprout up between them. "Though I must admit I much prefer your penchant for wildflowers. Far more practical, though just as beautiful."

But his focus wasn't on the plants Meg had harvested. Instead, John watched her, and she felt a flush creep up her throat and into her cheeks. His eyes flicked between hers. How had she never noticed how brown they were? Like the color of rich, freshly turned soil—a safe place to grow. She swallowed, and his gaze fell to her lips. He reached a hand toward her mouth, his thumb gently brushing the skin, and she felt herself leaning toward him.

"You had a bit of violet," he breathed. He held his fingertips there for a few seconds, before he cleared his throat, and stepped back, cheeks pink and eyes bright. He ran a hand through his hair and held it at the back of his head. His deep, soft laughter unwound something in Meg's chest.

"Here I am in my kitchen, with my wife and our two children, and I don't feel like a husband at all. I feel like a boy again." He shook his head. "It's nice."

"It is," Meg agreed. Had they ever had a moment like this, she wondered?

"Something's changing in you," John said. "You're becoming . . ." He paused, searching for the words, but coming up short. "I don't know. But whatever it is, it feels a bit miraculous being here to witness it. Like watching a flower bloom when you didn't realize what its petals would reveal."

"You, sir, never told me you were a poet," Meg said.

Again that laugh, like a secret meant only for her, and she realized what this feeling in her chest was, this sensation that went all the way down to her toes and came back up again, making her head light and her heart soft.

Meg was falling in love.

Voluntary Motherhood

W hen Meg arrived at Sallie's house the next day, it was just as Sallie had promised. Ned was nowhere to be found, and even the servants were scarce. Sophie met her at the door, quick to take the twins off Meg's hands.

"It's good work, what you're doing," Sophie said.

"It's only what's been done for centuries, long before they put that law into place," Meg replied. The words were borrowed, something Rebekah had said as she'd walked Meg through the process. She'd had Meg repeat back the steps more times than Meg could count, which Meg had been doing since she left the other woman's house two days ago. With things as they were, it was best that nothing be written down, to protect everyone involved.

Sallie and Annie appeared at the top of the steps, and Meg hurried up to meet them, basket in hand.

"I've got Annie set up in one of the unused bedrooms upstairs," Sallie said. "There's a fireplace which should work to heat water. Sophie and I put the hip tub in the room, and we brought up several pitchers full. I already have a pot boiling."

Meg nodded. They'd need the water for both the tea and the steam. The tub would help to catch and hide any initial bleeding, but Annie would have to manage most of that on her own.

"I also kept the sheets from the birth," Annie said. "I . . . I wanted to remember. Even if Mr. Miller did not. I thought those would work well since they're already stained. I can put them on the bed tonight—make sure he has a bit of drink before we go to sleep—and he shouldn't notice them."

"Well, we won't have any shortage of sheets," Meg said, as she opened her basket to reveal her own birthing sheets, packed at Rebekah's suggestion for the same reason, along with several of Rebekah's stained rags, as Annie would likely bleed for a week or two once Meg's work was complete.

Annie wrapped her arms around Meg and nuzzled her face into Meg's neck. "Thank you for doing this."

"Thank you for trusting me." Meg let herself breathe in the scent of her dear friend. The smell of lavender and rose water a reminder of easier times, before husbands and children and the picture of womanhood their mothers had sold them. She only hoped Annie would find the same sort of life Meg was finally starting to grow in her own home.

When she pulled back, she found Sallie ready and waiting. Meg reached for Sallie's hand and gave it a fierce squeeze. "Thank you for sending me to Rebekah."

"I'm glad she was willing to help," Sallie said.

"She seemed relieved to find someone to pass her knowledge on to," Meg said.

"We need more women like her in this town," Sallie said. "I'm not surprised you're becoming one."

"You set me on this path."

But Sallie shook her head. "You've always had a talent for plants. All I did was notice you eyeing that book."

"You got it into my hands," Meg said. "You brought me here, for Annie."

"For all of us," Sallie said, taking Annie's hand, too. "We're in this together."

Meg nodded fiercely. "Then let's get to it."

Sallie led them up the stairs to the room she'd prepared, and Meg set to work. First, she measured out the appropriate amount of herbs into the mug, making sure Annie was watching.

"You'll want to drink a full cup four times a day. It needs to steep for at least twenty minutes, but I would prepare it how you do your daily tea," Meg explained as she spooned the mixture. "That way if anyone notices, they won't think anything of it."

She poured the boiling water over the plants and left them to steep, then turned her attention to the tub. She filled the bottom of the basin with the contents of the jar she'd prepared. Once the herbs were spread evenly across the surface, she went back to the tea, dipped a pinkie finger into the water, and took a taste. It was exactly as Rebekah had told her it would be. With a nod, she turned and held out the mug to Annie.

"Are you sure you want to do this?" Meg asked. "Once we start there's no turning back, and there's always the chance that things could go wrong."

Annie nodded, resolute. She pressed her hands to her stomach and said, "Either I survive these plants, or I don't survive the birth." Then, she reached out and accepted the mug. She sat at the end of the bed, with Meg on one side of her and Sallie on the other as she sipped.

"I'm sorry you can't trust your husband to understand all of this," Meg said. Then to Sallie, "Or yours."

Sallie tilted her head. "I think if I were in Annie's situation, Ned would be amenable to it. But in his eyes, Annie is another man's wife, and he wouldn't like us keeping this from Mr. Williams."

"As if a woman isn't her own by right," Meg murmured.

"What about you?" Annie asked. "Would John understand were you in my place?"

Meg tilted her head as she considered this. "I don't know," she admitted. "But I'd like to think so."

Annie nodded sadly as she finished off her tea. Then, she took a deep breath and lay back against the bed, staring at the ceiling above them. Meg and Sallie fell back to join her.

"Will it work?" Annie asked.

"It has for other women," Meg said.

They lay that way in silence for a few minutes, the sunlight falling across the bed.

"What now?" Annie asked after a while.

Meg stood. "Now we let the herbs begin their work inside you and help them along with a bit of steam."

She offered Annie a hand up. Then, she and Sallie helped Annie out of her day dress. Annie took a deep breath before she stepped out of her drawers, and Meg led her to the tub. The basin sat low to the ground, curving up in the back.

"You won't sit all the way in." Meg placed the commode chair over the tub. "The water has to be hot enough to steam, so you'll just want to hold yourself over it, legs on the outside. It'll help loosen you up and hopefully make the next few days easier."

Annie nodded as she situated herself in the chair, and Meg went to get the pot hanging above the fire. Together, she and Sallie maneuvered it to the tub and poured it over the herbs. As the water hit the plants, the steam rose up, pungent and sweet, with the promise that soon Annie would be free of what was taking hold inside her—what might kill her should she continue to let it grow. Meg and Sallie sat on either side of her. Every few minutes, Meg added more water to the basin to keep the steam fresh.

"You should start to feel like you're opening up," Meg said. "Like before Andy was born, right after your water broke."

Annie nodded as she pressed a towel to her face. She'd begun to sweat from the steam. "There's certainly a shifting."

"Good," Meg said. Rebekah had told her to check in throughout the steaming.

Annie winced and doubled forward. "Oh," she said. "That was . . . that was uncomfortable."

"Cramping?" Meg asked.

Annie nodded.

"That's a good sign," Meg said. Rebekah had said it could happen all at once, or it could take a couple of weeks. No two bodies were the same. She'd suggested the steam—the same one Culpeper had listed in the book, though Rebekah had added a few herbs to the recipe and clarified the necessary amounts—to hurry things along.

"Do you mind if I take a look?" Meg asked.

"Not at all," Annie said.

Meg lifted Annie's chemise. Steam rose up in a cloud around them. Meg waited a few seconds for it to dissipate before she ducked her head. A thin line of blood had started to make its way down Annie's thigh and drip into the basin full of herbs.

"It's working," Meg said, her voice coming out all in one breath as the tightness in her shoulders shifted. She poured one final pitcher of hot water over the herbs. Annie doubled over with another cramp, and Meg gently rested a hand on her shoulder. Annie gripped it with her own.

After a few more minutes, Annie took a deep breath, then stood, wiping the blood from her inner thighs with one of the rags Meg had given her, before folding several of the cloths into a sort of diaper, the way she might were this truly her monthly course.

Meg turned to her basket and pulled out a jar of boiled chickweed and marshmallow, made into a poultice with fenugreek and linseed. "This should help with the chafing."

Annie glanced up from her work, now complete, letting her chemise fall over the rags. "Now this I wish I'd had sooner." She winced, placing a hand over her lower belly. When Meg reached toward her, Annie waved her away with a strained smile before standing upright. Together Meg and Sallie helped her back into her dress.

"The bleeding should continue, as if it's your monthly course, albeit a bit heavier," Meg said as she smoothed Annie's skirt into place. "If it's only sporadic, add another cup of tea. Once it does get heavier and steadier, you can stop drinking the tea."

Meg pulled out another jar from her basket, containing a mixture of echinacea, nettles, and raspberry leaf to strengthen Annie's health. "That's when you'll switch to this."

Annie accepted the jar with a smile, then a wince. She pressed her hand to her stomach once again. Meg's work might be complete—and done in a way that she knew would make Rebekah proud—but Annie's was far from over. Worse, it was work she'd have to undergo alone.

Word about Meg's herbal beauty tonics had started to spread. There was nothing illegal about making teas, but if the wrong person drew the connection between her garden and Annie's bleeding, Meg's newfound profession would be over before it began. Lucky for them both, no one yet knew about the pregnancy. Still, they couldn't be too careful, particularly after they'd already spent two of the last three days together. So Annie would drink her tea as instructed, and in a week, Sallie and Meg would visit her.

"If you could come with me to the Dovecote..." Meg started.

Annie gripped her hand. "We can't live our lives with ifs." She leaned in, pressing her cheek to Meg's shoulder, and they stood like that for a few moments in silence, until Meg took a deep breath and gathered her things.

"I will see you in a week," Meg said.

Annie nodded. "In a week."

A Letter Between Sisters

Meg spent the next few days without word from Sallie or Annie, working out her worry in the garden and the kitchen, harvesting and drying and packing and pouring as she filled their pantry with teas and tinctures and oils. Already she had orders coming in from the friends of the women who'd attended Sallie's gathering. The work served to distract her from her thoughts of Annie, but when she was alone in the quiet, stirring a decoction or nursing the twins, the fear crept in, spreading itself like pollen until Meg was covered with it.

Were this a little over a month ago, Meg would have found herself at Orchard House, her heart laid bare before Marmee, but that was no longer a possibility. What Meg set out to do was an evolution of her mother's own suffrage efforts—after all, a woman's freedom wasn't only in the right to vote but in having autonomy over her own body. As much as Meg hoped Marmee would approve of that, she didn't know what her mother might do if she knew the truth of Meg's work, how she might use it to control Meg, to shape her into the daughter Marmee wanted rather than the woman Meg was becoming.

That left Meg here, at the Dovecote, alone.

"Is it supposed to be boiling that hard?" John asked as Meg sat on a stool next to their stove.

Meg blinked. She hadn't even heard John come into the room.

"What?" she asked.

"Your water." He pointed to the stove, where her light simmer had started to bubble so strongly it threatened to spill out of the pot.

Her heart stuttered. She jumped up and quickly lifted the cast iron from the stove until the water stilled. She peered in at the contents and muttered a curse. She'd have to toss the whole thing. With a heavy sigh, she sat back down, her head between her hands.

John pulled a chair from the table and set it across from her. He gently rested his palm on her shoulder. "It's alright," he said. "It could have been worse."

Meg looked up at him. "You're thinking of the jelly."

He held a hand over his heart, eyes wide. "I'd forgotten all about the jelly."

Meg offered him a wry smile, and they both laughed softly. It had been one of their first—and worst—arguments. Meg, convinced she might become the wife Marmee told her she ought to be, tried making jelly for the first time, without any sort of teacher, and ended up making a mess instead. It had been the first time John had brought a friend home for dinner. Meg had been suggesting he do so for weeks, but she'd forgotten all about it when she got caught up in the kitchen.

It had been an embarrassing disaster for them both.

In the end, they'd both apologized and laughed over the whole affair. It was the first time Meg had realized life with John, while not the happily-ever-after she'd spent her childhood dreaming of, might at least hold some joy.

"It's certainly less of a mess than the jelly." John stood as he looked into the pot of ruined herb matter. "Surely something can be done with it?"

"Once it cools, I'll return it to the earth," Meg said. "At least there it can nourish the plants."

"What was in here?" John asked. "I can help you pick some more."

But Meg shook her head. If she continued as she was, she'd just ruin another. "I'm too distracted for this right now."

John nodded slowly. "You've seemed a bit out of sorts the past few days. Did something happen?"

As much as Meg wished she could unburden her heart to him, she couldn't take that risk. So she shook her head and said, "I'm missing my sisters is all."

John opened his mouth as if to reply, but ultimately closed it. "You know you can talk to me, Meg."

"Of course, I can," she said a little too brightly. "I'm your wife!"

John tilted his head to the side. Meg stood, and his hand fell to his side.

"I'll make dinner," she said.

John looked once more at the pot. "How about I make dinner tonight?"

Meg arched an eyebrow. "Don't trust me at the stove?"

John bit his lip. "I just don't want you to"—he paused, searching for the words—"be disappointed? Besides, you can write to Amy while I fix something for us."

Meg's eyes brightened. Now there was an idea. She couldn't tell Amy everything, should the letter fall into the wrong hands, but she could at least share some of what weighed on her. She reached for John's forearm and gave it a gentle squeeze.

"That would be perfect," she said.

His eyes widened. "I was distracted by the boiling, I almost forgot to give you this!" He withdrew an envelope from his pocket. Across the front, Meg's name and address had been written in Amy's flowing script. Typically, Amy included Meg's letters in with the others sent to Orchard House, but this had been sent to the Dovecote directly, to her.

Meg's brow furrowed. At least now she had something else to distract herself with.

> *Concord, Massachusetts*
> *My dearest Amy,*
>   *I've just read your most recent letter. Hearing of your exploits in Europe, of getting permission to copy in some of the best collections in Europe, is perfectly fitting for you. You are just as diligent in pursuing your art now as you ever were. I'm sorry I didn't see it when we were younger. Back then it was so much easier to view your passions as frivolous, as if it was my responsibility to guide your path as your older sister, rather than trusting your heart to do it for you.*
>   *I know, of course, that as women following our hearts is so rarely possible, but if I can offer you any advice as you travel Europe in the company of Mr. Vaughn and Marmee's expectations, it is that you do, in fact, put your heart first. Both for love and for passion outside of love. As I mentioned in my last letter, I did neither in making my choice to marry Mr. Brooke, instead letting my own stubbornness guide me along the road carefully laid by our mother's expectations. She might have wanted the best for me—to be married to a good man—but I*

wish I had known then what I've come to know now.

Thank you for sending your letter to me directly at the Dovecote. I still have not seen Marmee since last I wrote you, and I've no doubt that she would have read your letter before delivering it to my doorstep herself. It's funny how being away from her, from Orchard House, has lifted a veil from my eyes, helping me to see things as they are rather than as she presents them.

It makes me wonder what she's instilled in you. Your determination to make the match that I didn't and Jo won't. I understand you want to do what's best for all of us, but I hope that you find what's best for you along the way and only wish that I could have given you that advice sooner. That I could have been the older sister you needed rather than the one Marmee molded me into.

No matter what Marmee has made you feel, caring for this family isn't your responsibility, and it is unfair of her to put that weight on your shoulders. Still, you might be tempted to seek riches given how I've mentioned my discontent with John's income. I've started to realize that a wealthy man's finances wouldn't have filled the void in me any more than a good man's striving. It seems only I can make my own happiness.

What I can tell you is that, like I said in

my last letter, I've been discovering things about myself and my marriage to John that hadn't occurred to me before we spoke our vows. That, had I realized them sooner, I might not ever have ended up at the Dovecote at all.

I was not in love with John when we married. Recently, though, I find my heart turning over, and it may very well have been John's heartfelt apology and his subsequent interest in my endeavors in the garden that are softening a part of me toward him that I never expected to open up. It would seem that my ambitions matter to him, and that is making all the difference in the world. I only wish I'd discovered what I wanted from life before I accepted his proposal. Who knows how that might have changed things between us. Perhaps it would have been a marriage borne of love rather than mother's guiding hand.

My advice to you: Trust your heart. Trust your intuition. Trust yourself. I only wish I'd done the same.

While the Dovecote, I'm certain, is not nearly as exciting as Europe, it hasn't been dull! So much has happened in the few weeks since last I wrote—much of which I can't put on paper and will have to divulge when you return home.

My garden has only grown and grown since my last letter, much like the twins. I've found a teacher to help me in ways that Culpeper's book cannot. We're meeting twice a week, and she's showing me what she knows—how to prepare the plants, what herbs cure what ailments. After being a teacher myself for the Kings for so long, it's fun being on the other side of things again, returning to the place of student. What's more, I'm taking what I'm learning and applying it to women's needs. It seems there is at least one thing Marmee instilled in me that I don't regret—helping women.

Sallie held a tea so I could bring my work to some of her friends, and you wouldn't believe how excited they were! It turns out maybe I didn't need a man to meet my needs as I once thought. John, of course, is providing for our family, but the things I want for me . . . I might actually be able to purchase them without lingering guilt. That is, once I have time to shop! The work itself takes up so much of my days, but I find I enjoy it. Between that and raising two children, it's a wonder I even have a chance to sit down and pen this note. Funny enough, John is making dinner tonight so that I can do just that.

The tincture I made for Beth is almost ready. I'm nervous to bring it to her. Not because I'm afraid it won't help; I do think she'll find strength in it, but because I don't know that I'm ready to see Marmee just yet. Jo once confided in me that Marmee has a well of anger in her. I never believed it, thinking Marmee had told her as much simply so Jo wouldn't feel alone. Now, I'm *afraid of what it might mean if it is true. If Marmee were to discover . . . Well, we can discuss that when you return.*

I wish you were here. With the three of us together—me, you, and Beth—I know I'd feel strong enough to stand up to her should the need arise. Sending you all my love.
—Meg

Important Work

Writing to Amy calmed Meg's heart for the night, but she still had half a week before she could check on Annie—and while she was desperate for news, at this point no word was what she wanted. It meant Annie was safe, that the herbs were working as intended. But that morning, with the sun bright and the world turned fully to summer, Meg needed more than no news. She needed to feel useful.

She needed a distraction.

She stood in the kitchen at the Dovecote, holding the tincture she'd created for Beth up to the light. It wouldn't be at its fullest strength, but after a month in the jar it was usable, which meant she had no excuse to further avoid Orchard House. If words on paper to one sister could buy her a good night's sleep, what might a full in-person conversation do? Aside from that, Meg wanted to see Beth. To talk with her after her insights about their mother and her marriage—to recognize how much the things she thought of Beth came from the way Marmee had taught Meg to think of her. She owed her sister that much, even if she wasn't ready to see their mother just yet.

With a grounding breath, Meg strained half of the contents of her linden tincture into a dropper bottle, then sealed the cap once more and set it next to the row of jars she'd prepared with that year's flowers—more than enough to get Beth through to next summer.

She wrapped Daisy in a sling around her front, secured Demi to her back, and started her walk to Orchard House. It was barely midmorning, but already the sun settled into Concord, its heat a tangible thing against the weight of the twins, so much so that Meg's cotton work dress might as well have been wool. She ran the back of her hand over her forehead as she stepped off the road and made her way, instead, through a meadow that was at once a shortcut and a balm to her soul. Here the wildflowers were in full bloom, and Meg found herself stopping every so often to add a few cuttings to her basket—brilliant blue chicory flowers (which Daisy had pointed out with a delighted squeal), soft white yarrow blooms, and bright pink bee balm orbs.

Her path led her through the woods, to the old post box they'd set up as children. She lifted the box, and while it was empty of letters, she found it full of memories. Of her sisters, of Laurie, of a time of freedom that once would have left her feeling lost and lonely in her current life, but now hit her heart with a sweet nostalgia that made her smile rather than cry. She pressed a hand to her heart with wonder at the change the past month had wrought in her, when a familiar voice broke her from her reverie.

"Meg?"

She glanced up to find Beth walking through the trees toward her.

"Beth!" Meg said, a smile splitting her face. "What are you doing out here?"

"I've just come from Mr. Laurence's." Beth's voice came out a touch defensive.

Her sister wore a blue cotton dress, not unlike Meg's own, and her light brown hair hung loose about her shoulders. She looked thinner than she had the last Meg had seen her, and it was clear even the short walk from Mr. Laurence's had put a bit of color in her cheeks. But there was a brightness behind her eyes.

"I'm so glad to hear you're still playing," Meg said. "Was the walk . . ." She paused, then shook her head. "I can't help but ask after your health, but I also know if the walk was too much you wouldn't have undertaken it."

Beth tilted her head, eyes flashing. "Or I *would* have undertaken it and brought a picnic so I could rest along the way." She held up a basket for Meg to see, setting it at her feet and wrapping both Meg and the twins in a hug. "It's been so long since you've been by. Hannah's been making me the tea you brought."

"I'm sorry I didn't get a chance to deliver it myself," Meg said. "Has it been helping?"

"I'm out here, aren't I?" Beth said with a grin.

"Should we get you back home?" Meg asked.

Beth arched an eyebrow. "Based on your avoidance of Orchard House and the state Marmee was in after the last time you visited, I'm not certain that's really where you want to be."

Meg glanced over Beth's shoulder, glimpsing the house through the trees. "Is she home?" Meg asked.

"She is." Beth pulled a quilt from her basket and laid it on the forest floor between them. Then, she went around behind Meg and started to pull Demi from his place before she sat right in the center of the quilt with him in her lap. He reached up, gripping her hair in his hands, and though several strands came free in his fist, Beth only kissed him on the forehead.

She truly *was* a dear, but so much more.

Meg sat across from her and pulled the bottle from her own basket.

"This is for you," she said.

Beth looked it over, her smile slipping. "I've had quite enough of the medicines Marmee insists I take, sometimes they help in the moment, but . . ."

Meg shook her head. "This isn't like those. It's the same as the tea but more concentrated. That way if you don't feel up to drinking so much, you can take a few droppers full instead."

Beth's eyes brightened. "More of the linden?"

Meg nodded. "It's heart strengthening. So, it won't help with the pain the way the medicine does, but it might give you more energy."

"It's wonderful," Beth said.

"Beth," Meg said, "I'm so sorry."

"You didn't cause my illness," Beth said.

That, in itself, was debatable. If Meg had gone to see the Hummels back when Father was sick, she might have recognized the scarlet fever and not have allowed Beth to go at all, never exposing her sister to the thing that sapped her strength and threatened to pull her from their world every passing day. Meg opened her mouth to say as much, when Beth stilled her with a hand.

"We can't change the past."

"I'm sorry for not seeing you," Meg said, tears burning in her eyes. "There's so much life in you—the way you play, the way you move through the world. Marmee was so focused on your weakness, that none of us took the time to consider your strengths. You deserve better."

Beth swallowed, then laughed softly. "I wish Marmee thought as much." Then, she clapped a hand over her mouth.

They stared at each other for a moment, the words hanging between them. "Enough of me! What of you? And John?" Beth asked, a little too brightly.

Meg was tempted to press, to get her sister to spill every dark thought she'd had about their mother, but in satisfying her own discontent over Marmee with her sister's discontent, Meg would be doing exactly what Marmee had done to her. No, if Beth wanted to talk of their mother and their childhood, Meg would be there to listen. But she wouldn't force that upon her sister.

"I dream of being young and in love like you, but with things the way they are . . ." Beth trailed off as she freed the now-loose strands of her hair from Demi's grip and held them in front of her, before letting the wind take them away. "At least allow me to live vicariously."

Meg started to respond, then paused, biting her lip. Beth narrowed her eyes. Meg knew she could weave a pretty story for her sister, but Beth deserved the truth.

"That's why Marmee and I fought," Meg said. "John and I . . ." She tilted her head back, trying to find the right words.

"You don't love him," Beth said slowly.

A small sound escaped Meg's throat, and Beth reached for her hand.

"Not yet," Meg admitted.

"But if you don't love him . . ."

Meg shrugged. "Marmee thought I should be with a good man and not a wealthy man."

"So, you married a good man," Beth said, sadness in her voice.

"Whatever that means."

"It seems Marmee has her own ideas and plans for all of us, whether they're what we want or not," Beth said. "I worry about Amy looking for a match in Europe."

Meg nodded. "At least Jo is happy, finally writing in New York, away from all this."

"But are you happy?" Beth asked.

"I'm getting there," Meg said. "I thought I was supposed to dedicate my life to John, to the twins. To become a little Marmee. Then one day when they're grown, I could go on and do some great work like what Marmee's been doing with suffrage, but I can't wait for that."

"We don't know how much time we have." Beth held up the tincture. "Hannah said the flowers were from your garden?"

Meg nodded. "And there's so much more. I've been reading—"

"Reading?" Beth asked with a grin.

Meg threw a leaf at her sister that didn't make it more than an inch before the wind caught it up and took it away from them. "I may not be some literary genius, but I do care about more than dresses and parties."

Her sister offered her an apologetic, albeit mischievous, smile. "There's more to all of us than what we thought, hm?"

Meg pulled the book from her basket and handed it to Beth. "I'm learning to work with plants. There's a woman, Rebekah Mayer, who is teaching me. It's not writing or painting or composing..."

"But it's healing," Beth said, taking Meg's hand, her grip stronger than Meg expected. "And that's important work."

A Weight Lifted

Meg had prepared the twins an hour ago, and now she paced the length of the foyer waiting for Sallie. As they planned, Sallie was to pick her up to go visit Annie together. Meg hadn't heard from either woman since they last saw each other, and while she took it as a good sign that no one felt the need to send word, the silence had done little to soothe her nerves.

She heard the carriage outside the Dovecote before Sallie ever made it to the door. She wanted to throw it open, to run out and ask Sallie everything, but while Sophie could be trusted, they didn't know about Sallie's driver, Christopher, and they couldn't risk anyone thinking anything was out of the ordinary.

Meg gripped the edges of her simple gray-green day dress while she waited. After a few minutes, the bellpull sounded. She took a deep breath and pulled open the door to find Sophie at the threshold.

"Mrs. Brooke," Sophie said with a nod.

Meg searched her face for any sign of distress. "Annie . . . ?" she whispered.

"From what we've heard, all is well," Sophie said.

Meg felt a weight lift off her chest and leaned against the door frame in relief. She knew her worry wouldn't fully loose its grip until she saw Annie herself, until she pressed a hand to her cheek and tucked her hair behind her ear. But now Meg no longer felt as if she was being crushed.

Sophie reached for Demi while Meg lifted Daisy, and together they made their way to the carriage. Sallie leaned over the edge, waving. As soon as Meg slipped inside, Sallie took her hand and grinned. She leaned in and whispered, "You did it."

When they arrived at Annie's house, it took every bit of Meg's restraint not to push Daisy into Sallie's arms and run up the stairs. As they reached the door, Annie opened it wide. She stood with little Andy resting on her hip, her eyes bright, the worry that had creased the corners no more than a memory. Meg adjusted Daisy to one arm, then wrapped the other around Annie. She pressed her face into Annie's blond hair and took the deepest breath she had in days, Annie's familiar scent of lavender and rose petals washing over her, and under it a hint of mugwort, sharp and heady—an herb she would forever be grateful for.

"Come in, come in," Annie said when they finally broke apart. "There's tea in the sitting room and cakes from that bakery Sallie loves."

Annie handed Andy to one of her servants, Gemma, an older woman with graying hair. Sophie took Meg and Sallie's children, leaving the ladies alone with their tea. As soon as they were gone, Meg took the seat next to Annie. She leaned in close, examining the color in Annie's face—the pallor she'd had only a week ago was now gone. She pressed a hand to Annie's forehead, then her cheek.

"I was so worried," Meg said.

"I wasn't," Annie said. "I knew you'd take care of me."

"You seem . . . lighter," Meg said.

Annie laughed softly. "I suppose I am." She brushed a thumb over Meg's cheekbone. "You've been spending time outside. Though I must admit, you look lovely with freckles."

Meg flushed at the compliment. She'd considered using her own oils to undo the work of the sun, but now she thought she might just leave it.

"Was it terrible?" Meg asked.

"It wasn't easy," Annie admitted. "But it was far better than birthing Andy."

Sallie gripped Meg's forearm. "I'm so sorry we couldn't send word."

Meg shook her head. "Don't be. We did what had to be done to protect all of us. Does anyone suspect?"

Annie glanced toward the door. "After my first day of bleeding Gemma mentioned she'd been worried and was glad to see my course finally came. She was at my side the entire time with Andy. She knew how hard it was on me."

Meg nodded slowly. "And Mr. Miller?"

"I've always had a difficult time with my monthly pains," Annie said. "Mr. Miller is none the wiser. We're in the clear."

"I, for one, think this is a sign we need to start seeing each other more frequently," Sallie said. "Twice a week at least. Then we won't have to worry should we find ourselves in this situation in the future."

"I wouldn't mind that," Annie said with a soft smile over the rim of her teacup.

An Unexpected Visitor & An Unwanted Visit

After the success of her work with Annie, Meg felt not only at ease, but for the first time in a long time, content. Happy, even. She still hadn't divulged the truth of her work in the garden to John—and likely never would—but it didn't matter. She was helping women. She was helping *herself*.

Thanks to her teas and tinctures, she'd finally been able to start purchasing the things she'd gone without, the things she'd once hoped a husband would provide for her. A new silk for Sallie's next tea; two new work dresses for her days in the garden that, while airy and practical, fit just right; a new basket for her herb gathering; a journal in which she was recording her own findings with the plants so that one day she and Amy might just make the compendium they'd written about. She'd even started to set aside funds for Daisy so that when the time came for her daughter to begin making her own way in life, she would have the sort of choices Meg had been shielded from.

Over the next several weeks, Meg spent her Mondays and Fridays with Sallie and Annie; her Tuesdays hiding in the woods with Beth and the twins; and her Wednesdays with Rebekah, learning as much as the woman could teach her before enjoying an afternoon cup of tea with her housemate, Marianne. It was at Rebekah's urging that Meg had begun to prepare tinctures for the fall before the first leaf turned brown so that Meg would have plenty of medicine ready for all of the sniffles and fevers that come with the changing of the seasons. That was how Meg now found herself in the kitchen preparing echinacea on a Thursday. She hadn't gathered quite enough flowers for this particular batch, so she wiped her hands and headed out to the garden to harvest a bit more.

When she opened the door, she found John and Marmee on the steps out front.

Meg stopped in her tracks. Her chest clenched, and she gripped her skirts at the sight of her mother. She knew this day would come—knew she couldn't avoid Marmee forever—but she'd intended to reunite with her mother on her own terms.

"There's my Meg," her mother said, as if the last time they spoke Meg hadn't left mid-conversation and never looked back. "Your father and I were hoping to have you all over for dinner tonight. I thought I'd drop by and extend the invitation myself."

John looked up at Meg with a tight smile and troubled eyes. It seemed she wasn't the only one who'd enjoyed their break from Orchard House.

"How thoughtful of you," Meg said, voice flat.

"John, of course, told me he thought you'd be delighted. Though he seemed to think you weren't home." Marmee narrowed her eyes. John started to speak, but Marmee barreled on. "I'm certain Beth misses you dearly."

Meg quirked an eyebrow but didn't speak.

"And your father has been asking after the twins," Marmee added. "You can't keep them from their grandparents forever."

Meg crossed her arms. She could, in fact, keep her children from Marmee forever, though she hadn't yet decided if that was what she wanted. But as she stood talking to her mother, there was a squeal from inside.

"Mar!" Daisy called, recognizing Marmee's voice.

"Mar!" Demi echoed.

With a heavy sigh, Meg said, "Let me ready the children, and then we'll head that way."

"I'm certain they're just fine as they are," Marmee said, looking up at the sun, which had made its way across the sky. "Why not gather them up now and we can all make the walk to Orchard House together?"

Before Meg could stop her, Marmee was pushing past Meg into the house. Meg turned and stared after her and tried not to scream. John gripped her fingers.

"I was trying to send her away before you came to the door," John murmured.

Meg waved a hand because she simply didn't have the words. She and John may have not talked about Marmee since he wrote Meg that apology almost two months ago, but it seemed they were united in their feelings on the matter.

"I can send her away," John said. "I wasn't sure what you'd want . . ."

Meg shook her head. "It'll be fine. The twins already know she's here, and it will be good for them to see Father and Hannah."

Marmee insisted on carrying "her little Daisy" for the walk to Orchard House, and John took Demi, leaving Meg's hands free. Before they set out, Marmee's eyes swept over the garden Meg had cultivated, which already was reaching around the front of the house. One day, Meg hoped, it would rival what Rebekah Mayer had fostered at the edge of Concord.

"You've been busy," Marmee said. "Now I see why no one has been to tend my roses."

Meg bristled at her choice of words.

"I thought Meg planted those roses," John said. Meg rewarded him with a private smile.

"Well, seeing as she's left them behind in Hannah's care..." Marmee trailed off. "This is not the sort of garden I expected of you."

"I thought I'd foster what was already growing here, rather than trying to force it to become something else by my own hand," Meg said. The cuttings she'd taken from her first garden had already rooted, their flowers beginning to bloom on the other side of the gate. Even beautiful plants had their use, and roses in particular were a perfect addition to Meg's home apothecary. Not that her mother needed to know that.

"Not only is she tending it all, she's making use of it, too," John said, his eyes finding Meg. "Always in the garden or in the kitchen mixing up herbs."

Marmee pressed her lips thin, and part of Meg wished John would keep quiet only because she didn't want her mother sticking her fingers in this new part of Meg's life. But the pride brimming in his voice and the warmth it brought her might be worth just that. Besides, if she was going to find a way to coexist with her mother, Marmee would learn of Meg's garden sooner or later.

After supper, Meg and Beth had gone out to the old garden behind Orchard House. Their mother was right, the roses were overgrown and tangling with everything in sight, as if now that there was no one to tell them who and where to be, they'd finally realized Orchard House couldn't hold them anymore.

"That wasn't terrible," Beth said, with a nod to the house.

Dinner conversation had been, if not pleasant, uneventful. Father did most of the talking, which was just as well.

"I much prefer our forest picnics," Meg said.

Beth laughed. "You and me both."

"Girls!" Marmee called from the back door. She turned her head back inside and shouted, "I've found them."

"So much for hiding out here," Meg murmured.

Beth leaned her head against Meg's shoulder, and Meg

wrapped an arm around her sister's waist. "Just getting some fresh air!" Meg shouted back.

Within a matter of moments, the entire party had filed outside, Demi on Father's shoulders and Daisy clinging to John. Hannah laid out several quilts as the sky turned the wild orange of sunset. Demi let out a loud cry, and Hannah reached for him instantly.

"Someone need a change?" she cooed. But as she laid him on the blanket, her face clouded. She pressed the back of her hand to his forehead. Then, with one hand gently resting on his chest, she said, "John, can I see Daisy?"

Meg watched as Hannah placed the back of her hand first to Daisy's cheeks, then her forehead. At Hannah's furrowed brow, Meg dropped her hold on her sister and started for the children, but Marmee got there first.

"You're checking them for fever," Marmee said.

"Demi was a bit warm—"

Marmee scooped Meg's son into her arms before Meg could reach for him. She touched a hand to his face. "It's definitely a fever."

Meg brought her own hand to his skin. He *was* warm. She took Daisy from John only to find that she, too, had a bit of heat to her. She took a deep breath. In the past, at the first sign of illness in her children, she'd gone running for a doctor. But Meg had the tools to handle this. Rebekah had walked her through most of the common illnesses among children. Meg pressed a hand to Daisy's ear to check for pain, but the girl only smiled up at her. She swiped a finger under her nose and found it slightly damp.

"Trust me," Marmee said. "I've raised enough children. If it's scarlet fever . . ." Her eyes flicked to Beth.

"They aren't coughing," Meg said. "Just a bit of runny nose. Likely it's nothing to worry over, but I should get them home. I have a borage oil that should be ready. I'll get them fixed right up."

Meg hoisted Daisy up higher in one arm, then reached for Demi, but Marmee pulled him back.

"You'll do no such thing," Marmee said.

Meg stopped and stared at her mother. All around her, the others had fallen silent except for Demi's soft cries and the sound of Marmee's hand against his back.

"I'm sorry," Meg said at last. "I must have misheard you. Because I thought you said I won't treat my own children's illness."

"You're not a doctor, Meg," Marmee said. "You think picking wildflowers and tending weeds makes you fit to risk my grandchildren's lives with a hobby you've been playing at for, what, a month? Two?"

Meg pressed her lips together. "It's more than a hobby."

Marmee looked her over. "Yes, that much I can see. I don't think John's salary is quite enough to cover the cost of your new work dress and boots. Nor that basket you so haphazardly filled with wildflowers on your way over."

Meg caught John looking her over, his eyes narrowed.

"You didn't realize they were new, did you?" Marmee asked.

He opened his mouth, but didn't speak, shaking his head instead.

"I thought as much," Marmee said. "What else is Meg keeping from you, from all of us? You're making medicines out of your own garden. I heard you were even selling the sort of herbs a pregnant woman ought to avoid."

Meg's eyes widened a fraction. Beside her, Beth gasped.

Meg intended for word of her work to spread in the right circles, to help the very women who needed that work. Her mother, of course, was in those circles. But to mention it here? This was the sort of conversation that, with anyone else, could result in Meg behind bars, especially if anyone tied it back to what she'd done for Annie. Meg thought she knew her mother, thought a lifetime with Marmee had shown her the woman's character, but at every turn she realized Marmee wasn't who she thought. Her fingers extended into Meg's life like nightshade, beautiful and tempting with their sweetness, but ultimately a poison.

Meg schooled her face neutral. Would her mother, the suffragist, protect her? Would she protect Annie? Even the suggestion of what Meg had done in front of John and Meg's father put both women at risk.

"Many herbs that can help can also harm," Meg said, her voice surprisingly steady. "Of course I warn the women I work with what herbs not to take if they're with child. I would think given your own work, you'd understand the importance of educating women."

"And I think you'd understand the importance of listening to your mother," Marmee said.

Meg scoffed, every conversation she'd had with her mother over the past several years turning over in her mind. Before two months ago, all she'd ever done was listen. It wasn't until she stopped listening that she'd finally been able to hear herself. She wasn't about to go back to that way of living.

She pulled Demi from her mother's arms. When Marmee held on, Meg said, "Let my son go, unless you want to hurt him."

"I would never!" Marmee said, finally relenting.

Meg pulled Demi close, hugging both her children to her chest.

"What's all this about?" John asked.

"This is about my mother trying to decide my life for me," Meg said. "And now that I'm finally doing something for myself, she wants to sabotage it—even risk having me put in jail for it. We're here because of her, and I don't mean that as a compliment."

"Well, I—" Marmee started.

"No," Meg said. "It's time for you to listen, Mother. You've steered every step I've taken since I was a child without any thought of my ambitions or my desire or even the consideration that I might want a life that looks different than yours. When I was a girl, I wanted to be an actress! Or a singer! But you pushed me to care for my sisters, the same way you cared for us as children. You have never forgiven Father for spending his fortune on others. Rather than tell him—rather than hope for a different life for your daughters—you pushed me away from a man that might provide me with the wealth you didn't have. You sought to replicate yourself in me because you couldn't bear the thought that my life might outshine yours."

"Meg—" Marmee tried to interject.

"Little Meg, named after her mother. And look at me! I named my own daughter after both of us." Meg laughed sardonically as angry tears pricked her eyes. "She will not be a little you, and neither will I. Now if you'll excuse me, I'm going to take care of my children."

With that, Meg clutched her children tightly and started through the meadow toward the woods that would eventually lead to the Dovecote.

A New Understanding

As much as Meg wanted to stomp the whole way home, she was painfully aware of her footfalls and the life growing at her feet. Plants like these had given her something she could be proud of, and she didn't intend to punish them for her mother's actions. That, and she was carrying the twins without having strapped them to her chest and back.

But with each step she took, she couldn't believe she was walking alone—just her and the children, no John. While she hadn't fully expected him to take her side, things *had* been changing between them over the past two months. It had seemed like the more Meg found herself, the more they both softened toward each other. Yet he'd chosen her mother over her.

No, Meg hadn't told him how much money she'd been bringing in from her work, but she also hadn't spent any of *his* hard-earned money in nearly two months. Marmee *would* find a way to turn that around on her and stoke the very anger that most often had resulted in their arguments.

She'd been wrong to think things had been changing, to believe for a minute that she could find happiness in anyone other than herself. Of course John hadn't followed after her. He'd never been her choice. Her mother had hand-selected him for her, and to her mother he'd be forever loyal. As Meg reached the back of the Dovecote, she reached for the latch on the gate to let her into the garden. It took several attempts to open with the twins in her arms and angry tears blurring her vision. When she finally unhooked it, there came a rustling from behind her.

Meg turned, expecting to find a fox hiding in the brush. Instead, she caught sight of John running toward her.

"Meg!" he called before he finally reached her.

"Do not, for one second, think I'm going back there to apologize to my mother," Meg said. "I meant every word of it."

John nodded but was still catching his breath.

"I know it might hurt you, but I can't hold it in any longer. I need you to know I never intended for this life. I meant it when I turned you down the first time you asked me to marry you. It was only Marmee's words in my mind that had me talking back to Aunt March, that had me accepting your proposal to spite her. It's been Marmee all along, turning my eyes on you before I was even ready to consider marriage. And to think she could tell me how to care for my own children? As if I am still a child myself?"

She looked at her husband warily. "Don't tell me she sent you after me so you could stop me and call a doctor."

Meg waited for John's response, but he only shook his head and held up the basket she'd left behind at Orchard House. "Tell me what I can do to help."

"I . . ." Meg blinked. "I'll take that. You put the twins down." Then, she handed him the children.

Once John was gone, Meg harvested several fresh borage leaves from the garden, then headed into the kitchen where she began to prepare them into a poultice. As she ground the plants with her mortar and pestle, her anger finally shifted into something less harrowing though no less righteous. Still, she felt a slight sadness at what she'd said to John. The words had been true—and she'd needed to say them—but that didn't mean John was her enemy. He'd been her mother's pawn in all this.

John appeared in the doorway, his hair rumpled, and his hands deep in his pockets.

"The twins?" Meg asked, without taking her attention from the herbs.

"Asleep instantly," John said. He crossed the distance between them, rested his palms on the table, and waited for Meg to pause her work.

"Meg," he said, when she didn't.

With a sigh, she set the pestle down and looked at him. "I'm sorry if what I said hurt you—"

He shook his head. "No," he said. "Do not apologize. You were right, and I'm sorry. For the first time in a long time, I'm seeing things clearly. What you said . . ." He paused, ran his hands through his hair, then laughed with just a touch of bitterness in his voice. "Your mother hasn't only been directing your steps. When your father was sick, and I went to D.C. with her . . ."

"Marmee said you did that for me," Meg said.

"I did it because your family was important to me and to my employer," John said. "But I had no designs on your heart."

"But my glove," Meg said.

John laughed. "Yes, I kept your glove. I *did* have feelings for you—I *do* have feelings for you, still—but I wasn't on a path to marry you, or anyone for that matter. Not for many years. I enjoyed teaching. I liked having my own room and board and not having to worry about putting a roof over anyone's head or being a respectable enough man for marriage. But . . ."

"Marmee," Meg whispered.

"She asked after my plans for the future in just the right way. She told me I couldn't tutor Laurie forever—he'd be off to college soon. Then where would I be? I had intended to find another pupil with Mr. Laurence's recommendation behind me, but the way your mother positioned my life . . . it sounded lonely. And what father would willingly hand her daughter over to a man without a home? Of course, your mother assured me there were some young women out there who didn't care for riches, like her sweet Meg."

Meg scoffed at that. "I've always enjoyed the finer things."

John's lips tilted up.

"She pushed you to me as much as she pushed me to you," Meg said. She pulled out a chair and sat, dropping her head into her hands. She knew Marmee had directed her own steps, but John's, too? A part of Meg knew her mother thought what she'd done was for Meg's good, but it didn't change the fact that Marmee had never stopped to ask Meg what it was she wanted.

John crossed around to the other side of the table and took the seat beside her. He reached toward her hand. "May I?"

She nodded numbly, offering it to him. As he gripped it between his, he said, "I know this isn't the life you wanted."

"But it's the life I have," Meg said.

"It doesn't have to be," John said. "I'll . . . I'll find a way. If you want to leave this place, we'll make it happen, no matter the cost. I know you have your own money now, but you'll have mine, too. Whatever you need. And I'll be here to help with the children, to offer whatever legitimacy you need for your work."

"My work . . ." Meg trailed off.

"Your mother's accusations were thinly veiled at best," John said. "But helping women in that way—even helping yourself should you ever feel the need to—I support it fully. The work you're doing isn't only bringing you life. It's caring for others, and the last thing I want to do is get in the way of that."

But where could Meg go, a young mother with two children? Even between them they didn't have the funds for another home for her to run on her own—if that was what she wanted. Worse, she wasn't the only person who had been led down this path.

"What about you?" she asked. "Would that make you happy, being a bachelor again? Teaching? Being free of me and the children?"

John blinked at her. He shook his head slowly. "It's not my happiness I'm worried about."

But, for the first time in a long time, Meg found *she* was worried about it. Because even if she could have a life of her own, something in her heart would ache for this man who had seen her grow into this new sort of woman, who even now promised to keep her secrets.

"Then it seems, Mr. Brooke, we may be stuck together," Meg said, gripping his hand tighter, with tears in her eyes. "Because I'm not quite ready to let you go."

A small cry escaped his lips, and Meg brought his hand to her mouth. She kissed it gently. Then she leaned her head against his shoulder.

"You really like my work?" she murmured.

"I love it," he said. "I love who you've become in doing it. You are so much more than my bride or the mother of my children, and I'm sorry I ever treated you as only those things. You are a force, Meg March Brooke."

And, Meg realized, she was exactly that. It might take years to undo the damage her mother had wrought on her heart, on her sister's hearts. But now that it was out in the open, she might actually be able to heal, to help them heal, to help John— *her* John—heal.

And, as it turned out, she wouldn't have to do it alone.

PART THREE

~ Beth March ~
A Dear, and Nothing Else

A Little Ghost

Beth smoothed the handwritten letter flat against the music desk of her cabinet piano. She pressed the crease of the page where it was folded and let her eyes skim over the words, reading it the way she read sheet music—chaotically and all at once. Her eyes snagged, like a fishhook, on certain words. The way the ink bled around the word *Paris*, knowing that her sister pressed harder here as if ink alone was all that kept her buoyed in that strange city. There was much about "their dear Laurie" and Beth smiled a small, slightly worried smile. When she was a girl, Beth knew that Amy had feelings for their neighbor and now it looked like that had not changed. Was her sister falling in love even if she did not realize it? The people who do the most talking never seem to be able to pay attention to what happens in the spaces between the words. It is there in the silences that the meaning settles like so much snow. It was in the silences that Beth came to understand the world. She had always lived in the liminal, in-between, spaces. Her sisters had always been so achingly solid. Beth frowned. She also knew her little sister wanted to stand in this world as her own thing, not as a thing that was owned. Could a woman do that in a match? Even if it was with their beloved Laurie? Aunt March certainly hadn't. But Aunt March had money. Something she and her sisters did not.

She thought of Meg's garden work and of Jo's last letter. How Jo said she had been writing of the past; how her sisters were out in the world making something from nothing. Beth lifted her hands, stretched her long fingers out, feeling the pop of her bones shifting into place. She still lovingly touched the black and white keys just as she had the day this surprise instrument entered her life—a gift from the old man who once scared her but was now a dear friend. She laid them on the smooth ivory of the keys and with a breath, she let her eyes return to the start of the letter, and she began to play a song.

It was a lilting song, one that she had started composing years ago and one that she continued now to play and tinker with, thinking in some ways that it might never end. It was a song about wild theatricals and feet pounding upon well-trod staircases. It was a song about winter and Christmas and also about spring and kittens, about parents and sisters. It was a song about marriage and heartbreak, of proposals and promises. It was a song about the way the smell of bread and music can both fill a house. It was a song of writing and stories and candle wax, burnt fingertips, and hands cramped from sewing. Sometimes it was a song about sickness and fear. But mostly it was a song about childhood, something that she couldn't really believe was over.

It was their song. A song about those girls, Beth and her sisters, this family which their father used to call his Little Women.

In her head, that is what she called the piece.

"Little Women," an original composition by Beth March. She smiled to herself knowing how silly it would sound to actually put onto paper this rambling piece that lived inside her. She had never composed anything. She wasn't like her Shakespearean sister, crafting something from nothing, nor like Amy, painting to life the Europe of her dreams. She wasn't even like Meg, working her garden into something that could heal a person. Beth had this small passion. But sometimes, late at night when she added a new section or tweaked a chord, she told herself she would write it down and the next time she and her sisters, Meg and Amy and Jo, were finally all home and together again she would play it for them and see if they heard it too.

If this little song by their own Beth March was indeed the song of their girlhood.

She hadn't played it for anyone. Not even kind Mr. Laurence. Though she still visited him regularly. When she first started playing the cabinet piano over at his house, which always sounded so much better than her own, he used to linger at the staircase or in the doorway as if she were a ghost that would disappear upon being seen. After he gifted the piano to her, there was little reason for her to bundle up in her shawl and walk the quick easy path from her house to his. But she still did. By then, Mr. Laurence had become her friend. And, Beth realized sadly, one of the only ones left.

Meg was off and married to John now. Of course, Beth still saw her; but the thought of it sent a cold chill down Beth's back. She couldn't imagine lying so close to a man. The rough scratch of his beard, the width of his back. Beth preferred the openness of her bed, the way she could fill it herself. She wondered at times what it would be like to be held, as she had been held when she was younger, but that didn't matter now. Meg was married. She was Mrs. Brooke. A name like a neighbor that Beth waved to briefly from the front window. Beth remembered Jo's fear about Meg marrying, about how it would divide the family. But Jo also left. As did Amy. It seemed like everyone was prone to leaving. Except Beth. There was nowhere for her to go.

Amy was so far away that sometimes thinking about it made

Beth a little sick to her stomach. How vast and huge the oceans seemed. When she went there with her sisters it was fun to play on the shore but to think of Amy, having boarded that boat and sailed all those many miles over endless ocean, filled Beth with dread. What had she dreamt about those nights when there was nothing but water and more water—as far as you can see and as vast as you can imagine—until it met the sky? What was Europe like? For Beth, even Concord sometimes seemed too big. It was as if Amy turned into one of the characters from the stories that Jo wrote; a pirate or a vagabond, a cunning countess striking out on her own to find her fortune.

And lastly, there was Jo off to the wilds of New York City. Beth missed Jo most of all. She loved all her sisters, but with Jo gone it felt as if a part of Beth had vanished too. That wild girl had packed a suitcase, and inside it was a piece of Beth's heart which now lived in that strange city with her. Getting letters was nice but nothing compared to their late-night talks, when Jo would tell her whatever incredible story she was thinking about writing next. Something about ship captains and ladies in danger. They were fun and they made Beth laugh, reminding her of when they were little. Sometimes, Beth wondered if her sisters thought about the past as much as she did. Did they miss it? Would a story about their girlhood ever be a tale that Jo would tell? It wouldn't be dashing and exciting but Beth thought that in Jo's capable hands it would be good. It would be the story of four girls and what it means to grow up with all the joy and sadness that girlhood offers. It would be about home and sisterhood.

To Beth, it would be the whole world.

While music was what Beth cared about more than anything else, to her, music was fiercely personal. She never wished to play for anyone else. Just her sisters and her parents. Just something to fill the space. Something to carry them. She shook her head and lifted her fingers off the keys. When the music stopped the house rang empty without it. She rose from the bench and lovingly brushed the keys again before heading toward the kitchen.

She poked her head in. The kitchen was warm, the cooking stove already stuffed with wood, the light of it dancing across the walls. In the corner stood the sturdy table ready for bread making. "Hannah, I'm going next door to see Mr. Laurence."

The sweet older woman looked up at her; a slight dusting of flour always seemed to find its way to Hannah's hair or cheek or clothes. Beth felt as though Hannah never changed. She had seemed to be an old woman when they were children, and she was still an old woman now that they were grown. But time had always felt a little strange to Beth. It was as if her family still saw her as that little girl, but to herself, she was already so grown, so much older even, heavy with the burden of illness. "Of course, my love. Your mother is expecting guests later."

Beth's stomach tightened. Guests were the hardest part of her parents' activism. Beth had gotten used to the crowds at her father's sermons. She could disappear in them and listen to the townspeople chatter like songbirds. But whenever guests were brought into Orchard House, it was like a hand reached up and clamped over her heart. She knew they were doing good important work, but meeting people and making small talk was more than Beth could manage. When her sisters were home it was easier for her to disappear. Amy and Jo would fight for any guest's attentions. But when she was alone . . . "I will take supper in my room."

"Your mother won't have it, dearie. You're the only little flower she's got left to show off."

"I make for a poor flower. Trod upon and half wilting. No one would be interested."

"Nonsense. It will be a fine supper. And maybe you'll play us a bit of music," Hannah paused before adding, "if it's not too much."

Beth smiled. This was Hannah's way of asking her how she was feeling. Hannah, unlike Mother and Father, didn't ask in that blunt way they had. Beth would see the worry creasing their brows, the shared exchanged glances between them, before one of them would press a hand to her cheek, call her their pet and ask if she needed to lie down. Beth didn't like to fib, but more than that she didn't like to be watched this way, hovered over, handled like a broken thing. So even when she wasn't well, she would smile and offer up a contented, "Fine."

But with Hannah it was different. She was softer about it. Sneakier even. If she wanted to know if Beth was feeling well she would ask her to play something, if it wasn't too much. And even when her bones felt as if they had been lit up on fire and all she wanted to do was crawl onto the sofa with a kitten or two, Beth did her best to oblige. Sometimes she worried more about other people worrying about her than anything else. Even more than she worried about herself.

"I think I can manage," she said.

"That's a good girl," Hannah said, returning to slapping the dough before her. Beth smiled. Hannah was still here. Hannah and Mother and Father and kind Mr. Laurence. That was still a family, even if it wasn't her sisters. She lifted her shawl off the hook near the door and folded Amy's letter up and slipped it into her pocket. Her boots had been left near the fire so they were dry and warm after the last snowfall. She slipped them on and opened the door to Orchard House.

Beth stepped outside, feeling, for the first time in a while that she wasn't just a ghost haunting her own memories, but in fact a real live person. A woman with bones and muscles and a heart that still thrummed inside her. Damaged though it may be, it still beat. She smiled up at the sky, breathed the cold air into her lungs and delighted at the crunch of snow under her feet as she made her way to Mr. Laurence's house. She passed the small post office box that Laurie had wedged into the split of a tree trunk between their houses. Even though she knew it was empty she always lifted the lid, just in case, and was always a touch sad when there was nothing. If there had been something, an apple or a small seashell, Beth would have felt transported back in time, back to when things were so much easier. So much happier.

This is because you are the only one left, she thought to herself as she walked. *Nothing but a little ghost haunting an empty house.*

Though she tried not to think about it too much, it was hard, especially on days like this when the sun shone bright and the birds sang just so. It was hard not to see how much had changed for the worse. The stomachaches had increased, so now she ate even less than she used to. She tried at the table, if for nothing else than to not have to see that sad, worried look in Father and Mother's eyes. But she felt herself getting thinner, the way her energy was leeching away almost daily. Then there was the sickness, the vomiting. When she brushed her long hair so much of it came out that she kept it tied back now for fear of anyone noticing. She'd taken to wearing bonnets, something she'd loathed as a child. All of it made her irritable, and that irritation banged up against her calmer disposition. It made her snap at people she loved. She tried so hard to be good and then this weakness overtook her and the words that came out didn't feel as if they could have been formed by her lips. If there was one thing she hated the most about what her sickness had done to her it was that. She could accept turning into a ghost. She couldn't accept turning into a mean, bitter thing.

When she arrived at Mr. Laurence's she didn't bother knocking. There was, at this point, no need. She carried her music with her and creaked the old door open.

"Mr. Laurence?" she called, her voice echoing through the empty rooms. With Laurie gone the already empty house felt even emptier. Jo had made no mention of what happened be-

192 Linda Epstein, Ally Malinenko, and Liz Parker

tween her and Laurie in her letters, so the family was all rather confused. Their wild girl just left. And then, just like that, Laurie was gone too. Jo once told Beth that she and Teddy—her pet name for Laurie—were the two halves of Jo's heart. Poor Jo. Always running away for the sake—and probably also the sheer pleasure—of running.

"Mr. Laurence?" Beth called again, passing through the parlor and into the drawing room. The concert piano was there and Beth gave it a polite nod, like greeting an old friend, and settled on the bench. Before Mr. Laurence had given her the cabinet piano, she had avoided the concert one. When she was little it felt too big, too male, too much. But she wasn't a little girl anymore, regardless of what Meg and Mother or Father might think. She was grown, she could feel it in the very finger-bones she set against the cool ivory, inhaled, and played. The notes painted the room, filling in the space, moving from room to room, the same way it filled Beth. As she played, she thought about that time, which seemed both forever ago and still not too long, when this house and the men inside it frightened her. How strange that seemed now. Little Beth once afraid of her own shadow.

But then everything had changed. That winter got colder than ever, Father was serving as a Union chaplain and he had gotten sick, and Mother had left to care for him. And Beth alone tried to continue the good work they had started. She asked her sisters to come with her to visit the poor Hummel family, but they had said they were busy with work and school. Beth had been busy, too, but in a way that didn't seem to matter as much to them. Meg was a governess, Jo was Aunt March's companion, and Amy was in school. What was Beth doing other than helping Hannah run the household? If she was the stand-in mother, then shouldn't she do what her mother did? That was certainly how her sisters saw it. So she did. Or at least she did her best.

And then everything tipped.

When she closed her eyes, she could still see the form of the dead baby in her arms. She could still hear Mrs. Hummel, desperate, her hands clenched tight, speaking words she couldn't understand in a language that was composed of raw grief. She had stood in the doorway of their tiny home, the windows uncovered, the wind and snow getting in. The other children already looked pink and feverish, probably sick themselves, shivering from both the breeze and fear, because the baby had gone terribly quiet. So painfully silent, like no baby should ever be. And then because she could not help herself, she had looked down at the infant in her arms. How stiff and cold it had been. All she had wanted was to feel it breathe, pull and push warm soft air. The way its lips seemed so frozen. The eyes that stared up at her, seeing nothing. Not Beth nor the trees nor sky behind her. The way the snow fell, landing on those eyes, dusting eyelashes that did not and could not blink. Beth had held that dead child in her arms, feeling herself shake against it, until she was sure she would come apart and float away into the stars. In many ways it felt as if she had never put that child down. That she carried that still baby even now, like a ghost in her arms. And then, somehow the fever that lingered in that empty baby found its way to Beth, nestled inside her and took hold. Beth knew that was the moment when her life changed direction. When, like a carriage without a horse, it rolled off on its own. She thought of it as a cleaving. A separation. There was the life that was supposed to be and the life that now is.

A sick life.

A shortened life.

She stopped playing the piano, her hands resting on the keys, the ache in her chest sharper than the notes.

"Hello Beth," Mr. Laurence said. She turned and he stood behind her, a little more slumped than usual. A little more tired. Beth smiled, knowing in many ways she felt the same. Weakness comes to you like that. It comes in waves.

It comes like the tide.

"I wasn't sure you were home."

"I haven't anywhere to go these days."

"You must miss him terribly." She hated thinking about poor Mr. Laurence, alone now in this big empty house. It was the reason she still came over to check on him. To make sure he knew someone was thinking about him. She doubted Laurie did a very good job of writing home. He didn't seem the sort. He probably didn't realize there were other broken hearts out there.

"Yes. I didn't think that I would miss him as much as I do. He was a rather stubborn young man and certainly not fit for business, but he did leave a mark, in this house and on this old man. A house that was once empty became full, only to empty again, and it is impossible not to notice. And I worry."

"That he'll get hurt?" Beth asked, tapping a single note on the piano, listening to the way it rang through the big empty house.

"No, I worry he'll get distracted over there."

Beth cringed. "Do you know anything about what happened between him and Jo? Mother and Father told me they couldn't get a word out of Jo before she left. And she's mentioned nothing in her letters. I am too shy to ask."

"He was rather tight-lipped with me too. But he is upset and it seems as if he and Jo are speaking very rarely. I do hope that lovely friendship was not harmed. Teddy would hate that."

Beth noticed that Mr. Laurence only called him Teddy when he was out of earshot. Otherwise it was always Theodore.

"Whatever it was will heal eventually. You'll see."

"I don't doubt it. Things always do. What he needed to do was shift his concentration. Hence, the traveling. I hope he is well out there."

"He is with Amy. She will take good care of him."

"She always has, hasn't she?" Mr. Laurence said with a smile. "Do you think he shall become a great composer?"

Mr. Laurence smiled. "I fear Teddy does not have the discipline for composition. He is too easily distracted. He's never been good at sitting still."

"Like our Amy."

"Not more like Jo?" Mr. Laurence asked.

Beth gave it some thought before saying, "No, to be honest I think Laurie and Jo are alike, but in all the ways that don't work."

"Indeed," Mr. Laurence said, taking a seat nearby. Even sitting, the man seemed older, his hair a full shock of white now—no longer the gray he had in her childhood. But he had the same kind smile he always did, the same eyes that disappeared in wrinkles and the creases of soft skin.

"How are you, my child?" he asked. There was something about the way he said it, that Beth did not mind. She bristled when the others talked about her as if were still too young to understand it. But with Mr. Laurence, with his kind grandfatherly face, she did not mind. But there was also the way his eyes searched her face. Beth knew he saw it. The way she looked haunted—lighter, as if she was disappearing. The way the hollow of her bones seemed to glow beneath her skin. Even though the question was meant with love, in many ways Beth was tired of answering it. Mostly because, depending on the minute of the day, the answer could shift and change. And also because the answer was rarely, if ever, good.

But that was something Beth couldn't, or more often wouldn't, talk about. What was the point? All it did was upset everyone. She knew though, deep down inside, she wasn't going to get better. Sometimes she would say the word, to herself, late at night. Test it out on her tongue. Speak it aloud, though quietly, and see if the walls shook.

Two syllables. Dying.

Such a small word for such a huge undertaking.

But Beth couldn't talk about these things with anyone. Instead she had to be strong and fight back against her illness as if it was some enemy. But it didn't feel like an enemy. It felt like a companion. More than anything though, Beth wanted her parents and Hannah and her sisters to realize that this thing she walked with, they walked with too. Death comes for everyone. She was not unique, not even in dying.

But these were all thoughts that bounced around her head and certainly not words she could say aloud. So instead, she smiled.

Instead, she told them what they wanted to hear.

"I'm doing well. Thank you, sir," Beth said, the smile, still slightly forced upon her face. And then, because sometimes she felt like if there was anyone she could confide in it would be him, she said, "Though to be honest I still dream about the baby."

"The baby?"

"The baby with the fever. The one that . . . died."

Mr. Laurence nodded. "Death is haunting. When I lost my granddaughter I saw her everywhere. I still do. I see her in you. Grief is both a wide black storm that fills your sky and also a smoky invisible thing that seeps inside you. When it grabs hold, there is little to do but try to ride it out. You were so young when death first came to you."

Beth was startled by his frank speaking. "Do you mean . . . the fever?"

This was the closest she'd come to talking with anyone about everything that happened.

"Yes the fever, but also your solitary trips to help the German family."

"The Hummels."

"Yes, of course. It was very good and brave of you to go there."

"It didn't help. It didn't . . ." Beth paused as the image of the baby's face floated before her eyes. "It didn't save her. It didn't keep that baby alive."

"No, sadly, goodwill and wishing isn't always enough. But you helped. You still helped. You were there when they had no one else. Those kindnesses are not forgotten."

Beth gathered up her courage like so much cloth between her hands. She took a breath and then another and said, "I think I see her sometimes . . . amongst my dolls. Just sitting there like another doll, but then when I look back, she's gone."

They sat in silence for a few minutes before regret and fear clawed its way up her throat. "Is that a terrible thing to say? Am I a dreadful person?"

"No, my dear. As I said, you were very young when death showed itself to you. I can't imagine it not having altered you. Those were hard times. The war made monsters of us all in a way. Maybe we all could have done more. Maybe I could have." Mr. Laurence looked out the front window, with such a sadness in his eyes that Beth was sorry she brought any of it up. So she did what she always did when words failed her.

She played.

Her fingers danced over the keys, and when she was finished, she felt as if something good and cool, some kind of soft breeze, had blown through the Laurence house and swept all the ghosts back into their corners.

Grief cannot be destroyed, she knew that. It lived and breathed next to her at all times. But it could be tempered. It could, at times, be tamed. Art, and music especially, helped soothe it. She wasn't sure why this was but wondered if maybe art allowed us to tell a different kind of story, one in which we have just a little more control over the harshest winds. Maybe it lets us turn down the storm for a moment. Is that what Jo did with stories, Amy with paintings? Is that what Beth did with music?

"I should be going back. Hannah has informed me that we'll have guests for supper this evening."

"Well, that's quite disagreeable," Mr. Laurence said with a smile.

"Only to me it seems. I never know what to say."

"Being silent is not a sign of weakness or ignorance. In fact, being more keen to listen than to talk is a gift, my Beth. And not the kind of thing you should worry about."

He kissed her softly on her forehead. "Come again soon. My door is always open, and my heart feels lighter when you play for me."

"I will, sir."

"Someday I'm going to convince you to call me Grandfather."

Beth smiled, adjusted the hood on her shawl as she noticed the January afternoon brought snow, and headed out the door. She took her time getting home, meandering along the path, trying to catch snowflakes on her tongue. She wondered if it was snowing in New York City. Or in Paris. What about Meg? Was she outside catching snowflakes on her tongue? Did her sisters wonder about her as much as she wondered about them? Was it because she was the one that was still home, haunting these bedrooms and woods? Was it because it felt like yesterday that childhood had still been in full bloom and they were racing down a road that would never end?

Guests Have Arrived

"Hannah, I'm home," Beth called, knocking the snow off her boots. She rubbed her hands near the fire that crackled in the fireplace, warming them. Because she had taken her time, her fingers felt it. She was always careful to keep them warm. She had pain in so many other bones, across her legs, threading up her spine, but she didn't want it to reach her fingers. If she lost the ability to play the piano she wasn't sure what she would do. Then, life would just be an endless stream of household chores until death—the shadow that lingered in every corner of this once cheerful home—finally claimed her. Beth shivered though the fire was warm.

"Hello, my love."

She turned to see Marmee standing at the table, preparing the linens and plates. Beth watched her now, the way her hair had turned just a touch gray at the temples. It was the same with her father. How had time managed to slip by so quickly? Sometimes Beth felt as if she was standing in place while time and everyone around her sped up. Growing into a future she knew she would not have.

She hugged her mother and then gathered the plates to help. "Did Hannah tell you we're having guests?"

"Yes," Beth said, biting her lip.

"And you feel as though you could join us? That you might be up to it?"

Beth nodded, but didn't look at her mother.

"Darling," Mother said. She opened her mouth as if to say something else but instead she forced a tight smile and returned the nod. Beth wasn't sure but for a second, she thought her mother might cry. Sadness welled inside her, but along with it was something else. A small bubbling stream of anger. This was the look she could not stand. The look of pity. The look that said she was broken.

"Who are our guests?" Beth asked, swinging into the kitchen, picking up the bread, and depositing it on the table.

"Friends of your father's. Mr. and Mrs. Ronson and their daughter. Mr. Ronson just graduated from Harvard Law School and Mrs. Ronson is an activist. They are visiting Concord to work with our local suffrage group."

"Oh, Marmee," Beth said, a terror inside her. "College educated? I won't have anything to say. I'll be just a mute little doll. Just a dumb little thing. I might as well not even be here. Maybe I should take my dinner in my room."

"I know you're afraid, little one, but we have to learn to conquer our fears. Besides, the Ronsons are bringing their daughter, Florida. You are the same age. I think Florida will feel much better here in a strange town at a strange table if she had someone to talk to. You can do that, right? For me? You can make her feel welcome in our home?"

Beth nodded, trying but mostly failing to swallow her fear. She twisted her hands behind her back, a habit since childhood.

"That's my good girl," Mother said, kissing her head. "My sweet little cricket."

Within the hour there was a hearty, if not friendly, knock on the door. Father opened the door wide and with a flurry of skirts and coats and hats and chattering, the Ronson family found their way into Orchard House. There were only three of them, but to Beth it felt as if her home was full again. Full of chatter and the shuffling of shoes, bouts of laughter and general sweet chaos. It reminded her how quiet things had been without her sisters and she felt an ache knotting in her chest, like a second heart.

"Welcome!" Mr. March said, shaking hands and collecting coats. There was a blast of conversation, everyone talking over each other, snow knocked from boots, hands grasped, that it took a moment for Florida to even get to Beth. They were the same height, though still so different. Florida wore a smart dress that both Meg and Amy would have envied. Her hair was plaited in cunning braids. She was a beautiful Black girl, cut so closely from the cloth of her equally beautiful mother. But it was more than just being pretty. Yes, she was a girl that Laurie would have shamelessly flirted with, but at the same instance she seemed much more than just a girl. She seemed to glow. As if she was full of words that she was dying to share. It wasn't the firelight or the chill of a cold November night, it was something inside her that lit her up from inside. Her eyes were bright, her smile easy. Beth found her absolutely radiant.

When Beth realized what it was, a sad, awkward smile found her. It wasn't just that Florida was beautiful; she was healthy. She glowed the way she imagined her sisters did. With youth and vitality and the careless, cruel way people free from sickness take for granted. Beth wondered if she ever looked this way. If, before everything happened, before she became washed out and wan, there had been no difference between the way Florida or her sisters and herself looked. And in this brief moment she wondered if she could ever look or feel this way again. Was she doomed to feeling dim? The light inside Beth felt so small, like someone turned down the flame to barely a flicker. She wished she could disappear.

But then Florida was there, her hand thrust out in formal greeting. Beth could remember Meg scolding Jo, saying that no one shook hands anymore, but she happily took this girl's hand in her own. Though it was cold out, Florida's hand was warm, and she squeezed Beth's with a hearty kindness which felt different. She didn't touch Beth as if she were made of glass and might shatter the way everyone, even kind Mr. Laurence, did. And that was because Florida didn't know. To her, Beth was no different than anyone else. When the fever had touched her all those years ago, it left a mark, like a burn scar, that everyone in Beth's life could see. But Florida only saw another young woman before her, hand outstretched for the taking. And in that grasp, Beth was thankful to have this part of her remain invisible.

"I'm Florida Ronson. Nice to meet you," she said, her voice lilting with a slight accent Beth couldn't place. It was musical. She immediately wondered if the girl could sing.

"I'm Beth March. It's lovely to meet you, Ms. Ronson."

"Just Florida. My mother is Ms. Ronson."

"Now," Mr. March said. "This is my wife, Margaret. Margaret, this is Mr. George Ronson and his wife, Josephine Ronson."

"Call me Jo," Mrs. Ronson said, reaching out a hand and shaking Mother's.

Another Jo. Beth couldn't help but smile.

"So nice to meet you, Jo. And you must know we have a Jo of our own," Mother said, ushering the family into the dining room.

"Oh, how lovely," Mrs. Ronson said. "Will we be meeting her tonight?"

"I'm afraid not. She's working in New York City."

"I want to go to New York City!" Florida said. "Mother, you were there, weren't you? Last summer? You said we could go."

"And *this* is our daughter, Florida," Mr. Ronson said. "She wants to go everywhere."

"Not everywhere, Father. But New York City for sure. And out West. And maybe South America. And definitely to Canada. How long has Jo been in New York?" Florida then gasped with an excitement that reminded Beth of Amy. "Is she attending *school*?"

"No. She's working as a governess," Mother said.

"She's a writer. She's the greatest writer who ever lived," Beth added, her voice louder than she meant it to be. "And she's a great teacher. Jo can do anything she tries to do. Anything at all."

"And this," Mother said, "is my Beth. The only one of my flowers still at home."

"Lovely to meet you, Beth," Mrs. Ronson said.

"Come sit. Welcome to Concord," Mother said, ushering everyone to the table. Beth noticed that Mr. Ronson took Amy's seat, Mrs. Ronson took Meg's, and Florida took Jo's. Right next to Beth. "How were your travels?"

"The train from Cambridge was lovely," Mrs. Ronson said.

"They have a little truck that they wheeled down the aisle to bring you sweets," Florida added. Beth watched her, the way she spoke so freely. It must feel nice, she imagined. To not have everything you think somehow get stuck inside you until it's just a big knot of words and sentences that you'll never untangle. Words that filled your mouth until breathing, let alone talking, felt too hard.

Hannah served the roast, which smelled lovely, and Beth listened as her father and Mr. Ronson discussed his time at Harvard and the abolitionist movement. A lot of it was more than Beth understood but after dinner when the two gentlemen retired to the parlor, Florida and Beth stayed behind to help their mothers clean up.

"I think starting a chapter of the WSA in Concord is a smart move, Margaret," Mrs. Ronson said. Beth followed them, bringing in dishes and plates.

"I agree, but there are still so many people here who resist forward thinking. They don't want progress."

"That is because they are too comfortable in their lives. They don't see, or maybe they don't care, about how other people live. Especially how *my* people are living. It is intrinsically linked to the suffrage work that I have been doing. We need to join forces and come together because our fight is one. Our women's movement is led and directed by women for the good of women and men, for the benefit of all of humanity," Mrs. Ronson said.

"I couldn't agree more. If we can call together a meeting, I'm sure we can gain some support. But you must know this isn't Boston. There are many here who will not have the same viewpoint. Many that will be hard to engage."

"Your mother speaks so passionately," Beth whispered to Florida.

"Yes, she does. Sometimes too passionately. She often gets carried away about the rights of women and freemen and suddenly the dinner is burned, or we are late for some meeting or another."

Beth glanced at Florida's warm smile and then back at Mrs. Ronson. She had long seen her own mother argue passionately about justice, as her father did from the pulpit. The words they shared with their own daughters made their way into his speeches, but that was different from the way Mrs. Ronson spoke. For her, this fight wasn't about justice, it was about her life. It was about the lives of people she loved. Beth looked at Florida, realizing it was about Florida's life too.

Mrs. Ronson smiled. It was a sad smile, stitched from the exhaustion of repetition. "Ms. March, my journey has been nothing but an uphill battle of convincing freemen that women are their allies and convincing white women that suffrage is their cause too. I'm well aware of what we are up against."

Mother smiled. "I meant no offense. You are absolutely right. We can arrange for the meeting to be here while you are still in town. Now, shall we have some tea and music? Hannah, can you put the kettle on? Beth, would you mind?"

"Oh, you are musical?" Florida asked, practically vibrating. "How exciting!"

"Oh . . ." Beth hesitated. "Just a little."

"Nonsense," her mother said. "Our Beth is a wonderful piano player and without a doubt has the finest voice amongst her sisters."

"Marmee!" Beth gasped as the heat colored her cheeks. "I'm quite sure Amy is a better singer."

"I'm quite sure she's not," said Mr. March, passing through the kitchen. "She may be a better painter than the rest of you, but you, my angel, have the voice of one."

"Father, stop it."

"I for one would be delighted to hear some music, if Beth does not mind," Mrs. Ronson added.

"If it would please," Beth said softly. Suddenly Florida hooked her arm through Beth's and gave it a squeeze. It was such an intimate movement, as if they had known each other for ages instead of having only shared a single meal and a handful of exchanges, but Beth didn't shy away. It felt nice to be touched playfully and not with the worry that her parents' caresses now held. It felt light and casual and exactly what she needed.

Everyone collected their seats and Beth moved to the piano and pulled out the bench. She took a deep breath and considered which piece to play and then decided on Mozart. Her fingers lightly grazed the smooth ivory keys before her hands became their own entity and Beth felt as if she were far from her body, far from this living room, now floating in a world that was made only of music and color and light. Each note brought a different color. Pink A's and warm green B's. A yellow C-flat and a bright red D. Each note coloring her vision, her eyes closed, lost to the music. It had always been her release and her passion, but since the Illness, as she thought of that dark feverish time, it had also become her escape. Here, in the music, Beth was no longer a sick thing, she was hardly even a thing. She was nothing but light and laughter and passionate beauty. Music had always saved her, but now, it also transported her.

When she did come back to herself, fleshing out the final notes and resting her hands in her lap, she was afraid to open her eyes. The room was silent. An old fear gripped her: What if she had played terribly? What if the fever all those years ago had ruined her brain and made her hear something that was not there? Would her parents tell her the truth? Or would they just grimace through a terrifying performance, their once musical Beth now just pounding the keys like a wild woman no longer hearing what she used to be able to do?

Beth was afraid to open her eyes. She exhaled. She was sure her nightmare had come true. She should run. She should get upstairs and close the bedroom door and never show her face again.

But when she opened them, everyone in the room was full of smiles. Big smiles. Wide-open ones where you forget that your teeth were showing.

"Beth," Florida said, her voice breathy as if she had run a long distance. "That was . . ."

Beth knitted her hands together in her lap and dropped her gaze. Were they just being nice?

"That was incredible," Florida finished before hopping to her feet and giving a rowdy applause. The others joined her, first Mr. Ronson, then Mrs. Ronson, then Mother and Father. All of them stood and clapped and Beth felt her cheeks go pink. She thought she saw Mother wipe away a tear but she couldn't be sure. If she did Beth prayed it was only because she was moved by the genius of Wolfgang Mozart and not for any other reason. She both wanted to run away from this much attention and savor it. A tiny part of her, the part she considered to be the most like her sisters, loved it. She had talent. Her fears were untrue. The rest of her wanted to hide under her piano until their eyes fell on something else.

Something better.

"Please don't," she said, softly. "All the applause goes to the genius of Mr. Mozart."

"Untrue," Florida said as the clapping died down. "I am quite sure you can teach those notes to anyone, and they would not sound as they did coming from you. Your . . . *passion.* It was visceral. Like something you could taste."

Beth stared hard at the floorboards, unable to look at Florida speaking this way of her playing. She was blushing so much she thought she might faint as her heart did a little flutter in the hollow of her throat.

"I know for a fact that I could never do what you did," Florida said.

"Darling, you could if you tried," Mr. Ronson countered.

"That's true. It's really about practicing. It's just a matter of learning," Beth said. "My playing piano isn't like my sister Amy's painting or Jo's writing. It doesn't come from an innate talent."

"Oh, Beth," Florida said, her eyes shining. "I promise you, it does. It absolutely does."

"Your Beth should give lessons," Mrs. Ronson said.

Both Mother and Father exchanged a look. It was brief and fleeting and by no means would their guests have noticed, but Beth did. It was a look of worry. It was a cringe. It was fear. And Beth knew why. They didn't think she could do something like that. They worried it would tire her out. Make her weak. No. Make her weaker. Beth felt it down to her bones. And they were right. She knew that. To be honest, most days Beth had to rest, if not in her bed then on the couch, or if the weather was warm, on the comfy seat outside where the kittens played amongst the woodpile. It was a look that said she couldn't do it. Not that she wouldn't, because she was shy, but that she couldn't. That she was too sick. Too frail.

Too little.

Like a feather, caught up in a breeze that was floating away. Something that couldn't decide where it could go but only be swept along, endlessly.

No, Beth thought. *Like the tide. Like the tide that goes out. When it turns*, Beth thought, *it goes slowly but it can't be stopped.*

She felt something shift inside her. It was an angry feeling, buzzing like a hornet. She may be sick, but what if that wasn't the thing that defined her? What if she got to live just like everyone else? What if she was allowed to try things and fail or succeed on her own without this extra layer of protection that her parents wrapped her in?

"You really should do lessons, Beth. I'm sure you would be a most excellent teacher and what a cunning and smart way to utilize your talent," Florida pressed.

"I doubt very much that our Beth wants to teach," Father said, frowning. "It's not in her nature. She is a quiet girl and not prone to giving instructions or criticism. She is our House Angel. Every home needs one and she is ours. That is her purpose."

Mother smiled at her now so sweetly that Beth felt something hitch and ride up her throat. Her vision swam, narrowing and flexing back in waves. How strange it was to stand in a room and be talked about as if you weren't here. As if you were invisible.

"I think that is for Beth to decide," Florida said flatly. "Besides, she is not an angel, she is a young woman."

"Florida!" Mrs. Ronson snapped. "You're being unkind to our gracious hosts."

"No, she's not," both Mother and Father stammered at once. A strange silence fell over the room. Beth could feel how everything was ruined. They had had such a lovely dinner and now everyone had their eyes locked on her, as if her next move, her next comment would determine everything. The Ronsons were staying in Concord for a few weeks. The March family would be seeing them regularly. And now, their first meeting, and already it was ruined by Beth's playing. She felt her throat go dry.

"I . . ." Beth started

"Yes," Florida prodded.

"I . . ."

"What is it, love?" Mother asked.

All their eyes burned through her.

"I . . . I have to . . ."

Florida's eyes lit up. Beth wasn't sure what she was expecting but she was quite sure that it was not this. "I . . . have to go lie down."

Mother and Father's faces crumpled like a balled-up handkerchief. Florida tilted her head, giving Beth a questioning look.

"I'm sorry, please . . . please forgive me. I don't, um, feel like myself at all." Beth heard her voice going softer and lighter, as if she was disappearing.

Like a ghost.

She felt a lump form in her throat, and the hot prick of tears. She placed the sheet music, which she realized was getting wrinkled in her ever-tightening fist, back on the piano and tried to smooth the paper out.

"It was quite lovely to meet you all," she said stiffly, staring at the floor. She opened and closed her mouth a few times before forcing the words out. "Good night."

Beth beelined for the staircase, each step feeling like a mountain's worth of climbing. She left behind the silence and the wondering and the awkwardness. She left behind Florida's beautiful but forceful disposition, Mother and Father's sadness, and the Ronsons' confusion. She climbed the stairs and entered her bedroom, staring at the empty bed that was once Jo's. She closed the door behind her, climbed into her bed.

And then, as quietly as possible, Beth wept.

Amy's Letter

She woke a few hours later. The sun was long gone, the downstairs quiet as can be. Beth assumed the Ronsons were gone by now. Neither Father nor Mother had come up to check on her. She felt Orchard House like a living thing in this moment. A tired, sad house that missed the days it was full of girls, full of questions and screeching laughter, missed even being full of tears and arguments.

Orchard House, Beth thought, missed being full of life.

A sad smile swept across her face as she lovingly placed a hand on the wall near her bed. *Me too, old home*, Beth thought. *Me too.*

She sat up in the quiet and strained her ears, but the silence was so pervasive it seemed to have its own song. She reached over to the nightstand and, striking a match, she lit a candle. From the pocket in the folds of her skirt she pulled out Amy's letter.

Paris
Dearest Beth
It is another cold day in Paris, the kind that bites through any extra layers. I like the city but I find myself missing the quiet

of Concord. While amused by the hustle and
bustle of all the people and the carriages,
sometimes there is so much noise that one
can barely think! I haven't done much
painting, or copying at the museums, and
my fingers are itchy with the want to make
something. I miss Orchard House, and
Mother and Father and dear old Hannah. I
miss Meg telling me what to do even. Sometimes on the loneliest of nights, I even miss
Jo. But most of all, Beth, I miss you. While I
know the busy Parisian streets would over-
whelm you, Beth, I do wish, you, of all my
sisters, were here with me. Cousin Florence
is a fine enough companion, but I feel like I
am never relaxed.

When we were little and I always said I
would marry rich, I didn't realize that you
fall in love, like a tumble. Not like
something you pluck off the shelf and wear
like a hat. I suppose it takes time, though.
Fred and I, we don't laugh much. Is that a
silly standard to have? I worry that he sees
me not as myself but more as a treasure.
Please don't tell Marmee though. Maybe I
just miss my sisters and home feels so far
away.

I know Mother did her best but I wonder
if there were lessons we were not taught.
Things, not just about society, or being good
little Pilgrims, but about the heart. About
finding our own way. Or maybe it is every
woman's experience. Maybe figuring it out
alone is the only way. Or maybe I have
been away from home for too long.

Regardless, how are Mother and Father? How is Hannah? Have you seen much of Meg? She talks so much of her garden I wish I could see it. Have you been to see Mr. Laurence? I'm sure you are caring for our dear friend. You have always been there, Beth. Steady, like the North Star.

Please write soon. Tell me stories of Orchard House so I will not feel so lonely and homesick all the time. I know why Marmee sent me here. Always, to make a good match. I cannot stop hearing her say it in my head, but it could be for more, could it not? It could be to study and learn and become a—well, I feel foolish saying it but since it's only to you I will. To become an artist. If Jo can be a writer then can't I be an artist? I take comfort in the cultural life here. I feel as though it feeds a part of my soul that needed nourishments. Something Concord couldn't give me. But the peace of Orchard House and the comfort of my family is still an ache, like an old injured bone, that I cannot seem to lose. No amount of dancing or parties will change that.

Be well. Write soon.

And please do not forget your dear little sister.

Love,
Amy

Beth slipped out of bed, putting the letter in the trunk at the end of the bed that housed all her childhood dolls. Even though she was no longer a child she still pet each doll carefully and lovingly and then climbed back down the stairs. The house was quiet and cold; no fire burned in the hearth. Beth wondered what time it was and the clock on the mantelpiece told her it was midnight. She slipped her cloak over her shoulders and her boots onto her feet, and as quiet as a mouse she opened the creaky door to Orchard House. The front step had been swept clean of snow and Beth pulled the door behind her and sat down. It was cold but not so cold that she couldn't bear it. It felt good, actually. It felt real, as if it could cleanse her and freeze out all the bad sad thoughts, leaving nothing but the crisp good ones. Or maybe it could change her. Turn her back into the girl she had been before the fever.

There were no lights on in Orchard House nor in Mr. Laurence's, so the darkness spread like a blanket. Above her the stars swirled. She wondered if Jo was awake right now, down in that strange wild city. Was she writing? What did the stars look like in New York City? What time was it where Amy was? Had she already left for Germany? Was Meg sleeping well?

She missed her sisters so much. When they were younger it seemed like childhood would last forever. And even in her timidity she had felt as though she was a part of something bigger than herself. Like sisterhood was armor she could fashion to protect herself from the rest of the world. But then those days had ended. And now, everyone had left.

And Beth was just a happy little phantom, haunting herself.

She may not have been as brave as the rest of them, striking out on their own, but she did not like being left behind with nothing of importance to do but housework. At least Meg had a family to raise, a garden that healed, the delights of two darling children to greet her each morning. Beth woke to empty rooms and quiet halls and hushed and worried glances.

She felt as though she was waiting for something, but for what she couldn't be sure.

Beth glanced up at the stars again. They seemed so far away.

Just as her sisters seemed so far away, glowing like stars in their other lives. Lives that Beth only truly knew through letters and occasional visits. Everyone was *doing* something.

Everyone but her.

She was just waiting.

For what? For death?

She shook the dark thought out of her mind. She thought of what Florida said about giving lessons. Could she? Could she sit with some small child and teach them how to play piano? Could she impart to them the gift that soothed her? Florida thought she could. But her parents did not. She thought of her father calling her a House Angel. He meant it with kindness, she knew that, but she wanted to be more than an angel. She was a grown woman! Her younger sister was off finding a husband! Beth wanted to do something too. She wanted to be someone who would have adventures, and maybe love, even. How could Florida, a girl she just met, already see that and her parents could not? Were they so afraid that they would keep her at home, like a pet? Or was it just that Florida didn't know the truth? Didn't know that Beth was broken.

She shuddered, unsure if it was the cold or not.

She looked up at the stars again, picked three that were clustered together, and named them after her sisters. "Good night, Amy and Meg and Jo. Maybe tomorrow, I will be brave like you."

Beth got up and went back inside, the cold of the winter night settling into her bones.

Another Face

"Good morning, Cricket," her mother said when Beth joined them in the kitchen the next morning. Mother was scrubbing clothes in the sink, and on the table was the dough for Beth to knead.

"Good morning, Marmee," Beth said softly. She was feeling anxious about last night. It had been rude of her to just run out like that. She worried what the Ronsons must now think of her. She was worried that Mother and Father were disappointed.

"How are we feeling this morning?" Mother asked, wiping off her soapy hands and giving Beth a hug. She pressed her cheek against Beth's forehead. It was cast as a loving gesture and while it was, Beth knew there was more to it. That day, years ago, when Beth figured it out, she nearly cried. Her mother was casually checking to see if she felt feverish.

"I'm so sorry about last night, Marmee," Beth said.

"You have nothing to be sorry about. You played beautifully."

"It was terribly rude of me to run out of the room like that. They were just too interested in me. I wanted to . . . disappear."

"I know, Cricket," Mother said, getting back to the clothes

she was scrubbing. "But they thought you were talented. They were complimenting you. I know it's hard to have so many people looking your way, but if the look is with love and admiration, it's not that terrible, is it now?"

"I guess not. Florida . . ." Beth paused, mustering up her courage. "She thinks I should teach."

"I know she does."

"Is that something . . . that you think I could do?" Beth asked, her voice even quieter than usual. Her heart was in her throat. She wasn't sure which answer she wanted from her mother.

Mother paused in her scrubbing. She pressed her lips together until they turned into nothing more than a thin white line. When she spoke, it was with measured care. "I . . . I think if that is something *you* want to do then we could talk about it. But you must remember, my Beth, that is a commitment. People would pay you. Which means you have to be ready each time for the lesson. You have to be willing to host them here or venture to their house. You have to be . . ."

Her mother trailed off but Beth understood. You have to be strong. You have to be healthy. Those were the words that floated around the kitchen between them. The kind that didn't need to be said. Beth turned her back and let her fingers sink into the dough. She wondered if this was it. If this tedium of housework—the washing, the sewing, the baking, the cleaning—these never-ending tasks, was all she would have until all her days fell down like leaves in autumn?

"Marmee," she said, glancing over her shoulder at her mother. "Sometimes I want something more."

"I know you do, Cricket. I want more for you too."

For a brief moment Beth thought she would talk to her mother about how she still saw the Hummel baby, its dead, empty face staring at her from among her dolls or from a shadow in the corner of the room. Was she a ghost haunted by other ghosts? She wanted to ask Marmee if she believed in ghosts.

But her mother looked up at her and smiled and said, "I

think you are a good, kind, generous person who always tries to do the right thing and never has a cross word or a bad thought about anyone. And I think that is the best kind of life you can live."

Beth nodded and smiled and swallowed down her thoughts. She loved that her mother thought that, but she also knew it wasn't true. She had a number of wicked thoughts that she would never share with anyone. She had in her lifetime swallowed what felt like an ocean full of anger and regret and, worse, pity.

Pity for herself. Anger at that baby, followed by more anger at herself. It was a constant cocktail of dark emotions, secrets she told no one. Let them think she was the House Angel. Maybe that was better for everyone, because if they knew the rage that Beth sometimes felt shaking inside her, they wouldn't recognize their own daughter. Sometimes when Beth looked in the mirror, she wondered about this other self, living just below her skin. The way she flickered and pulsed there, another face of Beth March. And mostly she wondered what would happen if that Beth came out.

A Walk to Town

Because Beth was feeling physically okay today, she took the walk with Hannah to the market to get groceries. It was another cool day, and she was thankful for the slow, steady way that Hannah had. It allowed her to not get tired out but also to be able to watch the commotion of Concord unfurl around her. Not counting going to Mr. Laurence's, it had been a while since she was out of the house, and the walk into town felt good. With the cooler weather, she'd had to give up her visits in the woods with Meg. The sun was strong in the sky and the winter birds were still flitting about unbothered by the cold. Beth liked those hearty birds the best. The stout little brown ones— were they nuthatches or chickadees? she wondered. All the same she liked the fact that they would plod along through the coming hardship of winter still squabbling over what they could find. Beth had slipped a handful of seeds into her pocket before they left, and she took them out now and tossed them into the path. The birds swooped down, wings fluttering from the trees straight into the path, giving Hannah a fright.

"Beth!" the old woman gasped.

"Sorry, Hannah," Beth said, locking arms with the her. "But look how they hop! I just love them."

The duo made their way through the squabbling birds and down Lexington Road right into the center of Concord. They stopped at the post office but there were no waiting letters, which heaved Beth's heart. They stopped at the butcher's and the green grocer and just as they were about to return home, Beth heard someone shouting.

She glanced through the crowded marketplace and saw a cheerful yellow gloved hand pop up over the crowd of heads, waving frantically.

"Beth!" someone cried. Beth was sure that it could not be for her. She ventured out so rarely and when she did the orbit was so small. But then she heard her name again, this time louder and the yellow gloved hand bobbed above the crowded market until Florida burst through the crowds and grabbed Beth into a quick but warm embrace.

"Beth," Florida gasped, laughing. "I'm so happy to see you."

"Hello, Florida," Beth said, nervously shifting her basket of groceries. "I'm sorry about last night."

"Last night? Ha. Yesterday is long gone and tomorrow will be here before we know it, so we better get today going."

"That's . . . quite a philosophy."

Florida swatted a yellow-gloved hand. "It's my mother's. If I'm not out there constantly being a better person or making the world a better place, then I'm wasting my one precious life."

Beth smiled. "Sounds a lot like my parents."

"Yes, I do believe they are cut from the same cloth. Shall we go for a walk? You can show me about town," Florida said, hooking her arm into Beth's. It was just like the other day, how casual and simple she did it. As if they had known each other for so long. As if they had already shared all their secrets.

"I can't, I'm afraid I must get home," Beth said, though she did not mean it. The sun flitted through the trees as if daring her.

"Oh please, you must! It's Hannah, yes?"

"Ma'am?" Hannah said.

"Please, Hannah, it isn't too much for you to carry back, is it? So that Beth can show me around this beautiful town of yours. Take pity on me, I don't know anyone else."

\Hannah locked eyes on Beth. Soft eyes surrounded by wrinkles; the skin underneath seemed paper thin. "Is that what you would like, Beth?"

"Oh please, say it is!" Florida said, nearly squealing. She gripped Beth's upper arm and bounced on the balls of her feet.

"Yes . . . I think I would," Beth said. A smile broke across her face. It was wide and broad and normally she would have been embarrassed and covered her mouth, but she didn't. Instead, she looked at Florida's sweet brown eyes and said, "Hannah, do you think you can manage?"

"Of course, dear."

"I won't be long," Beth promised. "Don't worry Marmee."

"Enjoy yourself, love," Hannah said, gathering up the baskets, and then in just a whisper, "You deserve it."

Those three words slipped through Beth's ear and buried like a treasure inside her heart. Florida gave Beth's arm another loving squeeze. As they watched Hannah head home, she said, "Where shall we go?"

"What do you want to see?" Beth asked.

"Everything," Florida replied with a grin.

As they walked, turning down Main Street toward River Street, Florida peppered Beth with so many questions. The girl would have a new one ready to fire off before Beth even finished answering the last one. She wanted to know who lived in each house and what they did and where business was conducted and if there were any scandals. She was an even bigger gossip than Amy! They walked, arm in arm, the swish of their skirts lining up made almost as lovely a noise as the crunch of snow under their boots. They laughed, and at one point, Florida bent down and packed together a snowball. She threw it hard and fast at a nearby tree. She missed and nearly hit a person, and the girls, barely able to control their laughter, slipped down the lane, yelling half-meant apologies to the startled pedestrian.

"You remind me of my Jo," Beth said, leaning into Florida's shoulder. Beth noticed her skin smelled faintly like fresh-cut peaches.

"Tell me about your sisters. I would love to have sisters. Being an only child is okay, but I feel as though I might have missed out on something special. Or brothers! I would love to have two rough and tumble brothers!"

"Well, I practically had two brothers. Laurie, the boy who lived next door, was basically our brother, and Jo was always more brother than sister. In fact, she called herself our brother-sister."

"That is the one in New York City? The writer?"

"Yes. I love all my sisters, but I miss my Jo the most. I miss her stories and how rambunctious she is. She's like a hurricane!"

"How long has she been gone?"

"Months."

"That must be hard," Florida said, shooting a sideways look toward Beth. Her eyes had flecks of gold in them, and they shone like the sun. Much like looking at the sun, Beth had to look away. Her breath caught and in her belly was a feeling she did not recognize. "Tell me a story about when you were a little girl."

Beth chewed the inside of her lip. "There are so many. Would you like to hear about the plays Jo wrote? Or when

Meg went to the theater and met Mr. Brooke? Or when Amy fell into the pond? Oh! What about when Amy *burned* Jo's book!"

"Those all sound nice . . . except maybe that book burning one." Florida paused and turned toward Beth, taking both her hands in hers.

"Well, she was awfully sorry about it. Jo never let it go though."

Florida rubbed her gloved thumb over Beth's, once slowly, and then again. The whole time she did it she held Beth's gaze until Beth wasn't sure if she was still breathing. "I want to hear a story about *you*, Beth."

The dead baby's waxy face flashed before her eyes. "I-I . . ." Beth stammered. She released Florida's hand and then instantly regretted it. Her heart rabbited inside her. "I don't have any good stories."

"I don't believe that."

"I don't. My sisters, they're the ones that did all those things. I was just sort of there."

"Beth March, I will not take a single step forward until you tell me one story about you."

Beth racked her brain. And then she remembered a story. "Okay, I have one, but I was just a baby."

Florida hooked her arm into Beth's again and they continued on their walk. "That's fine."

"I was very little, maybe only two years old. I was a quiet baby. Easy to care for."

"I find that very unsurprising," Florida said.

"One day, my sisters thought it would be funny if they took all of Father's books off the shelf and built a tower of books around me. Apparently, I was so agreeable that they covered me completely and I was content to keep playing, stashed away in my tower of books. My sisters, being children themselves, eventually lost interest in the game. Later Mother became frantic and couldn't find me and finally my sisters remembered. When they dismantled the book pile, there I was, curled up, having fallen asleep under all those stories. Perfectly fine!"

Florida stopped. "That's . . . quite a story."

Beth laughed. "Indeed. My family likes to make mischief. More than likely it was Jo's idea. She's always seen me as her own dear little toy."

"Indeed, thinking of you buried under your family's stories like that. The way you just . . . *disappeared*."

Something about the way Florida said it—so flat, so blatant—snagged at her, like a fishhook, but before she had time to ask what she meant, Florida turned and looked at her with a hard, serious stare.

"What is it?" Beth asked, suddenly afraid she had said something wrong. The idea of upsetting Florida physically pained her, and she wasn't sure why.

"I would like you to teach me how to play piano, Beth March."

"Me? Teach you? But I'm sure you've already had music lessons."

"I don't want music lessons, Beth. I want you to *teach* me."

"I . . . I . . . I don't understand," Beth stammered.

"I can get lessons from anyone. My parents can afford it. I have never had the slightest interest in learning until now. But I want to hear the music like you do. I want to feel the keys the way you feel them. I want to learn from you, Beth. I want to know what it feels like to contain that much passion."

"I don't." Beth shook her head, embarrassed. "I'm not passionate."

"Oh, but you are," Florida said, lifting her hand and gently tracing the curve of Beth's jawline as if she were drawing her to life. Beth shivered. "You are absolutely full of passion, and I want a taste of it."

A cold wind whipped Beth's hood up. "I should head home."

"Promise me."

Beth turned down the path, her heart beating wild and fast. This had been a mistake. She should have gone home. Florida was too much. She wanted too much. Stories and conversation and now lessons. Beth felt bone tired. And beyond that, she was terrified of the feeling swirling inside her, dark and un-known.

"Promise me!" Florida yelled as Beth lifted her hand, her heart in her throat, and waved frantically at the girl.

Almost as if she could erase her.

A Little Bit Wild

That night she dreamt about the dead baby again, her waxen face and matted, sweat-soaked hair. The way her little mouth puckered open, waiting for a cry that was never coming. The dilated pupils of eyes that stared into forever now. In the dream she kept trying to find a place to put the baby down, someone to take her and fix her. Someone to bring her back from where she went. But everyone she ran to and showed the baby to acted like everything was fine, as if it was still a living, breathing infant with a full span of uncharted days ahead of her. When she tried to tell them the baby was dead they just laughed. When the baby's mother turned to Beth and said, "My child is fine. It is you that is dead," Beth woke, sweat-soaked and gasping.

She lay in bed, detangling herself from the dream that echoed with such cruel laughter. She could tell even from those first few moments of wakefulness that today was going to be a painful day. She ran her hand through her hair and more strands caught between her fingers, long and light brown. Tilting her hand, she watched them float gently, soundlessly, to the floor. Another part of her that was sloughing off. Eventually there would be nothing left. The effects of the belladonna, perhaps?

Beth rose, put on her dressing gown, and took the few painful steps from her bed to her dresser, upon which was an assortment of bottles and tinctures. She wondered if the pain was because of the venture into town, which made her think of Florida, so she immediately tried to think of something else. Something that wasn't so intense. She picked a bottle up, uncapped it, and let the liquid spill into her hand. She rubbed it first on her hands—always she must protect her hands—and then on her ankles, which hurt, and her elbows and shoulders, which also hurt. The smell was foul and would, of course, alert her mother to her pain, but this was not the kind she could grit her way through. She thought of her family's philosophy on medicine—homeopathy; the law of similarity, like attracts like. If the medicine produces the same condition as the malady then it must be helpful. She wondered though. The truth was, years after the baby, her pain had only increased, her breathing become more labored, more hair fluttered out of her head, and Beth could see that she was thin.

Thinner than she had ever been. She ran a hand over a hip bone that jutted like a hunk of china from below her flesh.

"You are wasting away," she said to the reflection across from her, a ghostly pale wisp of a young woman. "Soon you will be nothing but a lovely little skeleton." This made her laugh a dark laugh. Though she knew if she dared say anything like it out loud her family would be horrified. Instead, she hid her pain and smiled though the discomfort to keep them happy and to keep their worry at bay. But late at night in her darkest moments she hated them for it. She looked at her reflection again and her face changed, and she saw the Other Beth now. The one full of anger and resentment and pity for herself. The one that instead of bearing what she had been given, wanted to scream at the universe until her throat split open.

And when she allowed herself to feel like this Other Beth, she would chide herself for being a terrible daughter and sister, who had the most loving, generous family in the world. How could she be angry at any of them? It was not their fault she got sick. It was her own fault, or maybe no one's. It was the price she paid for trying to do the right thing. It was just terrible luck. And each time she thought that—while she reminded herself that her charity and kindness toward the Hummels was in fact, the right thing—a smaller, darker voice of Other Beth whispered that it was still unfair. That she could still be angry.

She remembered once when they were young, before all the troubles started, Meg had been chastising her sisters, calling Jo a tomboy and Amy a goose. Beth had in that moment asked Meg what she was. She remembered how much she longed for an assigned personality, for Meg, ever the little mother to the girls, to look at her and decide what part of Beth stood out the most. What did her sisters see when they saw her? Would it be her kindness? Her silliness? Her talent for the piano? Jo was certainly a tomboy and while Beth wasn't sure why Meg picked a goose for Amy, it did seem to fit. Something about honking and preening. What would Meg pick for her? So when Meg answered that she was a "dear" and "nothing else," Beth felt something inside her wilt, wither, and then die. And then everyone, even Jo—even beloved Jo, who Beth was sure could see into her heart of hearts—agreed that she was in fact a dear, and nothing else.

Nothing else.

If her sisters didn't see her, who did? Who could possibly ever see her if not them? And now that they were gone there was no one left to even try to see her, to peer into her heart and see that she, too, like her father's beloved poet, Walt Whitman, contained multitudes.

A ghost, Beth thought to herself, looking in the mirror. "Nothing but a ghost, haunting myself. Nothing else. Just an empty little ghost." She held her hands up, her fingers splayed out, and whispered, "Boo!" at her own reflection, before dropping them sadly.

Beth got dressed and descended the stairs for what she knew would be another day of endless chores. Hannah was already in the kitchen, preparing breakfast.

"Morning, love," Hannah said.

"Hello, Hannah," Beth said quietly. She knew Hannah could smell the liniment but she appreciated that she did not say anything. Beth turned her back, facing the basin before her. The dishes waited.

"I can brew up some of that tea Meg made, if you would like? If it helps," Hannah said softly.

Beth nodded but didn't answer. It would help. But it could not stop what was happening. Beth knew that. What had Father called her the other day? The House Angel. She heard clearly, then, Florida's response, her blatantly saying, to a strange man no less, that Beth was no house angel. That she was a young woman. How did a stranger who knew nothing about her see her more plainly than her family did?

Beth scrubbed the dishes and wondered, if she was so meek, that they didn't notice her. So gentle and agreeable that she could be buried under a castle of books and no one would notice. She thought about the look Florida gave her when she told that story. How she said the word *disappeared*. How there was something more than amusement there. How there was sadness, an inkling of pity. Beth didn't want Florida's pity. In fact, she hated the idea that Florida might pity her, might see her as broken. Because the truth was there was something about the way the girl looked at her, the way she *touched* her, that made Beth feel alive.

Maybe more alive than she'd ever felt.

The idea that Florida would look at her and see anything less than that broke her heart.

She flexed her hands, feeling her knuckles pop and settle. She glanced over her shoulder and checked on Hannah. But the woman was busy with her own work. Then, she lifted up a single plate and dropped it on the floor. It shattered, sending shards skittering about the kitchen floor. Hannah, startled, jumped into action, checking to make sure Beth wasn't hurt and picking up the pieces.

This, she realized, is what thinking about Florida did to her. It made her just a little bit wild.

And then, standing there watching the pieces be swept up, Beth knew fully and with her whole heart that she would teach Florida Ronson how to play the piano.

Something hopeful, like a bird, fluttered in her chest. She couldn't remember the last time she felt this way.

That evening she sat down to write Amy.

Orchard House, Concord, Massachusetts

My dearest Amy,

Whenever I receive one of your letters my heart sings. I love the stories you tell me about Paris which, even with all your wonderful details, still, to me, feels like a terribly big unknowable place. I think about the places you have been, all the streets and the way they must stretch infinitely with no end in sight, and I shiver. I'm glad to hear you're painting, which is the most important thing of all. You are so far from Concord, just as you used to dream when you were a girl. I pray you're experiencing everything. I miss you dearly, Amy. And I am glad Laurie is there with you, He can be a little bit of home to you.

There isn't much to report from here. The days slide into one another, drifting by like leaves falling from trees. Doesn't childhood feel both as if it happened yesterday and also a hundred years ago? Father and Mother are well, as I'm sure they tell you in their letters. We carry on as we always have. Orchard House standing stoic for another season. Did Mother tell you that Father has made a new friend, Mr. Ronson? Mother and Mrs. Ronson (who goes by Jo, which as you can imagine put me at ease during dinner) are doing suffrage work. They are trying to start a chapter of the organization that Mrs. Ronson started in Boston. Also, they have a daughter named Florida. She's really quite delightful. She's full of so much spirit and laughter and bravery. We have quickly become friends, which I'm sure surprises you as you know how shy I am. But I can't help it. Her enthusiasm is gripping and she's got the prettiest eyes I have ever seen. One could get lost in them. You'll never believe this, but she wants me to teach her to play piano. Of course I couldn't. You don't think I could, right? Mother and

*Father do not. They worry about my consti-
tution and my health, which I'm happy to
report is just fine, as always. I told Florida
that she could learn piano from any number of people but she looked me right in the
eye and said she wanted to learn to play
with the passion that I have. Passion, Amy!
I blushed.*

*Also, I have visited with dear Mr.
Laurence. He sends his best and he hopes
his grandson isn't being too much of a
bother!*

*It is strange though, to be here without
Meg and Jo and you. Meg comes by, but
married life busies her. I see her changed,
grown, which is good, but I feel when I look
at her that she is now so far from the girl
we played with. She seems to carry some secret knowledge in her. She has made me
tinctures, from her own garden, for my
heart. They help. I suppose that is what is
meant for us all though, isn't it? Jo is not so
far away but it feels as if there is an ocean
between Concord and New York City. Then
I think how there really is an ocean
between you and me, and I shudder when I
think of the size and depth that separates
us. I wonder at times how my letters can
even reach you? My sweet baby sister,
grown and so far from home.*

*The house is empty now with just Mother
and Father and me, wandering from room
to room. Sometimes it feels so quiet, I have*

to stop myself, pat down my own dress and realize that I am still here.

That I'm not just a ghost, haunting these halls.

Wouldn't that be funny? I could be a ghost spying on you and your paintings at night. Floating over to Meg's to watch her manage her new strange life and to ghost-chat with the babies. I suspect babies understand what ghosts say, being so close to that other side, don't you? I wonder how it feels to sleep somewhere other than Orchard House. What it must be like to sleep next to Mr. Brooke.

Father would be horrified that I ever thought this. Even you would be scandalized, wouldn't you? These are the things I say to you in my head, not the things I say in letters. But I do wonder. I think if I had to choose, which thankfully I don't, I would take soft warm arms, supple skin, over the scratch of a man's beard and his wide back. Warm, womanly arms are the only arms I could sleep in. I hope you understand.

Funny idea, me teaching, isn't it? I mean to say, Jo teaches and Father preaches, but they are both so bold and so manly that it makes sense. What could a little ghost like me possibly teach anyone? It is a foolish idea and I shall forget it at once. But Amy, if you will indulge me, I must say the way Florida (such a sweet name, isn't it?) looked at me after I finished playing just a short piece by Mozart, well, you would think I was standing on a grand stage somewhere! The fuss she made. And the way she talked about me and my playing afterwards, even so bravely to Father. Of course, me being me, I turned as red as a tomato and ran and hid. But, if only to you, and you must keep it a secret and not tell Father or Mother, for they will think me prideful but . . . I will say it felt nice. I know when we were young, I was always much too shy to speak lines in the theatricals we staged. All three of you were much better for that sort of thing. But music is different. It fills me in a way that I can scarcely describe. I've never had an audience bigger than my sisters and dear Mr. Laurence, so to play for strangers was terrifying. But it was terrifying in a way that also felt good. Is that how you felt boarding a steamer and crossing all that unimaginable water? Is that how Jo feels, walking the streets of New York City? Is that how Meg feels growing and harvesting herbs to heal?

I know I can never be as brave as you or Jo or even Meg, but I do wonder if I could be brave enough to teach Florida—sweet gentle Florida, who seems so taken by me, like I am her little pet—if I could teach her just a few things.

I suppose I will always wonder. I must lie down now, my dear sister. Please write

soon and tell me everything that is happen-
ing, especially about your art, which mat-
ters most of all.
All my love,
Your Beth

She folded up the letter and slipped it under her pillow. To-morrow, she knew, she would hide it amongst her dolls, like a secret diary, and write another letter to Amy, one that would sound more like the House Angel her sister left behind. One that did not talk about pretty eyes, supple arms, or ghosts. She slept fitfully that night, pain nested inside her, feathery.

The Northern Lights

The following day the Ronsons were coming by again. They were to meet with Mother and Father about setting up a group to focus on suffrage in Concord. Beth woke, unsure about giving lessons to Florida. Earlier, over the drudgery of housework, it seemed a possibility. It seemed like an escape. But now Beth whispered a small prayer that Florida wouldn't ask again. At least not in front of everyone.

Beth got through her day, finishing the darning and washing and letter writing, the whole while checking the clock, waiting for the inevitable knock on the door. And all day the question flopped back and forth inside her like a frantic stranded fish.

Then, just like that, the hour arrived, and the Ronsons appeared, as warm and welcoming as the setting sun, and the table was alive with chatter. Beth, though quiet, once again enjoyed the opportunity for Orchard House to be abuzz. Even Hannah enjoyed it. The way everyone was talking at once, hands waving about to emphasize points, glasses lifted in good cheer, the scrape of forks against plates.

"You're awful quiet," Florida whispered into Beth's ear. The warmth of it, the gentle tickle, startled Beth so much she dropped her fork.

"Didn't mean to scare you," Florida added with a smile.

"Oh no, it's fine. I just . . . your family is so interesting. It's refreshing. I sometimes feel like there are so few people in Concord that are like my family. Father is always coming up with new philosophies and Marmee is always fighting injustice in her own way. She works so hard for those that have less than us. But sometimes it feels as if they are the only ones. I was taught by my sister Jo growing up, but Meg often told stories about what other children said about the poor and . . ."

The silence was thick for a minute.

"People who look like me," Florida said, her face solemn.

"Yes."

Florida nodded. And then said quietly, so as not to draw the attention of the others at the table, "My father and mother have done work that will change this country and for it I am eternally grateful. But we need people like your family to talk to those other families. They do not listen to us, not even to Father with his fancy law degree." She smiled a sweet smile and looked fondly at her father, who was talking with Beth's father.

It struck Beth then what it must be like for Florida and her family to move through the world. What assumptions people made about them. The way others decided who they are or what they can do before they even knew them. What a cruelty it was. But was it much different than with her parents? The way they decided what she could do or couldn't do. An anger, fiery hot, rose in her chest.

"What do you want to do, Beth?" Florida asked without lifting her eyes off her father.

"Do?" Beth asked, distracted by her own thoughts. She looked at her mother. She thought about the way her whole life has been framed by having the fever. She felt the Other Beth shift below her skin.

"Yes, with your one dear and precious life. What do you want to do?"

Beth froze, looked down at her hands, which nervously played a small concerto on her lap. This happened when she got nervous. Music was her refuge, even when she was not at the piano. She finally managed to whisper.

Florida leaned in because Beth spoke so softly. "Again?"

"I don't know what you mean by *do*."

Florida laughed, a touch too loudly, and then cleared her throat. "What do you want to do? For instance, I want to travel. I want to see New York City and meet this infamous Jo. I want to go to New Orleans and then sail to Europe, like your Amy. I want to see the Northern Lights. I want to stand on that frozen wasteland and watch the night sky dance with color."

Beth didn't know what the Northern Lights were, but she understood now what Florida was asking. She wanted to know what her plans were. The way Jo was in New York City, and Amy painting in Europe, and Meg, growing her plants. They had always had plans. She was sure that Jo would one day be the famous writer she wanted so badly to be. And that Amy would be a renowned painter. Meg might not be doing what she had dreamed about as a child, but she tended a garden that healed people. What greater thing could one do? No one ever asked Beth what she wanted to do. In fact, once she overheard Jo telling their mother that she wished she could be more like Beth and have no wishes. Have no ambition or dreams but just be happy in her little sweet life. It hurt her but she would never have said that then. She couldn't even say it now. This was how they all viewed her. Mother and Father. Amy and Meg. Even her most dear Jo. She was just a doll. A thing that was propped up somewhere, a thing that made other people smile. A thing that had no dreams of her own. What kind of person doesn't have dreams?

The ghost kind?

"I'm still that child buried and forgotten under all those books," Beth said. It took her a moment to realize she had said it out loud. In fact, she had said it so loudly that the rest of the table heard.

Mother smiled and furrowed her brow. "What was that, dear?"

Beth stammered as all their eyes fell upon her. She felt the tears start to prick their way forward. Her joints lit up suddenly, a lightning bolt of pain, before settling back down.

"Oh, Beth was just telling me a story about her childhood," Florida said loudly, pulling their eyes toward her. "The tales she has told me about her sisters makes me long for siblings of my own." Under the table Florida took Beth's hand and gave it the gentlest of squeezes. "Beth, darling," Florida said, fixing her eyes upon her. It was a deep look, like a rope thrown to a drowning person. "Before it gets too dark shall we take a quick walk? I do love the look of the snowfall in the moonlight."

"I . . . should help clean up."

"Nonsense," her father said. "Go, enjoy. Get some air in those lungs. It will be good for you."

"Beth, darling," Mother said, gently laying a hand on Father's arm to silence him. "Are you sure you feel well enough?"

Beth looked at Florida. She didn't know if she did, to be honest. She had been in pain all day and she was already feeling tired and drained. But there was something about the way Florida looked at her, something that said she believed Beth could do this. That maybe Beth could do anything. And this was enough to make her rise up from the table and say, "A walk sounds lovely, if you don't mind."

Florida let out the tiniest squeal of joy and stood up. "We'll be back soon." She looped her arm into the crook of Beth's just as she had in town the other day. She did it with ease. She did it with pride. And the two of them headed out the front door into the crunching snow and chilling air. And for just a little while, Beth's bones stopped their daily song of pain, and the girls watched the moon flit between clouds.

They had fallen silent, watching the winter stars wink on across the blanket of night. After a moment Beth quietly said, "Do you think my sisters see the same stars I do?"

Florida was quiet for a moment before nodding. "I think we're all looking up at the night sky as a whole, regardless of where we are in the world. You miss them, don't you?"

"Terribly."

Florida took Beth's hand in hers. "Which one is Amy?"

"She's the one in Europe."

"No," Florida said with a laugh that nested inside Beth's chest. "I mean which one is she?" Florida pointed up at the stars.

Beth smiled. How did she know? "I imagine that one, there, the small but bright one in that cluster of three is Amy, because she's always going to be the baby of our family."

"Let me guess then," Florida said, shifting her arm slightly higher. "So that one that's a bit pulled away from the cluster. That would be your Jo?"

Beth blushed. "Yes! How did you guess?"

"Well, Jo is the one that's always striking out on her own, no? Always looking in a different direction."

"Indeed, she is. My brave Jo."

"So that is Meg. Hmmmm." Florida frowned. "So where is Beth?"

"Oh no. My sisters are stars. I'm afraid I'm terribly earthbound."

Florida watched her and in the darkness of the night her gaze intensified. It shook Beth, as if she was looking directly into the sun. She couldn't look away and she also knew she couldn't keep looking.

"Your sisters may be stars, but you, Beth March, you are the Northern Lights."

Beth felt her face redden. "What are those?"

"Oh Beth, it's like magic. Up north, way up north, suddenly night becomes day. Great green lights shine through the night sky."

"How?" Beth asked, gazing up at the stars and trying to imagine what Florida described.

"It has to do with the sun. And winds. Great bands of green light flash across the sky, lighting everything up. It's like magic. At first there is nothing and then, *whoosh*, flickering bands of green streak across the sky. I'm not completely positive what the science behind it is, but I desperately want to see them. I know I will someday."

Beth returned her gaze to Florida, studying the girl's face. She saw it there—the assurance she had, the faith in her words and actions that told her this wasn't just an empty promise or a wish. She would go. Florida would one day stand on the snow-packed ice of some distant land and watch the night turn into day.

"You will," Beth said. "Florida Ronson, I don't think there is anything that can stop you from doing what you wish."

Florida turned to her and smiled. "I know."

It was a small thing, but if she could, Beth would eat those two words like seeds. She would savor them in her mouth and keep them inside her forever, where they would grow, fueled by Florida's faith until they blossomed into the kind of confidence that took you across the world.

"I will teach you," Beth said, holding her gaze.

Florida flinched as if she had been struck and then pulled Beth into such a hard and fast hug that it seemed as if Beth were the only thing keeping Florida from floating away. When she let her go she traced Beth's cheek, lightly with the back of her index finger, and the feel of it lit Beth up.

"This is the most beautiful gift I have ever been given," Florida said softly. "Thank you." And then after a beat, "Do you think your parents will approve?"

Beth pressed her lips together and then said with a resolution she wasn't quite sure she felt, "It is not their decision."

Piano Lessons

When she finally gathered up the courage to tell her parents that she would be teaching Florida Ronson to play piano, she did so with a steady voice. She remembered Florida's advice about holding their gaze. They had concerns, as Beth expected, but she made her points as clearly as possible. In the end, they agreed, though they did so through tight lips. But Beth didn't care. She was proud of herself. She wanted to do this, and she showed them that she could. Now she just had to believe it herself.

But that belief was drowned out when, that evening, she overheard her mother talking to her father.

"I just worry she hasn't the strength," Mother said. "What if this sets her back? What do we do then?"

"We can't forbid it, my love. If this is what Beth wants, we must allow it. I . . . I can think of her as our House Angel but the truth is, she's a young woman whose life has already been deeply affected. She isn't asking for much. In fact, she never asks for anything. If it were Meg or Jo or Amy, we wouldn't think twice . . ."

There was a brief moment of silence and then, when Mother spoke again, Beth could hear the break in her voice, the hitch and catch of tears. "But it's not. It's Beth. Our Beth. And you know she isn't well, regardless of what we tell ourselves."

Upstairs Beth pulled the pillow over her head so she wouldn't have to hear anymore. She told herself she could do this. She kept saying it until it sounded true. Inside it felt like a bird had been set free within her ribs.

She sent word to Florida that their lessons would begin the following Sunday and that they would meet each successive Sunday for a few hours and Beth would teach her how to play. Florida insisted on paying, but Beth demurred. Hours before Florida's expected arrival, Beth fidgeted. She pulled a number of pieces out, flipping through scores, trying to find a good starting point. She discarded a number of Mozart pieces that were too complex. She needed something gentle, something repetitive so that Florida could get accustomed to the piano, the feel of the keys under her fingers, the fluidity of hand placement. She shuffled through a few more, pacing around the room as she did.

Hannah, who was in the corner knitting, watched her fret. "You'll wear a hole in the floorboards if you keep pacing like that, child."

"What?" Beth said, pulled out of her thoughts.

"The floorboards, love. You'll worry yourself right through them."

"Oh, Hannah, I'm so sorry. I just don't know what to start with. I need something simple so she doesn't get too frustrated if she falters, but interesting enough for Florida. Isn't she interesting, Hannah? I just find her so *interesting*."

"Quite interesting, that one. What about that one that goes *da, da, da, dum, dum, dum*?"

Beth cocked an eyebrow. "My dear sweet Hannah, I have no idea what you're talking about," she said with a gentle laugh.

"Oh you know. *Bum, ba, bum, ba, ba, ba, ba*. It's that lilting one. Has a bit of repetition in it. Sounds a bit like a lullaby."

"Oh! I know! You mean Bach's Prelude in C." Beth rushed over to Hannah and gathered her up in a hug, upsetting the woman's knitting. "That's *perfect*!"

"Yes, yes, yes," Hannah said, shooing her away. Beth dashed back toward the piano and started leafing through the sheet music until she found the Bach piece. She set it on the piano, sat down, and played the opening sequence.

Hannah got out of her chair and stood behind Beth, petting her old fingers through Beth's long hair. It was a comforting feeling for both of them. The old woman was kind and did not mention how much hair came out between her strokes.

"I think it's wonderful you're doing this, child," Hannah said.

"Mother and Father don't think I can," she whispered softly, lifting her hands off the keys. There was a beat and then another before Hannah spoke.

"They worry, yes. Your fever changed the course of your childhood, Beth. They thought they were going to lose you. That fear, it lives in them now, a terrible thing with teeth and claws. And sometimes it speaks for them. It is not that they think you can't do it, they just worry that it will wear you down. They just want you to be okay."

"But what if doing this, teaching Florida, makes me feel all right. Normal, even." Beth closed her eyes and exhaled. "I cannot let this house be my whole life, Hannah. I can't sit here until I'm dead, darning socks and being their House Angel. I cannot do it. I . . . I won't."

"I know, dear." Hannah kissed the top of her head. "That is why you're going to give these lessons. You know and they know too. Be patient with them, love. But also, follow what feels right for you. You have a kind, good heart, and you must learn to trust it."

"I just want something more."

"And you shall have it."

Florida's knock on the door was as chipper and intense as the rest of her. A steady and heartfelt *rat-tat-tat*. Beth opened the door, her heart fluttering in the hollow of her throat. The wind whipped both Florida and a whirl of snow into the doorway as she came inside.

"Concord truly takes winters very seriously, doesn't it? I thought nothing beat Boston, but apparently I was wrong," the girl said with a laugh as she unbundled her scarf and shawl and mittens. Beth attempted to help Florida shed her winter clothes, but it only ended in a confused jumble of arms and cloth.

"It is lovely in here," Florida said once they were seated. "The fireplace and the smell of bread cooking. Your house has such a nice feeling to it. Lived-in. Loved."

Beth looked around Orchard House. Florida was right. It was a lovely home, one that had been filled with laughter and love and the energy of four girls. At least she used to think of it that way. But now it felt more like a prison. Would she ever feel that way about her home again? Maybe when her sisters returned. Maybe when they could all be together. She felt her stomach tightening. What if that couldn't happen? What if those days were truly over? She tried to push these thoughts down into her toes.

"Thank you, that's very kind of you to say. Would you like anything?" Beth asked, her eyes looking at everything but Florida.

"Nothing other than to learn to play as beautifully as you do."

Beth felt her cheeks color. They got seated at the bench, the piano keys looking up at them in a smile. Florida was sitting so close to Beth that she could feel the heat of her body where their hips and shoulders touched. Beth couldn't stop thinking about it. She was quite sure she had never sat this close to some-one that wasn't her sister before in her life. It both terrified and thrilled her.

They covered the logistics of the sheet music first. They went through the staff and the treble clef and the bass clef and then each note. As Beth showed her the notes she played them one by one on the piano. Florida was a fine pupil, rapt and at-tentive. She laughed loudly when she made mistakes but even louder when she got things right. She threw all of herself into the lesson, as if there was nothing else she wanted more than to learn how to play this piano. Her enthusiasm at first over-whelmed Beth, who took to stuttering out her words, but then below that something inside her stirred. Something that felt just as thrilling as Florida's laugh. Something that felt more alive than Beth had felt in a long time.

Sitting there, with the small places their bodies touched, and the gentle way that Florida would mimic the fingering that Beth did across the piano keys, Beth felt something she hadn't in a while. She wondered briefly how it could be that just the other day she imagined herself a ghost. A ghost couldn't play piano or sit this close to Florida, or teach or laugh or touch. A ghost couldn't be seen the way Florida was looking at her; in-tensely and all at once. A ghost couldn't feel the way Beth felt when she looked into the deep pool of Florida's eyes. A ghost could certainly never feel as alive as Beth felt now.

When the lesson was over, they went for a walk. The wea-ther was a touch warmer at this time and the snow yielded to the sun, turning into slush, which splashed around their boots and wetted the hems of their skirts.

"So, my kind teacher, tell me, how did I do?" Florida asked, nudging Beth's shoulder with her own.

"Quite well for a first lesson. I think you'll be a quick study when it comes to reading music. You seem to have a gift for it."

Florida feigned embarrassment, which made Beth laugh. It

was such a light easy sound, it startled her a little. As if she couldn't imagine it coming from her.

"Well, I do have a gift for languages. I speak French as well as English and am currently learning German. I suppose music is just another kind of language, wouldn't you say?"

"Indeed." Beth wanted to add that when she herself felt the words bottle up inside her she often sat at the piano and played. Her sisters used to say that was Beth's main way of communicating. They thought it was cute, but she wondered if there was something to Florida's point. If music could be a way to say how you felt. A way to remember the past. A way to say that you love someone. But since she couldn't say any of this, instead she asked, "How did I do, having never taught before?"

"You were most excellent. Better than any other tutor I have had. I knew you could do this. You should take on more students."

"I can't."

"You say that a lot. But clearly, you can."

Beth felt something stir inside her and hot tears pricked at her eyes.

"What is it?" Florida asked, taking Beth's hand in hers. "What have I said that has upset you?"

Beth shook her head. "It's nothing."

"Clearly it's something, my dear Beth."

"I . . . am not good at talking about it," Beth said, barely above a whisper.

"Try," Florida whispered back, squeezing her hand gently.

"I am . . . not well."

"Oh, should we turn back?" Florida asked, as she gently laid a hand on Beth's cheek to check her temperature. "It's probably the cold."

"No, that's not what I meant. I mean, a few years ago, I was very sick."

"Oh," Florida said. It wasn't even a word as much as an exhale.

"I . . . recovered but . . ."

"I understand."

"You do?" Beth said, finally feeling the courage to look Florida in the eye—in those beautiful, rich eyes.

"Yes, that explains so much. Why you were reluctant to teach me, why you won't take on other students. Why your parents fret over you so much. It makes sense now."

"I'm sorry."

"What are you apologizing for?" Florida asked.

"For being like this."

Florida smiled. "You are not being like this. This happened to you, and you are carrying it. You are managing. You are doing your best."

"So you are not disappointed to have a teacher who is ill?"

Florida smiled with so much warmth that Beth couldn't stop herself from smiling back. "Disappointed? Beth, how silly. I think you are beautiful and talented and amazing. I hope to one day be lucky enough to be counted as your dear friend."

Beth looked away, unable to hold Florida's gaze. She had never known someone like this girl. Someone who saw right inside her and found nothing lacking. Not even her being a shy, sick girl seemed to matter to Florida. It was as if she accepted Beth exactly as she was. Relief flooded her. She realized for the first time how much energy it took to pretend all the time to be okay, to make it easier for Mother and Father and her sisters. It was exhausting. But right here, with Florida, a girl she hardly knew, she could just be Beth. She didn't have to pretend to be Well Beth. She could just *be*.

Florida seemed to sense this realization. "Now then," she said, once again hooking her arm into Beth's as the continued on their walk, "how long before I shall be able to play that Bach piece? If I practice every day? Also, when is our next lesson? Soon, I hope."

*   *   *

And so they went on. Meeting each Sunday, sitting side by side, hips and shoulders touching, hands smoothing out keys, knuckles cracking, whispered words and loud laughter, music sometimes beautiful, sometimes disjointed, filling the room until that Sunday when Florida arrived, and Beth was unable to stand.

Florida's first indication that something was wrong was that Hannah opened the door, not Beth.

"Oh, hello," Florida said, a touch surprised to see her. "Hannah, it's lovely to see you. I'm here for my lesson with Beth."

"I know, my dear. There wasn't time to send word to your family."

Florida stiffened. "Is something wrong? Is she alright?"

"She's not feeling well today, Ms. Ronson. I'm afraid we'll have to cancel today's lesson."

"Oh, of course. May . . . I visit her?"

Hannah pressed her lips together and shook her head. "I'm so sorry, love, but I fear it would be too much."

"But I . . ."

Hannah was surprised to see a tear roll down the girl's cheek. Florida brushed it away just as quickly.

"I would very much like to wish her well. I won't be more than a minute. Please, Hannah, it would mean the world to me."

Hannah glanced behind her as if she were about to be caught. "Mr. and Mrs. March are very strict about Beth when she has a flare-up."

"Please, Hannah. I won't be more than a minute."

"Well, seeing as how they are out right now . . . if you're quick about it, then go ahead."

"Oh, thank you," Florida said, about to race up the staircase when Hannah stopped her.

"You'll find her changed." She said it softly, her eyes never meeting Florida's.

Florida took the stairs two at time, but froze when she got to the doorway of Beth's room. There was an acrid smell she didn't recognize, and under that a sweetness that felt out of place indoors, especially during winter. Beth was nothing more than a lump under the blankets, a snatch of long tangled hair across the pillow. The worst was her breathing.

It was shallow and jagged, like each breath was taken through some sort of scrim. It sounded as if there was something wet shoved into Beth's mouth, and it frightened Florida.

"Beth," she called softly from the doorway. "It's Florida. Hannah told me you were ill so I just wanted to wish you well. I wanted . . ."

She trailed off as the thing in the bed that couldn't possibly be Beth stirred.

"Beth?" Florida leaned gently over the bed. There was a heat that felt inhuman radiating from the girl. Florida reached a hand out and gently touched her shoulder.

Beth jumped. It was like a spasm, and it startled Florida away from the bed. A low moan emanated from the girl in the bed, that Florida still could not believe was her sweet Beth. The moan morphed into a groan, growing louder, like a siren had been set off inside her.

"Beth? Can I get you anything?" Florida stepped closer and brushed some loose hair off Beth's face. When she lifted her hand the hair dangled between her now shaking fingers. She let it fall to the floor. When she looked back at Beth, her eyes were open. Two shocks of white.

"Beth," Florida said. "Can I get you anything?"

"Go away," Beth groaned. Her eyes darted about, unable to focus on anything, and Florida wasn't sure if she could see her or not.

"It's me. It's Florida."

"Go away." And then Beth began to moan again, low in her

throat. It sounded more like a sound that would come from an animal than a person. Florida took a few steps back. She looked around the room, her eyes finally landing on the jars and ointments and medication that filled the top of the dresser. The noise coming from Beth grew and Florida heard the steady pound of Hannah's feet coming up the stairs. She felt a panic, low and humming inside her.

"Oh dear, let's try some more," Hannah said as she burst into the room. She took a rag out of a bucket of water near the bed and pressed it to Beth's forehead. "Come, hold this," she said to Florida.

With nervous steps Florida approached the bed, knelt down, and pressed the cool rag to Beth's hot forehead.

"All her fevers are bad," Hannah said. "And the pain. The pain is everywhere."

Hannah rummaged through the bottles on the dresser, talking softly to herself until she found the one she was looking for. She popped out the cork and poured a clear liquid onto a spoon and then slowly slipped it past Beth's lips. She spoke to the girl softly as she did, and Beth started to settle down. Her breathing was still a jagged, raspy huff, but she was at least no longer moaning.

Florida stood up, dazed, letting Hannah take her arm and lead her down the stairs. When they got to the door, Hannah said, "She will recover. But when she spikes like this, it is overwhelming For her. For us."

"I had no idea. She told me that she got sick, but I didn't picture anything like this."

"I know, my dear. Who would? The fever of her childhood seems to have settled inside her bones, and when it comes back, like some sort of devil, she cannot stand it."

"Will she be better by next week?" Florida asked. It was so low, barely a whisper, as if she feared hearing the answer.

"Yes, love. The illness is hard, but it never lasts too long."

Florida thanked her and left Orchard House, stepping back out into the cold, feeling fundamentally changed.

For Beth, it went like this: The heat came first. She felt it in the night like a fog gathering around her. Every inch of her felt warm. She touched her head and her fingers slipped across the sweat. She pushed the blankets off her. She needed to get her medicine, but when she turned to sit up the whole room tilted and turned and fell. Pain radiated across her shoulder as her torso hit the floorboards hard. And then everything went dark.

The pain woke her again. She was back in bed, the pillow wet with sweat under her head. She heard the quiet murmur of voices, but she couldn't open her eyes. She tried to speak but nothing came out. When she moved, pain sang through her bones, lighting up everything inside her, until she saw spots in the dark like stars exploding. She thought of her sisters and then she thought of nothing.

There was a voice. She felt a hand touch her face and it felt so cold she flinched. When she moved, the pain moved with her, coming in waves. *Like the tide*, she thought and then didn't understand what that means. She heard her name. At least she thought she did. Was it Jo? Was Jo back? Would they take another trip to the beach? Her bones screamed, and the pain furrowed deeper inside of her, hot and white and permanent. It nested with teeth and claws. She tried to open her mouth, to talk to the face that swam in and out of focus before her. Was that Marmee? Did she leave her here, in all this hot, hot pain? But when the focus snapped to for a moment it was neither Jo nor her mother. It was a face she didn't recognize. A strange face. She wondered if perhaps it was death itself, but then it started to look like the baby. The dead, still baby. Is that how death would come for her? In the form of a voiceless, breathless infant? She thought she was screaming, screaming for the baby to go away. She wasn't ready to die. Not now. Not alone like this. *Go away*, she thought. Did she say it out loud? The face receded then, like a ghost, and Beth nearly laughed. She had scared away Death. Did that make her Death itself? Something cold ran down her forehead and then something bitter down her throat and then she felt nothing at all, and in that nothingness she realized she was free. Even if her freedom was death.

Beth Finds Her Voice

By the following Sunday, Beth was recovered, but drained. She was seated on the couch, a book and a kitten in her lap when Florida knocked. It was not the usual happy *rat-a-tat-tat* knock. It was timid. It was scared. And Beth understood. Hannah told her that she let Florida come visit her. Beth had no recollection of her being there, but she feared what Florida must think of her now. That once she saw that sick girl in the bed she would only ever see that. The way Mother and Father see it. Like a ghost that haunts her. *You're haunting yourself now,* Beth thought. She didn't move to answer the door. She was still weak, and truth be told she wasn't sure if she was ready to see Florida. What they had between them, when Florida saw her as normal, was a precious thing, and now that would be gone. Now she would see the sickness that everyone else saw. And Beth knew, on her face she would see pity. She hated that part most of all.

Florida knocked again, a bit harder, and through the wood, Beth heard a timid, "Hello? Hannah? Beth? Is . . . is anyone home?"

Beth rose, steadying herself on the arm of the couch. She

placed the kitten on the cushion, and it mewed up at her, showing a tiny pink tongue. She smiled and petted it and the kitten tried to climb back onto her. "Not now, little one."

Beth gathered up the blankets on the couch, wrapping them around her to prevent a chill and also so that Florida wouldn't notice the very drab, very slept-in nightclothes she was still wearing all these hours later. She should have been dressed by now, but she didn't see the point.

She walked slowly, a dizziness starting in the base of her skull. It hummed and buzzed like a swarm of bees. She touched the edge of a nearby chair to keep her balance. That had been one of the lasting effects of the latest bout of illness. She felt dizzy all of the time. When she reached the door, she pulled it open. She couldn't recall it ever feeling so heavy.

Florida had already turned to go and was halfway down the path. She could have let her go. She could have said nothing and waited for next week to see if she would come back for another lesson. But something about the way the girl was walking—so heavy—made Beth call her name.

Florida spun around as if a shot had been fired. She sucked in air and placed a hand on her heart. She seemed surprised and relieved all at once. And then she ran, down the path and up the steps and Beth flinched thinking the girl was going to crash right into her. But she stopped right at the doorway and grabbed Beth's hands with her cold ones.

"Oh, my Beth! There you are. You look wonderful," Florida said, petting a hand over Beth's matted tangled hair.

"I . . . look dreadful."

Florida squeezed Beth's hands in her own gently. "No, you are an absolutely radiant doll. You have no idea how much joy it brings me to see you."

Beth couldn't help but smile. "Would you like to come in?" she asked as the cold sent a shiver through her body.

"Oh, of course! Yes, let's get you inside where it's warm and away from this chill." Florida wrapped an arm around Beth and brought her back into the warmth of Orchard House. Beth, weak, leaned into her and Florida happily took up the slack. She steered her toward the couch, stopping to give a pet to the kitten. "Oh, what a little dear," she said.

When they were both settled and Beth pulled the blankets tighter around herself, she said, "Can I get you something to drink?" Even though she knew the idea of brewing even a cup of tea for Florida seemed exhausting.

"No, absolutely not. I need nothing more than to look upon your sweet face. I have missed you, my Beth."

"I'm sorry. Hannah . . . she told me you were here. When I was . . ." Beth trailed off and looked down at the floor. She worried what Florida had seen. What she thought now.

"I did come by, and Hannah was kind enough to let me come up and see you. I held a cool cloth to your forehead while Hannah gave you medicine. Do you remember?"

Beth thought back to last weekend but even her memories were burned up by the fever. She vaguely recalled seeing a face she did not know. "I don't think I do. But thank you for caring for me."

"I was happy to help." Florida said it as if she meant it, but there was something clipped in her voice, something shadowy in her eyes. Something that said Florida had been scared, maybe. Or worse, repulsed.

"I know that when I am in the midst of a fit I can sometimes say things I do not mean. My sister Jo one time told me that I said I absolutely hated Amy, and of course that isn't true. It's the fever."

Florida pressed her lips together and smiled, tilting her head to the side. She shook it slowly and said, "No, I don't recall you saying anything at all, dear."

Beth immediately appreciated the lie, but she couldn't help

but wonder why, after she had been so sick and probably said terrible things, Florida came back.

"Are you here for a lesson?" she asked. "Because I don't know if I am well enough right now."

"Oh no, of course not. I'm here to see you. That is all. I have spent a week worrying about you. Worrying if you were going to get better. Worrying if . . ,"

"I'm sorry to have made you worry so. I seem to do that to everyone I . . . care about."

Florida snapped to attention. "You care about? I care, too, Beth. I care very much and that is why I was worrying. The thought of you being in pain kept me up at night. I sat at my window gazing at the stars and trying to remember which ones you picked for your sisters and then thinking about our talk about the Northern Lights. All I wanted this whole week was to see you again, to talk to you." Florida took Beth's hand and pressed it to her own cheek and Beth felt herself blush.

They were quiet for a moment before Florida said, "May I speak frankly?"

Beth stiffened but nodded, a lump forming in her throat. She was both afraid and expectant for whatever it was that Florida was going to say.

"Will you tell me how? How it happened? How you got the fever that first time?"

Beth took a breath. The dead baby's face floated before her. "It was during the war. There was a poor family that I would bring food to. The Hummels. Their infant was sick. The mother, she had so many children and no food and they didn't speak English. She gave me the baby to hold. I caught it from her."

"What a terrible thing that such a kind act of generosity was repaid as such. Sometimes the universe makes no sense."

"Do you see me differently now?" Beth asked, dropping her gaze. "Like a broken thing?"

Florida made a small noise in her throat. She lifted Beth's

chin gently with her finger until Beth was looking at her. "You are not broken."

"That is how my family sees me. Even my sisters. When they look at me their eyes are clouded with worry. With the memory of what happened. It's as if they're all just waiting for everything to go bad again. And each time I get sick, each time I am feverish, that worry deepens. I worry they do not see me as me, but instead as a tragedy."

"If their fear has clouded their faces, it has not touched their hearts. They worry because they love you."

"I know, but I worry they just see illness when they look at me. And then I think that is all I am. I hate it, Florida. I get so angry sometimes." A single tear slipped down Beth's cheek.

"What if," Florida said, "instead of seeing yourself as well or sick you just let yourself be? Just be. Just like everyone else. We do not know what will happen in this life. We do not know our fate. What mountain might shake if you gifted yourself the space to just *be*. What if you stopped holding your breath and fearing another bout of illness? And what if you stopped worrying about them?"

"I don't understand," Beth said.

"Just be. Do the things you want to do. Rest when needed, but *live* too. Live outside this house, lovely as it is. Take risks," Florida said. And then, "Teach pushy, silly young women to play the piano even though they are probably hopeless at it."

Beth looked up to see the most beautiful smile on her face. Just be. Maybe she could.

"Have you been practicing?"

"All week, teacher."

"Show me."

Florida went to the piano and played for Beth. It wasn't perfect and she missed some notes and had to start over more than once but, in this moment, it was the most beautiful music Beth had ever heard. To think that she was the reason that Florida was playing the piano, clumsily as she may have been, filled Beth with a feeling she wasn't familiar with.

When the front door opened and Beth's mother came in, Florida stopped playing. Beth's mother looked from her to Beth on the couch, who instinctively pulled her blanket up higher. She felt exposed and couldn't understand why. It was something about the way her mother was looking at her and then at Florida. As if they were somehow wrong. As if they shouldn't be here in this moment together.

"Oh, Florida, it's lovely to see you again. I was just with your mother."

"Lovely to see you too, Mrs. March."

Mother put her basket down and kicked the snow off her boots. She unwrapped her shawl and hung it on the hook by the door and then crossed the room and knelt down by Beth. "Hello, Cricket. How are we feeling?" She pressed a hand to Beth's forehead, even though her fever had been gone for days.

"I'm well, Marmee."

Beth's mother furrowed her brow. "Are we sure we aren't over exerting ourselves?" She glanced at Florida. It was just a quick dart of the eyes, but Beth saw. And, worse, so did Florida.

"I should go," Florida said, getting up off the piano bench.

"It's probably for the best," Mother added, quietly.

Beth felt anger stir in her. "No, please stay. I like the company."

"I think it's time for you to rest, don't you?" her mother replied. The way she said it sounded more like a direction instead of a question.

Beth fixed her eyes on her mother. She was not like Meg or Amy or Jo. All of them had at some point in their childhood challenged their mother. Pushed back to understand where the line was. But Beth never did that. She always bowed her head, always followed her direction. She never spoke out, let alone up. But watching Florida gather her things and make polite chitchat, her anger forced her lips apart.

"Rest? What do you think I have been doing? What do you think my whole life has been?"

Her mother started as if she'd been slapped. "Beth, this doesn't sound like you."

"Maybe it does." She kept talking even though her voice dropped to just above a whisper. "Maybe I just never say it."

"Well," her mother said, looking flushed, "what would you like then?"

"I would like Florida to stay. I appreciate the company, especially as I have been alone all day."

"I see. But don't you think tomorrow would be better?" Beth's mother said.

"Florida, I would like you to stay." Beth didn't shout it. She didn't need to. Her anger was painted on each word. She wore it on her face like a shield. Florida stopped putting on her shawl and stood there, her eyes locked on Beth. "Please."

Mother looked at her daughter and stammered a quick, "Oh, of course," before crossing the room and heading up the staircase. As she went, she offered a quiet, "Let me know if you need anything."

Florida stood there, watching her go.

"Please," Beth said, holding out her hand, beckoning the girl to join her on the couch.

"Are you sure?" Florida said. Beth didn't recall her ever sounding so timid.

"Yes, please," Beth said, scooting over on the couch to make room for her.

"Wow, that was a Beth March I haven't seen," Florida said, as she sat and fiddled with the edge of the blanket.

"Was I terrible?" Beth asked softly. "I didn't mean to be rude. I am just tired of being told what to do all the time. I'm tired of being treated like I'll break."

"No. You knew what you wanted and you stated it. I'm very proud of you. If you want my company, I'm always happy to be with you."

"I don't . . . I don't like being told what is good for me all the time. I want to be the one who decides. They still treat me like a child. Like a sick thing."

"Well, you're neither. So good for you."

Beth smiled. But the truth was she was tired. Mother could very well be right that she should be resting. But she didn't want Florida to leave. Every moment she spent with her, she felt better. More fully formed. Like a real person. "Tell me a story, Florida."

"What about?"

"About your life."

And so she did. She talked about Boston and her family fighting for suffrage. She talked about the school she attended, one of the few schools in Boston that all races could attend. Though it was still hard for her. The white children were cruel. She talked about her fears and her hopes and her dreams of her future. And Beth listened, until exhaustion took her, and she started to doze. When she did, Florida stayed to hold her hand while she slept.

The Northern Lights

Their lessons continued and each week they sat together, sharing that piano bench, hip to hip and shoulder to shoulder. Florida was a quick learner and she was getting better at keeping up with Beth when they played together. When she completed a song, Florida clapped her hands and cheered for both of them, causing Beth to blush.

"You really must congratulate yourself more, Beth. You are very talented. You could play on the stage, you know."

"I couldn't. I've neither the talent nor the disposition That is for my sisters."

Florida leaned in close, so close that Beth's breath caught, and she felt something flutter in her throat. Florida's big brown eyes were like an ocean she could swim away in. She could get lost in them and happily disappear forever. For a moment Beth wished time would freeze and she would always be here, looking at Florida.

When she spoke, Florida did so softly. "I want to tell you something and I want you to know it in your deepest heart. I want you to lock it there and keep it forever."

Beth managed a nod.

"I don't see what happened to you when I look at you. And I'm not trying to say that it doesn't matter, because of course it does. It has shaped your life. It still does. It is important and I understand why your family focuses on it. But I don't see that. I see *you*. You are funny. You are the most generous creature I have ever met. You are sweet and thoughtful. You are also an immensely talented woman. Which, based on your descriptions, makes you no different from your equally talented sisters. I would give anything to show you how you look to me."

Beth smiled and then was struck with a deep sadness.

"What is it?" Florida asked.

"I miss them. I worry about Amy on her own and far from home. It feels as if she has been gone forever. I know she craves adventures and love, but she is my little sister, even if she is grown. I worry that when we were younger I wasn't a very good big sister to her. I was too busy following Jo around like a puppy dog. I didn't take good care of Amy. She and Jo, they argued so much."

"Enough that Amy burnt up Jo's manuscript."

"Oh, yes. I forgot I told you that. Amy regretted it the moment it happened. But Jo, well, she never let it go. I always felt stuck between the two of them. Even when we were little, Amy wanted nothing more than to grow up as quickly as possible. I worry that in those moments, when they were arguing that I took Jo's side too often. I was always so proud of her, of the stories she wrote and how different she was from everyone. I was so shy, and she was so brave that around her I felt a little braver. Amy was also brave, and talented. I think, for Jo, it felt like there wasn't enough room in our home for both of them. But I was Amy's big sister. I should have tried harder. I should have stood up for her."

"I'm sure Amy doesn't feel that way."

"I worry she does. It's been a while since her last letter."

"She's traveling. Letters take a long time to travel, especially over a big ocean. I'm sure that any day now you and I will walk to the post office and find a delightful letter from Amy detailing all her adventures and we will laugh at how silly you were for thinking her upset. I am an only child, but I know if I had a big sister there isn't a thing she could do wrong. She would be my idol."

"That's kind of you."

"What do you think it is like, where she is traveling?"

"I think it smells like roses everywhere. And all the gentlemen can play the piano. And women never have muddy dress hems."

Florida laughed, kicking up her own snow-stained skirt. "I would never fit in."

"Nor I. Do you remember when I agreed to teach you piano? Do you remember what you said? About me and my sisters?"

"I said that they may be stars, but you are the Northern Lights."

"What did you mean?"

"I meant, Beth March, that I think you are magic—the kind of magic that stops people cold. Stars are beautiful, but there are so many in the night sky. They are small bits of light that honestly can only awe when they are viewed as a whole. But the Northern Lights come when they want, flashing a brilliant green across the night sky and then, just as quickly as they came, they are gone. They are temporary, yes, but to those who have seen them . . ." Florida paused and took Beth's hand in hers. She lifted it to her lips and ever so gently, as delicate as butterfly wings, she kissed the back of her hand. She looked up at Beth and said, "To those who have seen them, they can never ever be forgotten."

Beth blushed deeply but could not look away. She whispered, "You make me believe I can do anything."

"That . . . that might be the sweetest thing someone has ever said to me." Now it was Florida's turn to blush and look away.

There was a beat and then another and it looked like Florida was going to say something, and for some reason this frightened Beth, so instead she said, "Shall we play?"

Florida cleared her throat and smiled a closed-lip smile as if there was something she needed to keep inside. "I would love that."

And so they did, with their shoulders and hips gently touching. The warmth of their skin coming through the fabric of their dresses, warmer today, as if they were both running a shared fever. At one point, a shy right pinky of Florida's hand grazed the even more shy left pinky of Beth's hand as they moved over the ivory keys, and for a moment Beth couldn't breathe and didn't care if she never did again.

An Unwanted Gift

The following Sunday, Florida was late to her lesson. Beth continued to peek out the window, waiting to see her come up the front steps. But one hour turned into two and there was no Florida. A sinking sadness started to fill her chest. She felt lonely, as lonely as she had before Florida and her family burst into the living room those many weeks ago. It was as if Florida was the daylight, the very sun herself, and without her Beth could not find her way. She thought about how scared she had been that day. How scared she had always been until now.

She continued to look out the window until a cold feeling settled over her. What if something happened? What if Florida was hurt? She pulled her shawl off the hook at the door and went into the kitchen.

"Hannah?" she said, as the old woman raised her head.

"What is it, dear? You look affrighted."

"I'm going for a walk. Let my parents know if they ask. I won't be long."

"Are you okay to go alone?" Hannah asked, but Beth was already through the kitchen door, making her way to the front door before she even got the words out. She knew that Florida and her family were staying with the Nelson family, up the road from the center of town. It was not a long walk but she had never taken it alone. In her youth her sisters were with her, or her parents, and now, if she went to town Hannah always came. But Florida did it every Sunday to see her and if she could do it, then Beth could do it.

She walked carefully, mindful of ice, and though her skirt hems were damp by the time she arrived she kept going, trying not to think about what to say, until she was standing in front of the Nelsons' door. She knocked softly at first but then louder.

The way Florida did.

A woman she recognized as Mrs. Nelson answered the door. "May I help you?"

"Hello, ma'am," Beth said, and offered a little curtsy because though she tried to be brave she was awfully nervous. She squeezed her hands together to stop them from shaking. "I'm terribly sorry to call unannounced, but I was looking for Ms. Florida Ronson. We had an appointment today."

"Beth?" a voice from behind the lady said.

When Florida peeked her head out, relief flooded Beth, filling in all the pocked empty spaces. Florida was okay. "What happened? When you didn't come for your lesson, I was so worried."

"I'm sorry, Mrs. Nelson," Florida said as she joined Beth on the front porch and closed the door.

"Are you ill?" Beth asked. Florida's eyes were red, and Beth knew starkly and fully that she had been crying.

"Come sit down," she said, motioning toward the bench on the porch. The sun was strong that day, so the wood felt warm beneath them.

"What is it?" Beth pressed. "You're scaring me."

"I'm fine. It's just . . . my father—" Florida's voice caught, and Beth took her hand. This seemed to help, and after making a small, strangled noise in her throat, Florida continued. "My father has been offered a lecturing position, to speak to other freemen about suffrage."

"Oh, but that's wonderful!"

"Not here."

Beth felt her stomach drop, as if she'd been pushed, violently, off a ledge. "Where?"

"Throughout the country and then eventually into Europe."

"Oh," Beth said softly. She stared hard and long at the wooden slats of the porch, the way the grain of the wood knotted and curled. The wood seemed to stretch away from her, the way time was now stretching away from her and taking Florida with it.

A small noise came from Florida. Something that pulled Beth out of her own thoughts. She reached up and brushed the errant tear away. "Oh, Florida, it's what you wanted."

"How can you say that?" It was barely whispered.

Beth forced herself to smile. She could be brave. "You'll see so many places. New York. The South. The West. And then to Europe, where everything will smell of roses and you'll drink fancy cocktails, and never have muddy hems and—"

"And," Florida interrupted, "I won't have you."

Beth smiled hard, as if that could hold back the tears that pricked at her eyes. "We'll write all the time."

"I'll be moving too much. Our letters will be lost."

"No, they won't. I'll send a new letter every day. It will be filled with my strange little stories of stupid old Beth puttering around the house, which of course will be of no interest to anyone." She wanted it to be a joke, but the words fell like little stones from her lips.

"I'm so sad to leave you, my Beth."

"We'll see each other again," Beth offered, but she knew it was hollow. Florida would be gone for a long time. Years and years, and Beth knew in the darkest part of her heart that she didn't have years. Not anymore. She knew it even if she couldn't talk about it. It pulled at her, like the tide. She was running out of time and now Florida was leaving. Why was everyone always leaving her?

"Promise me you'll keep practicing."

"How shall we move a piano to all those places?"

"Oh, come now, you're resourceful and terribly bright. You'll find a way." Beth offered a smile she didn't feel, and bumped the girl's shoulder. "You'll get to see the world, Florida. Just like you wanted. This is a gift."

Florida fixed her beautiful brown eyes on Beth and said, "Then why does it feel like something I do not want?"

This Little Love

That night, there was a knock on the door. Beth knew it was Florida even though the knock did not resound with the bright cheerfulness Beth had come to love. It was not a knock that said hello.

It was a knock that said goodbye.

Beth answered the door with a smile on her face. The last thing she wanted was for her friend to see her sad. She was happy for her. As she was happy for Jo and Amy and Meg. She was just tired of being the one left behind.

"Shall we play, or shall we go for a walk?" Beth asked.

"I would like to play just one more time with you."

Beth opened the door wider, and Florida stepped inside. Beth tried not to think about how it would be the last time. Her parents were at the Ronsons' helping them to prepare for the tour. Her parents were delighted when Beth told them the news and they had rushed over right away, chattering about how Mr. Ronson alone could change the hearts of this seemingly cold nation. Beth did not feel as confident. She had heard Florida's stories. She knew that her neighbors, even in the north, saw them as unequal. Her own futility in the face of such ignorance filled Beth with a rage she would never have the words for.

"Let me," she said to Florida, taking the girl's cloak off and hanging it by the fire. She was careful with it, as if it were more than a piece of fabric, but something precious and a part of Florida. They sat at the piano together, knees and hips and shoulders touching. Beth tried not to think about how this would be the last time she would feel her, the way her body pressed, almost purposefully, against Beth's. She felt a longing she wasn't familiar with, and she wished she had the words to ask for the thing she didn't know how to name.

The thing she needed.

They played beautifully, fingers gliding over keys in perfect syncopation. Beth even caught a small smile on Florida's face. "You do have a gift," Beth whispered.

"I have what was given to me. It is your gift," Florida said, lifting her hands off the keys. She turned toward Beth. The whole of her thigh was now pressed against Beth's and she couldn't help but notice. It was as if she could feel her skin through the fabric. "In return, I'd like to give you a gift."

Florida threaded a ribbon that was weaved through her braids, out of her hair. She took Beth's left hand and tied it around her wrist. "So you don't forget me."

"Oh, Florida, I could never forget you. I do not need any such token."

"Just take it. Wear it always."

"I will." Beth touched the soft satin. She knew, instantly, she would never take it off.

"One more gift. But for this one you must close your eyes."

Beth smiled and did so, a giddiness dancing inside her. Being with Florida made even the saddest things more manageable.

She felt Florida shift on the bench and then she felt the lightest touch on the side of her face. A finger grazed her cheek, traced her jawbone, and then brushed lightly over her lips. Beth felt her heart quicken.

It was featherlight until it wasn't. Florida's lips tasted sweet, like cherries. Beth's hands went up and with her eyes still closed, found the girl's face as if she could hold her here, forever, locked in this kiss. As their lips parted and found each other again a fire lit up in her, hot and bright, as if she could burn away to nothingness.

As if they could burn together.

She didn't want it to end. Ending would mean it was finally over and she would have to say goodbye. Florida pulled back gently and looked at her. "Promise me, you'll never forget."

"I could never," Beth said.

Florida turned and gazed out the window. The snow had started again, and it was drifting slowly and lazily outside. The flakes taking their own time to find their place on the ground.

"I have a gift for you too," Beth said.

"My Beth, I want for nothing. You know that."

"Gifts are not for wanting. They are for accepting." Beth reached down and opened the small basket that contained her sheet music, and from it she pulled her only precious thing. She handed it to Florida, who looked it over, eyebrows raised.

" 'Little Women' by Beth March," she read.

"You asked me to tell you a story about me. This is my story. I don't have words to speak it, so music tells it for me. This is the only story I have, and I want it to belong to you."

"Oh, I couldn't," Florida stammered, flustered. Beth could see the tears forming in her eyes.

"I want you to play it. Every Sunday that you can find a piano in your travels, and when you can't, I want you to play it on your lap or on the tabletop. Every Sunday. And I will play it too. And it will be like we are still sitting here, just you and me, playing our story together."

Florida let out a stifled sob and hugged the music to her

274 Linda Epstein, Ally Malinenko, and Liz Parker

chest. "I promise. Every Sunday my soul will be spent with yours."

"And mine with yours."

Florida looked out the picture window and watched the snow tumble to the ground. "How beautiful everything is tonight."

Beth watched her, studied the gentle slope of her jawline, the soft pucker of her lips, the way her ears were just a touch tilted. She studied the girl, stitched her into her own heart so she would remember this in the end. So that when it finally was the last and truest goodbye, Florida would still somehow be there.

"I never planned anything."

"Pardon?" Florida said. "What, my Beth?"

"I like it when you say 'my Beth.'"

Florida laid her hand against Beth's cheek and Beth wanted to sink into it, to always be in Florida's hands, safe and loved.

"I never planned anything. I wasn't like my sisters. They all planned to marry or to go off and have great adventures. I never saw that for myself. And now, I think it is too late for plans."

Florida smoothed Beth's hair back. At first, she worried that loose strands would come out in the girl's fingers, and she felt a pang of embarrassment, but it faded just as quickly. Florida already knew. She knew immediately the way Beth knew. And it never frightened her.

"It's never too late for plans. There is only one cutoff point, you know." Florida winked at her. Beth smiled at her dark humor. "And you know that is the case for everyone. One life, correct? So, what would you do with this one precious life? What do you want to experience more than anything else? What great adventure have you dreamed about?"

"I think it just happened," Beth said, laying her forehead against Florida's.

Florida sighed deeply. "You are my Northern Lights, Beth March."

"Promise me, I will always be that to you."

"Always, my love."

It was no small thing, this little love. Beth wasn't sure when it started, how Florida had, like a seed, taken root inside her and grown to fill in the empty spaces. The spaces that Beth feared would never be filled. She wished they had started sooner, that they had more time. But she also knew even if she had decades it wouldn't have been enough. Beth wished the night would last forever, stretching out in an infinite moment where there was nothing but her and Florida and this feeling that lay inside her, feathery and light like their promise. She knew it couldn't, that nothing was permanent—not the night, or this feeling, or her life—but she wished for it, hard, all the same.

They stayed like that for a while, arms wrapped around each other, foreheads touching, still as a statue of two lovers, as the snow fell outside, covering Concord in a new fresh blanket of white.

PART FOUR

~ *Amy Curtis March* ~
Redux

When Genius Burns

Uncle Edward had a comprehensive list of tourist sights he intended for them all to visit, gleaned from his very studious reading of Baedeker's guide to the Rhine and Northern Germany. Traveling by railroad and carriage, they had been touring at a quick clip. They stopped in Koblentz for a brief time, then a whirlwind few days in Nassau. Finally Amy and her aunt, uncle, and cousin had arrived in a lovely hotel in Frankfurt, where they planned to stay for a couple of weeks. The previous day they had done quite a bit of walking throughout the city, including a visit to Goethe's house.

As they had trod through the childhood home of the great poet and playwright, Amy couldn't help but think of Jo, scribbling away in their attic back home in Concord when they were children. Goethe was a genius. Jo would certainly agree with that. But as Amy peeked in the rooms where the young Goethe had lived as a child, her mind returned to the *genius born or genius nurtured* conversation that plagued her.

Would Goethe's genius have had what it needed to manifest, had he been born into a family without means? What if he had not been given the advantage of years of private tutors and lessons? If he hadn't attended university at Leipzig and Strasbourg? Would that genius have had what it needed to flourish, without the security of financial support from his family? Perhaps.

And if Goethe had been born a woman? What then? Would the world still have *Faust* or "Prometheus" if the world told Goethe, from childhood, that his highest ambition should be having children and looking beautiful? What if Goethe's singular purpose, out of necessity, had been to put food on the table for the family? Amy thought back to Jo, who viewed her scribbles as a way make money. Amy thought Jo might have genius within, had she not been so busy writing thrillers and sensational stories to sell to magazines. What might Jo be able to write if she had the luxury of learning and studying and honing her craft? That's where she and her sister were different.

For what of herself? Did genius burn in the soul of Amy Curtis March? She didn't know. But genius or not, Amy knew her soul was that of an artist. And she couldn't, she *wouldn't*, put a monetary value on that. She didn't have the advantages of a wealthy family or of being a man. But she knew one thing she did have was the ability to choose. As a young girl she'd determined she would marry a wealthy man, because she knew that was the only way she might have the leisure and the means to be faithful to her artistic soul. But if she were to marry would she also have freedom? After they left Goethe's house, had one asked Amy anything about the particulars, she wouldn't have been able to answer. She had been in such deep contemplation, holding her cousin's arm and letting Florence lead the way, that the young artist who usually noticed everything in detail had paid attention to nothing.

Today Aunt Mary was staying back at the hotel, claiming a headache. Amy suspected her Aunt would rather spend the day in the hotel atrium, sipping tea and reading her well-worn copy of *The Queen: The Ladies Newspaper and Court Chronicle*, which she'd carried with her since they departed London. Uncle Edward's proposed itinerary for the day was slightly daunting, but Amy and Florence were game, being the young and enthusiastic girls they were. And so the three intrepid tourists embarked on another sight-filled day, and Uncle Edward happily ticked off entries on his checklist.

He was particularly keen to see Dannecker's famous statue, *Ariadne on the Panther*. It was to be their final destination of the day. Uncle Edward hired a carriage, as none of the three were interested in the hour-long walk to and from the country estate in Friedberger Landstrasse, which housed the marble lady. She resided in a building built exclusively for her exhibition, called the Ariadneum.

Uncle Edward and Florence were strolling the gallery and chatting. Amy stood before the great statue alone, sketchbook in hand, wondering at the marble princess draped across the back of the panther. She was transfixed. Ariadne's crossed leg was tucked beneath her thigh, toes peeking out behind her hand, which casually rested upon the foot. Amy gazed at these touch-points of princess on cat, which the artist had imbued with breathtaking, casual beauty, as if they were a landscape. Dannecker had described his sculpture as an expression of the idea of wildness tamed by beauty.

When Amy, Florence, and Uncle Edward had first looked at the statue together, Amy couldn't recall the story of Ariadne. She had been too embarrassed to say so though, for even Florence seemed to somehow know the significance of the great cat. As she stood alone before the statue now, considering it, Amy only remembered Ariadne helping Theseus out of his maze troubles with the Minotaur. That took her thoughts back to Fred and their adventure in the hedge maze at Hampton Court, which then reminded her of the imminence of his arrival in Frankfurt any day.

Before she had left Paris—and before her final rendezvous

with Laurie at the Louvre and their unexpected kiss—Amy would have looked forward to reuniting with Fred. But that kiss had left her confused and conflicted. What did it mean? She'd gone over it repeatedly in her mind and couldn't come to a conclusion. She had known Laurie since she was a little girl. She had always loved him and knew it if she thought honestly about him.

It wasn't just his generosity to her family, which of course had been extraordinary. Besides being her great protector against Jo's merciless teasing, it was that Laurie truly knew her and had *always* recognized who she was. She remembered back to when she was banished to Plumfield to stay with Aunt March when Beth was first ill. It wasn't only that Laurie had visited every day and taken her out gallivanting, as he'd promised. Yes, they had gone on long walks on the grounds of Plumfield, out for drives in his carriage, and even to the theatre. But all the while they talked and laughed, and he never treated her as silly or frivolous or someone not to be taken seriously.

When she had written her childish last will and testament, to dispose of her worldly goods were she to meet an early demise, he hadn't mocked her. Of course she had nothing of substance to leave anyone when she was twelve years old. Yet of all the things she might have written, she had thought to leave Laurie her art. She smiled, remembering her model of a clay horse, which Laurie had correctly critiqued as lacking a neck.

Her thoughts and her gaze returned to *Ariadne on the Panther*. She admired the sleek fierceness of Dannecker's wild cat. It was true. She had always loved Laurie because he could see her heart. Would that she could see his, too, so she might understand what the kiss meant.

Later, when they returned to the hotel in early evening, they were hungry and tired, but satisfied with a full day of sightseeing. Aunt Mary met them at the lobby.

"This came in the post," Aunt Mary said. "It looks like

young Mr. Laurence has written you from Athens." Amy's heart began to race, and she wanted to snatch the envelope from her aunt's hand. She was so practiced, though, in hiding her true emotions that she serenely accepted the letter and merely said, "Oh, thank you, Aunt." But she needed to turn her face away because she couldn't control the blush that was quickly rushing from her neck to her cheeks. She placidly followed Florence up to their room so they might change out of their day dresses, and with each step she took her stomach did a flip-flop.

Florence sat on a chair in the corner of their room, unbuttoning her shoes. "I told Mama I would meet her in the hotel solarium before dinner," she said. "Will you join?"

"You go ahead, dear," Amy said. "I think I will rest for a moment before going down."

Amy felt as if the letter, which she had placed atop the bureau, were magnetic, and it took all of her restraint not to rip it open. Instead, she folded her gloves neatly and put them in the bureau drawer.

"Perhaps I will draw a bit," she said. "I promised my sisters I would pile heaps of drawings at their feet from every city where we traveled. London and Paris are well represented, so I can't let our quick pace through Germany trip me up."

Florence gave Amy a quick hug. "You are single-minded, Cousin," she said. "So dedicated to your sisters and your drawing."

Amy patted Florence's arm. "As you are to your parents and to me," she replied.

When Florence left, Amy sat on the edge of the bed. She tried to take a deep breath—at least as deep as her corset would allow—then she opened the letter.

Letter From a Friend

Athens, Greece
My Lady,
　I trust you are well and that your
journey to Germany has presented few difficulties. I hope the itinerary your uncle or-
ganized has been pleasant for you and
Florence, and that you are able to visit all
that you wish to see and experience. Frank
arranged our travels to Greece through
Thomas Cook and Son, a new sort of agency
which offers excursions for groups of travelers. As such, we have been relieved of any
duties to set our own itinerary, find accommodation, or procure transport. The
freedom from having to attend to the particulars of travel has been quite agreeable.
Frank and I are united in our fondness for
a bit of carousal, and as such have been
greatly enjoying a pleasant anise-flavored
aperitif throughout our travels.

The small smile that had rested on Amy's face as she had been reading Laurie's letter wavered for a moment. She paused in her reading, brows furrowed in concern. She hoped Laurie and Frank weren't being *too* intemperate. Coming from a family that only drank spirits medicinally, Amy had learned to adjust her judgment of European alcohol consumption since traveling abroad. She couldn't help feeling uneasy though, knowing Laurie's voracious appetite for living life to its fullest and hence not always exhibiting restraint when he ought. She continued to read.

He wrote to her about the quick pace at which their group was traveling and the wonder of visiting ancient Greek sights he had only read about. He wrote, *At the Temple of Athena Nike, I thought of you and how much you'd love to see where the Elgin Marbles had originated.* She smiled at the thought of Laurie standing in the Temple of Athena, thinking of her.

He told her about the exotic foods they had tasted, how balmy the weather was, and how pleasurable it was to travel with Frank, who he described as *a like-minded soul.* Amy thought about Frank and Fred and how different the brothers were. It was hard to believe they were twins. On and on Laurie's letter went, in his slapdash yet elegant scrawl, chatty and informative and friendly.

Toward the bottom of the last page, under a smudge of ink that hadn't been adequately blotted, Amy slowly read the last few sentences of Laurie's letter.

I must apologize, he'd written, *for my actions last we met at the Louvre. I behaved in a most ungentlemanly manner towards a friend I cherish dearly.* Amy sniffed and swiped at the corner of her eye, which had unexpectedly teared up when she read the word *friend.* She hadn't known what to make of the kiss. She had pondered and wondered and spun myriad explanations and fantasy stories about the resulting repercussions it might have. She had begun to lend more weight to the reservations she'd been trying to suppress about an impending proposal coming from Fred.

He continued, *My dearest wish is that our friendship remain that of bosom friends. You may count on me to not speak of it again and I sincerely beg your pardon. Ever yours, Laurie*

Amy slowly refolded the letter, thinking about the kiss and how she had been surprised, but not unpleasantly. She remembered running her hands through his hair and the feel of his body against hers. The softness of his lips and then the urgency of the second kiss. How her heart had raced. How right it had felt. Rising from her perch on the edge of the bed, again she tried unsuccessfully to draw in a deep breath. She cleared her throat.

With a determined step and a resolute expression on her face she strode to the bureau and placed the letter in her drawer, beneath the packet of correspondence from home. Then, with the dexterity of a young lady who has refined the art of suppressing unwanted feelings, she said out loud to the empty room, "Well then, friend it is, and that will be that."

As she said it, something fractured in her heart, but she refused to pay it any attention.

Like in a Romance

Heidelberg was a very beautiful city and from where she had stood on a terrace at the ruins of the great castle, Amy had very much appreciated the view. It had been nearing sunset. The soft music of an Austrian band drifted up from below and the Neckar river slowly rolled its way through the valley. Florence and Amy had come to Heidelberger Schloss with a group of young people with whom they had been keeping company. They had all poked about the ruins, viewed the enormous tun, and ambled the decrepit gardens which, despite the decay around them, had retained their beauty. When the others had gone to look around inside, Amy had stayed on the great terrace, trying to draw. Fred had gone to the poste restante to pick up his letters and was to meet them after.

A slight breeze had ruffled the page in Amy's hand, and she had breathed a small sigh of relief as she welcomed the bit of solitude. For weeks they had been on the move, each day delightfully crammed with activity, and Amy had barely taken time to draw, let alone put brush to paper. Since he'd met them in Frankfurt, Fred had been resolutely courting her and Amy had made the purposeful decision to enjoy it and try not to think too much. Aunt Mary and Uncle Edward were very encouraging of the progressing relationship.

From Frankfurt they had traveled to Nassau and Bad Ems. There they enjoyed the excitement of the casino, strolled the footpaths and curated vistas surrounding the Kurhaus, and partook of the famous spa, where they drank, bathed in, and took inhalation treatments of the celebrated mineral waters. Then on to Koblentz, where they had met some like-minded young travelers. Their days were full, visiting tourist sights, shopping, and making excursions into the countryside. On a boat down the Rhine, Fred had befriended some students from Bern, expanding their circle even wider. Amy had gotten caught up in the dizzying frenzy of activity.

But even as she was enjoying a tranquil moment, Amy had found it almost impossible to concentrate enough to create even a passable rendering of a delicate vine of coral honeysuckle, which had intrepidly climbed a stone wall on the terrace, and prettily obscured the relief of a lion's head.

Laurie hadn't written again after the newsy letter from Greece, culminating in his effective erasure of their kiss in the Louvre. Little by little Amy had succeeded in putting him out of her mind entirely. That had felt like a much more practical pursuit than delving into an examination of her feelings about the kiss, about Laurie, or about what she might want. Instead, she had let herself be swept away by Fred's courting.

It only took a bit of effort to overlook all the small ways Fred irritated her. She had tamped down any furtive misgivings that were trying to make themselves known and had allowed herself the indulgence of starry-eyed fantasies of being Mrs. Fred Vaughn. It was easier to do when she was thinking about Fred, rather than spending actual time in his company.

Sitting sketchbook in hand on the terrace, waiting for Fred's arrival, Amy had felt as if she was in a romance. She had imagined what it might look like were someone to sketch a picture: a golden-haired young lady in a cornflower-blue dress, at sunset, waiting for her lover to arrive, just like in a fairy tale. Finally Fred had come hurrying up and found her.

And here they were now, Fred holding her by both hands, and she felt flooded with emotion. Unfortunately, they weren't the sentiments she might wish for.

"Amy?" he said. His pale blue eyes searched her bright gray ones.

"I'm sorry, what?" she replied, flustered. She had been trying to focus on him, on this young man in front of her, but thoughts of that other young man kept intruding. She returned her gaze to Fred, with his fair skin and ashy-blond hair parted neatly on the side. She let one of his hands go and reached nervously to fuss at her own hair. She looked from his eyes to his chin, which was full of whiskers, in the English style. She thought his beard a bit anemic, even for a young man of twenty-two years. Touching her mouth, she wondered what it would feel like to finally be kissed by him. Then she remembered Laurie's smooth-shaven cheek, the silkiness of his chestnut-brown hair, and the softness of his lips against hers.

She blinked, trying to clear her head. He wasn't Laurie. This wasn't Paris. And she would *not* allow herself to destroy this. This was Heidelberg and Fred, who marched through his life so sure of himself, knowing exactly what he wanted. He might not be musical or artistic or make her laugh. He might not be a romantic Italian full of emotion and impulsivity and vivacity. But Fred was as dependable as the whole British Empire, devoted as an Irish setter, and had been absolutely steadfast in his courting of her.

He took her nervously wandering hand in his own and squeezed her fingers gently, bringing her gaze back to him and his earnest eyes. "I said I shall soon come back—you won't forget me?"

"But why would I forget you?" she said. "Where are you going?"

"I must go to Greece." He sighed and looked away, but kept ahold of her hands. Then he turned back to her with a resolute demeanor. "Frank has taken ill. I must go care for him until he's well enough to travel. My parents have requested that I deliver him home."

She had often heard that Frank wasn't well, but she had never known the nature of his illness. Neither Fred nor any of the Vaughns had ever mentioned it.

"But he's with Laurie," Amy said. "I'm sure Laurie is caring for him."

"I promised my parents I would go and bring him home," Fred said again, with a nod of his head.

"But Laurie has always been such a great help to my family," Amy said. Fred was shaking his head in a way that suggested he had something to say but was holding back. "I'm certain he would nurse Frank back to health," Amy said. "They've always been such great friends to each other."

"Oh, Amy," Fred said, "you dear, innocent girl."

Amy frowned. If there was one thing Amy couldn't stand, it was being condescended to. She pulled her hands from his and leaned away from him.

"Mr. Vaughn," she haughtily said, "of *what* am I being innocent?" She stood, throwing her shoulders back, and as a slight breeze passed, it sent a ripple through her loosely pinned hair. She was never more beautiful than when miffed.

"I'm afraid my parents don't trust Laurence with the task," Fred said, a mean little laugh escaping.

"Not trust . . ." Amy didn't finish the sentence as she shook her head in puzzlement. For once she was speechless. Then she said, "What on earth are you talking about, Fred?"

Amy knew Laurie could sometimes be given to a bit of overindulgence, but he was never unreliable. He lived his life as an adventure, and wanted to experience everything profoundly. It was one of the things she loved about him. He had always been a breath of fresh air in a home that often felt onerously laden with rules and judgments. Yes, sometimes he would drive his carriage a tad too fast, drink a little too much champagne at a dance, or become so enamored of a bit of music or a poem, he could hardly concentrate on anything else. Back home in Concord he was considered the most honorable and generous of young men, and someone the whole March family counted upon.

Fred cleared his throat and looked away.

"If Frank is ill and with Laurie, it makes no sense that you would need to go care for him or collect him. Theodore Laurence is dependable and capable. He's an honorable person and I would trust him with my own life," Amy said.

"I know that Laurence has been kind to you," Fred said, still looking away. "And I am too much of a gentleman to engage in indecorous conversation with a young woman whom I admire very much." He sniffed and cleared his throat again. "Please understand that . . ." He shook his head and didn't finish the sentence. Amy had never seen Fred look so uncomfortable.

Still not meeting Amy's gaze Fred said, "My brother and Laurence share proclivities which . . . they have a predilection for . . ." He finally turned back and looked imploringly at her. She frowned, still not understanding to what he was alluding.

"Frank has sometimes suffered from a weakness of disposition," he finally said, "and I would prefer not to malign the character of either my brother or Laurence." Amy leaned toward him, still trying to grasp what he was saying without saying it. He continued, "But ever since our days at school, their friendship has sometimes lacked propriety." He purposefully nodded his head, as if he had finally made himself clear. Which he hadn't.

"And so, my parents would rather I went to collect Frank

than entrust Laurence, who—although a great friend to you and your family—has been known to contribute to that frailty of temperament."

It was frustrating that he wouldn't come out and just tell her to what he was alluding. It was so very British. Was Fred—who was known to overindulge in the drink himself, leading to more than a few unwise choices in gambling—passing judgment on Laurie as unreliable or suspect due to intemperance? That seemed unlikely. She just couldn't guess what he was talking about, so she decided to surrender to not knowing and reflect upon it later.

Taking up her hand, Fred said, "Let's not argue, my dear." She drew in a deep breath. "I say again, I shall soon come back, and I ask you not to forget me." She gave his hand a slight squeeze. Tilting her head, she forced a small smile. And although Amy didn't promise him anything, Fred seemed satisfied with the way she looked at him.

A Letter to Mother

Heidelberg, Germany
My dear Marmee:
  Having a quiet hour before we leave Heidelberg for Switzerland on our way to Rome, where we will spend the winter. I hope all is well at home. I'm sorry I haven't written as much as I ought. Since leaving Paris we have traveled at a rapid pace, each day filled with more liveliness than the last. I'll try to fill you in on everything, for some of it is quite consequential, as you will see.
  Frankfurt was delightful; I saw Goethe's house, Schiller's statue, and Dannecker's famous "Ariadne." It was very lovely, but I should have enjoyed it more if I had known the story better. The baths at Nassau were jolly, although Fred lost some money, and I scolded him. He would do well to have

someone to look after him. His sister Kate said once she hoped he'd marry soon, and I quite agree with her that it would do him well.

At Koblentz we had a lovely time, for some friends with whom Fred had got acquainted, gave us a serenade. It was a moonlit night, and Florence and I were awakened by the most delicious music under our windows. We peeped behind the curtains and saw Fred and the others singing down below. It was quite romantic, Marmee--the river, the bridge, the boats, the great fortress opposite, moonlight everywhere, and music fit to melt a heart of stone. Afterwards I wanted to reproduce it in pastels, but I hadn't the time, as we were soon off on our next adventure. I don't think I could have evoked the romance of it though. The beauty of the moonlight would have been lost, I fear.

When the boys were done singing, we threw down some flowers, and saw them scramble for them, kiss their hands up to us and go laughing away--to smoke and drink beer, I suppose. The next morning Fred showed me one of the crumpled flowers in his vest pocket and looked very sentimental. It begins to look like his feelings toward me are growing.

The sail down the Rhine was perfect, and I enjoyed it with all my might. It was just as Father's old guidebooks had described. I haven't words beautiful enough to evoke it, but I keep thinking I might be able to capture it with pencil or pastel.

Fred has been so kind, and I have grown quite fond of him. I haven't flirted, Mother, truly, but remembered what you said to me, and have done my very best. I can't help it if people like me; I don't try to make them, and it worries me that perhaps they are enamored of an idea of Amy March rather than of me, myself. Jo says I am too sensitive and haven't got any heart when it comes to others. Now I know you will be relieved, although my sister will probably say, "Oh, mercenary little wretch!" but I've made up my mind, and, if Fred asks me, I shall accept him, though I'm not madly in love.

I like him well enough, and we get on comfortably together. He is young, sometimes clever, and very rich, which I know will be helpful to you and father. I know his family won't object, for they are all kind, well-bred, generous people, and they have been quite encouraging of our friendship.

You've always said that one of us must marry well; Meg didn't, Jo won't, Beth can't yet, so I shall do as you and father hoped, and make everything cozy all round for the family. I wouldn't marry a man I hated or despised. You may be sure of that, and, though Fred is not my model hero, he does very well, and, in time, I imagine I should get fond enough of him, as I can see he is

very fond of me. I trust he will let me do
just as I like, painting and sketching. So I've
been turning the matter over in my mind
the last week, for it was impossible to help
seeing how much Fred likes me.

Last evening we went up to the castle
about sunset--at least all of us but Fred,
who was to meet us there. When he finally
arrived he came hurrying through the
great arch to find me. He looked so troubled
that I forgot all about myself and asked
what the matter was. He said he'd got a letter and he needed to leave, for Frank is
very ill in Greece; he was going on the night
train, and only had time to say goodbye.

I know he's been meaning to speak, but I
think, from something he once hinted, that
he had promised his father not to do
anything for a short while. We shall soon
meet again in Nice; and then, if I don't
change my mind, I'll say "Yes, thank you,"
when he says, "Will you, please?"

Of course this is all very private, but I
wished you to know what was on the hori-
zon. Don't be anxious about me; remember
I am your "prudent Amy," and be sure I
will do nothing rashly. I know you will send
me all of your advice; I'll use it if I can.
Love and trust me, Marmee.
Ever yours,
Amy

Rome

To Beth

Rome, Italy
My dearest Beth,
　We are settled in Rome and although the temperature has been fairly mild, at least as compared with our cold Massachusetts winters, it has been wet and gray all week. We have taken an apartment in Piazza Barberini where, until it began to rain, it was very bright and cheerful. One can see the fountain of the Triton from our window, which is a very attractive view.

　It is a comfort to have our own rooms once more and stay put for a while, after lodging in hotels and pensions these past months. The swiftness with which we were travelling was exhilarating yet quite tiring. Now Flo and I are huddled near the stove, trying to ward off the chill, and having a pleasant, lazy afternoon reading and

drawing and writing long letters home.
With every day an adventure, sometimes
it's nice to stay home and have a simple cup
of tea and toast with jam and not worry
about things such as the correct fork to use
or if I want to eat snails.

Now that we are not busy being tourists
for a moment, I also have time to miss
home, and when I think of home I think of
you. I think about you keeping the hearth
fire warm. Sweet and loving. Reliable as
the north star. It's a comfort to me, knowing you are always there. At the Borghese
Gardens, Florence and I both thought of
Meg, who would have surely known the
names of every blossom, blooming or not.
And even though I believe she's already
read Mr. Hawthorne's The Marble Faun, I
have picked up another edition for Jo, as
here they were published with the title
Transformation: or the Romance of Monte
Beni and I think she might care to have
that.

The other day Uncle Edward had us visit
the Roman catacombs and Aunt Mary
hadn't begged off, which she often does, and
while we were down there she nearly
fainted. If I hadn't been concerned for her
health it might have been humorous. He
has us set to see the Coliseum in the moonlight. The longer we travel together the
more Uncle Edward surprises me. Doesn't
it all sound so romantic, Beth? And of
course it is! Every which way one turns

there's a piazza with a Baroque fontana, a palazzo brimming with Renaissance masterpieces, or another via ending in picturesque ancient ruins. I feel so spoiled to say that for the moment I may have had enough seeing of sights. I believe I've become benumbed!

In all the time I've been away, this is the first time I wish I were back in Concord. If I were home, you and I would crawl under the afghan together on a rainy day such as this, cuddling as we used to, on the settee in the parlor. We might be children again for a moment. Remember how Hannah would sneak us a spoon of honey to suck? At the moment nothing seems sweeter than that memory.

Has Jo returned home? I haven't had a letter from her in quite some time. I look forward to hearing more about her exploits in New York and hope she hasn't gotten herself into any scrapes. When you visit our Meg, please give the twin cherubs a squeeze from their Auntie Amy and pick me a blossom from her garden to enclose in your next letter.

Uncle picked up the post just the other day when our mail finally caught up with us. I noticed your letter was written in Marmee's hand, Beth, although I could tell the words were your own. I like to imagine you had been practicing too many hours on the pianoforte and needed to rest your fingers. I try to think that is why Marmee

took up the pen for you. Please take good
care and stay well. I know you pride yourself on being helpful to Mother and
Hannah, but promise not to work too hard,
dear.
With much love and tenderness,
your sister,
Amy

Draped Model

Perhaps the travelers were growing travel weary or perhaps they were becoming weary of each other, for once they were settled in the apartment in the Piazza Barberini, they often went their own ways. Aunt Mary sought respite from the cold, damp weather, which did not agree with her constitution. She was content to stay put and pass the time in peaceful solitude, paging through Italian fashion periodicals. If the sun peeked through the clouds and the rain stopped she might venture out to visit with the Misses Smythe, spinster sisters to whom Katherine Vaughn had given her introduction.

Most days Florence happily visited with two English young ladies she had met in Paris during their mutual infatuation with porcelain painting. They were lodging with their families at the Hotel Costanza in the Piazza di Spagna, also known as the British District, where one might buy a kidney pie or enjoy a Sunday roast in the shadow of the Spanish Steps. They spent much of each day shopping, gossiping, and playing Italian card games.

Uncle Edward had joined the archaeological society, with

whom he would venture out exploring Roma Vecchia. He was intent on unearthing an undiscovered treasure to bring home with him. When it was too rainy to dig, which it often was, he frequented a gentlemen's club, where many an afternoon was spent in pursuits that only men who belong to gentlemen's clubs are privy.

With all of the Carrols otherwise occupied, Fred off in Greece, and who knew where Laurie was, Amy had thought she would be able to put all of her focus into studying art. Sadly, her good friend Mary Cassatt had gone to London for the winter, which was most disappointing. Free of suitors and distracting family friends, without a vigorous sightseeing itinerary designed by Uncle Edward to follow, she was unhappy to have found Rome to be a place better suited to a student of sculpture rather than painting.

But there was a Mr. Crowninshield from Boston, who had opened his studio to a class of ladies in sketching from nature, and Amy availed herself of it. With easels strapped atop a packed landau, they went on excursions to the *campagna* to draw en plein air. And so, with the other young ladies, Amy sketched the pastoral beauty of the most painted landscape in Europe. But Amy yearned to paint, and unlike in London and Paris, copyists did not flourish in the great galleries of Rome during the cold weather.

The viewing of a masterpiece in a museum or palazzo was fine if one wore an extra wrap or two. But it was impossible to spend the time needed for copying in the stone-floored rooms, which were quite frigid, as they were heated only by small earthenware braziers that did nothing to ward off the damp and cold.

One evening, Amy joined Cecilia, a young woman she'd met at Mr. Crowninshield's, to an evening class at the studio of an Italian painter. He occasionally allowed female students, so young ladies aspiring to improve their watercolor took any chance they could to paint from a draped model. Though Amy wished very much to paint a nude model, to fully capture the human form. It irked her that because she was a woman that simply wasn't an option. A draped model was the best a female art student could expect.

Accompanied by a few other young women, Amy and Cecilia sat behind the primary students, who were all men. As the men painted they smoked cigarette after cigarette, and a haze hung over the large room. And whilst the group of young ladies softly spoke amongst themselves in French or English as they worked—about painting and technique and the natural beauty of the model—the young men loudly talked to each other while they painted, laughing and gesturing and singing in Italian.

At the end of the evening, after packing their paints and brushes, Amy and Cecilia awaited the arrival of Cecilia's father, who was to accompany them back to their respective lodgings. It was unsafe for a lady to traverse the deserted Roman streets at night unescorted. The model, who was probably only a bit older than them, lingered near Amy and Cecilia, also waiting for someone.

"*Grazie, signorina*," Cecilia said haltingly with a smile. The young woman shyly smiled back at the girls. "*Voi siete coraggiose*," the model replied, nodding toward the young men, who seemed to be staying on. Their singing had increased in volume, and they had apparently added wine to accompany their cigarettes. "*Non sono sempre carini.*"

"Oh, what's she saying?" Amy asked.

"I don't know," Cecilia replied to Amy, then, "*Non parlo Italiano*," to the young woman. "Only English," Cecilia said, pointing to herself and Amy.

"*Français alors?*" the young woman replied, looking from Cecilia to Amy.

"*Je parle français*," Amy said.

And in broken French heavily accented with Italian, the young woman said, "Be careful with these painters. They talk of your painting all night, and then of your person."

Amy's eyes grew wide, and she felt herself blushing.

"Of your face and your . . ." The young woman gestured up and down with her hand.

"My body?" Amy replied in English, then, *"Mon physique?"* switching back to French.

"Sì, signorina, il tuo fisico," she replied. Then, heavily accented in Italian she said, "Not nice," and shook her head.

They looked at each other, across differences of culture and language and social class, acknowledging that anywhere a woman went she was potentially at risk. A young man arrived, with the same dark features and blue-black hair as the model, clearly her brother, and she turned to leave. Amy reached out and touched her shoulder. *"Grazie,"* Amy said. She sighed, turned back to Cecilia, and recounted what the model had said to them.

The arrival of Cecilia's father and a friend of his, come to take the young ladies back, halted any further conversation they might have had concerning the subject, as neither of them wanted to be forbidden to attend class again.

Palazzo Barberini

As the weeks went by, they all fell into a satisfying routine. Amy took painting and sketching classes, as they were available. When Florence and Aunt Mary busied themselves with social engagements, she began to decline their invitations and spent time painting or drawing in their cozy apartment or en plain air, weather permitting. Uncle Edward kept himself very busy between his gentlemen's club and the archaeological society. And sometimes, all together, they would visit a must-see Roman attraction.

The rainy winter was becoming slightly less rainy, and it felt like spring might be right around the corner. Soon, their time in Rome would end and they would move on. Uncle Edward had insisted before they did that they must all visit Palazzo Barberini together, given its close proximity to their lodging.

Florence gazed up the long, winding staircase of the palazzo, then at Amy. Amy smiled at her. Florence pursed her lips and looked at Aunt Mary, who returned her look. "Mother?" Florence said. Aunt Mary glanced at Uncle Edward, and then said, "Eddie?" He sighed, his shoulders sagging dejectedly. Then Uncle Edward looked at Amy, who tried not to laugh.

"Don't worry, Uncle. I'll go," Amy replied, taking hold of his elbow. Uncle Edward smiled down at Amy, patted her arm, and the two began their ascent of the winding staircase.

"I believe both your cousin and your aunt will end by leaving Rome without having viewed the second floor of this spectacular palazzo," Uncle Edward said. "And all because they'd rather find some English-speaking tourists to have a cup of tea and a gossip than walk up Borromini's masterpiece of a staircase."

"Perhaps if they knew that it isn't as demanding of one's stamina as one might think then they might give it a try," Amy said, as they rounded a turn.

"That is because of the helical design," Uncle Edward said, proud to be able to share his knowledge. "It follows the principle of turning around an axis of rotation," he continued. They rounded another turn. "The longitudinal flattening allows for an easier ascent than a circular staircase might," he finished, clearly satisfied with himself.

As the weeks had turned to months and finally to over a year of traveling with the Carrols, Amy found herself growing more and more fond of Uncle Edward. Amy and Uncle Edward were amiable companions, with a similar enthusiasm for art. For although they didn't necessarily share the same taste or interests — Uncle Edward tended to appreciate more ancient things, holding antiquities in high esteem, while Amy's interest was mostly focused on painting and more current sculpture—they were each glad to accompany the other on expeditions to contemplate a masterpiece from any era.

Today their objective was to view a portrait of a woman that was believed to be painted by the Baroque artist, Guido Reni, although who the woman actually was and if the painter was in fact Reni were both the object of much speculation. What wasn't speculation was the fact that viewing this portrait had inspired more than one man of letters to wax philosophical about it. Charles Dickens had said it was "almost impossible to be forgotten."

As they approached the painting, Amy said, "For all of its notoriety, it's not very large, is it?"

Uncle Edward furrowed his brow, thinking. "I don't think the painting is considered disreputable," he said. "It's more that the story surrounding its subject deals in such unsavory issues."

They stopped in front of the portrait and were quiet for a moment, gazing together at the pale face of a young woman, her hair wrapped in a white turban, looking over her shoulder at the viewer. Amy thought her face emanated hopelessness, her despair almost palpable. Her eyes looked red rimmed and slightly puffy, as if she'd been crying. There was an innocence to her countenance that belied the account of her tragic life, and the brutality of her death by execution.

"Do you think it's true," Amy said. "The story about her?"

Uncle Edward patted her arm, which he was still holding.

"The story of the House of Cenci is certainly true," Uncle Edward replied. "There is some debate though whether this is actually a portrait of Beatrice Cenci, which is an entirely different conversation."

Looking closely at the portrait, Amy tilted her head. Beatrice Cenci had been executed in 1599, along with her stepmother and brother, for the heinous murder of her father, Count Francesco Cenci, who had violently abused them all. He was known to be a cruel, dissolute, and savage man and had even been jailed. Among other brutalities, Beatrice accused him of repeatedly raping her.

Amy trembled. Although it was chilly in the gallery, it was Cenci's story that made her shiver. Legend was that on the night before the anniversary of her execution by decapitation, Beatrice haunted the Sant'Angelo bridge holding her severed head in her hands.

Percy Bysshe Shelley had written *The Cenci*, a five-act verse drama, after viewing this portrait and Hawthorne's *The Marble Faun*, written when he lived in Rome, debated at length the nature and scope of Beatrice's guilt. Amy hadn't read either but of course Jo had. Amy had listened though, and paid close attention when the story of Beatrice Cenci was discussed by others. She took a step nearer to the painting, and as she was still holding her uncle's arm, he stepped with her.

"Do you think people are drawn to this portrait because of the story of Cenci," Amy asked, "or do you think it's the painting itself?"

"Well, I am no philosopher," Uncle Edward answered. "Nor am I an expert on art or art history," he said, "but as you know I have a deep appreciation of ancient artifacts and classical antiquities."

They both kept looking at the painting.

"I take pleasure in gazing upon objects that human beings touched or lived amongst hundreds or even thousands of years ago."

Amy noticed that the delicateness of the young woman's features was accentuated by the turban atop her head, balanced by the draping of material over her shoulder. She thought it lent her an air of vulnerability. Beatrice Cenci or not, Amy thought, she certainly looked quite tragic.

"Why is that, Uncle Edward?" Amy asked, turning to look at him.

"Before we embarked on our travels, I had never questioned *why* my interest in ancient artifacts is so keen," he answered. He looked down at her and a small smile illuminated his face, his eyes crinkling a little in the corners. "And it's only been here, in Rome, that I began to find an answer."

Amy waited. She never would have guessed her uncle was so introspective. "What I've come to," he said, "is that it affords me an opportunity to be imaginative."

"Imaginative?" Amy asked, turning to look back at the portrait.

"Exactly," he said. "There are not many avenues for a man such as I to give life to one's imagination." He paused, thinking. "I'm not artistic or unconventional in any way." He chuckled. "I believe many in my social circle, perhaps even in the family, consider me a bit orthodox and boring." Amy tried not to smile. Before traveling with Uncle Edward she might have said exactly that. He had always been so quiet.

"But I find, I'd rather say nothing, than engage in conversation in which I frankly have no interest."

"I see," Amy said. "And how does this relate to antiquities and imagination?"

"Ah, yes!" he replied. "You see, when I look at an ancient object—a Greek vase, Roman coins, a statue from ancient Egypt—I like to think of the people who handled these objects or walked amongst the buildings that are in ruin now. They had full lives that we know nothing about. They were men and women with passions and interests, who loved and hated, who . . ." Although he was still facing the portrait, Uncle Edward's eyes were unfocused, his thoughts—his imagination—clearly engaged elsewhere.

"Uncle Edward," Amy said, "I believe you are a bit of a romantic."

Uncle Edward shook his head a bit, as if to clear the fog.

"Perhaps," he said, nodding a little. "So in answer to your question, I think people are drawn to the *sensationalism* of the Cenci story. And since a connection has been suggested between the story and the painting, our imaginations are engaged, and our view of the portrait becomes informed by that story."

Amy was dumbstruck. She had been traveling with her aunt, uncle, and cousin for over a year. And she was just *now* finding out that her uncle's interest in checking off as many places as possible from his list of tourist sights was actually rooted in his curiosity about the world. Back home in Concord she had no idea he was such an interesting and interested person. She had only ever thought of him as Florence's father, not a man with a surprising passion for learning. And not only that, but apparently Uncle Edward was a deep thinker, too. She couldn't imagine *how* he'd ended up with Aunt Mary.

A Certain Something

They would be leaving Rome soon. Amy wasn't sure she was ready to say farewell just yet though. It was interesting because in all their time abroad it was only here that she'd allowed herself to focus on art and only art. She hadn't attended many of the social functions that Aunt Mary and Florence went to, dances and balls and the like, and Uncle Edward usually told them to go on without him as he was content to stay back. He'd been inspired by the notebooks of da Vinci, and had taken to recording his thoughts and insights on all that he was seeing in a small journal. He'd begun to make small sketches and drawings, which gave Amy nice justification for staying back with him. They spent many an evening in quiet companionship, as Amy painted and Uncle Edward pondered and chronicled his travels.

Amy rifled through the stack of letters she'd received since being abroad. Many from her parents and Meg and Beth, a few from Jo. Aunt March had written a number of times. And of course Laurie. There were quite a few from him, but not any recently. She hadn't received any after that one from Greece, the first and only letter he'd sent after their kiss. She touched a finger to her lips and sighed. Then she reread Fred's note.

London, England

My dear Miss March,

I take pen in hand to assure you, lest you worry, that my travels to Greece and our return journey to Great Britain was quite uneventful. Frank and I are three days returned to London and will be off to the country house where Frank may convalesce through the springtime. I trust your time in Rome has been pleasant.

As it is my preference to make haste so you and I may reunite sooner, I will not be attending the Epsom Derby. This annual race is a favorite of my family, and I haven't missed it once since I began attending as a lad of ten years. I share this information to impress upon you the degree to which my affections are yours.

Whilst in our Surrey home I have a meeting with my father regarding a certain something I have requested from our family jewels. I hope to be able to share more about it when you and I meet again.

I very much look forward to that moment, when the weather will be fine, and I might gaze at your pleasing face once more. I imagine your golden hair set against the blue of the Mediterranean Sea. I close this letter now thinking of that day.

I remain, dear madam,
your sincere and affectionate admirer,

Fred W. Vaughn

A *certain something*, she thought. She felt a little dizzy, thinking about it, as if she were in a boat that had unexpectedly caught a current. She had put herself in this boat and had decided the destination would be acceptable. She closed her eyes and took a deep breath to steady herself. Then she opened them, gave a nod, put Fred's letter with the others, and tied up the whole stack with a ribbon. She put the stack in her trunk and continued to pack up to leave Rome.

Nice

Promenade

Amy and the Carrols had had a very nice routine in Rome, coupling tourism and sightseeing together with mundane but relaxing days where each went their own way. It didn't take long to get into a similar rhythm once they were settled at their hotel in Nice. Only in Nice the weather was lovely, the days were sunny, and the mood of the town was much more focused on leisure and amusement. When Fred arrived he ensconced himself in a nearby hotel and resumed his attentive courting of Amy, as if it had never been interrupted in Heidelberg.

One afternoon Uncle Edward had arranged to meet with some men he'd befriended back in Rome at the archeological society. They were off to the Muséum d'Histoire Naturelle de Nice, a destination Aunt Mary had absolutely no interest in attending. Fred had proposed strolling the Promenade des Anglais and was coming to collect Amy and Florence at the hotel. But Florence claimed a headache and didn't want to go. Aunt Mary was wavering on whether to allow Amy to walk with Fred unchaperoned, especially on a route where everybody who was anybody might see anybody else who was anybody. As the day was quite warm, Amy knew Aunt Mary would have difficulty avoiding the lure of staying put in the comfortably shaded hotel courtyard, with a fan and a magazine.

She readied herself, arranging a delicate layer of netting over the skirt of her hydrangea- colored day dress, trying to spruce it up a bit, as it wasn't of the very latest fashion. Amy would welcome spending some time alone with Fred, even if it were in a public setting. Knowing his proposal was imminent—she knew he had brought that *certain something* with him—all of a sudden it felt important that she get to know him better. It would soon be progressing from an abstract idea of marriage and what there was to gain or lose, or how to best position herself within it, to a concrete reality. It would be her, Amy Curtis March of Concord, Massachusetts, saying yes to Mr. Fred W. Vaughn, a graduate of Eton, an oldest son who would inherit homes in London and Surrey, plus a substantial yearly income. And that would be for the rest of her life. Would she feel as if she were in a beautiful fairy tale, living happily ever after? How much did that matter? How much *should* it matter?

She looked at herself in the mirror, tucked some loose locks of hair into place with pins, and pinched her cheeks a bit to brighten them. She turned her head this way and that, examining her nose, pressed a finger on each side of her nostrils, then let them go. She smiled, thinking about how much she'd disliked her nose as a child.

She thought about the married people she knew well—her parents, Aunt Mary and Uncle Edward—and wondered what their relationships had been like before they were married. How well had they known each other? She had no idea how long her mother and father had courted before they married, nor Aunt Mary and Uncle Edward. She wondered if Aunt Mary and Uncle Edward's relationship had been based on economics or love. Perhaps both? Certainly her own mother had given up financial stability when she married Father, although

Amy didn't know if her mother realized that before or after she married Father. Her sister Meg had certainly not married John for money, but based on the letter Meg had sent last summer, she hadn't married him for love either. As far as Amy could tell, she'd married John just to spite Aunt March, who had adamantly insisted Meg shouldn't marry him at all.

Fred finally arrived and Aunt Mary gave her permission, so they began a leisurely stroll adjacent to the sparkling Mediterranean Sea. Amy protected her fair skin beneath a parasol. Although the sun was bright, there was a slight breeze coming in off the water, which made the increasing warmth tolerable. It felt lovely to be walking with a gentleman along the Promenade des Anglais, politely nodding to passersby, who were mostly other tourists chattering in English. She remembered the first time she and Fred had walked together, in London, and how anxious and uncomfortable she had been, and not simply because of the soot in her eye. It felt like so much had changed since then. She had changed, although she couldn't say why that was or when that had happened.

They walked quietly together, side by side, having run out of subjects for conversation. Fred had told her all about the Epsom Derby, which he again mentioned he had missed because he was so eager to come see her. He went on and on about a new opera he was eager to take her to when they eventually returned to London, by Giuseppe Verdi, that was being discussed by many in his social circle. Then he asked her if she'd been to the opera when she'd been in Italy, but as she hadn't, the conversation petered out. When she began to tell him about the excursion her uncle had arranged when they were in Rome, viewing the Coliseum by moonlight, before she knew it they were talking about the Parthenon, and how he had made sure to pop in to take a look when he'd gone to fetch Frank home from Athens.

As they walked Amy told herself it was a *good* thing, to enjoy the company of a suitor in amiable silence. But soon their lack of conversation started to feel uncomfortable, and Amy was just about to start telling Fred about sketching in the Campagna when they stopped to say hello to a young man who apparently knew Fred.

"Miss March," Fred said, gripping her elbow a bit proprietarily, "please meet Mr. Hugh Davies-Taylor. We were schoolmates at Oxford."

It was a shame Florence had stayed back because Mr. Davies-Taylor was attractive in a way Florence liked. That is to say, he was impeccably dressed in the most fashionable of men's attire, and had an air about him that reeked of family money, which never failed to impress her. He and Fred had been chatting for quite some time, while Amy politely listened, as she stood perspiring under her parasol, which could only do so much against the warmth of the day. Finally they had all begun to walk together, the men still chatting and catching up on some of their school friends, until they reached the hotel where Fred was lodged.

He turned to Amy and said, "Shall we go in? We can get a cold refreshment."

"That would be lovely," she said, looking forward to being alone with Fred again. Mr. Davies-Taylor hadn't even looked her way, let alone spoken to her, since Fred introduced them and he'd said, "Charmed," and gave her a quick nod. They entered the coolness of the hotel lobby and Amy started to feel annoyed when she saw that he had followed. The three were sat at a small table on a shaded terrace, which caught a breeze coming in off the Mediterranean. The scent of jasmine danced in the air, mixed with a pleasant briny sea smell. A waiter came by and offered Amy a fan, for which she was grateful. Fred ordered lemonade.

As they sat at the small table Davies-Taylor kept talking and talking. Amy smiled and nodded, smiled and nodded. When she thought her cheeks might break from holding the polite smile, she'd retreat behind the fan. Besides the fact that both Davies-Taylor and Fred were basically ignoring her, she wouldn't have been able to get a word in edgewise. After a while Mr. Davies-Taylor's clipped Eton accent began to grate on her nerves. She might scream if he uttered one more sentence that didn't hold an article or pronoun.

At last he seemed to notice that he and Fred weren't alone when he asked where Fred and Amy had met. Amy was about to answer, but Fred jumped in saying, "Well, you know Theodore Laurence." Davies-Taylor looked quizzical. Fred went on, "Chap I introduced to you to at Boodle's?"

"Top chap," Hugh said. "Bit of a nancy though, eh?"

Fred glanced at Amy, then away. "Don't think so," Fred said, then cleared his throat. There was a pause for a moment, then Amy pounced, wanting to add something, anything, to participate in the conversation. Her cheeks hurt from smiling so much. "I've known Mr. Laurence since I was a child," she said. "His grandfather lives next door to my family." But Mr. Davies-Taylor paid her no mind, continuing his conversation with Fred as if she hadn't said a word.

"Americans at Boodle's," he snipped, literally looking down his nose and shaking his head. Fred glanced at Amy again and looked uncomfortable. Finally, Mr. Davies-Taylor excused himself for another engagement, and Amy breathed a sigh of relief.

Fred smiled at her, now that Davies-Taylor was gone, reached across the table and took her hand in his. She didn't pull it away.

"Goodness! I didn't understand half of what you and Mr. Davies-Taylor were talking about," Amy said. She very much didn't like the feeling of not knowing.

"You needn't bother yourself with it," Fred said, gently squeezing her hand. "Just idle chitchat." A slight breeze blew across the terrace, which was refreshing. Amy withdrew her hand and took a sip of her lemonade.

"Fred," she said, "tell me, what is Boodle's? And what is a nancy?"

He swallowed and looked slightly uncomfortable. She didn't like seeing him uncomfortable so she playfully said, "Please assure me that Mr. Haughty Davies-Taylor isn't someone in your very inner circle." Then she smiled wholesomely at him.

Fred laughed and reached again for her hand.

"Hugh and I are not friends," he assured her. "His grandfather belongs to the same gentlemen's club as mine. Boodle's, it's called."

"That's reassuring," Amy had replied. "I would hate to think you would *purposely* seek out the company of someone who doesn't allow room for a woman to speak."

"Indeed," Fred replied laughingly. "And do you, my sweet Miss March, count yourself a follower of Mr. John Stuart Mill?" He looked pleased with himself and continued. "The author of the philosophical treatise *The Subjection of Women*?" Amy saw that he was trying to impress her, to win points as it were for dropping Mr. Mill's name.

"Perhaps I do," Amy replied, glad to see him relaxed again. She wondered if he'd read it, or had only heard about it, but she didn't want to make him feel bad if it were the latter, so she didn't ask and just smiled.

"And a nancy?" she asked. "What does that mean?"

Fred started to blush. "I dare say I'd rather not discuss that with a lady," he said, looking uncomfortable again. "Sometimes Davies-Taylor forgets his good breeding."

"Oh! Well then, please tell me," Amy said. "What was he saying about Laurie?"

Fred didn't reply, but all of a sudden took great interest in his own lemonade, which he made a big show of sipping.

"We Americans are proud of our directness," Amy said. "I'd much rather know."

He looked away from her, lowered his voice, and said, "Davies-Taylor was asking if Laurence is . . . you know . . ."

"I don't know," Amy said, truly innocent of what he was talking about.

"Remember the Jew artist Simeon Solomon," Fred said. "We saw some of his paintings together in London?"

Amy remembered seeing Solomon's work when she and Fred had visited the Royal Gallery. She had greatly admired Solomon's paintings of subjects from the Hebrew Bible, as well as his beautiful depiction of the ancient Greek poetesses, Sappho and Erinna.

"I don't follow," Amy said, remembering the art but not anything about the artist.

Fred sighed. "Davies-Taylor was asking if Laurence is a bugger," he said.

For a minute, she didn't understand what he'd said. But when his words finally registered she was genuinely shocked. She stood.

"I'm sorry, Amy," Fred said, still seated and looking up at her, "but you insisted on your American directness."

"I think . . . I think I'm ready to return to my hotel," Amy said. She could feel her fair skin blushing and couldn't look directly at him.

"I'll escort you back," he said. She glanced at him and saw his brows knit in consternation.

She straightened her posture, drawing up to her full height. "I'd prefer to go alone," she said, finally looking him directly in the eyes.

He looked distressed, and stood up to speak to her. "Amy, I ask as friend to both you and Laurence," he said, "are you upset at Davies-Taylor's lack of manners?"

She frowned.

He continued, "Or are you upset because you think there might be merit to it?"

She sniffed and replied, "Laurie is a gentleman of good breeding."

Fred answered, "Agreed. Laurence is certainly that. As is my brother." At that she turned away from him, crossed the terrace and walked inside the hotel. Fred caught up to her and in the dim coolness of the hotel lobby they stood for a few moments, facing each other.

"You know, Amy . . ." Fred cleared his throat. "Frank and Laurence have been close friends for a very long time." He looked past her, toward the window beyond which you could see the sparkling blue of the Mediterranean. Amy's brow furrowed. She felt like the ground was shifting under her feet.

"Close friends?" she said. All of a sudden she felt so young, so naïve. Almost imperceptibly he nodded. Apparently, there was so much going on around her—and always had been—of which she was unaware.

"Since we were boys, really," he said softly, "before Laurence went to live with his grandfather." She could feel tears behind her eyes, which she willed into submission. She would not cry in in public.

"I see," she said. She blinked quickly, trying to remain in control. She gave a short nod then began walking across the lobby. At the door she snapped open her parasol. Fred walked with her for a moment, down the Promenade des Anglais, which led directly to her hotel. But before they parted, they stopped, and he took one of her hands in his again and with the other tipped her chin up so she was looking directly at him. He said, "Dear Amy, I very much look forward to seeing you tomorrow." He nodded at her meaningfully. Each time they had met since he had gotten here she wondered if it would be the day he asked for her hand. She searched his eyes and he nodded again. Her heart sped up and for a moment she felt lightheaded.

He was the eventuality she knew was hers. She'd decided it

would be okay, that it would be the best thing. So it was confusing when her emotions wouldn't align with this decision. She leveled her gaze at him. "And I look forward to that, Mr. Vaughn," she said.

As she walked down the promenade, she gazed out at the sea, hiding beneath her parasol. A breeze came off the water again and the briny smell of sea salt tickled at her nose. It reminded her of visits to the ocean with her family. How she wished she was with her sisters right now. A stray sunbeam reached her fair, unblemished face, and she adjusted her parasol. She thought of Meg's plump cheeks, which always looked bronzed and healthy from the sun, and Jo's practical face, with her strong features and smooth Italianate skin.

At home when the family went to the sea, if she and Beth didn't huddle together under an umbrella, by day's end Amy would be blistered and salmon colored. Beth would be stippled with a thousand freckles to add to the constellation that already populated her sweet face. She missed Beth so much. A day at the ocean with her family sounded so much less complicated than trying to understand everything that was swirling around in her head.

She could feel the sand through the soles of her soft kid shoes as she slowed her walk, to look at the fishing boats bobbing prettily in the turquoise water. She turned the conversation over and over in her head. Was she upset at the unbearable Davies-Taylor's lack of manners, gossiping about Laurie, as Fred had asked? Or was she upset because she thought there might be merit to it, and to what Fred had implied about Laurie and Frank?

Another gentle breeze blew in from over the water, stirring the netting she had laid carefully over her dress. With one hand she patted it down. It was hard to examine her feelings, to determine which aspect was actually upsetting to her.

As she strolled the short distance back to her hotel, she

hoped Aunt Mary and Cousin Florence wouldn't plague her with a million questions about her afternoon when she returned. She needed to think. She wasn't ready to go in and face her family. So she sat beneath her parasol, shaded enough on an iron bench with a view of the water. The sun was dazzling on the surface, reflecting like so many diamonds. That comforting briny smell came in off the water once again and she heard the dusty ruffle of the palm trees, as the fronds rubbed together.

To think of society talking about Laurie, that he was the subject of gossip, was unbearable. It was the audacity and impoliteness of the arrogant Mr. Davies-Taylor that made her angry, for the more she thought about it, the more the truth of it seemed likely. Knowing Laurie, as she did, it just didn't seem far-fetched. She remembered him telling her that Jo had inferred "certain things" when she'd proposed a marriage of convenience, and he'd said he wouldn't deny them. She hadn't known then what he was referring to.

But then what of their kiss? This was the part that was perplexing. Amy touched her lips with her fingers. Laurie had kissed her. She closed her eyes, remembering every part of it. And then, what had happened between them at the Louvre replayed in her mind, as if it had happened yesterday. It was as if all the months that had passed, her travels in Germany and Italy and then back here in France hadn't happened. Because even if it was confusing, she had loved everything about that kiss, the surprise of it, and then the second kiss, the passion of it. Her eyes brimmed with tears.

But why was she thinking about this *now*? Laurie had said it was a mistake. If what Fred said was true, then Laurie had been being truthful. She couldn't be upset with him for not being more forthright with her. If she thought about it he'd tried to tell her a number of times, but she hadn't wanted to understand.

Then she thought, *What if what Fred said about Laurie and Frank is true*? And she realized she didn't care. Because if it was true it didn't change one thing about who Laurie was to her, how she thought of him, or any of the reasons he was so special to her. Coming to that conclusion felt comforting. She loved Laurie and if that was how his heart worked, of course it was fine. She thought of how well suited Rosa Bonheur and Miss Micas were, how unmistakable their love and devotion for each other was. She thought of how much she wished her sister could find someone, too, and have an arrangement like RB and Miss Micas. A Boston marriage. Oh, how she wished Jo would find someone to love and to be loved by. So just because Laurie was a man, it was no different. It was deplorable to think that people couldn't see that; it was offensive that who one loves, whether man or woman, would be a topic for gossip or something anyone should feel shame about. Didn't everyone deserve love?

Declination

The next day Amy waited in the sitting room of their suite at the hotel. She felt lightheaded. Was her corset laced too tight? She drew in as much of a breath as she could, sat up straighter with her shoulders back, crossed her ankles, and folded her hands in her lap. She could feel her heart beating in her chest and for a moment she was afraid she might actually faint. She hadn't felt this nervous in a very long time.

Aunt Mary had tea and cake sent up and excused herself, saying she and Florence and Uncle Edward would return in one hour precisely. Amy stood up as Fred entered the room. She tried to smile as she anxiously twisted her hands together. He looked nervously at her, which was not a way she'd ever seen him before.

"There's tea," she said, pointing lamely at the tea and cake.

"Oh, thank you," he said. He cleared his throat. "Please," he said, gesturing at the settee. "Do sit."

They both started speaking at the same time.

He said, "I think we must speak of . . ." while she was saying, "Remember that time at the Louvre?"

"I'm sorry," he said. "Must we talk about the Louvre? Paris seems so long ago."

But since their conversation the previous day, Paris had been plaguing Amy. In fact, it was all she had been able to think about. Laurie at the Louvre. Fred at the Louvre. Painting at the Louvre. She knew this was it. Fred was going to ask her, and she had to clear this up.

He said, "I think you know how I feel about you, Amy," then paused. She gazed back at him and thought *Why isn't he asking me how I feel about him?*

"Actually," she replied, "I'm not certain." He looked genuinely surprised. "Sometimes I think I know, but then I question if I am correct."

"I've been quite sincere with you, always," he said.

"But at the Louvre," she started to say again.

He looked irritated. "I want to speak of the *future*, what's to *come*, not some incident you've been holding on to from Paris," he said, his brows drawing together.

"An incident I've been holding on to?" she said. She thought she might *actually* faint. Had their conversation been that inconsequential to him? Steadying her shaking hands she picked up the teapot and poured them both tea. He nodded thanks, took his cup, and gestured to the sugar.

"Please?"

Delicately she picked up a cube with the sugar tongs and dropped it into his cup. "Thank you," he said. He stirred and took a small sip.

She added cream to her own and took a sip.

They looked at each other and her heart was beating so strongly in her chest she thought it might be audible. Again, they both started speaking at the same time.

"Please, do let me speak first," he said. "Whatever is concerning you about Paris surely can't be of as great significance as what I must say."

She put her teacup down, folded her hands in her lap, and again tried to take a deep breath. She just nodded.

He started again, as if he had rehearsed what he was going to say. "I think you know how I feel about you." She bit her lip, not allowing herself to question him this time. Then he dropped to one knee and said, in the most heartfelt way, "Miss March, it gives me great pleasure to ask for your hand in marriage."

It was happening. She had imagined when he asked her she would feel joy or elation, or even just relief that the waiting was over. And yet she felt none of those things. What it felt like was that she had a knot lodged under her diaphragm. Of all the things Amy had thought she might do or say when Fred proposed, almost fainting had not been one of them. Was her corset, indeed, laced too tightly?

He had followed her to Paris, to Frankfurt, and throughout the Kingdom of Germany. He'd returned to France to be with her here in Nice. He had attentively courted her across the Continent, and even at times had been romantic; Heidelberg truly *had* felt like a fairy tale. He might have asked her then, before he'd gone to Greece to sort out his brother. What would she have said?

It wasn't her corset that was confining her after all. She wanted to be able to say yes, and make everyone happy. She had thought she could do it. But what she'd realized the previous day is that yes, everyone does deserve to love and be loved, but more, they deserve to be known. His words to her at the Louvre all that time ago were the knot lodged in her gut, and she couldn't bear it. Those words echoed in her mind. *Perhaps your interest in painting will wane when someday you have a nursery full of babies of your own.* If he really knew her, if he really loved her, he would never have said that.

And so, much to his dismay, Amy declined Fred's proposal. When she explained to him, recounted their conversation from that long-ago afternoon, he didn't understand why she felt it was so important. That fact, in and of itself, was exactly the problem.

One hour later, precisely, as Aunt Mary had said, the Carrols returned. The door to the sitting room was flung open and in rushed Aunt Mary and Florence, their matching smiles already in place, followed by Uncle Edward, who walked into the room in a more measured pace.

Breathlessly Aunt Mary said, "We just want to wish . . ." She and Florence stopped so abruptly Uncle Edward almost bumped into them. They both looked frantically around the room.

"Where did he go?" Florence whispered loudly.

"Amy?" Aunt Mary said. "Didn't he . . ."

Behind them, Uncle Edward looked Amy directly in the eye. She stared back at him, then raised her eyebrows. He nodded at her. She gave the tiniest of shrugs. Then he gently smiled and nodded again.

A Letter to Mother

Nice, France

Dear Mother,

I haven't had a letter from home in some time. I suppose the post hasn't caught up to us here yet. I imagine when it does, I'll have plenty to read though! I look forward to hearing from you and hope you have included in your letters every little detail about my niece and nephew, how Meg and John are doing, if Jo has had any further luck with publication, and of course all about Father. But mostly, I long to hear of our Beth. It was concerning that her last letter to me was in your handwriting. I hope she is well. Please hug my angel of a big sister for me. I miss her.

I have news, Marmee, that perhaps might disappoint. As expected, Fred Vaughn has asked for my hand in marriage. I know you and Father were hoping I would find a husband of some means whilst abroad. Please don't say you weren't, I know the truth of our family's financial circumstances. Aunt March has always been candid, speaking of these matters to me, even if you and Father tried to be more circumspect. She still hasn't forgiven him for his financial mishandlings and has been very outspoken about the burden he's put on you and the rest of us. All that is to say, even though you never stated it directly, I know you were counting on me to marry well. And yet, I declined Fred's proposal.

One of the many things I've begun to realize since I'm here is that whether I'm genius at it or not, living an artistic life is really all that I've ever dreamt of. I don't want to hurt you or Father, but I also can't accept living half a life. That is what I would have been choosing, accepting Fred, or any man who doesn't understand that about me. It would be the slow death of my spirit. I've met women here who are unabashedly ambitious in their pursuit of art. That is the life I choose, and I can't apologize for it.

I know I am blessed to have the love of you and the rest of our family, as well as many kind friends. It is my hope that you, who tend the fires of my home, will come to honor and encourage my firmness of purpose. I speak the truth of my heart when I say if choosing art over marriage

means art is all I have, that will be enough
for me.
I remain, as ever,
your loving daughter,
Amy Curtis March

Amy reread the letter one last time, folded it, and sealed it, finally satisfied that she'd said what she needed to say.

The Color of Memory

The thing about painting in watercolor is controlling your wash. What's laid down first, what's underneath, can't be covered over, for in the end it will show through. When Amy closed her eyes, she could see the painting she wished to paint so very clearly. Gone was the vivid blue of the Mediterranean. Vanished was the crisp way the sunlight played with the shadows of the balustrade of the small balcony where she sat, just outside the double doors leading to their rooms on the third floor of the pension. Behind closed eyes she visualized the colors and tones she would bestow upon the page—shades of olive and tan and ecru. She could see how she would frame the image with tree branches in the foreground, as if she and the viewer were taking a long view. She knew where the shadows and light would fall.

Viewing the finished painting wouldn't feel like looking at something intimate, although her relationship with all that it represented would inform it. She thought of her family and her home. Trying to paint Orchard House from memory, it was difficult to separate the facts of the two-story clapboard from all that it embodied. So much of what she was grappling with—the narrowness within which women were expected to exist, the expectations of her family—felt too immense to contend with. She opened her eyes, looked down at the blank page, and dipped her brush in the water.

When she was finished, she exhaled. It felt as if she'd been holding her breath for a very long time. Painting the house, placing it on the page, she was free from the weight of it. The thing about painting in watercolor is controlling your wash and allowing the light from underneath to come through.

Amy had really done it! She felt as if she'd gotten out of the boat that had been caught up in a fast current leading only to marriage and money and Fred Vaughn, or someone else just like Fred Vaughn. It was both exhilarating and frightening, but she finally felt as if she could breathe. Aunt Mary and Cousin Florence had been shocked when she told them she'd declined Fred, and no matter how many times she tried to explain it to them, they would not or could not understand. Uncle Edward understood though, and then told her he never much cared for Fred. When Amy asked him why he hadn't said anything to her, he told her he hadn't wanted to unduly influence any decision she might make. She was grateful for that. It felt as if she'd made a mature decision, having come to it on her own.

When Amy had painted her childhood home it felt as if by putting Orchard House on paper she had purged something. Like something had gotten unstuck in her, and then out spilled paintings and sketches, works in charcoal and ink and pastels. It was as if a blindfold had been taken off of her eyes and all of a sudden she could see magnificence in even the most mundane of things. All the world was beautiful, and she would do her best to express it on paper or canvas.

Expect Me

One afternoon Amy and Uncle Edward came back from an outing to Villefranche-sur-Mer. On their return they were to meet Aunt Mary and Florence at tea. Amy went up to the room she and Florence shared to change into something more appropriate. Atop her pillow was an envelope. She picked it up and turned it over to see her name in the elegant handwriting of Mr. Theodore Laurence, written, as always, as if there wasn't a moment to waste and it had been quickly dashed off. Carefully opening it, she saw the shortest of notes, which read, in its entirety:

> *My Lady,*
> *My travel plans have changed, and I will soon join you in Nice. Expect me.*
> *Ever yours,*
> *Laurie*

She turned the paper over, to see if there was anything else. How perfectly strange it was to receive such a perfunctory

334 Linda Epstein, Ally Malinenko, and Liz Parker

note, after not hearing from Laurie all of these months. Where was he? What had his plans been? Why had they changed? Regardless of any of those questions, she would be very glad to see him.

There was so much she wanted to talk to him about! First, she wanted to let him know that Fred had told her of his inclination toward those of the same sex and to apologize to him for not understanding when he had alluded to it. That must have been difficult for him. She wanted to set his mind at rest if he was worried that knowing this about him might make any difference to her, which of course it didn't. Laurie was Laurie, and she adored him.

She sat down on a small chair near the window of the room, looking at the note, forgetting all about changing her clothing and going down to tea. She smoothed her finger across the letters of her name, and imagined him addressing it. She wanted to tell him, in person, that she forgave him for the errant kiss. She wouldn't tell him that she wasn't sorry it had happened though. Or that it probably meant something different to her than it meant to him. Or that she had hoped . . . well, she wasn't going to think about what she had hoped.

And, of course, she wanted to tell him that she had declined Fred's proposal. She thought back to their picnic, which now seemed like a lifetime ago. He'd said to her then that if she married she should choose someone who could see her as the artist that she is. He had said *if* she married; he hadn't told her she *must* marry, like everyone else told her. She wanted to tell him that she'd made the hard choice, and she chose being an artist. She knew she would figure out how to do that, without losing herself, without marrying for money, without marrying at all. One day a painting by Amy Curtis March *would* hang in the Paris Salon. If anyone could see this and understand her decision, it was Laurie. She patted the note on her lap. She was very glad she would see him soon.

*   *   *

When Aunt Mary and Florence tired of going on outings with Amy so she might paint, Uncle Edward hired a sweet low basket barouche with a pony for Amy to drive so she might take herself here or there to work. Aunt Mary balked, saying it wouldn't be proper, but when Uncle Edward pointed out how many fashionable young ladies were driving themselves around in all sorts of carriages, Aunt Mary agreed to allow it.

When Laurie arrived in Nice a few weeks later he called at the hotel, but they were all out and about. Amy had gone up to Castle Hill to draw. On her return though, as she passed an entrance to the promenade, there he was, standing at the crossing. She saw him, halted the carriage and said, "Oh, Laurie, is it really you? I thought you'd never get here!"

Seeing her, his eyes lit up. He climbed into the carriage and with no destination in mind, they slowly drove through the streets of Nice. Although there was so much she wanted to say to him, she found herself tongue-tied, and he seemed shy or reserved. Their conversation felt halting and awkward. He asked after Florence and her aunt and uncle. She wanted to hear what news from home he'd had. Finally, she dropped him at his hotel, and they agreed to meet the next day.

They sat on a bench by the sea, watching the boats. They could hear the laughter of a young woman as she was serenaded by the gentleman rowing her in a pretty white dinghy.

"You're apologizing to *me*?" Laurie said.

"Well, yes," Amy replied. "I believe you tried to tell me a number of times." She glanced at him. "But I didn't understand," she said. "I just . . ." She looked down at her lap. "I just didn't know that men could . . . that you meant you . . ."

He smiled and nudged her with his shoulder. She smiled shyly, looked at him again, then back down at her lap.

"But I understand now," she said. "I'm sorry it took Fred

explaining it to me after hearing gossip from that pompous, odious . . ."

"Anyone who knows him knows Davies-Taylor is a condescending snob," Laurie said. "Frankly, I don't care a hoot about anything he says."

"And nor should you!" Amy said, looking up at him. "It makes me so angry," she continued. "What business is it of his, or anyone's for that matter, that you . . . well . . ." She wanted to be able to say it aloud, but she stumbled again, not because of what she felt, but more because she'd never heard anyone talk about this in plain language, with no judgments attached to it. It just wasn't done. But this was important, and she wanted Laurie to know that she loved and valued him just the way he was. She cleared her throat. Her eyebrows drew together as she tried to find the right words. ". . . that you are romantically inclined to those of your own sex," she said. She looked up at him. "Is that right? Is that how I should say it?"

Laurie looked at her, held her gaze, then shook his head a little, as if she *hadn't* gotten it right.

"It's not that simple," he said. His voice caught. He cleared his throat and said, "It's true that I am." He took a deep breath. "It's also true that I'm romantically inclined to the fairer sex," he continued. He tilted his head. "I know this might be confusing," he said. And Amy *was* confused.

"I just . . ." Her eyes welled with tears. She swiped at them with her fingertips. "I just never knew there were so many variations of romance and attraction, Laurie." He moved a little closer to her on the bench. "And I certainly never realized it wasn't at all straightforward for so many people, especially people who I know and love."

He took her hand. "There are so many variations of love," he said. "I don't know why it's not considered polite to discuss," he continued, "but so many of us don't fit the classical idea of love."

"Like Jo, too," Amy said. "I don't think she's exactly like Rosa Bonheur."

"No, I don't think so," Laurie said.

"But Jo is Jo, and that's fine."

"It is," Laurie said.

Amy sighed and then looked up at him again. "So then, when we said goodbye at the Louvre . . ."

He turned away and bit his lip.

"It's okay if you don't love me in that way, Laurie," Amy said. But it hurt her to say it.

It was his turn to swipe at his eyes. He shook his head again.

"Amy," he said, and turned on the bench, so he was facing her. "I do love you in that way," he said. "I think I have always loved you."

"But then why . . ."

"Perhaps it's too much to hope for," he said. "But I want to be loved for who I am." He took her hand in his. "I don't want to be a solution to your financial situation."

"Oh, Laurie!" Amy said. "You're not!" She gripped his hands tightly. She looked around, to see if anyone was watching them, but it was getting later in the afternoon, so there weren't many people about. Those who promenade, and those who watch those who promenade, had all retired to tea or supper or a late afternoon nap. "I don't care a fig about money!" she said.

"Amy March, who declared when she was twelve years old that she must marry rich so she could have fine things, doesn't care about money?" Laurie smiled. "Really?"

"You're making a jest," Amy said. "But I'm serious." And she was. She sat up tall on the bench next to him and turned so she was facing him, too. "When I said no to Fred," she said, "I chose to be true to myself." She nodded. "I want to be loved for who I am, too." A breeze came in off the water just then, and rippled at her hair. "I would rather marry nobody, to be a painter," she said. "I chose art."

His smile, which had begun as a teasing sort of smile, slowly turned to a smile of wonder.

"Does it have to be one or the other," he said. "Art or love?"

"I don't know," Amy said. "But I will always choose art, if I have to choose."

"What if you don't have to choose?" Laurie said.

"I never imagined that as a possibility," Amy said.

"I choose art, too," Laurie said.

Amy looked quizzically at him.

"I choose you," he said. "So I choose art because without art you aren't you."

Amy had been in love with Laurie for so long, even if she'd only recently acknowledged that fact to herself. For years she'd suppressed those feelings, in fear of upsetting Jo. She hadn't ever entertained the thought of Laurie being the object of a marriage of convenience. Learning of his inclination toward other men, she'd locked something away in her heart, never imagining it might have the opportunity to be let free. When she finally distinguished what she, Amy Curtis March, needed and wanted for herself and her life, it was as if a clearing had been made. She had thought that clearing would *only* be filled with art. Either/or. In her experience women didn't get to have it all.

"You choose art," she said. "I see." It was her turn to smile. "Will you do something for me?"

"Anything," he said.

"First, I want to go somewhere more private, and I should like to kiss you again." He raised his eyebrows. "I do," she said, with a big smile. "I rather liked it. And then . . ." With a flush in her cheeks, she whispered something in his ear.

To Sketch a Model

Amy stood on the landing outside the door with her hand on the knob and felt the warmth of her blush climb her neck, spread over her fair cheeks and radiate up into her hairline. She straightened her back, pulling herself together. She righted the plain linen smock she'd tied on over her royal-blue afternoon dress, as if straightening her clothing might somehow ease her embarrassment. She smoothed her hands down over the smock.

She thought of Rosa Bonheur, who had haunted slaughter-houses so she might learn animal anatomy. If Amy truly was going to be an artist, learning how to do this was essential. She stood, hand on the door handle. She wasn't little Amy March anymore, a girl from small town Concord, Massachusetts. Whatever her parents had intended for her when they'd allowed her the trip, she knew why she'd come.

She closed her eyes for a moment, took a deep breath, and turned the knob. She strode confidently into the studio, where he was posed. He was perched sideways on a wooden chair, facing away from her, his arms resting on the chair's back. The sun shone in from the open window and a breeze ruffled his silky mahogany hair. His chin rested on his crossed arms, his face hidden, pointed toward the far wall. He didn't pick up his head or turn toward her. He cleared his throat but didn't say anything. His skin was swarthy, arms tanned and healthy from time spent in the sun.

Amy swallowed, as her eyes followed the lines of muscle that started at his neck, which was slightly sunburned, and flowed down his spine, the delineation between the taught trapezius and the rise of his deltoid at the shoulder. Then down his strong, narrow back, from shoulders to waist, a dip at the small of his back, and then even further down to his smooth buttocks. She felt her heart speed up. She swallowed again.

One leg was in front of him, out of her view. The other was to the side. She felt a wave of heat rush up her body when she saw the fine dark hair that started heavier on his thigh and traced a path to his ankle, growing sparser as it rode down his lithe muscular leg. She'd only ever seen a man's calf at the beach, never a thigh, which was always covered by a bathing costume. His skin looked smooth and well cared for.

She cleared her throat, walked to the easel and picked up the charcoal. She was grateful everything was set up for her, waiting for her to sketch. She would have felt awkward moving about the studio preparing, or being in the room when he disrobed. She felt a little dizzy. A naked—no, a *nude*—man was right there in front of her. She wasn't someone who usually couldn't find the right words, but she found herself tonguetied.

So all she said was, "Thank you for letting me do this," and began to sketch. She observed him taking in a deep breath and watched his latissimus muscles slide over the ribs on his back. She imagined his lungs filling with air. Her hand swept across the paper as she tried to capture in charcoal what was before her eyes. "Of course," he softly replied.

She changed her paper and he changed his position slightly.

She started another page, endeavoring to capture the lines of his beautiful muscles, the narrowness of his waist, the spread of his shoulders, the outline of each muscle grouping. And then his hand delicately resting on his thigh. She soon forgot they'd even spoken, and all one could hear was the soft scratch of the charcoal on the page, and outside the open window the flower girl at the corner calling her wares. *"Fleurs! Fleurs! Jolies fleurs!"*

Nothing existed but Amy's hand, the charcoal, the paper, and the subject. He was no longer an unclothed young man. He had transfigured into Subject. He was neck into back. Flow of an arm—deltoid, tricep, bicep, forearm—and the alluring, challenging intricacies of the hand. He was beauty and form, shadow and light, an artistic challenge to master.

When she was finally done, she felt spent. He lifted his head and turned his face toward her. "Thank you for asking me to sit for you, my lady," Laurie said.

She smiled at him but didn't answer. He smiled back and nodded his head, as if some unasked question had just been answered. She wiped the charcoal dust from her hand onto the linen smock, unbuttoned it, took it off, and placed it on a chair. Then in silence she turned and left the studio.

Walking slowly down the steep staircase leading to the courtyard at the center of the building she imagined Laurie dressing himself. She felt herself begin to blush, then softly laughed at herself. She waited for him in the courtyard beside the large double doors leading to the street.

She wondered, if Father and Mother or Aunt March could see her now, would they think her disgraceful? And what of her sisters? She couldn't begin to guess what Meg and Beth might think. But Jo would no doubt laugh at her. Silly Amy still believing she could be anything other than a pretty face with a bit of artistic talent. She knew she could never say a word about this to her cousin Florence. She thought of Rosa

Bonheur, who would probably commend her, saying, *"Bien sûr!"* while lighting a cigarette, or dear Mary Cassatt, who no doubt would applaud her.

As she thought about it, her guiding person had always been Laurie—when she had felt suffocated by Mother's moralizing; when Jo had looked down her nose telling Amy she was spoiled and selfish; even when Aunt March had insisted she unwaveringly adhere to the rules of social etiquette—Laurie had been there. He had been the one to encourage and support her artistic aspirations. He really did understand her.

Back in the studio Laurie's body—the model's body—had transformed into a pure study of form. She had been filled with the possibility of living independent of the confines of social expectations, outside the limited condition that a woman might expect to experience. As she was drawing she had felt as if she existed apart from her identity as a woman, or sister, or friend. She had just been an artist.

As she waited for Laurie to join her and escort her back to the hotel, she wondered if on her return anyone would be able to see that she'd changed. For she had. She wasn't the same person who had anxiously stood outside this studio door. She wasn't the young woman who agonized over all the ways she might misstep. She cared much less about the good opinion of others. For she had stopped fooling herself, stopped trying to be someone she wasn't, to satisfy the needs of other people. Perhaps her life might have been easier and more predictable had she gone ahead and married Fred Vaughn. Had she done, she would have had to give up everything. What she hadn't expected was that in choosing art—choosing herself, choosing to live her life her own way—she could also have love.

A COMPLIMENTARY CLOSE

And so, dear readers, we leave you here. You may already have knowledge of what happens next in the story of the March sisters, how events we've touched upon here are about to unfold. As you ponder what else you might know of Meg, Beth, and Amy's stories, do take care to remember from whence your information has been gleaned.

Remember, authors take liberties with their fictions, crafting stories from shadows of the truth. But now that you're privy to some of the confidential conversations, intimate and undisclosed connections, private moments, and correspondence, perhaps a different light has been cast on these fictions.

Perhaps we've given the other March sisters a moment in the spotlight of their own stories—free from a certain sister's interpretation and a certain mother's expectations. After all, no one can be all things to all people, and while some might have sought to craft these sisters into their own ideal of little women, we think, just maybe, they'd have liked to make the decision of who they were and who they would become for themselves.

Authors' Note

Louisa May Alcott gave us such a gift in her penning of *Little Women*. Writing this book, diving into her original work and expanding upon the stories she told, was both a joyful and a humbling exercise. *Little Women*, while not exactly an analogue for Louisa's own life, was inspired by her family and her sisters, but Jo is the heart of that story. Together, we've sought to bring voice to Meg, Beth, and Amy and, in doing so, voice to Louisa's sisters: Anna, Lizzie, and May.

We pulled from both Louisa's original work and her sisters' lives, and we would be remiss in not sharing at least a bit of a look into that process and, of course, giving credit to our inspiration.

The story we've crafted for Meg pulls much from the original text of *Little Women* as far as Meg's passions go. More than once she enjoys the flowers, the greenhouse, and even mentions fairies. This dovetailed perfectly into giving her a life as an herbalist. Anna Alcott Pratt, the sister for whom Louisa took inspiration for Meg's character, was an avid reader, so it only seemed natural that she would find her way into work in the garden through a book. Nicholas Culpeper's *Complete Herbal*—first published in 1652 and reprinted many times, including in 1860—was the perfect fit.

As a teenager, Anna wrote in her diary, *I have a foolish wish to be something great and I shall probably spend my life in a kitchen and die in the poor-house. I want to be Jenny Lind or Mrs. Seguin and I can't and so I cry.* This, combined with a journal entry that Anna wrote on her twenty-eighth birthday reflecting on how little of value she'd accomplished for herself or others made us want to give Meg something of value in her story that extended beyond her family and the four walls of the Dovecote.

While Meg found discontent in her marriage, Anna seemed to find much joy in hers, especially as it gave her stability she never truly felt in her family home (even if she was poorer than she'd have liked to be). It was from this kernel of discontent, and her shared wedding anniversary with her mother, that Meg's relationship with Marmee came to life on the page, and Meg was ultimately able to find the love in John that Anna found in her own John. Unlike Meg, Anna was not terribly social, and her diaries suggest she struggled with having close friendships, so we pulled the friendships from Meg's girlhood into her adulthood, giving her the support system she deserved while her sisters were away.

We have very few of Elizabeth "Lizzie" Alcott's letters, but from what we do have, we can easily see that while many of the events in *Little Women* historically track—both Beth and Lizzie contracted scarlet fever, which weakened their hearts, leading to an early death—that is where the similarities seem to end.

Even in death Lizzie was not granted the sweet and simple passing that her literary counterpart experiences. Instead, Lizzie lashed out angrily at her family as they plied her with morphine to dull the pain. And in life, as we can see from some of her letters, Lizzie had a dry wit. In one she wrote, *"Miss Hinkley"*—presumably a nurse—*who "was horridly shocked at my devouring meat . . . and stared her big eyes at me. [She] will probably come to deliver another lecture soon. I don't care for the old cactus a bit."*

In this story, we tried to give our Beth a little bit of Lizzie's darkness. A little bit of anger at her situation. The Other Beth. We wanted to honor the woman who died and whose memory was turned into a very different version of herself. She was a woman who lived and made art and was snarky and funny and suffered and died angry. The story that Beth tells regarding being covered up by the books came from Lizzie's own life, and we are indebted to Carmen Maria Machado and her *Paris Review* article, "The Real Tragedy of Beth March" for bringing it to light.

Louisa's youngest sister, Abigail May Alcott (Nieriker), was "the other Alcott sister" engaged in the arts. She was an accomplished painter, who achieved some of the goals that our Amy aspires to.

In *Little Women* Amy and Jo butt heads and have a sometimes contentious relationship, whereas May had a close one with Louisa. We leaned into the *Little Women* version because it was much more interesting for our story! But in reality, May's European studies, where she came into her own as an artist, were financed by Louisa's success with *Little Women*. In 1877 May had a still life exhibited at the Paris Salon (the only painting by an American woman that year), and in 1879 the Paris Salon exhibited May's final painting and what is now considered her masterwork, *La Négresse*.

May studied in London, Paris, and Rome, as our Amy does. The other places Amy travels were taken from mentions in *Little Women*. We used some words, phrases, and reworked sentences directly from *Little Women* in our story. In addition, we borrowed liberally from a travel guide for women artists that

May wrote, *Studying Art Abroad, and How to Do It,* which was published in 1879. Our Amy takes classes from some of the teachers May recommends in her guide, visits places mentioned, and has experiences based on May's descriptions. Caroline Ticknor's 1928 memoir of May includes her journal entries, which also supplied inspiration as well as words and phrases in May's voice.

One of the big challenges Amy faces in *The Other March Sisters* is whether a woman can marry—that is, have love—and still be an artist. May was able to find that balance when she married Ernest Nieriker, a businessman sixteen years her junior. He was fully supportive of her work, but sadly, after only two years of marriage, May died shortly after giving birth to their daughter. We tried to honor May's artistic legacy by imbuing Amy with some of the drive and seriousness of purpose with which she studies art, in a way that *Little Women* did not.

And while not an on-the-page character in *The Other March Sisters,* Jo's influence in our work cannot be overstated. Jo, whose sisters referred to her as their brother. Jo, who chose a shortened version of her name over her full name of Josephine, in much the same way that Louisa's sisters called her Lou.

While the language of queerness wasn't as defined when *Little Women* was first published in 1868, the themes are clear on the page to an astute reader. Louisa herself once said in an interview, "I am more than half-persuaded that I am a man's soul, put by some freak of nature into a woman's body [. . .]." The queer themes we've included in her sisters' stories are meant to honor Lou's own legacy. As queer authors ourselves, we hope they'll serve as a reminder that queer people have always been here and will continue to be, both on and off the page.

ACKNOWLEDGEMENTS

From All of Us

Collectively we would like to thank Louisa May Alcott. Without Lou's masterpiece, our book would not exist. We hope you would have appreciated the stories we created for Jo's sisters, and the way we challenged assumptions. With our 21st-century gaze we saw so many queer themes in the subtext of *Little Women* that perhaps you weren't aware you were putting there. Or maybe you were? We will never know but we hope you would have enjoyed the way we took them and ran.

To our editor, Wendy McCurdy, thank you for falling in love with our Meg, Beth, and Amy, and for giving their stories a home. To everyone who helped make a good idea into a book and then get it into readers' hands, and especially to our team at Kensington who shaped it into its final form, thank you: Michelle Addo, Robin Cook, Vida Engstrand, Tory Groshong, Lauren Jernigan, Kristine Noble, Rena Rossner, Kath Rothschild, Sarah Selim, TKCover Artist, TKDesigner.

From Linda

This was a hard book for me to write. First conceived right before the pandemic as just a fun romp, I had no idea what would be in store for me in the following years. I wrote most of Amy's story while experiencing multiple losses and undergoing monumental changes in my life. Throughout it all Alison Green Myers was by my side. You reminded me I'm a writer, and sometimes writers need time to pause and ponder; sometimes writers need to just feel their feelings; and sometimes writers write. We talked plot points, character development, queer history, and how we bring something of ourselves to everything we write. For this and so much more, but especially for your friendship, I am grateful.

It feels impossible to adequately thank Ally and Liz. I can't do it in a couple of sentences. Do I tell you how talented you both are? Do I say how lucky I feel to have my name on a book with both of you? Do I mention how much I value our friendship, born from this collaboration? Yes, yes, and yes! Also, huge thanks for understanding when my anxiety won the battle.

Thanks to Amber McBride, for your generosity of spirit, friendship, and faith in me as a writer. I must have done something pretty awesome in a previous lifetime to deserve your friendship.

I've had the good luck to have long talks with Tracey Bashkoff, a brilliant art curator and family friend. You probably don't remember this, Tracey, but you once told me that I know more about art than most people. That *one* tiny comment gave me a bit of confidence that my thoughts and feelings about art might have some validity. I couldn't have written Amy's story without that.

Robin Arzt and I talk on the regular about creative process, how painting and writing are comparable, and not. I adore our art talks, Robin. Thank you for being a dear friend to me for more than half my life, for your support and encouragement of my writing for all these years, and for your paintings, that surround me on the walls of my house.

Gratitude to David and Christi Nelsen-Epstein. You provided a home for me and held me safe until I could do both things on my own. So grateful for that and everything that's come after. I love you.

As always, I'm grateful to my mom, who gave me my first (purple) copy of *Little Women*. She encouraged me to be a voracious reader by her example, and *always* bought me books. She would have been so proud to see the writer I've become.

I am indebted to May Alcott Nieriker and her fictional counterpart Amy Curtis March; the first because her dedication to living an artistic life, and her success as a woman artist in the 19th century, is an absolute inspiration to me; the second because she was always secretly my favorite March sister. I hope I've given the die-hard Amy-haters something to ponder. Eternally grateful to readers for being willing to take the ride with me. I appreciate you.

Lastly, thanks to my partner, Nan Tepper, who brings out the best in me in all ways. I couldn't have finished writing Amy's story without your patience, understanding, and love. How fortunate I am to have you as my champion. How lucky we are to have found each other. How unexpected and delightful that I get to live happily ever after with a fellow writer and book nerd even nerdier than myself. You have my heart and love, Nan.

From Ally

This book started as a "what if" conversation on Twitter before the pandemic. Over time it grew to be one of my favorite things I have ever written. It also grew in importance. Giving Beth a love story and making her more than her illness became the heart of this story to me. Too many times in books characters die to show other characters the meaning of life, but for Beth I wanted her to have her own life. I'm honored I got the chance to tell her story.

With that in mind, it would be impossible to adequately thank Linda and Liz. Working with you both has been a truly wonderful experience and I love the way we brought the other March sisters to life, and gave them stories of their own. I'm very proud of us and I hope you are too.

To Elizabeth Alcott, you were funny and I wish more people knew that. You had a dry sense of humor and you joked about death and illness. You called yourself, "the little skeleton." I can only hope you would have found joy in the story I wrote.

To Amber McBride and Aly Ames, you are my friends, my beta readers, and the people who remind me that yes I can really do this. I cannot thank you enough. Your encouragement means the world to me and I would never be the writer I am now without your guidance. A Team forever!

To my sisters, Stephanie and Jennifer, thank you for always supporting me and believing in me when I struggle to believe in myself. I love you both very much.

Mom and Dad, you didn't get to read this one but I know you're proud. Thank you for always encouraging me to read, for the weekly trips to the library when I was growing up and always telling me that I could be anything I wanted to be in this world, even a writer. Your faith carries me now. I love you more. I will miss you forever.

To Jay, my rock. You're with me on all those early mornings as we plug away at our laptops. Without your support and belief, I don't think I would be where I am today. You have never wavered and when I do it is always you that holds me up. You are my best friend and there is no one I would rather spend this crazy life with.

And finally, to all the readers out there who have struggled with an illness, I see you. You are more than your diagnosis. And you have your one beautiful life to live – just like everyone else. I believe in you and I love you. Thank you for going on this journey with me. I hope Beth gave you a little hope too.

From Liz

My confession: I'd never read *Little Women* until Linda and Ally asked me to write this book with them. Thank you for bringing me in on this novel—for asking me to write Meg's story and then loving the Meg I brought to life. The first email I received about this project was titled "Looking for Meg March," which in itself became the inspiration for "Finding Meg March." I'm so grateful to have my name on the front of this book alongside both of yours. This is something we'll have forever, and I couldn't have asked for better co-writers.

To Anna Alcott Pratt, I know that you are long gone, but I hope you found the purpose in life you sought in your journals. I can only dream that you would've loved the story I've given Meg.

Amber McBride, you convinced me to write this story (and to take our herbalism class), so without you, there would be no Meg March Brooke the herbalist. Our friendship means the world to me, and your thoughtful critique always makes my work better.

Rebekah Faubion, you are one of my best friends and biggest champions. We will forever scream about each other's books to anyone we can (and forever read those books ourselves to help each other pull the very best out of our stories). Obviously, I named Meg's bisexual midwife teacher after you.

Alison Ames, you are an angel, you are a star, and you have become such an important person in my life. Thank you for being excited about this book from the moment I told you about it all the way until it hit the shelves and for always having thoughtful (and usually hilarious) critique.

Tracey Neithercott, thank you for your excitement over this project (and really everything I've ever written—the feeling is mutual). I still remember when Greta Gerwig's *Little Women* was filming when I came to visit you! Sara Biren, I love having you in my life—your astute eye, your sarcastic wit, and your endless optimism. Yes, the two of you were the namesakes for the characters at Sallie's tea.

To my readers—those coming to find my words for the first time, and those who have been tireless in sharing about my work since my debut. There are many of you, but I especially want to shout out Jacqueline (@purposelyunperfect), Kat (@itskatsteele), Joanna (@lifewithprinceman), Emily (@booksandbedtime), Emily (@emilyisoverbooked), Britt (@brittyoreads), Jennifer (@shereadsatnaptime), Erin (@erinsbookspot), Brianne (@books_withbri), Laura (@manosfrias.reads), Holli (@bohemian.tea.pedler).

Dad, thank you for teaching me to be brave, to follow my heart, and to always be true blue.

And to Nick. You are the love of my life and my best friend and the person I adore most in this world. With you, I learned what it is to love and discovered that marriage can be (and *is*) a joy, something I infused into Meg's story. Thank you for always pushing me forward, cheering me on, making my work better, and having ideas all your own (like the title).

Discussion Questions for

The Other March Sisters

by Linda Epstein, Ally Malinenko, and Liz Parker

These suggested questions are to spark conversation
and enhance your reading of *The Other March Sisters*.

1. While *The Other March Sisters* holds true to some of the text in *Little Women*, it draws from the real lives of Alcott's sisters, giving a different view of them than Alcott provided. How do you feel when you read a new take on a classic book? Do you like when authors reimagine beloved characters, or do you feel they need to be left as originally written?

2. Have you read other books that have reimagined classic novels? If so, how do you think *The Other March Sisters* measures up?

3. How are Meg, Beth, and Amy in *The Other March Sisters* similar to the portrayal of their characters in *Little Women*? How are they different?

4. While many adaptations of *Little Women* portray Amy as Laurie's second choice, a number of scenes in *Little Women* show his love for her long before they meet up in Europe. In *The Other March Sisters*, Laurie didn't only love Amy first, she was the only March sister he had romantic feelings for. Why do you think the authors made this decision and how did you feel about this interpretation of the proposal between Laurie and Jo?

5. Amy's view of her own artistic ability is colored by Jo's role as the "genius" in the family. How is she able to separate herself from her family's expectations and pursue her art without the shadow of Jo hanging over her?

6. Amy reflects on her decision to burn Jo's manuscript when she was a child, something she regrets deeply. Did you ever do something terrible as a child? Were you forgiven? How did that shape your relationships going forward?

7. Meg is often considered the most traditional of the March sisters, with many adaptations portraying her has satisfied with her marriage—wanting nothing more than a life as wife and mother. The original text points to a greater discontent, which the authors explored in more depth in this novel. What makes it possible for Meg to find satisfaction in her life and love in her marriage in *The Other March Sisters*?

8 *Little Women* calls Beth a house angel, often forgotten and always facing her illness with grace. How did *The Other March Sisters* challenge this portrayal?

9. Beth knows that she is dying but is unable to speak about it with her family. How does her relationship with Florida help her become more than just "a dear" not only to her family, but to herself?

10. While not often portrayed in mainstream history, queer people existed in the 1860s. All three sisters' stories feature queer themes, much like Jo's story (often referred to as a brother by her sisters)—from Laurie's bisexuality and hints at a relationship between Meg and Annie in their girlhood, to Beth's romance with Florida. How does the role of queerness and queer identity play into the larger themes of *The Other March Sisters*? How did you feel about the inclusion of queer characters in this book?

11. There are a number of queer side characters in the novel who help the sisters see the world in a different light, including Rosa Bonheur (a real artist of the time) and Rebekah Mayer (a fictional Concord midwife). How do these women help Amy and Meg define themselves and the paths they wish to take in life?

12. In 1845, the Massachusetts statute "Procuring Miscar-riage" made performing an abortion punishable by up to 20 years. Meg is faced with a difficult decision to help her dear friend Annie when it becomes clear another preg-nancy could jeopardize her life. How did you feel about this being portrayed in *The Other March Sisters*? How might you have handled this situation?

13. While many adaptations of Little Women have painted Mrs. March (Marmee) in a feminist light, the original text of *Little Women* shows her having a heavy hand in her daughters' choices. How do her expectations impact Meg, Beth, and Amy's stories? Were you a mother in the 1860s, how might you have approached your own daughters dif-ferently?

14. Beth and Meg come to a shared understanding about Marmee during their picnics in the woods, and Meg and Amy write about Marmee's expectation that Amy find the right match. How do these interactions among the sisters shape their decisions to live their own lives rather than being the "little pilgrims" they were raised to be?